LONG SHADOWS

AN ADAM ALBA MYSTERY

JOSEPH ONESTA

Pittsburgh, Pennsylvania
Integrity HPI

ISBN: 979-8-9872548-2-0
Library of Congress Control Number: 2025910494

DISCLAIMER

This book is pure fiction—crafted from my imagination, early-morning musings, and a touch of escapism. The characters, places, and events within these pages exist only in this world of words. If you think you recognize someone, a place, or a moment from real life, I assure you—it's just a trick of your mind. (I should know.) Any resemblance to actual places, events, or people—living, dead, or in between—is purely coincidental.

Now let's go!

ONE

The bus pulled into the degraded parking lot of a half-empty strip mall, just one of the many rural or small-town stops on the way from one city to another. Adam looked at his watch. He had been on buses for over twenty-four hours and had not slept.

The unsettling feeling of being watched dogged him. He called it the "shadow" feeling. It felt like he was being observed and followed from a distance. At times, he became the observer, seeing himself from behind and watching his life happen. For fifteen years, ever since his accident and the brain trauma that came with it, he had been trying to either shake the feeling or shake the tail.

The injury cost him a year of his life and had forever changed it as a consequence. Sometimes the shadow feeling was barely noticeable. Other times it was impossible to ignore. He clung to logic, trying to rationalize the feeling away but there seemed to be a truth that he couldn't ignore. Sometimes the shadow feeling was significant; he just didn't know when that was.

He took a deep breath. The acrid smell of the chemical toilet in the back of the bus made him recoil and hold his breath.

Every time he began to settle in somewhere, inevitably he'd have to move on, go somewhere so new that he was distracted by the newness of it. Once he settled in his new place, it would all calm down—for a while.

He had just moved New Orleans into history. It was now a memory obscured by hours of landscape seen through a grungy windowpane. Like every place eventually, New Orleans had closed in on him. He had to move on.

At least, Adam thought, *this town has a proper station.* Most stops along the way were at gas stations or convenience stores. This strip mall had obviously seen better days, and by the look of things, those days were long gone.

Three empty storefronts with soaped-over windows were bookended by two remaining viable businesses. One was the bus station, the other a laundromat. Old and faded signs on the vacant store windows read "For Lease." The largest empty unit still had a tempera-painted window that read "Ur Community Thrift Store, Donations Accepted." *What must have happened to the economy of a town for a thrift store to go out of business?* The parking lot was cracked and potholed, and in places, sizable weeds grew from between the gaps in the cement. There were no other cars in the lot.

The driver turned off his radio, a transistor that he might have had since he was a kid. He sometimes had to fiddle with it to get a better reception, but it was always country music that was not loud enough to listen to but just enough to be aware of. It was certainly enough to keep Adam awake.

A young girl wearing a Texas Wesleyan hoodie, who had boarded the bus in Fort Worth, gathered her things and keyed a call on her phone. She flicked brown hair away from her ear, making room for her phone. "Hi, just got here. We're a little early."

The driver opened the door for her and watched her descend the steps. He announced that the bus was ahead of schedule and would leave again in about ten minutes. "Restrooms and vending machines inside." He followed the girl off the bus to get her luggage from under the carriage.

Of the three other people on the bus, two were sleeping, and one, a gaunt woman with short wavy hair and thick glasses, was reading. No one even looked at the driver. Adam stood up. He wasn't used to sitting for so long. It was too much like waiting. This was a chance to move, to stretch and loosen up, and to breathe fresh air.

Outside, it was hotter than he had expected. He stretched, first bending over, then bending back, then side to side. Torquing his body to stretch his oblique muscles. A few squats and lunges to loosen up a bit more. Adam could feel the eyes of the woman who had been reading, half-watching him through the crusty bus window. Looking up, he smiled at her just to let her know he had seen her looking at him. She pretended not to notice.

Adam was a handsome man with a powerful figure and well-used to people looking at him for that reason. He thought he could sense the difference between admiration, lust, and sometimes jealousy.

He continued stretching. Walking and raising his knees high to hold them against his chest, stretching his hamstrings, then grabbing one foot, then the other from behind and pulling it back to stretch his quads. Arms fully extended, he leaned against the bus to stretch his calves and Achilles tendons. He took a deep breath, filled his lungs with the steamy air, and held it for a long time. Letting it out slowly, he could feel his entire body begin to relax.

Adam's palms were black from leaning on the bus. Inside the station, the driver was leaning on the counter, smiling and chatting with a middle-aged woman behind the ticket counter. She wore a brightly colored floral top and was well-coiffed, her hair in gentle curls draped to her shoulders. She reminded Adam of his own mother who used to dress and put on make-up to go to the grocery store. She seemed to enjoy the bus driver's conversation and attention and the opportunity to gossip. Clearly, they knew each other; perhaps they even had something going. Adam smiled to himself, wondering if arriving at this stop ten minutes early hadn't been planned.

The men's room was amazingly clean for a bus station restroom. It was small, just a toilet, sink, and urinal. A small shelf by the sink held a stack of paper towels. Adam washed his hands and dried them. Standing at the urinal, he unzipped, arranged himself, and felt the relief of emptying his bladder. Once again, that sense of being watched rose to the surface. In such a small room, knowing that there was no one else there, he still wanted to look back over his shoulder.

Life never quite goes according to plan, and Adam knew that better than anyone. Every time life got comfortable—friends, a decent place to live, a decent way to make a living—something would just mess it up. It just went too far, demanded too much of him and then that shadowy feeling that dogged him would push him. Then there would be a new plan, a move, and a change.

Adam splashed water on his face and ran his fingers through his tousled hair. His beard stubble looked like several scruffy days of growth. He looked into his own deep blue, almost cobalt, eyes. Three generations removed from a young man who boarded a boat and sought a new life. Adam sometimes wondered who he would have been if young Adamo Alba hadn't left Italy. Still, he always liked the person who seemed to be looking back, not at him, but *into* him.

Flagstaff was at least another two days. He had to change buses in Oklahoma City and Albuquerque, New Mexico, with a million tiny stops along the way. A deep breath turned into a long sigh. He tossed the paper towels into the wastebasket by the door and stepped back out into the lobby. The smell of fresh coffee wafted over him. The clerk was pouring a pot of coffee into a thermos for the driver.

That coffee smelled good. The vending machine didn't look as promising as the fresh coffee smelled. He noticed she was half-watching him and asked, "Any extra in that pot? It smells amazing, and the alternative…" He threw his eyes back to the vending machines.

She had a motherly smile. "Sure thing, sweetheart. All I got is black, though. No milk, no sugar."

"Just the way I like it."

She emptied the pot into a foam cup and handed it to him. "Sorry, I don't have a lid for this."

Adam reached for his wallet.

She smiled and shook her head. "Honey, it's on the house. I can't drink coffee this late in the day. It would just go to waste."

He sipped. The aroma and taste were heavenly. "Good coffee." Thanking her for a second time, he stepped out of the air-conditioned station into a blanket of steamy heat. He watched as the young college girl climbed into an absurdly large pickup truck. She glanced at him and nodded as she pulled the door closed. The diesel engine revved before winding its way through the cracked, cement parking lot.

Back on the bus, Adam began to fear the hours on the bus ahead of him. He could feel his muscles tightening as soon as he sat back down in his seat. He just didn't want to do it. He hadn't slept well the night before his trip, and he hadn't slept on the bus so far. He knew sleeping on a bus never worked for him. He'd sleep better even if he were sleeping rough in a field somewhere.

He had noticed a motel near the highway ramp and if they had a room, he could make a clean start tomorrow. *Fuck the ticket*, he thought. He just wanted off the bus.

The driver was walking back to the bus with his thermos of hot coffee. Adam waited by the door.

"Let's go, pal. We're on our way," the bus driver said.

Adam shouldered his rucksack. "I've decided to get off here. I've had enough buses for today."

"Odd place for that. Pretty country but the middle of nowhere. Are you sure you don't want to hang on to Oklahoma City? Lots more choices there." The driver clearly felt uneasy.

"There was a motel near the highway. I saw the vacancy sign. And like I said… I'm tired of buses."

"I can drop you there if you'd like. I'm just getting back on the highway."

"No, thanks, the walk will do me good. It's only a half mile or so." He just couldn't get back on the bus. "Mine is the green duffel." Adam pointed at the undercarriage luggage compartment.

Manda Lamano looked up from her computer to notice her husband's truck out in the parking lot of the bus station. She looked at her watch. He wasn't supposed to be there to pick her up for another hour. He was just sitting in the cab, smoking a cigarette. He had parked with the driver's side away from the station as if she wouldn't notice his smoking. She pressed a few buttons on her cell phone.

"What the hell are you doing here so early? Don't you have anything better to do?"

"Blake called me. Some guy got off the bus unexpectedly. He thought it was fishy."

"He seemed nice enough."

"Said he was going to walk to the motel, but he never got there. I checked. I drove back and forth between town and the motel several times. Never saw hide nor hair of him. I just thought I'd wait around in case he came back."

"You're overreacting." She sighed.

"Probably, but better safe than sorry."

She was tired of her husband hanging around and was relieved that he didn't try to wait for her inside the station. She didn't like him smoking and didn't like the smell. She knew he thought that opening the window was enough, but the cab always smelled like stale smoke. It clung to his clothes and sometimes, she thought, to his very skin.

The last bus of the day pulled into the lot. Another college student coming home for Memorial Day weekend. He had a backpack slung over his shoulder. She recognized him and waved. It was Junior Delgado. As the bus pulled out of the lot, she saw the young man leaning on the open passenger-side window talking to her husband.

She keyed in the number of his phone again.

"What's up?"

"Why don't you offer Junior a ride to the church? His parents are probably at services. It's Friday night."

"Don't want to leave you."

"Don't be silly. The church isn't far. You'll be just a few minutes."

"I don't know."

"Go on. That pack looks heavy. Do the boy a favor."

He hesitated, and then she heard him offer the boy a ride. Junior accepted, dropping his backpack into the bed of the pickup and climbing into the cab.

She was locking up the bus station when he got back. He parked and got out of the truck. She saw he was wearing his sidearm, his hand awkwardly close to the revolver.

"Don't you think you're overdoing it with the gun?"

"It's an open carry state. Don't want to lose you." He put his arm around her.

The door of the laundromat was propped open. As they approached, they saw the stranger, bare-chested, in a folding chair leaning back against a dryer. Blaine moved his hand toward the pistol at his side.

"Don't be crazy," she admonished, slapping his hand away from the gun. "It looks like he's asleep. He just decided to do his laundry."

"Nobody gets off an interstate bus just to do laundry. I'm coming in with you."

"The hell you are. Give me a few minutes. If he's asleep, I'll wake him up. Last thing anybody needs is to wake up looking at your scowling face while you're waving a gun around."

"You never know about these drifters, Manda."

"And you can go to jail for shooting a drifter. I don't want to lose you either. We don't know anything about this man. Land o' Goshen! You're suspicious of everybody. All that man has done so far is to get off a bus."

"But Blake said… "

"I don't care what Blake said. You and your brother never give anyone the benefit of the doubt. So suspicious! The two of you! You're here. You're armed. What the hell do you think is going to happen? Just wait outside."

"He's naked, Manda."

"He's shirtless, Blaine. It's hot as hell in there. And he's a damn sight better-looking than you are without a shirt, and even you go around shirtless. Just go stand over there by the window. If anything goes wrong, you'll handle it but preferably without that damned gun."

She thought he looked so innocent, and he had been exceptionally polite. She could easily imagine this weary traveler trying to discreetly change his clothes in the laundromat to be able to wash what he had been wearing down to the socks and, she thought, his skivvies. He wasn't naked but nearly so. He wore only a pair of red running shorts. The heels of his bare feet rested on the empty duffel bag. His head reclined toward the dryer. His mouth was slightly open, and he emitted a barely audible snore. She imagined that the rhythm of the dryer had lulled him to sleep. *He must have been tired, bless him.*

"Sweetheart," she gently shook his shoulder.

He awoke groggily. He squinted at the brightness of the fluorescent lighting.

"You've fallen asleep, honey. Your laundry is done, and I've got to close up here. Sorry to bother you. Why don't you fold your clothes while I sweep up?"

"You're the lady from…"

"Yes, from the bus station. I do a lot of little jobs around here."

Sluggishly, he got up, untangled his duffel bag from the leg of the folding chair, and emptied his dryer. He pulled his still warm jeans over his shorts. Pulling a T-shirt over his head, he noticed the man wearing a sidearm standing outside furtively glancing through the window every minute or so.

She saw his reaction. "That's my husband, Blaine. He came to pick me up."

"He looks…"

"Like your bus driver. That's his brother, Blake. Twins, not identical, but unmistakable. You got family around here?" she asked though she knew he hadn't. In Ur, everyone knew everyone, and if this man stayed more than a day, everyone would know about him.

"No, ma'am, not that I know of."

"Call me Manda. Everyone does. Never thought of myself as a ma'am."

"I'm Adam." He began neatly folding his clothes and layering them into the duffel bag. "You make a fine cup of coffee." He picked up the empty coffee cup and tossed it into a trash can. "Exactly where is here?"

"You mean you got off the bus and don't know where you are?"

"It must look crazy, but I'd been on buses for a whole day without sleep. I saw there was a motel near the highway and thought I'd get a good night's sleep before continuing my trip. I just wanted to take a break. Where am I exactly?"

"You're in Ur." She pronounced it like *your*.

"My what? I didn't get that."

"Not your what. It's the name of our town. Ur. It's spelled U-R but we say *your*. So, you're going to head out tomorrow; where ya headed?"

"Flagstaff."

"Pretty place. My husband and I took the kids to the Grand Canyon years ago when they were still kids. We spent a night just outside Flagstaff." She was cleaning dryer vents of lint. "Blaine, come in here and meet Adam. He's just passing through."

Blaine came in, a little on his guard. He reminded Adam of an inexperienced wrestler. Adam's eyes couldn't help looking at the gun. "Nice to meet you, sir." Adam extended his hand; a disarming move most people had trouble resisting. You can tell a lot about a person by their handshake. Blaine's hand was firm, a little too firm.

"Same here. Where are you from, Adam, and what brings you to Ur?" He sounded like he was trying to sound friendly.

"I'm originally from Pittsburgh. But I've been in New Orleans for the last year or so."

Adam went back to finish folding his clothing. Manda was now wiping down washers with a damp rag and opening the lids of the top loaders and the doors of the front loaders.

"He's headed for Flagstaff."

"Flagstaff is a long way off."

"That's why I decided to get off my bus." Glancing at the gun, Adam called out the apprehension he was sensing from this man. "Looks like that decision may have caused some concern. I'm genuinely sorry if I worried or scared you."

"Listen, buddy, I'm not worried or scared. I protect my own, if you know what I mean. That's all." He patted the holster at his side.

Adam had more than sized up this man. He was big but soft. His courage came from a weapon. He might have been accurate with the pistol, but Adam thought he could take him down and get that gun without much trouble. "I don't expect you'll take my word for it but, for what it's worth, sir, I'm no threat to anyone. I respect you, your life, and your privacy. I can only hope you respect mine, so, suffice to say, I had enough of sitting on a bus, and I decided to get a good night's sleep before continuing my journey. I've got lots of time to get to Flagstaff, and I'm in no hurry. The motel down the street looked like a place where I could get a good night's sleep. *That's all.*"

Manda felt the tension change in the room and broke in. "Honey, you may not be in a hurry to get to Flagstaff, but I'm in a hurry to finish this work. I've got to sweep and mop this floor before I can go home. If you could just wait outside for a few minutes, we can drop you off at that motel just as soon as I'm done here. That is, if you don't mind riding in the bed of the truck." She looked at her husband. "Blaine, you need to relax. Go smoke a cigarette, will ya?"

TWO

A blade of sunlight sliced through a gap in the curtains and cut across Adam's face, waking him. The digital alarm clock on the nightstand read 6:06. His dream still swimming in his head on the edge of waking.

It must have been riding in the bed of that truck to the motel. In his dream, he was eight or nine years old. Too many cousins to count were packed in the bed of a rusty, rickety pickup truck driving down country roads in Ohio to a soft serve ice cream stand next to an old-fashioned drive-in theater that, during the day, hosted a flea market.

He had been lucky to get a room. A very tired-looking woman in a sari and clacking flip-flops had checked him in and handed him the key to number six, the last room available. She locked the lobby door behind him. He noticed the "no" on the vacancy sign come on and the lights in the lobby go dim before he reached his room. He wondered if she would stay alert all night if the motel wasn't full or, if at a certain time, she'd just flip on that no vacancy sign and just go to bed.

There were three things wrong with the room. The first was that he could hear the couple in Room 7 getting lucky. The woman was particularly loud, a sound Adam found annoying. The second was a horsefly that refused to leave. He tried to shoo it out the door several times, but it would just bank a turn and head back into the room. It buzzed loudly like a bumblebee, banging into lampshades and light fixtures. The third was a musty odor mixed with stale tobacco smoke that billowed out of a groaning under-window air conditioner.

He had checked in around 10 p.m. The highway ramp came to a tee in the main road. On one side of the ramp was a McDonald's, and on the other was a gas station and convenience store combination. It was about 10:30 at night, and they were both open, but Adam had no appetite. More than anything, he needed a shower and a bed. *The middle of nowhere in a place called Ur*, Adam thought to himself. It was a toss-up between an open window, the sounds of the highway, and the heat of the night or the musty, fatigued noise and unpleasant smell of the air conditioner. In the end, he chose fresh air and the highway. He had opened the window as far as it would go.

He slept deeply and soundly, the sounds of the highway falling into the background like white noise.

He had kicked off the sheets in the night and lay naked on the bed. Scooching up on the pillow to get the light out of his eyes, he eyed the gap in the curtains. Someone could have looked in, seen him sleeping. He wasn't self-conscious about his body. Years of high school and college wrestling had stripped away any sense of modesty. More than once, he'd stood completely nude on a scale during a weigh-in, hoping he hadn't gone over his weight class.

The thought of someone peering through the gap in the curtains was creepy enough to slightly heighten that shadow feeling.

Deep sleep had left him feeling refreshed and energized. His body craved movement, a good stretch, and a workout. He didn't need a gym, weights, or machines; those had their place, but his usual morning routine of wrestling drills focused more on agility, flexibility, and stretching. All he really needed was a bit of open space—a small grassy patch, ideally— but even a parking lot would do. He pulled on a pair of red running shorts, socks, and sneakers. After tying his room key to the drawstring of his shorts, he stepped outside to find a spot to work out.

The sun was bright, the day was already warm, and the dew on the grass had already evaporated. He paced off an area large enough for his drills. The sun felt warm and bright on his skin. There was a slight breeze rustling the leaves on the trees. It felt good to move. Sometimes his routine drills felt like swimming through air with smooth, graceful, flowing movements. Each stretch, each practiced maneuver bringing him closer and closer to harmony with his environment.

After working up a decent sweat, his muscles warm and loose, he headed back to his room, showered, shaved, and carefully packed his bags. He rarely ate before noon, but McDonald's had pretty good coffee. He decided to walk across the street and get a cup before checking out. He set his packed bags on the floor by the door.

As he left his room, outside the open door to Room 7, he saw a portly woman, her hair wrapped in a scarf, her mahogany skin contrasting with the stark white of the sheets she was pushing into a laundry bag that was hanging off a cart.

"Good morning," he said with a smile.

She nodded and replied in kind. She had an accent that he couldn't place, and she quickly looked away. She grabbed a small stack of clean linens and turned to go back into the room.

"Excuse me," he said. "I'm here in number six. I'm just heading over to McDonald's. If you want to clean this room next, it's alright. I'll just come back in a bit for my bags, if that's okay with you. I have them by the door here. I just don't want to carry them with me to McDonald's."

She nodded again, with a smiling expression that was difficult to interpret.

The drive-thru line at McDonald's verged on absurd. It was so long that the last few cars in line were barely off the road. Yet, there was a single pickup truck parked in the lot. There was no wait at the counter. And the only customers in the dining area were three men huddled at a table.

Steaming coffee in hand, Adam debated whether to sit down and take time with his coffee or just head back to the motel to check out. The bus he had abandoned the day before had arrived in the late afternoon. There was, of course, the potential of an earlier bus, but if there wasn't one scheduled, he'd have hours to kill, sitting in that dismal little bus station.

He reminded himself there was no rush and slid into a booth with a clear view of the window and the rest of the dining room. The morning sun glinted and ricocheted off the tabletops. He watched the cars and trucks in the drive-thru line inch forward while more cars joined the line. He could also watch the only other customers—three men who looked like they were gearing up for a day's labor. Construction or road work, Adam guessed.

One had the weathered look of someone who lived under the sun—deeply tanned, his skin leathery and creased like old work gloves. The one Adam could see best was thickset with a belly that pressed gently against the buttons on his short-sleeved shirt; the tiny checks of the print stretched across the soft contours of his chest. He had a cheerful, round face framed by a close-cropped horseshoe of dark hair. He wound a baseball cap through his fingers back and forth, stopping at the brim and going back the other way. The third was the youngest. He had smooth, tanned skin and a physique that seemed sculpted more by barbells than blue-collar work—shoulders wide, posture proud. He was the quiet one.

They were speaking Spanish. Adam tried not to listen, but between his college Spanish and his Calabrian relatives, he understood more than he thought he could. When the sundried one said something snarky, Adam bit down on a grin, barely holding it in.

The cheerful one noticed Adam's reaction, and their eyes met. He sent Adam a big smile, and his eyes seemed to sparkle with delight. "You understood that?"

Adam felt his face redden. "I'm sorry, I didn't mean to eavesdrop but that was funny." He let the laugh out. They were all looking at him and seemed amused, even if Sun-Dried looked as embarrassed as Adam felt.

"My name is Tommy, Tommy Delgado. This is Luis." He pointed at the sun-dried man. "And this is Chucho."

Adam stood up and offered his hand to each of them. "Adam," introducing himself.

Tommy indicated the empty seat at their table. "Join us."

The one called Luis looked at his watch and glanced impatiently at Tommy.

"Where are you from, brother?" Tommy asked.

"Pittsburgh, originally. Just passing through." Adam sat down.

In Spanish, Tommy explained to Chucho that Pittsburgh was a northern city. Chucho seemed interested but said nothing.

Luis looked at his watch again. "Tommy, we really should get to work."

Adam started to get up. Tommy had a hand up to stop him. "We have a few minutes, Luis." Then to Adam, "Pittsburgh, huh? You are the first, uhm, what do you call someone from Pittsburgh?"

Adam reddened again. "Pittsburgher."

Now it was Luis's chance to hold back a chuckle.

"Really?" He beamed. "Pittsburgher, like cheeseburger?"

Tommy then switched to Spanish explaining the joke to Chucho, who feigned amusement but seemed embarrassed.

"Really," Adam admitted and joined in the amusement.

"Where are you headed?" Tommy asked.

"Flagstaff but my bus won't leave for a few hours. I could use something to do in the meantime if you have any suggestions."

"Not much to see these days," Tommy said, leaning back and cocking his head to one side. "Unless you're into casinos or Walmart. Not exactly the most exciting town anymore."

"Anymore?" Adam was interested.

"Not much left of town after Walmart opened. Lots of local businesses closed. The casino, well, let's just say it changed things around here."

Luis glanced at his watch and muttered something under his breath in Spanish. Tommy shot Luis a glance and nodded his head. Raising a calming hand to Luis, "Pocos minutos! We're putting a new roof on our church just down the road."

Luis gave a quick snort. He turned to Adam. "He's the deacon, and we are volunteers." He said the word volunteers as if the word came with meaningful air quotes. "Some of us have real jobs to get to."

Adam wondered if Luis was really pressed for time or if he was suggesting that a church deacon wasn't a real job.

Tommy's smile faded and his face stiffened. "Unfortunately, the corridor of corruption is about the only thing to do around here anymore."

"What's the corridor of corruption?" Adam looked around the table.

Tommy smirked. "Walmart on one side of the road and the casino on the other." He pointed in the direction of the bus station.

"Walmart." Luis added, "Right next door to his church." It sounded like a gibe. "Just keep going another half mile or so past the casino, and you'll come to town. Not much to see, but the Pioneer's Rest serves a great breakfast and lunch." Luis pushed his chair back hard, the legs scraping loudly against the tiled floor.

Chucho followed his lead and began gathering cups and food wrappers from the table.

Tommy, too, stood up. "I wish we had more time, but Luis is right. We do need to get to work. We can give you a lift in that direction if you'd like."

Adam waved the offer away. "Thanks, but I still have to check out of the motel, and I've got plenty of time. It was nice meeting you guys."

They shook hands again. Chucho just smiled and said nothing. Adam apologized to Luis. "Sorry to keep you."

Luis tilted his head so Tommy couldn't see the wink he sent Adam. "Hope you enjoy your trip."

Watching them leave, Adam sat back down in his booth to finish his coffee and watch the drive-thru line inch along. As cars exited the line, they exited the town, making use of the highway on-ramp. Maybe sitting in a drive-thru line was as important to them as sitting with his coffee was to Adam, but he doubted it. To Adam, most people went through life unconsciously either reliving, most likely regretting, the past or rehearsing the future, never really paying attention to the moment at hand. Those people, holding up their phones to capture images of events like concerts or Mardi Gras parades, what were they recording it for? To look back and relive something that they never really experienced in the first place.

If life had taught him anything at all, the lifespan of now, the moment we call right now, is short, fleeting, and can never be recaptured.

When he got back to his room, his bags were gone.

In the motel lobby, the same ill-tempered, sari-wrapped woman that had checked him in came out from the back room when he rang the bell on the counter. Her mood had not improved with a night's sleep.

"I have your bags here." She scowled at him.

"Sorry, I told the lady I'd be right back. I just went across the…"

She interrupted him with a shrug of her shoulders. She obviously wasn't listening and didn't care. He set the key down on the counter. She picked it up and handed him his receipt. "It's all on your card. No extra charges. Your bags are in here." She walked to a closet door just behind the counter. "Too heavy, you come and get them."

He slung the rucksack over his shoulder and grabbed the handle of the duffel. He tried to apologize once more. "I'm sorry. I didn't mean to inconvenience you."

Her face was indignant, her brow furrowed. Something seemed to be missing, an empty space behind her eyes. She was on autopilot. She just turned and walked away, disappearing through the door behind the desk.

It wasn't Manda working the counter in the bus station but a thin young man with delicate features. He was in his early twenties. As Adam entered the bus station, he noticed the boy's gaze trace his figure in an appraising way. Adam started to explain, but the boy interrupted it with an almost flirtatious smile.

"Manda said you'd be back today. You're real early, though. You can use the same ticket, but you'll have to reconfirm your connections when you change buses in…" he tapped at his keyboard, "… Oklahoma City and again in Albuquerque. It doesn't take long; just check in to make sure the buses aren't full and there's a seat available." Then, in confidence, "Don't stress over that; they are *never* full." He laughed to himself. "You're welcome to wait here, if you'd like. Your bus should be here at 6:20."

"I think I'll explore for a few hours. Can I leave my bag here?"

Claim check issued, Adam left the station feeling the young man's gaze follow him. The sun was high now, and it was warming up. He found himself slowing down in patches of shade to just appreciate the difference in temperature.

He saw the casino first. It was out of place, a garish construction in a beautiful rural setting. As he rounded a curve in the road, Walmart came into view. Ah, *the corridor of corruption*, Adam mused. Just past the Walmart parking lot was a small white clapboard church with roofers hammering away. *Must be those guys*, Adam thought.

Adam ducked into Walmart and bought a sub sandwich, a bag of chips, and two bottles of water. If he ate lunch at the restaurant the one guy mentioned, he'd keep the sandwich for the bus. He stashed them in his rucksack. Exiting on the far side of the store, closer to the small white clapboard church, he heard the thumping of hammers. They echoed back and forth. He watched the roofers. The day was already hot, and Adam thought it must be really hot up on that roof.

The boom box atop the cab of Tommy's pickup truck blared Christian music, its upbeat rhythm out of place against the quiet of the day. Adam slowed, trying to identify the three men from McDonald's working on the roof. Tommy, recognized by his girth, kneeled near the ridge, laying down the next shingle. Chucho stood up and straddled the ridge. Arms slightly extended, he balanced himself with an uneasy lack of confidence. He couldn't see Luis, but he noticed a bobbing head moving around on the other side of the roof near the steeple.

From the ground, Adam squinted, watching Tommy wipe sweat from his brow. He stood up, perhaps a bit too quickly, and swayed a bit. Then Tommy jerked unnaturally and fell back on his knees. Chucho crouched, and Luis stood up from the other side of the roof.

Adam barely had time to process what he was seeing before Tommy collapsed and rolled off the roof.

Adam's breath caught in his throat. Time shifted as Tommy tumbled down the roof in slow motion. His shirt caught on some guttering, pulling it away from the fascia. Tommy landed hard on the ground with a sickening thud. Adam couldn't have heard the thud, but he felt it.

Adam sprang into action. He sprinted forward instinctively, his heart pounding in his chest. He could see Chucho scrambling down the ladder, shouting something in Spanish. Luis was already running toward Tommy, his face pale, his eyes wide with panic.

Adam reached them just as Luis knelt beside Tommy. "Tommy!" Luis shouted, shaking him gently. "Tommy, are you alright?" Tommy was lying on his back. He didn't respond. At first, he just looked like he was unconscious.

Adam approached. Instinctively he laid his fingers aside Tommy's throat. No pulse. He tried his wrist. Nothing. A cold knot of dread twisted in Adam's stomach.

"I know CPR," Adam shouted over Luis' attempts to arouse Tommy. Adam knelt down and began chest compressions. "Call an ambulance, NOW!" Was it a heart attack? A stroke? But something gnawed at him, something about how Tommy jerked before he fell. And then he noticed the tiny bloom of red that seeped through the front of Tommy's shirt. "Call the police, too," he shouted to Luis.

THREE

For the first time in a long time, the puppeteer, for that is how he thought of himself, had a sense of real accomplishment. Most of his days were drudgery, a litany of routine events waiting for an opportunity to present itself. Today was not much different, but the feeling had changed, as if things, for whatever reason, had started going his way—the way he intended.

Instinct and cunning had taken him to the right place at the right time, and with the flick of his finger, he had eliminated two snags in his plan, a two-for-one sale.

It took a significant effort to sit down at his computer and review the surveillance footage of the laundromat. Cloud storage was expensive, so he reviewed the footage every day, and most days, he simply deleted it.

Something told him, however, that today might be a little different. No one had vandalized those machines for weeks. The new camera setup would make sure they were caught in the act. If the little bastards had been out for fun on a Friday night, perhaps, just perhaps, he caught them. Would he show the footage to the sheriff, or would he more enjoy showing it to the parents of the little vandals? What would it be like, he wondered, if he were to simply hold the footage over the heads of those little bastards? If they were willing to vandalize and steal, what else might they be willing to do? They'd be under control.

Most days he'd just speed through scenes of women from the trailer park overloading the machines to save a few bucks or a local using the big machines for rugs or comforters. If they, whoever they were, came in for some quick cash, he'd have them.

When he saw the stranger walk in with a duffel bag and a cup of coffee, he became curious. He backed up to when the guy walked in and played the video at normal speed. He watched the guy, a very handsome guy, empty his bag into a machine, shaking each garment loose and dropping it in. He bought a small box of detergent from the vending machine and emptied it into the washer.

Then, looking around a little apprehensively, making sure he was alone, he started to strip. First the shirt, revealing a muscular, well-defined chest. Off came the sneakers, socks into the washer, and to his anticipated delight, the belt slipped out of its loops. He slowed the video down. It wasn't a completely clear view, but he could almost feel the unbuttoning and unzipping of the jeans. He could imagine the sound of the zipper being undone. It excited him. Down the jeans came, revealing a pair of perfectly fitting jockey shorts, just like you see on the front of the package in the store. And what a package! This guy was hot, really hot.

He paused the recording, holding his breath. "Please, please, please. Don't you need to wash those, too?" he whispered to himself.

In anticipation, he clicked on the play icon. Instead of pulling off the jockey shorts, he pulled on a pair of red shorts over them. Closing the lid of the machine, he pushed the coins through and picked up his coffee.

Damn, he was fucking hot! He rewound and watched the man strip several times, each time enjoying it more. His eyes fixed on those jockey shorts, always taking his imagination one step further.

The ringing of his cell phone shocked him out of his reverie. As he answered, he moved the mouse to the download icon. This clip was a keeper.

FOUR

Adam sat cross-armed, legs extended and crossed at the ankles, in what he guessed was an interrogation room in the Ur substation of the county sheriff's office, where they asked him to wait. A card table and three folding chairs furnished the room. He noticed that feeling of being watched and scanned the room until he saw the security camera hanging from the ceiling in the corner of the room. There were no windows.

Adam could feel his body tightening, his mind starting to rev like an engine. Ever since he was a boy back in Pittsburgh, he'd had a habit of bottling up energy—and now, stuck in this bland room with nothing to do, the waiting was almost unbearable. He wanted to move; even something simple like jogging in place might help. But he worried that showing too much nervous energy on camera wouldn't serve him well.

He closed his eyes and pressed his finger into the cleft of his chin. A small smile tugged at his lips.

He thought of his Nonno.

His grandfather had a shed behind the house, perched on the steepest part of the backyard hill. It was barely more than a potting shed, but to Nonno, it was his workshop. Terraced rows of tomatoes and peppers spilled down the hillside below it, and on one of the shelves inside sat an old wind-up alarm clock with two brass bells and a hammer that danced between them when it rang.

One afternoon, when Adam was maybe six, he noticed the clock wasn't ticking.

"Nonno, did you forget to wind the clock?"

His grandfather set down his tools and lifted the clock from the shelf.

"No, Adamino," he said, his accent warm and familiar. "This time, I wind it too tight."

Adam's face fell. "Did it break?"

"Not broken," Nonno said, pulling Adam onto his lap. "Just... stuck. You help me fix, eh?"

Together they opened the back of the clock with a tiny screwdriver. Nonno pointed to the coil spring nestled among the delicate gears.

"See this part? This is the spring. It holds all the power. We wind it up, and it makes the clock move—tick-tick, ring-ring." He gave Adam's belly a playful tickle. "But today I give it too much. Now the spring, she can't move. Too much energy, all stuck inside."

With a gentle nudge of the screwdriver, Nonno released the latch. The spring unwound in a sudden whirl of motion. Adam jumped.

"Adamino," Nonno said softly. "Your teacher tell me sometimes in school you get up, move around, go bathroom too much, eh?"

Adam squirmed in his lap, unsure if he was in trouble.

"Is okay," Nonno said. "You have big spring inside you too. Gets tight sometimes."

Adam looked up at him, curious.

"You want to know a trick?"

Adam nodded.

"Close your eyes. Can you see the spring inside? Look for it."

Adam shut his eyes and gave a little wiggle. Nonno chuckled.

"Now—here is the trick. Everyone has a special button to help unwind the spring. You know where yours is?"

Adam opened one eye. "Where?"

Nonno tapped the little cleft in his own chin. "Right here. I have one, you have one."

He gently pressed Adam's chin, right in the center.

"When your spring gets too tight and you can't run around, you press here. Just like winding down the clock. It helps you be still. Just until it's time to run again."

Adam giggled, eyes wide. "Really?"

"Really. It work best when you close your eyes and think of the spring; let it go *slow.* You try next time, okay?"

Back in the interrogation room, Adam kept his finger on his chin. Just a light touch. He imagined the spring inside loosening, unwinding, quieting.

It still worked—sometimes.

The waiting was the worst part. His rucksack had somehow ended up behind the police caution tape and had been taken as evidence. He thought of the bottled water. He could use a drink about now. He pulled in his legs and straightened his back. He sat up, twisted in his chair until he heard and felt his back crack.

He felt his pockets for his phone. It was in his rucksack. *Shit!* He couldn't do anything without his phone. He stood up. He casually stretched. Before he could rest his palms on the floor, he stopped himself. He thought of the red stain on his one hand. He hadn't told them about that. The image of the small bloom of red he had seen on Tommy's chest popped into his mind. *It could have just been a scratch from the gutter. Hell, it could have been a zit.*

However, his mind kept going back to his first thought, *A clean shot that stopped the heart.* Adam shook his head as if to clear it. *It's all just speculation. Stop speculating. You did what you could for the man. Don't muddy the waters with speculation.*

The best way to describe what happened at the First Pentecostal Church that morning was ordered chaos. Adam had continued CPR until the paramedics arrived. They quickly took over. Adam and Luis stood at the side watching them.

Luis had appeared more angry than worried. "Do you think he'll make it?"

"I don't know." Adam didn't mention his thoughts when he first noticed the tiny blood bloom on Tommy's chest. He avoided looking at the patch of now dry blood on the ball of his hand.

"Fuck. I knew I shouldn't have come. My wife volunteered me." Raising the pitch of his voice, "It'll just be a few hours." Then back to his own voice, "She'll do anything for this fucking church! Fucking holy rollers! She's here four times a week! Wednesday and Friday nights and twice on Sunday. And now I'm stuck here because that fat deacon fell off the damned roof."

"What happened up there?' Adam asked.

Luis shook his head, baffled. "I-I don't know. It all happened so fast. One minute Tommy was complaining about the flashing. It pissed me off because I did the flashing around the steeple, and I did it right. Then the next minute, Tommy was on the ground."

"Where's Chucho?" Adam asked.

Luis looked around. "That lazy bastard." Exasperated. "No fucking idea."

Two police cars arrived. A sergeant and a deputy separated Adam and Luis, took statements, and then they were both brought back to the substation.

And now, Adam had to wait. He hated waiting. He tried the doorknob, but the door didn't budge. At once the deputy opened the door. "Do you need something?" She must have been standing guard.

She could not have been more than twenty-five. She was pretty in a wholesome and scrubbed way. She had a round face with jet black hair pulled back in a tight bun. He tried to imagine her smiling.

"Water, coffee?"

"I could really use a cup of coffee, but I'd like to wash my hands." He held up his hands. Her gaze lingered on the bloodstain for a fleeting second. "I'll be right back."

Adam hoped that she would return with a cup of coffee, but instead, she had a swab kit and a gunshot residue collection kit. She led him over to the table. He noted that she positioned them so that the swabbing of his hands was in full view of the camera. She dabbed both his hands with sticky tape and placed the tape into right and left hand receptacles. She did the same with the swabs. It wasn't unexpected. If Tommy had been shot, they'd want to know if Adam had fired a gun recently. But why would an assassin stick around to do CPR?

She was efficient and formal. "Wait here. I'll be back in a minute. I need to escort you to the restroom so you can wash your hands." Adam wondered if she'd have to come in with him. He didn't care if she did, but she was so young, he felt for her. *That stern demeanor is part of the job*, he thought. *I bet she's really pretty when she smiles and lets her hair down—literally and figuratively.*

Sergeant William Baxter was tall, broad-shouldered and muscular, a combination that would intimidate anyone. Adam put him in a level above what used to be his own. Baxter's thick, cropped, jet-black hair looked like fur. His complexion was a rich, deep copper brown. He had a strong, broad face and wore an inscrutable expression. The deputy followed him into the room and stood in the corner.

Adam set down his coffee and offered Baxter his hand.

"Have a seat, Mr. Alba. I've gone over the statement you gave to Deputy Isi earlier. I just want to go over it again to see if anything new comes to mind. Sometimes details get clearer after a little time has passed."

Adam knew better than to comment on the passing time. There was no rushing this process. He sat back down and picked up his coffee. The warmth of the cup was calming. "Sure thing."

"You don't mind if I record our conversation?" Baxter smiled. "Most people talk faster than I can write."

Adam glanced at the camera strategically placed in the corner near the ceiling tiles. Baxter pulled a voice recorder from his breast pocket and put it on the table. Looking down at it, Adam said, "I give my full permission."

Adam admired the way he asked for permission to record the conversation. It was clean, unabashed, and honest. Of course, their interaction was recorded anyway by that video camera. Adam gave his permission and repeated it when Baxter turned on the voice recorder. He repeated his story, and Baxter peppered his account with questions.

"How were they positioned on the roof?"

"Chucho was standing. Tommy and Luis were kneeling."

"Can you describe their positions relative to one another?" Baxter asked.

"It looked like Chucho was just standing there at the ridge of the roof, Tommy was at his feet, and Luis was on the other side of the church roof. I couldn't see him until he stood up. I could see Chucho's face, but Tommy had his back to me, and like I said, Luis was on the other side of the roof."

"So this Chucho was closest to Tommy on the roof, and he was standing up."

"Looked like he was straddling the ridge, but I can't be sure."

"By the way, how did you know which was which?"

"Tommy had a bigger build."

"No, I mean, how do you know their names?"

"Oh, sorry, I should have mentioned that I met them this morning at McDonald's. I had some time to kill and asked if there was anything to do around here. Tommy mentioned the casino and Walmart. He called it the corridor of corruption."

"The corridor of corruption?" Baxter seemed to think that description amusing.

Adam nodded. "That's what he called it. He said they ruined the town. I don't remember exactly how he said it, but I got the idea that the town was just a bit past the corridor of corruption. I just thought I'd check it out."

"Anything else about the conversation? What about the other guys?"

"Chucho never said a word. Luis complained about not getting paid and wanted to get to work so that they could finish the job."

"Can you describe Chucho for me?

"Luis can probably do a better job. I don't think he spoke English. He never said a word to me. Never ever really looked at me more than a glance. The others only spoke Spanish to him, and I know enough Spanish to know they were translating for him. He was about as tall as Tommy, thinner, fitter, like a sporty guy, and darker-skinned than Tommy, lighter than Luis. His clothes were kind of baggy, but you could still see he worked out."

"Any scars, tattoos, or anything else that might identify him in more detail?"

Adam shook his head. "Not that I noticed. All I know is that he was up on the roof with Tommy and Luis, and he was the first to come off the roof. They were crouching around Tommy. I started CPR. I didn't notice Chucho was gone until the paramedics arrived."

"Tell me about the blood on your hand."

Adam flushed. "From the CPR. I saw the blood, but Tommy didn't seem to be breathing, and I couldn't find a pulse. I just went into automatic mode. There wasn't that much blood at first, but the pressure of the chest compressions made it worse."

The interview came to an end. Baxter signed off on the recording. "Mr. Alba, you're free to go, but you'll have to stick around for a few days. The sheriff will want to talk with you, most likely tomorrow. Where can I reach you?"

Nonplussed, Adam said, "My cell phone is in my rucksack. When do you think I can get it back? I have no idea where I'll stay. Probably the motel, I guess."

"I'll see what I can do about your rucksack. I'll ask Deputy Isi to make a few calls for you. That motel usually fills up on the weekends."

FIVE

osie Valez, her hair up in a scarf, dumped the bucket of dirty mop water in the alleyway behind the Pioneer's Rest. Her great-grandmother bought the business, hotel and saloon, back when some folks still used the hitching post in front of the building on Main Street. She kept the place running out of sentimentality and to have something to do.

She used the standing tap to rinse out the bucket and mop. Henry, the short-order cook, was done for the day. He always left the kitchen clean and tidy and put the dining room chairs up on the tables so that she could sweep and mop the floors. He'd take them down again the next morning when he came in to do the prep work. She wrung out the mop, dumped the water again, and stowed the mop and bucket against the back wall.

It was nearly four in the afternoon. The Rest was open from eight to two, breakfast and lunch only. She and Henry worked seven days a week. If either of them were to ever be sick, a sign on the door would be sufficient to elicit the understanding of the patrons. But neither of them was ever sick.

She climbed the back stairs to her rooms on the third floor. Just before COVID hit, she had converted two guest rooms into a cozy apartment for herself. There were still two guest rooms on that floor, but with so few guests, they were never used. One had become a de facto storage room. She gave the other one to Henry as part of his wages. He was alone in life. He was safe and reliable even if he drank a little too much beer occasionally.

Only one guest occupied a room on the second floor. A guy named Jesus Ramirez. He was from Mexico, paid the weekly rate, cash up front, a month in advance. She hadn't seen him much. He had never taken advantage of the free breakfast she offered guests of the Rest.

According to Manda Lamano, the woman who cleaned the guestrooms and the lobby on Monday mornings, he was very neat and tidy, and made his own bed even when he knew the sheets and towels would be changed. What more did Rosie need to know? Her mother always said, "Curiosity killed the cat. If you don't need to know, don't ask."

She sank into her favorite chair and reached for her television remote. She recorded her favorite soap opera every day and watched it every evening. Her eyes closed. Her head fell sideways, resting on the wing of her chair.

Her cell phone woke her. It was that nice girl, Aya Isi, the new deputy at the substation. She had a stranded traveler who needed a place to stay. She didn't say why the traveler was stranded or how long he'd be staying.

"Of course, I've got a room. Give me ten minutes. The lobby door should be open. Tell him to wait there." She checked herself in a mirror and slipped into a comfortable pair of slippers. She descended the front stairs to the lobby.

Deputy Isi led Adam to the lobby door of the Pioneer's Rest. "There is a vacancy here. It's kind of old-fashioned. If you don't like it, you can get back to the motel on Monday night. It's the only other place in town. The owner said she'd be about ten minutes, you can wait for her in the lobby."

He thanked her and stepped into the lobby. It was illuminated by sconce lighting that had been converted from gas to electric. The floors were polished planks. A Victorian settee and two chairs were centered on an ornate area rug. To one side there was a roll-top desk flanked by a curio cabinet filled with ruby glass goblets. In the corner was an old player piano with the scroll visible. Adam pressed a few out of tune keys.

Rosie descended the front stairs. She saw a young man leaning over the player piano. He plinked a few keys.

"It's out of tune, but it still works, but only with a gold coin," she teased.

He turned around smiling. "I've never seen one before, at least one that wasn't a movie prop. Is it a real one? I mean, is it an authentic antique?"

"Yes, honey, it is. But it's not the only authentic antique around here. At least I feel like one sometimes."

He cocked his head as if he couldn't tell if she were joking. He smiled at her. "I'm Adam Alba. He offered her his hand.

"I'm Rosie Valez. I run the place." Saying she owned it was something she rarely admitted. In her mind it still belonged to her father.

Close enough to see his eyes, she realized that he was both older and more handsome than he appeared from a distance. She ignored a sensual feeling that surprised her. For a brief second, she felt like a schoolgirl seeing a very cute boy for the first time. She hadn't felt that kind of reaction for a long, long time. She hoped she wasn't blushing.

"It's like something out of the Wild West." He gestured around the lobby.

"If I had a dollar for every person who said that. " She smiled back at him. "The whole first floor, restaurant, and this lobby, used to be a saloon back in the day. The old bar is still there on the restaurant side, though I don't serve liquor anymore."

Shaking his hand, his touch sent feelings through her that were oddly sharper and softer at the same time, like an unexpected shock of static electricity that makes both people laugh. "Let me show you how much like the Old West the Pioneer's Rest is. Come on." She thought her tone sounded a little too coquettish and reined herself in. After all, he was a stranger. She led him up the stairs. She flirted all the time when she was waiting tables. It was part of the job, and the old coots liked the attention, but no one in the restaurant took her flirting seriously. There was no telling how this guy might react.

She forced herself into business mode. Pointing at a red velvet rope partially blocking the third-floor stairs. "All guest rooms are on the second floor. Don't go up there. It's not really safe."

She opened one of the rooms in the front of the hotel. "All the rooms are the same except for air-conditioning. The rooms to the rear have window units. The front rooms, like this one, have a view of the park and get a nice breeze. If you prefer air-conditioning—"

"I'm fine without air-conditioning." Adam interrupted her, thinking of the stale smell coming out of the unit at the motel. "I prefer fresh air."

"Each room has a sink for washing up." She pointed at a small sink under a wall-mounted mirror. Next to it there were towels of varying sizes hanging on a rack. "Two bathrooms with showers are down the hall. They're marked Men and Women, but if one is occupied, use the other one. There's only one other man staying here. Just leave them the way you found them—clean."

Adam tested the bed to have something to do. It was adequate for sleeping, but for a man accustomed to rough sleeping, his only concern would be if it were too soft. There was a table and chair to one side and a dresser with a mirror to the other. "Seems fine. How much?"

"How long are you planning on staying?"

"Not sure," he said honestly. He didn't think he should say that he was waiting for the police to let him leave town.

"Thirty-five dollars a night or $160 for the week." Rosie rattled automatically.

"That's incredible." Adam blinked.

"It also includes one meal a day in the restaurant downstairs. It's open from eight to two every day."

"I'll take a week. Can I pay you now?" He stood up, reaching for his back pocket. "I'll go and get my bag in a bit." He didn't lie but something told him not to mention he was getting it from the bus station.

Another cash-up-front guest, she thought, *and eye candy to boot.*

He plucked eight twenties from his wallet and exchanged them for a key.

She took his driver's license, filled out a brief form on her clipboard, and asked him to sign it.

"Rooms are cleaned, and towels and linens changed on Monday mornings. No cooking in the room. There is a little communal kitchen at the end of the hall with a fridge and microwave. If you need extra towels, they are in a closet next to the kitchen. Help yourself."

He thanked her and watched her leave.

Back in her apartment, she breathed deeply and put the tea kettle on the burner. She hadn't reacted to a man that way in years. Most of the men from around town were older, sun-scorched, overweight, wearing baggy clothes and bola ties. This Adam wore clothes that actually fit his body. That kind of body deserves clothes that fit. She chuckled at her own silliness.

Adam looked at his watch. It was nearly five and he was hungry. He thought of the sandwich and chips in his rucksack. He thought of his phone. He thought of his bus ticket. If he had his rucksack, he could eat that sandwich. He could call his sister in Pittsburgh. Hell, he could get on that bus at six twenty, though he knew he wouldn't get far without being labeled a fugitive. He locked his room behind him and set out. There'd probably be food in the casino, and if not, there was Walmart.

He had to pass the substation on his way back out of town. *I'll let Baxter know where I'm staying, where I'm headed, and when I should be back in case he has my rucksack.* Two thoughts volleyed in his mind. Should I have told Baxter to call DuPuis back in the New Orleans Police Department? Should I have told him what I thought about the blood?

When dealing with the police, he knew it was best to answer their questions without embellishment or speculation—unless they ask for it. On the other hand, being asked why he failed to mention something might later be cause for suspicion. In any case, he knew he had nothing to hide, not really.

He wrestled mentally until he had reclaimed his duffel bag from the bus station. It was Manda behind the counter again, and when he walked into the station, she seemed pleased to see him. Adam thought he detected a hint of compassion in her face, and she wasn't surprised to learn he was extending his stay in Ur.

"Where are you staying? The motel?"

"No, I've got a room at the Pioneer's Rest."

"It's old-world Ur. You'll be comfortable there. So, you've been captivated by the beauty of Ur?" she said over her shoulder as she walked to a back room to get his bag.

Adam wasn't sure if she was sarcastic or sincere. Perhaps she was fishing for details about rumors she'd already heard. He played it safe. "It is really nice here. People are nice. The weather. A good place to spend a few days."

Hoisting his bag up onto the counter, she chuckled. "Most folks around here have been here all our lives." She winked. "Enjoy your visit, now."

He thanked her and left the building. *Back to the corridor of corruption*, he thought.

Coming from the opposite direction, the church looked serene and peaceful. The image of Tommy Delgado's fall played on an infinite loop in the back of his mind, and he did his best to not allow it to come forward.

He chose to check out the restaurant in the casino first, thinking a hot meal was better than a cold sandwich wrapped in plastic. Adam wove his way through the parking lot toward the main entrance. As he approached, an automatic revolving door began to spin.

Stepping out of the door into the main room of the casino, he was at once pelted with the sounds of slot machines, one-armed bandits, though the arms had been replaced by buttons and the clicking slots replaced with garish animations.

He was surrounded by cool air and the lingering odor of stale cigarette smoke. The immediate assault on his senses was so unpleasant he almost backed out of the place, but hunger got the best of him. A guard stood at the door, and Adam asked him for directions to the restaurant. Whether a natural stoic or completely disinterested, the guard merely pointed to the far corner of the casino. Adam wondered where all the people came from. He navigated through the crowded betting tables and passed by a poker tournament area near the restaurant. Adam noticed a small corridor that had restrooms and a separate entrance. He'd be sure to leave through that door to avoid the chaos of the casino.

The restaurant was quiet, nonsmoking, and very pleasant. He was seated by a middle-aged woman with a raspy smoker's voice. She asked him if he had a preference of seating.

"I'm alone. It doesn't matter."

"Will you be wanting the buffet?" She indicated a large salad bar area with people lined up on both sides.

"Can I order from the menu?"

She nodded and led him to a small table near a server staging station and a set of swinging kitchen doors. She grabbed a menu from the staging area and handed it to Adam. "Leanne will be with you shortly."

Leanne looked like she should be doing homework rather than waiting tables in a casino. She was a slight girl, with thin arms and bony hips. Her thin, mousy brown hair was tied back in a short ponytail. Several strands had come loose and framed her face. She used makeup to hide the fatigue; a more natural look would have betrayed her. Adam noticed an engagement ring on her left hand. Perhaps she was older than she looked; perhaps not. Adam felt sorry for her.

He ordered a steak, baked potato, and salad. He would normally be more conservative with his cash, but after the day he had, a splurge was in order. "Um, I need to use the restroom. Can I leave my bag here, or should I take it with me?"

"I'd say it's safer here than in the bathroom. I'll keep an eye on it for ya."

SIX

Adam woke in the middle of a dream that first morning in the Pioneer's Rest. He waffled in and out of the dream, trying to figure out what it was about. In the dream, he saw Ken Griffen, his last wrestling opponent, walking down the road in Ur, past the Pentecostal church and the corridor of corruption toward town. He wore that red singlet and strutted confidently away from Adam, casually looking back to make sure Adam was still following him.

Ken had blamed himself for the accident. While Adam was still hospitalized and unconscious, Ken had tragically ended his own life. In the dream, he kept trying to catch up to Ken to explain that the accident was just an accident. That it wasn't his fault, not at all. Adam had weighed in too far over his weight bracket and was offered the choice to either sit out the match or to face an opponent in the higher weight class. He shouldn't have done it. Griffen was a wrestling legend, and wrestling him while at the bottom of the weight class was Adam's own mistake.

It wasn't the first time Ken had entered Adam's dreams. He climbed out of bed, pulled the red running shorts out of the top of his duffel bag. In Adam's view of the park across from the Pioneer's Rest, it looked like a good place to exercise. There was room enough to do a full series of wrestling drills—those practiced movements that left Adam feeling limber and strong.

It was well-maintained and clean, with ornate benches of wood and wrought iron in both shady and sunny locations. Cement walkways meandered among tall trees and grassy areas. A white wooden gazebo stood proud in the center of the park that occupied an entire town block. Adam imagined people dressed in their Sunday best, strolling through the park on a warm, pleasant afternoon. Perhaps buying snow cones or ice cream from a vendor with a cart. He thought of Tommy, who had said coming to town had been a real treat.

For the first time in days, he had the luxury of working up a real sweat and taking his muscles to exhaustion. He worked fast, getting his heart to pound. As he finished, he could feel his muscles tensing and releasing.

He showered in a claw-foot bathtub with a circular curtain that barely surrounded his body. The hot water drew the curtain in, and it tended to cling to his flesh. After rinsing off, he luxuriated in the hot water just running over his body. He felt agile, flexible, and loose. He turned off the hot water tap and braced himself for the cold. It came quickly. He stayed in the shower long enough to get used to the temperature. Invigorated, he turned off the tap and reached for his towel.

The pile of dirty, sweaty clothes on the floor reminded him that he should have brought a change of clothing with him to this communal bathroom. He wrapped the towel around his waist and hoped he wouldn't run into anyone in the hallway. Though it didn't really matter. Rosie said that there was only one other guest, and he was a dude. So far Adam hadn't seen him.

His room didn't have a phone. No one worked at the front desk. There was no front desk. They hadn't yet given his rucksack back to him. *What could be taking so fucking long for them to go through it? It was just normal stuff.* The worst part was it had his phone. A thought startled him. *They are going through my phone.* He gasped, wondering if he were someone considered a suspect in an unexplained death.

His heart sank. How long would it take to access it? What if they had to wait for a warrant? It was a holiday weekend. It could be days! He pulled a clean pair of jeans and a fresh T-shirt from the top of his duffel. He considered his steps. He had no idea how long he'd be in Ur. He could walk back to Walmart and buy a cheap prepaid phone so he could at least call his sister. He would stop by the substation and give his permission and his PIN for them to search his phone. That should speed things up.

He had to dig for a clean pair of underwear almost to the bottom of the bag. Something didn't feel right. His underwear wasn't where he thought it should be. He had just done laundry two evenings ago, mostly because he hadn't had time to do it before leaving New Orleans. Some of the clothes he had packed were dirty, and he had been wearing the clothes he had on for more than twenty-four hours. The laundromat just solved the problem. Clean clothes and a good night's sleep were what he had wanted—had needed.

He always packed his duffel bag strategically, especially when he knew he'd be traveling and not returning to a home base. Unpacking to find something he needed was too much work. If you just packed with a plan, you could find whatever you needed without unpacking the whole bag. But something was not right about this bag.

Adam looked down at the opening of the bag. It didn't even look right. Had he just been in a rush when that lady, Manda, hurried him along at the laundromat? Had someone gone through his bag? If they had, why? Had the police searched through his bag at the bus station without telling him?

He picked up the bag with the handles and examined it. It looked perfectly normal. There weren't any tears or cuts. No damage at all. He felt around the outside of the bag. If he hadn't known better, he might have guessed he had the wrong bag. It felt wrong. Nothing felt right. In one corner he felt something hard that shouldn't be there. He tried to think what it could be and came up empty.

He stopped and ran his mind over the last few days, including his last two days in New Orleans. Had someone given him something that he forgot about? Stuffed a goodbye gift into his bag? He shook his head. No one had a chance to do that. He also remembered emptying the bag into the washing machine. *I would have found it at the laundromat.* When making a move, everything he chose to keep became everything he owned in the world. It was all in the rucksack and the duffel bag. Every item he kept was the result of a decision—the bare minimum. It wasn't a lot of stuff.

His mind turned methodical. That hard thing wasn't his, and whoever put it in his bag had to unpack it at least partway to get it in there. What had they taken out? The bag was packed tightly. There wasn't a lot of room for additional items. That was what the rucksack was for—not the duffel.

He'd have to go commando. He hated going commando. He pulled on the clean jeans and T-shirt he had pulled from the duffel, slipped into his shoes, and slid his wallet and room key into his pockets. He grabbed the bag and headed to the substation.

Deputy Isi was sitting at the desk. The hint of a smile flashed across her face. "How's the Rest? Did you sleep alright?"

"Nice, but I have a problem."

She raised her eyebrows. "What do you need?"

"Is Sergeant Baxter here?" Adam asked.

She straightened her back. "It's me or nobody." The smile was gone.

"Sorry, I didn't mean it like it sounded." He set the bag on a chair in front of the desk. He tried to explain the problem the best he could, but he wasn't doing a good job of it.

"Wait, are you saying someone stole your underwear?"

"No. I mean, I don't know. They just aren't in the bag where they should be. And I noticed that someone, I don't know who, has moved things around in my bag. I felt the bag from outside and there's something hard in there that isn't mine."

"What is it?"

"I don't know, but… it shouldn't be there. I didn't put it in there."

She squinted. "Someone went through your bag and put something into it. Do I have that right?"

"Yep, call me OCD if you want." He ran his fingers through his hair. "When I pack my bag, I pack it in such a way that I don't have to unpack it to find what I need. Things have been moved around. And that hard thing isn't mine!"

"You're sure."

"Yes." Adam's tone was confident.

"Did anyone help you pack?"

"No."

"Has the bag been out of your control at any time?"

He thought. "Well, it was in the luggage compartment of the bus for almost a whole day." He traced his memory carefully. "I left it in my motel room when I went outside to work out and again when I went to McDonald's for coffee. It was about half an hour both times. When I got back from McDonald's, the bag was gone, and the housekeeper—I assume it was the housekeeper—had taken it to the lobby. That lady that works the desk…"

"Mrs. Patel?"

"I guess. Anyway, she was kind of rude."

"That's her. Don't take it personally."

Isi started taking notes.

"I also left it at the bus station. I was going to continue my trip on the evening bus. But then, yesterday happened. After I checked into the hotel, I walked to the bus station and picked up my bag. I stopped at the casino because I was hungry. After dinner, I walked back to my room."

"Did you leave the bag unattended at any time in the casino?"

"No." He tripped mentally. "Wait. For about ten minutes when I went to the restroom. The server, her name was Leanne, said she'd keep an eye on it for me."

"You left it at your table?"

"Yes. It's been in my room in the Pioneer's Rest ever since. I did go out and worked out again this morning, and I took a shower down the hall, but it was locked in my room. That's it."

She furrowed her brow. He could see the cogs in her brain working. Her eyes darted around in their sockets. Then the color drained from her face.

"Okay, I'm probably overreacting. I hope I'm overreacting." She said this out loud, but Adam didn't think she was talking to him. Looking directly at him, she said, "Mr. Alba, we're going to leave your bag on that chair. Please don't touch it again." She got up. "You and I are going to go outside."

"Huh?"

"You heard me. Leave the bag. Let's go outside." She got up, went to the door, and held it open for him. "Now!"

"Everything I own is in that bag except for the rucksack you guys took yesterday."

"Too bad. Do as I say."

He got up and walked out of the front door of the substation. Deputy Isi followed him and locked the door behind her. "Wait for me across the street." Isi began talking into the mic on her shoulder.

Isi tugged at the door to the post office. It was locked. She cupped her hands over her eyes to peer through the glass door. The woman who ran the post office, normally left the lobby open on Sunday for people to check their mail. She also tended to hang out in the back using the Internet. Isi could see light through the gaps in the Dutch door that served as a counter. Isi feverishly pounded on the door. Confused and unsettled, the woman came out, and they crossed the street together.

Does she think someone is trying to kill me? Does she think I'm trying to kill her? Is she just following procedure? Clearly, she thinks there was something dangerous in the bag. Adam unconsciously ran his fingers through his hair. *Does she believe me about the bag? Did they believe what I told them yesterday? Am I a witness or a suspect?* Adam tried to fit the pieces together. They looked like they should fit, but they didn't. *But why would anyone want to harm me? I don't know anyone here. All I did was see an accident! Right?* He closed his eyes and tried to pull himself together. That shadow feeling was back and strong. His mind floated somewhere above his body, looking down at an absurd situation. *Whoever did this did it before the accident or while I was in the interrogation room. It doesn't make any sense at all.*

Adam couldn't escape his first thought when he saw that bloom of fresh, wet blood. *Stop kidding yourself. You know what you thought when you saw the blood. What if it really was a gunshot? But it couldn't have been. There should have been the sound of a gunshot and more blood or an exit wound. What the fuck is going on?*

He looked at Deputy Isi. She wasn't exactly ignoring him, but she had things on her mind. She was pacing back and forth and keeping her eye on the front of the substation and the post office that shared the building. In between her talking to her shoulder, he could hear the wispy sound of the speaker lodged in her ear. Her eyes kept panning from one direction to another as if she were looking to cross the street. *She's waiting for backup or making sure someone doesn't go near the substation.* He could feel the tightening in his body. The benefit of that morning's workout was draining away.

The Pioneer's Rest restaurant was buzzing with the after-church crowd, but apart from the occasional car looking for a parking spot, there wasn't much traffic. The angled spaces in front of the Rest were full. Twice someone tried to park in front of the post office, but Isi sent them on their way. There were plenty of places to park, but the most convenient were already taken.

Within half an hour, two men in protective clothing, one leading a dog, approached Deputy Isi for the keys to the substation. Sergeant Baxter arrived shortly after they did. He spoke a few minutes to Isi and then pulled Adam aside. "Mr. Alba, let's take a walk in the park."

It was near midday. The sky was a bright blue without a cloud to be seen, but that shadow feeling lingered. Adam felt conspicuous. Some of the people sitting near windows in the Pioneer's Rest were watching with unabashed curiosity, like a cat waiting for a mouse to appear. Adam could feel their eyes follow Sergeant Baxter and him to a bench under the shade of an oak tree.

As they neared the bench, for a second Adam was again out of his body, observing Baxter and himself sitting down from a distance. He could have been sitting in the window of the Rest. He took a deep, slow breath to center and ground himself.

Baxter angled himself to look at Adam.

"Do me a favor, Sergeant. Make sure that thing is on." Adam gestured toward the chest cam he wore. "Let's just make this official."

Baxter raised his brows. "It already is. I'll take that as your consent. I got the gist from Deputy Isi, but I'd like it from you. Tell me about the bag."

Adam told him. Baxter's questions were a little more specific than Deputy Isi's, but they amounted to mostly the same thing.

"On your bus trip, were there any stops that were long enough for people to want access to their bags under the bus?"

"There were a couple of fifteen-minute stops, but I didn't see the bay opened for anyone except new passengers."

"Tell me about the housekeeper at the motel again."

Adam recounted the same story.

"And did you discuss with the housekeeper or the Patels about your destination or mode of transportation?"

"I tried to be friendly with that woman behind the front desk. I do think I said something about Flagstaff and the bus, but she didn't seem interested."

"And in the casino restaurant, was there any discussion with anyone at all about who you were, where you were headed, or how you were going to get there?"

"No, no one, not at all."

"Was there anyone there that you recognized, perhaps from the bus or the motel?"

"Not that I noticed. Sorry."

Baxter leaned back against the wrought iron armrest of the bench. He seemed to deliberate. "I spoke with Detective DuPuis of NOPD."

Adam's face betrayed his surprise. "Okay. And?"

"You had to figure we would check your background. Nobody here knows you or anything about you. Your arrest in New Orleans came up. It's on the record." Baxter's voice was intentionally calm.

"But they know it wasn't me."

Baxter raised his hand. "Yes, I know. The record indicates *No Disposition.*"

"What's that mean?"

"It means they didn't pursue it or there was no trial. It doesn't erase the fact that you were arrested. Anyway, I called DuPuis for the story and his impression of you. It's that simple. He told me all about it. He spoke highly of you, actually."

Adam relaxed slightly. "I sense a but coming."

Baxter nodded. "I'm going to share something with you. You would find out anyway. Because of that, I want your assurance that you won't engage in any risky activity like you did in New Orleans. If you have any ideas, any at all, share them with me, only me, in confidence. Don't act on your own."

"I have no intentions of doing anything other than cooperating with you. I can't even imagine… I don't know what's going on or why it's happening. I had a reason for doing what I did in New Orleans. Maybe DuPuis told you; maybe he didn't, but I don't see any reason for me to do anything now. I need my rucksack because it has my phone. If you want to look in my phone, I can give you the PIN. Whatever I need to do to get my stuff back, I'm ready to do it. I expected to leave here yesterday. I have already told you all I know."

Baxter breathed deeply. "I'm afraid you're going to have to stay here a while longer. I know your phone is in the backpack, but I can't get that for you now. If you need to make a call or two, you can use the landline in the substation."

Adam looked like he was about to protest.

"Let me finish, please. It'll get around soon enough, but what happened yesterday wasn't an accident; it was homicide. You need to agree to stay. I'd rather not detain you as a material witness."

Adam was deflated. "It was a gunshot, wasn't it? When I saw the blood…"

"We're going to keep that under wraps. Have you told anyone anything about your experience yesterday?"

"Not really. When I picked up my bag last evening at the bus stop, that nice lady, Manda, was interested in why I was staying, but I didn't tell her."

"If anyone else asks you about what you saw, and they will, you don't have to tell them anything, but you might be better off just giving them a shortened version of what you told us yesterday. Don't make anything up, and if you remember something else, tell me or Isi, no one else."

"Okay." Adam shrugged.

"And if someone tries to pump you for information, I'd like you to tell me about that. It's a good idea to keep using the word *accident*."

Adam was silent for a moment. "It's bigger than what happened yesterday, isn't it?"

Baxter didn't respond, which was itself an answer.

"Any idea how long they're going to be in there? I want my bag back." Adam gestured to the substation.

"No idea, but you aren't getting that bag back today."

It started as an airy snort that morphed into a chuckle and finished as a belly laugh.

Baxter looked quizzical.

"Look, everything I own except the clothes on my back and a pair of sweaty shorts, socks, and a T-shirt are in the possession of your office. I mean **everything**. Sweet Jesus!" He shook his head. "This is nuts."

SEVEN

There was a moment as Baxter regarded Adam. The sound of squirrels scurrying from tree to tree was all that filled the silence. A short, gentle breeze moved the leaves and dappled the bench with tiny dancing orbs of sunlight.

Adam was unsure of what he saw in Baxter's face. Was it pity, compassion, helplessness, or suspicion? "Please don't be offended, but I feel like I've stepped into a different dimension. In the span of two days, everything has gone crazy."

Baxter nodded. "I'm not surprised you feel that way. Mr. Alba, let me buy you lunch, and then I'll take you to Walmart where you can get a few things."

Adam snorted again, but this time he shook his head in resignation. "Good news for you, Sergeant, you don't have to buy me lunch. I get a free meal with my room."

As they pulled into the Walmart parking lot, Adam's eyes were glued to the First Pentecostal Church of Ur. They flitted from the roof to the ground where Tommy had lain. The crime scene tape had been removed, but the scene replayed in Adam's memory. He could even feel the intensity of the situation; the emotion, checking Tommy for a pulse, and the stiffness of his arms while doing CPR.

"Did you ever find Chucho?" Adam asked.

"No. No one seems to know anything about him except he was some guy Tommy was helping out."

"Even Luis?"

"Even Luis," Baxter admitted. He parked in the farthest reasonable space from the door of the store.

"I won't be long." Adam pulled the handle of the passenger-side door.

"I'm coming with you," Baxter said. "Might pick up a few things myself."

Adam looked at him skeptically. "You don't have to, Sergeant. I'm not going anywhere." He opened the car door, and humid heat poured over his body like a heavy blanket.

"That's not why I'm coming in with you."

"What is it? Some sort of witness protection?" Adam quipped.

"You could say that. Unofficial, of course. To everyone else, I'm just a cop helping an out-of-towner, a witness who has agreed to stay in town while we wait for the coroner's report on an accidental fall. That's the story. That's all of it. Some people around here might want to press you for more. To them you don't know anything more than he fell, you did CPR, and it wasn't enough."

Adam's heart sank and echoed the words, *It wasn't enough*. It pained him to think of it.

"Thing is, if they think there is more to the story, a few might want to take the law into their own hands," Baxter continued. "If I'm with you, they see the law. And they will feel less compelled to take care of things themselves. I'm glad the Rest was so crowded while we had lunch. That did a lot to quell speculation."

"What do you mean? Vigilante justice?" Adam remembered Blaine, Manda's husband, and his sidearm making sure to let Adam know that he would take care of his own.

"A fair number of the folks of Ur were there. They saw us together. This is a small place, and you are a stranger. By now, people are putting air quotes around Tommy's "accident." By Tuesday, when you see the sheriff, there will be a hundred different stories circulating. That's what it's like in a small town. Sometimes, it gets in the way. Sometimes it plays into our hands. I'm hoping for the latter."

Baxter followed Adam, pushing a cart around the store like a bored husband. Multipacks of colored T-shirts, socks, a multipack of Fruit of the Loom Y-fronts, a pair of jeans, and a button-down shirt.

None of this stuff would come with him to Flagstaff if he ever got his bags back. Too bad the Ur Community Thrift Store had gone out of business. He would have easily shopped there first.

Baxter took a call from his wife.

"She wants me to pick up a graduation card for her cousin's kid."

"How'd she know you were here?"

"Texted her."

Adam added toiletries to his cart—shampoo, shaving cream, disposable razors. Baxter's phone rang again. Adam could hear only Baxter's part of the conversation, which amounted to little more than a few grunts and instructions to get ahold of someone named Cody.

Reminded about his sister's youngest son, Jake, graduating high school, Adam too bought a card. He planned to send it off on Tuesday when the post office opened.

Baxter waited patiently while Adam purchased a prepaid cell phone and the clerk activated it. He got a new number, not wanting to deactivate his real phone. He handed a copy of the number to Baxter. "You can reach me at this number if I have reception. I assume there's decent reception in town."

Baxter nodded. "You might want to think about some food supplies for the next day or two. The Rest closes early, and I need you to stick close to the hotel for the next couple of days. Avoid isolated or unpopulated areas. I don't think you should be wandering around."

"Why not?" Adam tensed.

"Whoever put that package in your bag just might want it back."

"What was it?"

"We have to wait for the lab. Holiday weekend. My guess is drugs."

"The lab?" Adam ventured. "Is that the bigger picture?" He mouthed the word drugs.

Baxter didn't respond.

Intuitively, Adam said, "If it helps, I was supposed to change buses in Oklahoma City and Albuquerque, New Mexico." He knew that if he had gotten on the bus, those drugs would have gotten on with him.

"Thank you. That's useful information." Baxter didn't say that he already knew it.

"And how about the rest of my stuff? When can I get my bags back?"

"Maybe, eventually, but for now the duffel bag has to be examined for evidence."

On the way through the store to the grocery section, they passed a display of jigsaw puzzles. Adam stopped. Perusing the selection, he chose one with 1,000 pieces. He figured it would fit on the table in his hotel room. The picture on the box was a group of three teddy bears surrounded by other toys.

"You don't strike me as a teddy bear puzzle type of guy." Baxter was smiling.

"The picture doesn't matter. It helps me to relax and clear my head. It helps me think. I've done it ever since I was a kid." He looked around. "I need a roll of masking tape."

Supplies purchased and bagged, they got back in the car. As they made the brief drive from Walmart to Pioneer's Rest, Baxter set some parameters for the next couple of days.

"Your best bet is to act normally, be friendly and polite—not too friendly but overly polite. Avoid conflict. Do what you normally do but stay in town. Don't open your door to anyone you don't know. Don't take any unnecessary chances. If you need anything, even like you need to go back to Walmart, call or text me." He pulled out his phone and the paper that Adam gave him. "There, I just texted you. You have my number. I or Deputy Isi will get back to you. No one else. Remember to keep your phone charged. If anything happens out of the ordinary, call.

"I can work out in the park?"

"Sure. Just stay in town."

Out of the box, the prepaid phone had only enough charge to activate the service. Even at that, the clerk needed to plug in the charger. The first thing Adam did was to put the phone on charge.

Baxter's instructions cluttered his mind. It wasn't that they were difficult or onerous. He had been nice enough. More than once while talking with Baxter, he had thought of the advisor to his high school chess club. "It's important to understand the move your opponent makes, but even more important is the move they didn't make." It wasn't what Baxter said as much as what he didn't say.

Adam understood that he was a stranger in a town where the only strangers kept themselves mostly to a casino and perhaps a motel for the weekend. Being a different kind of stranger was automatically worthy of suspicion.

Getting off the interstate bus halfway through his journey—for no clear reason—had already cast him in a suspicious light. Being on the scene when a homicide occurred and quite literally ending up with blood on his hands only sealed his fate figuratively as well. Naturally, the locals would be wary.

If Sergeant Baxter knew more than he let on, he might well have eliminated Adam as a suspect, but then why hang on to the rucksack? If nothing else, he was a witness, perhaps a material witness. Adam had resigned himself to the plain fact that he, himself, was the only person in town who knew he was innocent of any crime. He'd be in Ur a lot longer than he had planned.

Suddenly Adam was grateful that his hotel room was not a cell. Though, based on what Baxter said about people taking the law into their hands, he might be safer in jail. He was allowed to roam freely, if only within the town, but was it as bait for the person or persons who put the presumed drugs in his bag?

His thoughts began to roller coaster, so Adam busied himself. He put the sub sandwiches he bought in the communal refrigerator. He washed out his red running shorts for tomorrow's workout. The lightweight material would easily dry before morning. He opened the multipacks of T-shirts, socks, and underwear and placed them in the top drawer of the dresser.

He laid his toiletries out on the top of the dresser and realized that he forgot to buy a hairbrush. He looked into the mirror above the sink and tried to use his fingers as a comb. It didn't seem to help much. It looked like he had just climbed out of bed.

Still waiting for his phone to charge, he emptied the teddy bear jigsaw puzzle out on the table and began sorting through the pieces, looking for the borders. As he found them, he put them off to the side in the lid of the box. When he found what he thought was most, if not all, of them, he swept the other pieces back into the box. One fell on the floor, and he was careful to pick it up. Out of superstition, he put that piece on top of the dresser. It would be one of the last pieces he'd fit into the puzzle.

Jigsaw puzzles had always been part of his life. They needed a kind of concentration that blocked out peripheral or inconsequential thoughts. They absorbed him but didn't stop his unconscious mind from working through things the way it does when someone is dreaming. Sometimes, resolutions to problems he wasn't consciously thinking about presented themselves the way they might do in the shower or while brushing one's teeth. Ideas just seemed to surface. For Adam, jigsaw puzzles were a kind of meditation.

When he was a kid, before he could buy his own puzzles, he'd put them together, then break them apart, mix up the pieces, and do it again. By the time he was in junior high, he had a stack of puzzles on the shelf in his closet. Each time he repeated a puzzle, it got easier and easier. They no longer required the concentration that freed his mind. That was when he started to do them face down.

The more time Adam spent with Sergeant Baxter, the more his thoughts seemed to tangle. Baxter had a way of asking questions—or making offhand remarks—that caught him off guard. Adam kept circling back to the moment he picked up the puzzle, and Baxter said something about the teddy bears. He could've shrugged it off, said the image didn't matter, and moved on. But he hadn't. He'd explained more than he needed to. Even Baxter's silences felt loaded, like they were asking questions of their own. Maybe that's why he hadn't thought about a hairbrush. Baxter had a knack for getting people to talk—a useful trait for a cop and a dangerous one for anyone with something to hide.

He was well on his way to finishing the border of the puzzle when his new cell phone sprang to life. There were two text alerts. One welcomed him to the service, offering him a discount for automatic renewals, and the other was the one from Baxter. Adam saved Baxter's number as a contact and logged into Google to download his whole contact list.

Having signed into Google, he checked his emails. As he expected, there were two emails from his sister expressing frustration over his lack of communication. He wasn't ready to talk to her. She'd have lots of questions, and he didn't have many answers, and that would inspire more questions. If he acted cagey with her, she'd know it. She always knew when he was hiding something, and being his big sister, she'd worry until she was satisfied.

A selfie and a few emojis would serve best. He often sent her selfies to show her he was all right. If he took one in front of the post office, with the name of the town and the zip code displayed, she'd know exactly where he was. She would know he was okay. She'd have questions, but it would buy him some time.

It was still light enough to get a good picture, and it would only take a few minutes. He bounded down the stairs to the lobby. Before stepping out onto the street, something checked him. Perhaps it was the unconscious effect of Baxter's instructions, but he thought he should be more cautious, more aware of his surroundings.

Adam looked through the window on the lobby door. He took in as much of the street as he could. He wasn't sure what he was looking for. The town was nearly vacant. The restaurant was closed. No one was around. There was only one young man sitting on a bench in the park staring at his phone. Adam watched him for a moment before stepping out. The young man looked up and around and stretched before going back to his phone.

Adam stepped out on the sidewalk, trying not to look at the young man sitting in the park. Just be normal, Baxter had said. *Just be normal. You're being paranoid. It's just a kid on his phone. No real reason to think he's there waiting for you.*

The road was empty. No cars. No open businesses. No pedestrians except for the guy in the park. Adam looked into the door of the substation. No one was there. He gently tugged at the door. Locked. A sign on the door read, "In case of emergency, dial 9-1-1." A little further down, he stood in front of the post office. And tried to put the selfie into focus. He had to stand a little in the street to get the name of the town and the zip code into the frame. He straightened his back and extended his arm for the selfie. He thought of a happy time and snapped the picture.

As he took the picture, out of the corner of his eye, he could see the young man in the park watching him. He tried to tell himself it was normal. Adam was the only other person in the street, and he was the only thing moving on that lonely Sunday afternoon.

Something about the way he was watching made Adam uncomfortable. Was a stranger taking a selfie really that interesting? A chill ran down his spine. It didn't have to make sense. It didn't feel like a stranger was just looking at him. It felt like someone was intentionally watching him. No matter what, he couldn't shake the feeling.

Adam repositioned himself in front of the post office. He switched the lens on the phone and, still extending his arms like he was taking a selfie, he snapped a picture of the guy in the park. *I'll send this to Baxter. He'll think I'm nuts, but better safe than sorry.* The truth was, Baxter had said just enough to keep Adam on the alert. *"Whoever put that package in your bag just might want it back."*

The boy lost interest in Adam and looked back down at his phone. Adam pulled the phone close and pretended to be examining the quality of the selfies. He had a decent picture of the boy and texted it to Baxter.

He tried to act unaware as he walked back to the Pioneer's Rest. Not too fast, not too slow. A casual glance at the park.

Back in his room, he texted his post office selfie to his sister, Cathy, with a note. "Just a little side trip. Quiet little town called Ur, pronounced *your*. Continuing to Flagstaff soon. Sending Jake's graduation card on Tuesday when the post office opens. No ATM close by. Take $100 out of my account and give it to Jake when he gets the card. The cell phone reception is sketchy. I have to find Wi-Fi. I'll call soon." *That should do,* he thought.

He recovered one of his submarine sandwiches from the fridge. He opened it and scooped most of the bread out of the bun, leaving the crust. He squeezed the little packets of mayo onto the bread, spreading it with the packet, then flattening the sandwich with his palms.

As he slowly ate, he stood a little back from the window, looking out at the park. The young man remained there, still staring at his phone. Every so often he would look at the Pioneer's Rest. Out of instinct, Adam backed even further from the window. Adam assumed the guy was either one of Baxter's guards or a lookout for someone else. Adam imagined him texting. *Subject is back inside the hotel.*

Adam sat down at the table and disappeared into his puzzle. It was a challenging one. The pieces were small. As dusk fell, he got up and looked once again out the window where the guy had been sitting. He was gone.

Adam switched on the desk lamp and continued his work.

A noise on the floor above startled him. Something heavy had been dropped on the floor. There was supposed to be only one other guest at the Rest, and the third floor was blocked off as unsafe. Who could that be, and what were they doing up there? As if in answer to his questions, Adam could hear the muffled sound of a broadcast baseball game. Someone was in the room above his own, and whoever it was, they were watching or listening to a game.

EIGHT

S houting voices woke Adam from a restless sleep. He had difficulty falling asleep, half torn between a boyish desire to strain to listen to the baseball game and the childlike fear of strangers occupying the room above his on a floor that was labeled dangerous. He must have fallen asleep sometime, but he woke up wanting to sleep more. What were they shouting about?

He got up, half stepped, and half leaned toward the window, being careful not to get too close out of modesty. There was a lot of activity in the park across the street. A crew of five or six guys was setting up canopies and pushing carts of metal folding chairs and tables from a truck parked on the lawn. Chairs were already placed in the gazebo, and a rotund man was placing music stands in front of them.

So much for my workout, Adam thought. It must be a Memorial Day event. He slipped on the red running shorts and opened his room door. There was no one around, and the doors to the two bathrooms were open.

He still hadn't seen the other guest. The thought of someone watching baseball in the room above his didn't feel so menacing in the bright light of day. The guest rooms didn't have television or Wi-Fi. Maybe upstairs was just a private space, and the sign threatening danger was a smokescreen. Perhaps Rosie herself was a baseball fan. After a visit to the bathroom, doing his necessary, as his dad used to call it, he took a quick shower.

Back in his room, he shaved in the wash-up sink, *a brilliant idea for a hotel with shared bathrooms*. He reminded himself how his fingers were inadequate as a comb. Still wrapped in the damp towel from his shower, he stood at the window brushing his teeth and watching the guys set up.

It reminded him of the church festivals that dotted the city of Pittsburgh when he was a kid. They had games, a kiddie ride or two, and sold ethnic foods. He loved those church festivals. He thought of his grandmother, who had dedicated every Friday to making pizza to raise money for the church, and during Lent, she helped organize the Friday fish fry. Huge pieces of batter-dipped cod on a bun less than half the size of the fish. His mouth watered thinking about it.

What he wouldn't give to sit at his grandmother's table just one more time. She doted on him, always watched to see what he ate, and often tried to make him eat more. He thought of his sister, who would be visiting and tending family graves today the way his parents had done before they died. He thought of his Nonno, who still lived alone in that little house on the side of the hill. He'd be sitting in the car with her retelling family stories. He missed his family, but he missed his Nonno most of all.

He picked up his phone to see the time. It was 8:45, and he had two text messages. His sister replied to his selfie. Thanks for the photo. Where the hell is Ur, and what is up with this new number? Jake's party is in two weeks. I don't expect you, but it would be nice if you were here, and Jake would love to see his favorite uncle.

Adam smiled, knowing she was using the same guilt trip their mother would have. He chuckled to himself. *I'm his only uncle, and Jake will be hanging out with his friends, getting drunk.* He replied, "Old phone acting up. Having it looked into. The new number is temporary. I didn't want to transfer my number to this cheap phone. It's just a backup for now."

It wasn't a complete lie. Someone was likely *looking into* his phone.

The other was from Sergeant Baxter: "That's Junior Delgado. Tommy Delgado's son. Polite kid. Very smart. State judo champ." He could have said more, but he hadn't. Adam's stomach sank. "So, was he really watching me or not?" Adam whispered to himself. State judo champ? Was that a warning or just an expression of local pride in the boy?

Adam dressed, pondering Junior Delgado. *He was too young to lose his dad. He couldn't have been more than twenty or so. That's way too young. Did he just want to see who I was? Perhaps he wanted to ask me about his father's death. Did he want to thank me? Or did he think I was somehow involved or responsible for his father's death? Or maybe, Adam* chastised himself, *he just wanted time to be alone and think and went to that empty park to have some space around him. Poor kid, I can only imagine what he's going through.*

Adam glanced at the puzzle on the table. There would be time to puzzle things out. For the moment, he was hungry.

Adam surveyed the restaurant when he stepped inside. In the back, near the kitchen door, was a group of three tables pushed together. He recognized one of them as either Blake or Blaine. He figured it was Blaine, as he was wearing a sidearm.

There was a table with two men near the front window. One was apparently supervising the men setting up the festival. Using a walkie-talkie app, in a voice too loud for indoors, he spoke instructions into his phone, and a guy in the park gave him a thumbs-up. Rosie was filling their coffee cups. She called to Adam. "Sit anywhere you'd like, honey. I'll be with you in just a sec."

Adam chose a table so that he would have his back to the wall and still see the door clearly enough. He had the shadow feeling lingering distantly in the back of his mind. He kept it at bay by telling himself he was a stranger in a small town. Naturally people would wonder who he was and why he was there. Out of the corner of his eye, he saw a few turn-around looks from the tables in the back. God knows what Blaine was telling those people. There were only a few people in the room, but it seemed filled with the sounds of murmured conversations and the scratching of cutlery on plates with the background of the dim rock music coming from the kitchen.

Through the window, the park looked increasingly festive. They were hanging candy-colored bunting, the plastic kind used by car dealers, between lamp posts. Almost everyone who walked past the restaurant windows came in to eat. The room quickly got crowded. Adam wondered how Rosie and the cook would manage. Groups of more than four pushed tables together. The restaurant had the feeling of a private club. Everybody knew the routine.

The day before, when he and Baxter came in to eat, they sat with their backs to the restaurant on high stools at the counter that had once been a saloon bar. Their conversation revolved around the package in his bag, and he hadn't paid much attention to what was going on in the restaurant except that he didn't like the vulnerability of giving his back to everyone. Then he figured that Baxter's presence added an extra layer of security.

Adam began to feel guilty having a table of four to himself when Luis and a woman entered together.

They looked around for a table, and Adam stood up and waved at them. The woman seemed a little confused, but Luis's face lightened. He led her to Adam's table. "Been wondering what happened to you. Eunie, this is… " he hesitated. "The guy who did CPR on Tommy."

Adam half stood up. He wasn't offended that Luis didn't remember his name. "I'm Adam. It's a pleasure to meet you, Mrs.… ?"

"Eunice." She shook Adam's extended hand.

"You two are welcome to join me. I've got this table to myself. And the place is filling up fast. I'd welcome the company."

Luis looked at his wife. She shrugged, and he held a chair out for her. "Thanks, you're very kind," she said to Adam.

Rosie approached the table smiling. She set three glasses of water on the table. "Coffee?"

They all nodded.

"Sunday menu today." She laid down a laminated, postcard-sized menu on the table. "I'll get your coffee and be back in a jiffy."

Eunice slid the menu toward Adam. "Weekdays Henry cooks to order, but on Sundays, the place is so crowded, you have to pick one of these. Today, being a holiday…"

Adam nodded. "I was here yesterday. Rosie really seems to enjoy her work when the place is full. I've worked in restaurants. Most people would be frazzled."

"Oh, Rosie was always the social butterfly. We grew up together. Very popular, if you know what I mean." Eunice raised an eyebrow. "It's not about the money either. She doesn't need it. She just likes people." She smiled at Rosie as she returned with the coffee pot.

Coffee poured, Rosie took their orders. As Rosie walked away, Eunice stood up. "If you'll excuse me, I'm going to wash my hands."

Luis leaned into Adam. "Whatever you do, do not bring up the church or religion, or you will be in for the sermon of your life. She's made my life hell ever since she 'found Jesus.'" He motioned quotation marks. "Always complaining, always criticizing, always nagging me to get me to do this or that for her church. I feel bad saying it, but Tommy Delgado took advantage of that."

"Tommy was the pastor?"

"Deacon. To be fair, he didn't ask anybody to do what he wouldn't do himself. He worked his ass off for that church and deacon isn't a paid position. He did it all 'for the Lord.'" He gestured air quotes.

Adam nodded and changed the subject. "Luis, I'm glad we ran into one another. They kept us separated while they were questioning us, and we didn't have much time to talk. What happened up there on the roof?"

Luis slowly shook his head. "None of it makes sense. I've gone over it again and again. I was working on the section of the roof closer to the steeple. Tommy was shooting nails, but he had a hard time walking the line, that is, keeping the shingles straight. Chucho stood up, straddling the ridge. I thought to see if Tommy was keeping the shingles straight.

"Tommy was complaining about the flashing, and it was pissing me off. That guy didn't even know how to use a fucking chalk line, and he's complaining about my flashing. I have been a roofer for almost thirty years. I put the flashing around the steeple myself, and there was nothing wrong with it.

"Tommy stood up and fell off the roof. That's all I know. Tell you the truth, with his complaining and his trying to be in charge, more than once I felt like knocking him off that roof." He rethought his phrasing and flushed with an emotion that Adam couldn't define.

"The church should have hired me. I offered to do it for the price of supplies, half of which I had left over and was willing to donate. I would have had to pay my crew. I still would have been working for free, and it would have cost me more because my crew wouldn't be on another paying job. Instead, Eunice *volunteered* me to lead the volunteers."

"I asked you to do it." They hadn't seen her return. She sat back down. "And you are still complaining about not being paid after such a tragedy!"

Luis sighed and put his coffee cup down on the table hard enough for some coffee to spill out onto the table. "Eunice, nobody would be dead if the church just coughed up a little money so I could pay my crew."

"Well, I didn't volunteer for you. I said I would ask you to do it."

"Well, when the pastor asked the congregation for volunteers, of which there were none, he made it sound like it was a done deal. When I asked you if you had promised that, all you said was, 'Luis, do it for the Lord.'" His tone was mocking, and Adam could see him getting a bit wound up. "If the Lord wanted me to do it, he would have provided the money for me to pay my crew."

The bickering was pointless, and Adam guessed that the same argument had been hashed and rehashed several times. The main thing that Adam got out of the conversation was that Luis didn't know that Tommy's death was not an accident. Thinking about how Tommy had jerked before he fell, he interjected. "The roof doesn't look that steep. What do you think made him lose his balance?"

The argument temporarily halted; Luis deliberated. "The cops asked the same question. There was nothing to trip over. He wasn't a roofer. He wasn't in great shape. Maybe he got dizzy when he stood up. I know he was taking medication for blood pressure. Chucho was standing there. He saw better than I did. Find Chucho and ask him. That's what I told the cops."

Rosie was setting down their plates.

"Looks delicious, Rosie." Eunice smiled.

Adam sensed a bit of sarcasm in her tone.

"It's hard not to talk about what happened." Adam said apologetically, trying to stay on topic.

"I can only imagine," she said, slowly shaking her head in that it's-such-a-shame kind of way. "Tommy was such a humble and kind man of

God. He and his family sacrificed a lot for the Lord. He was an inspiration. Not like others." She cast a sideway glance at Luis.

Luis let out a slow, silent sigh. "Pastor Lehman drives a Cadillac."

Eunice raised a hushing hand.

"And what about the other guy, Chucho? Have you seen him?" Adam pressed.

Luis shook his head, putting a forkful of beans in his mouth. "No. I didn't really know him. No one did. He was someone Pastor Lehman picked up. You know the type. One of those guys with a sign that says, 'Will work for food.'"

"He was homeless?"

"He didn't look homeless to me. He was clean. He didn't stink. And he didn't look hungry to me. He was strong enough to carry the shingles up to the roof."

Eunice cautioned. "Hard times can hit anyone anytime. He showed up at church a few weeks back asking the pastor for work."

Adam couldn't stop thinking about the blood bloom on Tommy's shirt. All Baxter said was it wasn't an accident. Adam knew he was in the thick of this, and he didn't want to end up getting fingerprinted again. Baxter asked him not to take chances, but wasn't he in a better position to ask questions? People might consider his curiosity appropriate. "I don't mean to suggest that Chucho pushed him, but were they close enough for that to happen from your perspective?"

Luis considered. "I think they were physically close enough. But I don't think Tommy knew Chucho any better than I did. I suppose it could have happened that way, but why? Chucho would have to be a psycho. Tommy was helping Chucho. No, my guess is Chucho was a mojado, a wetback, illegal. He had almost no English." Luis tilted his head. "The way he disappeared. I don't think the cops found him yet."

Rosie was back at the table refilling their coffee cups. The restaurant crowd was thinning, and some people were already strolling around the park as vendors set up their booths.

"He was staying here, wasn't he, Rosie?" Eunice looked up at her.

"Who? The guy from the church?"

Eunice nodded.

"I think he still is. I haven't seen him for a couple of days. Hasn't come in for his free meals."

"Have the police talked to you about him?" Adam asked.

Rosie nodded. "They asked me to call if I see him."

So Chucho was the other guest staying in the Rest. Adam's mind whirred.

"The church paid his rent, right?" Eunice asked. "They took up a collection."

Adam noticed Luis tense at the question. Adam could hear his thoughts. *They could have taken a collection to pay my crew instead of asking for volunteers.*

"He paid in cash, a month in advance! I didn't ask where he got the money." Rosie shrugged and walked away.

"The police have been asking around. They've talked to a bunch of folks from the church. Mostly it's that girl deputy they hired." Eunice leaned toward Adam as if in confidence. "There is a memorial service for Tommy at the Friday night service at 7 p.m. Perhaps you'd like to come. There's a social hour after with refreshments."

The ideas were piling up in Adam's head. Again, facts weren't fitting together. What had the police told the Delgado family about Tommy's death? Why didn't they tell Luis that they suspected homicide? What did Junior think? This guy, Chucho, well-fed and clean, shows up, asks for help and gets it, then disappears at the first sign of trouble. Did Luis ever think about the blood on Tommy's shirt? It may not have been obvious at first, but after the CPR it was.

The restaurant was rapidly emptying. Adam noticed furtive glances as some of them left. Were they looking at him, or did they think it strange that Luis and Eunice were sharing the table with him? Adam wondered how many people would approach them at the fair wanting to ask about the stranger in town.

Eunice glanced at the delicate gold watch on her wrist. It was more like a bracelet than a watch. It glinted in reflected light. "The pastor is going to give the blessing before the mayor opens the fair. It's almost time. We need to go, Luis." She pulled a small mirror out of her purse and checked her hair.

Adam became self-conscious again about his own hair. Untamed by brush or product, he was sure it was standing on end at odd angles.

Luis leaned forward to reach for his wallet. Adam held up his hands. "I got this. You two go on over to the festival." Luis halfheartedly protested. Adam could see that he was not used to others offering to pick up the tab.

"Really, Luis. It's my pleasure." Adam waved to get Rosie's attention and mimed asking for the bill. He could hear the music from the kitchen a bit louder than before. The drop in the din from conversation was noticeable. The very air seemed thinner.

Luis said he would get the next one, thanked him, and extended his hand. Adam shook his hand. He hadn't liked Luis much when they first met in McDonald's, but it was good to really talk to him. Luis' willingness to confide in him surprised him, but he imagined there weren't many people he could talk to so freely. In a town where everyone knew everyone else, there was more left unsaid than ever had to be said. Everything that was said was unlikely to remain in confidence.

In standing up, Eunice thanked him for breakfast while adjusting her clothing. "Please stop by our church booth. We've got the best chocolate chip cookies in town, and I'm sure Pastor Lehman would like to meet you." Her smile was more cordial than genuine. She was a difficult person to read in many ways. Friendly, but at arm's length.

Adam watched them leave and cross the street. *Of course the pastor would like to meet me. Everyone in town must be curious about me.*

Adam climbed the steps back to his room. He was looking forward to the fair. To sponsor such an event, the town of Ur couldn't be as empty as it appeared. If Ur was like most small towns, everyone would be there. It just might feel like one of those old church festivals. It wouldn't be the same, but it would be fun.

The door to his room was propped open, and a pile of linens lay outside it. A woman was inside tucking in sheets around his mattress. She sensed him standing outside the door. She turned toward him. A broad smile of recognition washed over her face. It was Manda. The contrast between her warmth and Eunice's stiffness struck him.

His surprise at seeing her must have been obvious. "I do a lot of little jobs around here. I'm almost finished. You can come in if you'd like." She plumped the pillows and ironed out the sheets with her palms. "Not much to do this morning. Only two guests." A warm breeze billowed the sheer curtains just as someone across the street began checking the audio equipment.

"I think I saw your husband in the restaurant."

"Yes, he's down there. Did he say anything to you?"

"I don't think he saw me."

She laughed. "Honey, everyone knew you were there. They might not have known who you were, but they knew they didn't know you. Many might have guessed that you were the stranger who tried to save Deacon Delgado."

"You know about that, do you?" He felt exposed.

"Just about everyone does. If they didn't before, they do now." She plumped the pillows and placed them on the bed.

"That's a comforting thought." He didn't try to hide the sarcasm in his voice.

"They mean no harm by it. Ur is such a small place. We all knew Tommy. Most people liked him even though he could be preachy sometimes. Now you are connected to him. There will be a memorial service on Friday evening, if you're still around and want to go."

Adam nodded. "I probably will be here… there."

She looked down at the table with the upside-down puzzle pieces. "I've never seen anyone put together a puzzle that way before. You are an interesting fella."

"I don't know how interesting I am. I find it more of a challenge. The shapes fascinate me. I get absorbed. Not much to do, really." It was more than that for him, the way some pieces seemed to fit but later proved to be in the wrong place. He would have liked someone to know that his life felt like an upside-down puzzle and everything he did or tried to do was about making sense out of his life. He could not share that with anyone, and he believed that the habit of putting puzzles together upside down had been a kind of divine gift to help him make it through life.

"Mind if I ask you a personal question?" The sound of concern in her voice disarmed him.

"Ask away."

"Were you robbed or something?" She seemed afraid to ask.

"No, why?"

"It's none of my business, but you had two bags when we dropped you off at the motel. They're not here. I just thought…"

"No, no, everything is fine." Adam interrupted her. She had caught him off guard, and it unsettled him. How should he have answered that question? She seemed genuinely concerned about him, but she asked about his bags. His mind went to the hard package that was in his duffel.

Had she been the one to go through his bag? Had she put the package in there? Was she hoping to recover the package while she cleaned his room?

Her question was reasonable. The rucksack and duffel were conspicuous in their absence. It was reasonable. Perfectly reasonable.

She sensed his discomfort. "Look. It's none of my business, and you can tell me to mind my own, but I just emptied your trash. All those tags from new clothes. I just thought something happened to you. I might be able to help. If you need things, I have the keys to the old Ur Community Thrift Store next to the bus station. You can have your pick. They're out of business and just left that stuff in there. I haven't had the time nor the gumption to clean it out."

Adam pulled himself together. "That's kind of you. Thank you for your concern. I don't really need anything right now, but if I do, I'll remember your offer." Adam thought it best not to explain more. If he told her the police had both his bags, it might raise suspicion about him. "You've been exceedingly kind, and I appreciate it. Truth is, I might eventually have to take you up on that offer." If his bags were kept as evidence of something, he would certainly do so.

She smiled and nodded at him. "Oh well, you just let me know. You can always find me at the bus station." She patted him on the shoulder and left the room.

NINE

Pastor Patrick Lehman, of the First Pentecostal Church of Ur, a spherical man with visible sweat on his brow, used a booming voice to get the audience's attention. He stood on the steps of the gazebo to lead the gathered people of Ur in a prayer. He thanked God for the valor of the soldiers who had given their lives in service of their country and asked God to bless and protect the members of the armed forces, especially those who called Oklahoma home. He asked for wisdom for the mayor and the town council. Claimed productivity and prosperity for the area over the coming summer and asked for it all in the name of Jesus.

As he prayed, soft comments like "Yes, Lord" and "Amen" could be heard in the crowd. Eunice and others had their heads bowed and their hands raised like they wanted to ask a teacher a question. Adam had seen this before, but it wasn't common in Mother of Sorrows Roman Catholic Church, where his family attended mass. The pastor then led the group in the hymn "How Great Thou Art," accompanied by a ragtag mixed group of musicians; some old-timers, high schoolers, and one girl, with a clarinet, looked young enough to be in junior high.

When he introduced the mayor, there was genial applause. The mayor said little beyond what the pastor had done. He lauded the sacrifices made by all veterans, including those who "aren't yet to be mourned but are today worthy of our gratitude." He encouraged people to thank veterans for their service. He welcomed the residents of Ur and nearby communities to the festival. He reminded them of the dates of the county and state fairs and encouraged them to attend and compete for prizes and do their part to keep the great state of Oklahoma great.

It was a bullshit political speech, and the crowd, which Adam guessed at about 200, seemed to know it. They didn't even wait for the mayor to finish speaking before they began murmuring to one another and dispersing. The mayor, sensing that he was losing the crowd, declared the festival open and directed the band to take over.

Adam saw Deputy Isi staffing the sheriff's booth. There were several other uniformed deputies throughout the crowd. They were just participating in the festivities, but Adam knew better. The sheriff, a good old boy if there ever was one, was out in the crowd shaking hands. After all, there was always another election coming. The mayor was doing the same thing, though it seemed to be less pleasant for him. Adam felt a twinge of pity for him. He was probably an official on the way out, and he looked like he knew it.

The sun was high, the breeze warm, and the leaves of the oak trees fluttered in the air. The music was light. He was amazed that the band sounded as good as they did. He wondered how long they would play. Adam wished he could find that little boy inside himself that would enjoy this festival just because it was a festival. He just couldn't erase the idea that he was stuck there, in the middle of an investigation that had nothing to do with him. And that law enforcement believed it possible that he was in danger.

The size of the crowd helped Adam feel less conspicuous. He noticed that neither Baxter nor Isi acknowledged him with more than an unfamiliar nod, as if he were just another face in the park. The other deputies did the same. Had they been briefed, or were they uninformed? The whole event had an air of somehow being orchestrated, that the festival was an act in a play and the audience, unrecognized by the actors, was waiting for something to happen. Was law enforcement surreptitiously watching him to see who, if anyone, would approach him? Perhaps to get back that package? What would they do if it happened? Or were there other people being watched? Baxter had at least hinted that his investigation went beyond the current circumstances.

There was a line for the snow cone vendor. He was shaving a huge block of ice with what looked like a hand plane. He fashioned near-perfect spheres of shaved ice in paper cones and poured vibrantly colored syrups over the top. It was a moment of nostalgia for Adam. On the north side of Pittsburgh, near the hospital and the Aviary, an old-timer sold snow cones to people in the park. It was a childhood treat that he remembered fondly.

When it was his turn, Adam handed two dollars to the vendor, who began shaving a cone for him. "What flavor do you want?"

"Just plain."

"It's just ice." His voice sounded unsure.

"I know. I don't really like those syrups. Too sweet. I guess I'm weird."

The vendor shrugged and handed Adam the cone. Adam walked away, scraping off bits of shaved ice with his teeth and feeling them melting on his tongue. He'd walk around until he found the church booth to meet Eunice's pastor. He thought he would ask the pastor, when remembering Tommy, not to single him out in any way.

He was really hoping to run into Junior Delgado. Friend or foe, Junior was still a question in his mind. In either case, he wanted to give Junior the opportunity to talk. As he thought of him, he spotted Junior sitting on a bench with two others of similar age. Adam's nerves tightened a notch or two.

Closer than he had seen him the day before, Adam could see he was a strong, handsome lad. *State judo champ*, Adam recalled. Under a gi, a competitor's muscles would be less visible than in a singlet, but they'd be there. Adam didn't know much about judo. He estimated Junior to be in a weight bracket just under his own. *If this becomes unpleasant and physical, it would be a fair match.* Adam felt ashamed of the thought.

The boy to Junior's right was the young man from the bus station. The other was a girl. She looked familiar, but at first, Adam couldn't place her. Not until she flicked her hair back over her shoulder with her hand did he remember. It was the girl from the bus.

Adam didn't want to interrupt or impose on their conversation, but he wanted Junior to see him and to have the opportunity to approach him if he chose to. So, Adam sat down on an opposite bench. Surely one of them would notice him, and eventually all three would. Adam tried to look relaxed, just enjoying his snow cone, but inside he was alert, just in case the encounter proved to be less than cordial.

Junior was leaning forward, his elbows on his knees, his hands under his chin in a prayerful pose. The boy from the bus station had his hand on Junior's shoulder, and the girl had hers on his back. They were almost huddling together. Adam waited. The band stopped for a break, and there was quiet.

Was it the strength of Adam's gaze at the group that made the bus station boy look up and straight at him? His eyes automatically scanned Adam, and he knew the boy recognized him. He said something to the other two, and they both looked up. The girl looked annoyed, while Junior's expression momentarily was blank. He muttered a few words and got up. He motioned to his two friends to stay put. As he approached, Adam's sinews tightened. His reflexes set to act.

Their eyes locked. Junior crossed the path. "Sir, may I speak with you?"

Adam nodded. "Certainly." The politeness of the boy's tone might have relaxed him if he hadn't anticipated the contact so much.

"Mind if I sit down?"

"Please do, son." The word *son* was natural, automatic. Adam wasn't sure where it came from and feared it wouldn't be well received. He wasn't in the habit of calling young men "son." It just happened.

As the boy sat down, tears began to flow from his eyes and dripped to the ground like blood from a broken nose. Men confront face-to-face; they communicate shoulder to shoulder. This wasn't going to be a confrontation but an opportunity to comfort the lad. Adam could feel himself relax as compassion for the boy filled him.

Gathering his strength and composure, he said, "My name is Tom. Tom Delgado. You're the guy that tried to help my dad, right?"

"I'm so sorry, son. I did my best." Again, he called him son. Where had that come from? Adam tossed his remaining ice onto the grass by the sidewalk and put his hand on the boy's shoulder. "I am genuinely sorry."

He spoke, doing his best to fight off tears. "I just wanted to thank you and to ask you about what happened. I thought… I hoped you could tell me more."

"I don't know much, but I'll answer your questions as best I can," Adam said with only a slight reservation. There would be things he thought it better not to say.

"Can you tell me what happened?"

"Here's something you might not know. I met your dad that morning in McDonald's. I was a stranger, and he was very nice to me. A little later, I was walking to town. I saw your dad and two other guys up on the church roof. Your dad stood up. It looked like he lost his balance and fell. I ran to help. I performed CPR until the paramedics arrived."

"They kept his body for an autopsy. Why would they do that for an accident?"

"I don't know, but they might want to know *why* he fell off the roof. Maybe there was some medical reason for him to lose his balance."

Junior nodded. "It was never supposed to be him, you know. Things like this shouldn't happen to guys like my dad. He was a great man, serving the Lord. Doing his best for God. He wasn't an old guy. It just doesn't make sense." The tears started flowing again in earnest. "I want you to know he was a good guy, and I'm thankful that God had you there."

"If it's any comfort. I don't think he suffered. He was unconscious when I got there. I couldn't find a pulse, and he wasn't breathing on his own. Like I said, I did my best."

"It helps. I'll tell my mom, my whole family." He stood up. "If you are still in town, there's a service for my dad on Friday at our church. I'm sure my mom would like it if you were there."

"Wouldn't miss it." Adam smiled consolingly. Adam watched him join his friends. They stood up, and he watched them walk away.

It sounded like firecrackers off in the distance. Then there was a disturbance in the crowd, a swelling of voices. Police radios sounded. A circle of people stood around the sheriff's booth. As Adam approached, he saw the sheriff clearing an area. Deputy Isi was talking into her shoulder. Baxter knelt on the ground next to the pastor, who was lying there. Adam could see blood on one side of the pastor's face.

Baxter stood up. Adam couldn't hear what he said to the sheriff, but he could read Baxter's lips. "He's gone."

Determined not to be detained again, Adam abruptly turned and walked away. The catharsis he felt after clearing the air with Junior Delgado was quickly replaced with a fishbowl feeling of being observed as if every eye in Ur were fixed on him. Every step he took felt scrutinized, his muscles becoming tighter and his movements feeling stiffer.

He hadn't been near enough to be part of the crowd surrounding the pastor. He took his opportunity, crossing the street, hoping it looked like he had been unaware of the seriousness of the event. He knew better, of course. Who wouldn't notice the most conspicuous person in town coming closer to see what happened? Over and over again he could see Baxter, standing up, turning toward the sheriff, and his lips mouthing the words, "He's gone."

Baxter and Isi would surely want to talk to him. They knew where to find him when they wanted him.

First a deacon and then the pastor. Only an idiot might think the two events were unrelated. Adam might have been one of the few people in town to know that Tommy had been shot. Though he couldn't have been the one to shoot the pastor, and unless he could magically make a gun disappear from the scene, it was impossible for him to have shot the deacon, that didn't eliminate him from conspiracy. After all, he was still a stranger, a person of interest, wasn't he?

When he opened the door to his room, there was an immediate cross breeze that would have been refreshing if he hadn't been so sequestered in his racing thoughts. He barely noticed that the bottom drawer of the dresser was pulled out slightly, and without thinking, he slid it back into place.

He left the door open. In the very unlikely event that Chucho came back to get his stuff, he could intercept him. If Chucho were still in town, equally unlikely, the festival would make a convenient distraction to sneak back, get his stuff, and slink off.

He was too wound up and wasn't in the right mind to answer questions. Surely it would happen sooner rather than later, but he wanted time—time to loosen up, time to clear his head, and time to pull himself together. He looked out the window, still cautious enough to stand back behind the sheer curtains so as not to be noticed. The park was full and chaotic. Most people had gathered around the sheriff's booth. He could see several uniformed deputies trying to manage the crowd. Blocked by the canopy of the trees, he couldn't see what was happening with the pastor's body. How long would it be before paramedics or, more likely, a medical examiner arrived? Or didn't they do that sort of thing in Oklahoma? He couldn't remember an ME arriving at the church.

He needed to move. Wrestling drills would be great. Wrestling drills, his drills, used just about every muscle of the body. And when he started his routine, he usually fell into a concentrated, almost empty mind, a kind of trance focusing his attention on movement and muscles. His room was too small, the lobby too public and cluttered with furniture, and the park out of the question. He surveyed the common guest area outside his room. There was just enough room in the center. It would be cramped, but it just might do.

He changed into his workout clothing. He didn't want to sweat in his street clothes. There was no telling how long it would be before he could get back to that laundromat. He moved to the center of the common area. Crouching, he began his routine. Move after move, first to the left and then to the right, stretching and pushing against his own muscles. He could feel the resistance in his sinews, his tendons, and his tense muscles. He pushed hard. He began and finished the entire routine and repeated it twice more, always keeping the sequence, always pushing himself further, stretching more. Flexibility. Agility. Looseness.

He worked his body for over an hour. Eventually, his muscles were loose again. Soaked in sweat, he needed another shower. He pushed himself up off the floor. In his room, he grabbed a towel, underwear, his key, and his jeans.

Through a small hole, left by a bolt that once held a sign that read "Emergency Exit," a dark-brown eye watched.

TEN

The hot water saturated his hair and cascaded down his body. He breathed in the steam and allowed his muscles to luxuriate and soften. When he thought he had enough, he turned off the hot water and turned up the tap on the cold. He could feel the pores of his skin close, and his private parts shrink from the cold and even more tension release.

When he stepped out into the common area, he saw the door to his room was ajar. He stopped. Tried to think. Had he not closed it all the way? Had he left it open? He jingled the key in his hand. He had intended to lock the door. Had he forgotten to do it?

His chest tightened as a cold ripple slid down his back, raising goosebumps in its wake. He crept forward, each step deliberate. Had someone returned for the package? Were they still in there? Holding his breath, Adam shifted his weight and peered through the crack in the door, trying to see inside before making himself visible.

A jolt of surprise. He could see Baxter sitting in the straight-backed chair at the table by the window. He faced the door and clearly saw Adam approaching.

"The door was open. I thought I'd just wait here," Baxter said.

"There's a sofa in the hallway." His voice was as thick as the tension he sensed in the room. He couldn't hide his annoyance. He wanted to ask if Baxter had a warrant and if he had searched the room while he was in the shower. Instead, Adam took a deep breath, sighed, and told himself he was overreacting.

"I didn't want anyone else to know that I was waiting for you. It might cast suspicion on you," Baxter offered in explanation.

"As if the entire town isn't already suspicious of me. Anyway, I'm the only guest here, apart from Chucho."

Baxter's face was acknowledgement enough. "Has he shown up?"

Adam shook his head. "I haven't seen him."

"I saw you leave the festival."

"Yes."

"It concerned me," Baxter said simply.

"How so? I was nowhere near what happened." Adam tried to read Baxter's inscrutable expression. "I figured if you wanted to talk to me, you knew how to find me." Adam hung his towel over the rack near his wash-up sink.

"So, I'm here."

Adam sat on the bed, raised his legs, and leaned back against the headboard. He put his hands behind his head and tried to appear as casual as he could. He was aware of his bare chest moving with his breath. He tried to control it, slow it down. "What do you want?" There was still a bit of an edge to his tone.

"Why did you leave the scene?"

"I told you. I was nowhere near what happened. It had nothing to do with me, and I didn't want to end up in that interrogation room all afternoon."

"Fair enough. I saw you talking to Junior Delgado. It might help me to know what you talked about."

The words "I saw you" were never completely benign to Adam. "I don't think it will, but I'll tell you anyway. Naturally, he's pretty broken up over his father. He thanked me for trying to help and asked me what happened."

"What did you tell him?"

"Basically, just the bare facts I told you two days ago. Specifically, I told him that I saw his father fall. I ran to help and did CPR until the paramedics arrived." He opened his hand as if to say, *That's all.* "He's worried or suspicious though."

Baxter nodded. "What makes you say that?"

"He asked me why his father's body was kept for an autopsy."

"What did you say?"

"That I had no idea, but the coroner might want to know the reason he fell. I thought that was true, that I wasn't lying, and vague enough that I wasn't telling him something he didn't already know."

"Anything else about the conversation that might be important?" Baxter repositioned himself in the chair and leaned in toward Adam.

"I know what I did not say." Adam met his gaze. "I didn't say anything about the blood on Delgado's shirt. Nor did I say anything about the accident being a homicide. I tried to comfort him. Hell, he's just a kid."

Baxter pondered. "I know him pretty well. He's the oldest and probably thinks he needs to be the man of the family now."

Adam continued. "I told him that I didn't think his dad suffered. I hoped he'd realize that his father was already gone. I hope that comforted him. He also invited me to the memorial service on Friday. It's like the third or fourth invitation to that event I've gotten."

Baxter paused. "I'm wondering if you can help me clear something up. Can you point out where you were when all the confusion started?"

"Sure." Adam got up but wondered if Baxter saw him talking to Junior he should know where it happened. He went to the window. The park was clearly visible. He could see the tarp of the sheriffs' booth through the trees. The other booths were being dismantled. Pointing, he said, "It's that one. The same place we sat yesterday. The one facing the bank. Junior was sitting with his friends on that bench across the path facing into the park. It looked like his friends were comforting him. I didn't want to approach him directly, so I sat down across from them in case he wanted to talk to me. I thought he might because of yesterday."

"So, you stayed there after Junior left you?

"Yep, still on that bench. I was thinking about that kid. He went off with his friends, and I was just thinking about him. What a terrible thing to experience." He added "... at any age."

"If you could, tell me what happened from the time he left until you left the park."

It was an interrogation again. *I'm in this up to my neck*, he thought. Adam resigned himself once again to cooperation. He knew that anything he said could be interpreted and reinterpreted in any number of ways, but to resist, to not be helpful, meant increased suspicion. The room suddenly felt smaller. "Okay, the kids walked out of the park, past the bank. I was sitting on the bench. I heard disturbed voices, people shouting. I got up to see what it was all about. The sheriff was pushing back on the crowd. I went close enough to see the pastor lying on the ground, and you were squatting beside him. I saw you stand up and say something to the sheriff. That's when I turned and walked away."

"Do you remember anything else?"

"I saw what you said to the sheriff."

"You *saw* what I said?"

"I didn't hear it. I saw your lips move, and it looked like you said, *He's gone.*"

Baxter seemed impressed. "Anything before or after that?"

Adam considered. "I came here. Before... " He concentrated. "Before I watched them go. I really felt sorry for Junior. I was thinking about my own parents and how it felt to lose them." Then he remembered. "I heard firecrackers."

"Firecrackers."

Adam wondered if Baxter was taking mental notes or if he was recording the conversation somehow. "Four or five. I didn't think much about it. It wasn't a whole string, like the way you buy them, but they were close together. I didn't count."

"Where were you when you heard the firecrackers?"

"Still on the bench. I hadn't moved." He furrowed his brow. Now it really felt like an interrogation, like Baxter was trying to catch him in a lie.

"Think carefully. Can you tell me what direction the sound came from?"

Adam closed his eyes and mentally put himself back on the bench. He raised his left hand. "There were echoes, but I think they came from my left."

"From the direction of the Pioneer's Rest?" Baxter asked for clarification.

Adam just nodded.

Neither of them was aware of Rosie standing in the doorway until she spoke. "Something I should know?" She had her hands on her hips. Startled, they both turned to look at her. There was silence for a beat or two. She fixed her eyes on Sergeant Baxter. "I saw you coming in a few minutes ago. I figured something was up."

Baxter nodded. "Yes, something is up. I'm glad you're here." It would be easier to test his hunch if she gave him permission to investigate. He didn't want to have to wait for a warrant. "Is there roof access in this building?"

"If you've got a long ladder." She sounded more cautious now.

Baxter nodded, pressing his lips together. He seemed to scan his thoughts. "How many rooms have a view of the park?"

The question surprised her. Her eyes moved to Adam. He shrugged his shoulders despite having a fair idea.

"If you don't count the restaurant, only four. This one, of course. One across the hall and the two upstairs. Henry's room," she pointed to the ceiling, "and a storage room."

So, it was Henry, the cook, upstairs, Adam thought.

"Would you mind showing them to me?"

"I'd like to know what this is all about."

Baxter looked away, once again out the window. It was a reasonable question, but he didn't like to admit he was working on a hunch, even a well-reasoned one. Saying too much might give something away or cause her to resist for any number of unknown reasons. He didn't want her to resist or insist on a warrant. "Just testing a hypothesis," Baxter replied enigmatically. If what he suspected turned out to be possible, the time for gathering evidence would be at hand. "If I could just see the rooms with a view of the park… " He started walking toward her, assuming she would show him.

"My pleasure." Her tone betrayed her slight annoyance.

She led the way across the common area where Adam had done his wrestling drills and unlocked the unoccupied guest room door. Adam followed them. He was curious, and no one had said he couldn't go too. Rosie unlocked the door and pushed it open. Before she could enter, Baxter motioned for her to stand back. He cautiously drew his gun from his belt and brushed past her.

Rosie's expression became even more serious. Her back straightened. "It's not occupied."

He didn't respond. He stealthily entered the room, scanning it for places where someone might hide themselves or something else. He pivoted around the dresser, under the bed, and the table. All was clear. The room was a mirror of Adam's. It was neat and tidy. After scanning the room, Baxter walked over to the window and looked out. The park was clearly visible, but there was no clear view of the area around the sheriff's booth. If the shot came from this building, it didn't come from this room. "Rosie, does anyone else have keys to these rooms?"

Rosie said, "Guests have a key to their room, of course. Henry has a key to his room upstairs. But I don't think he locks it. I have a master key on my keychain, and there's an extra master hidden in the laundry room off the kitchen downstairs. Manda Lamano uses it on Mondays to clean."

"Anybody else know about that?"

"Everybody knows she cleans for me on Mondays. She just cleans the guest rooms, the hallway, and the lobby. She did it this morning… while her fat, lazy-assed husband ate my food and *complained about it.*" She paused and muttered to herself. "… pain in the ass. He thinks it should be free while Manda is working."

"I meant about the master key."

"Oh, well, Henry knows. Manda knows, of course. It's well-hidden. I mean, I'd challenge anyone to find it. Just what's going on? Frankly, that gun scares me."

"Sorry about that. It's just a safety procedure. Like I said, I'm just testing a hypothesis. I really appreciate your cooperation. I don't mean to worry you. I'd like to see upstairs, please."

She led them past the rope and sign forbidding entry. "The sign is just to keep guests from exploring upstairs. It's a private space."

Baxter cut in front of her. "If you don't mind, I'll go first. Just in case."

"Just in case of what? Listen, Henry's up there. Don't you dare shoot him." She said it loud enough for anyone on the third floor to have heard.

Adam found this exchange amusing and had to suppress a smile. Though it was unlikely, clearly Baxter thought it possible that someone other than Henry might still be hanging around. *This scene would never have played out this way in New Orleans.*

Baxter looked her in the eyes. He was considerably taller than she, and he leaned in and spoke quietly. "Rosie, I have no intention of shooting anyone. I know Henry, and unless he points a gun at me, we'll both be fine."

"He doesn't have a gun. He's not allowed," she hissed.

Baxter blinked. "Okay. Let's go upstairs, please.

"Be my guest." She gestured. She turned and mouthed to Adam. "This is nuts!"

It was a conspiratorial action. Adam guessed she saw him on her side now. He followed them up the dimly lit stairs. There was a narrow window on a small landing halfway up. Baxter paused there briefly to take in the view. When Adam passed it, it looked like it hadn't been opened in decades. The floorboards creaked, and a threadbare carpet runner shifted under his feet. There was a gentle old-wood smell that Adam associated with bottom-tier antique and used furniture stores.

A lanky, bony man stood at the top of the stairs with hands raised above his shoulders and a broad, ironic expression on his face. He had close-cropped sandy gray hair that had been matted down by a baseball cap. He wore dingy, stained restaurant whites and carried a blue bath towel draped over his shoulder. "Don't shoot, Bax, I'm unarmed." Adam couldn't tell if his tone was playful, mocking, or both.

Adam had never met Henry. He looked crusty, rough. Like a guy you wouldn't want to mess with. He wasn't big, but he was wiry.

Rosie leaned to peer from behind Baxter's back. "Henry, Sergeant Baxter would like to see your room. Okay with you?"

Henry made a melodramatic bowing and sweeping gesture toward his open door. "As long as you don't make a mess." He chuckled and continued on his way to the bathroom. Adam wondered why he didn't ask questions before agreeing to what could have been a search of his room. *Either he has nothing to hide, or he's used to conceding to others, especially the cops.* Adam thought the latter was more likely. Henry reminded him of someone on parole who never ever wanted to end up in prison again. That was probably why he wasn't allowed to own a gun in an open carry state.

Baxter seemed to have let down his guard a bit. "Make a mess? Look at this place!"

The room was cluttered, the bed unmade, and a pile of laundry lay in the corner. Several meals worth of dirty dishes from the restaurant were stacked on the small table like the one Adam used for his puzzle. The furnishings were old and worn. Apart from a few pictures in cheap frames on the night table, the room was unadorned.

Adam and Rosie waited at the door. Baxter glanced out the window only for a few seconds, then walked back to the door. "Let's just check the last one."

The door across from Henry's room was slightly ajar. The room was unfurnished. Some large plastic storage bins were stacked against the interior wall. There was nothing else in the room. Baxter strode over to the window, looked out, and took a deep breath as if he saw what he had been looking for.

His curiosity heightened, Adam stepped into the room, wanting to look out the window. Baxter raised his hand. Please don't come in, and don't touch anything. He had found what he was looking for. That shocked Rosie, who visibly stiffened. Baxter spoke into the microphone on his shoulder. Then to Adam. "Mr. Alba, did you see anyone come out of the building when you were coming back from the festival?"

Adam shook his head. "No one."

"Miss Rosie, did you see anyone other than Mr. Alba or me entering or leaving the hotel?"

"I saw you, like I said. I didn't see anyone else."

"How about through the back, the kitchen perhaps?"

"I wouldn't know. I'm in the dining room the whole time we're open, and I clean it after we close. You'll have to ask Henry, but I doubt there was anyone other than Manda. She does the laundry down there. You might want to talk to her as well. But Henry would have raised a ruckus if someone he didn't know came through his kitchen. He doesn't like surprises. I think it comes from his PTSD. He was in Iraq, you know."

There was a long pause. Then, as if she had found the missing piece to one of Adam's jigsaw puzzles, she raised her head and looked straight at Baxter. "Wait just a minute. You think someone shot Pastor Lehman, and the shot came from here?"

Baxter sighed. "Pastor Lehman was shot. Everyone in town will know that by tonight. The people at the festival already know it. I don't know where the shot came from. This is just a working hypothesis while the crime scene techs do their thing in the park. But, frankly, it's more likely now than it was even a few minutes ago. There is a clear line of sight from this window."

Their eyes met for a silent second. Rosie looked like she had suddenly sobered up after having drunk too much. The atmosphere was thick with thought. It could have gone very differently. She could have demanded a warrant. Instead, she spoke very clearly and intentionally. "I give you my full permission to search this entire building from top to bottom, including my apartment if you feel the need. Mr. Alba, you're a witness. If that shot came from my building, I want the son of a bitch caught." She was undoing a key from her ring. "Here's my master key. It fits every door lock in the building, including my apartment.

His eyes flickered to Adam and then back to her. "Thank you, Rosie. I'm grateful for your cooperation."

"Of course. Do you need me with you? I'd rather not." Her face and demeanor had deflated. She now looked tired. She even looked older.

"No, ma'am. But just one more question, just to cover the bases. There is a municipal tornado shelter under this building. Correct?"

"Used to be, until they built the new one under the school back in the nineties. There's still a sign for it in the alley, but everyone in town knows to go to the school. We kept it up while business was busier before they built the motel. I stopped bothering after that. Not enough guests to worry about it. I haven't been down there for five years or more. If it's locked, the master key should work."

"Where is the entrance?"

"Under the last flight of the back stairs. You'll probably need a flashlight if you go down there."

"Thank you, ma'am." She walked away, unlocking a door to what Adam assumed was her apartment.

Before she closed the door, she said, "The back stairwell is marked *Emergency Exit*. If you need me, I'm here in my apartment."

Baxter spoke into the microphone on his shoulder and sidled past Adam. Adam got his attention. "Sergeant, I have something to tell you."

Baxter stopped and looked at him.

"The bottom drawer of the dresser in my room was slightly open when I came back to the hotel."

"You're sure you didn't leave it that way?"

"I've never touched it. I don't have enough clothes to fill the dresser."

ELEVEN

While the crime scene techs were around, the afternoon was filled with voices in the hallway, footsteps on the stairs, and an official vibration in the air. While they worked in his room, Adam went to the substation to be fingerprinted, ostensibly to eliminate his prints from potentially others found in his room.

After he was allowed to reenter his room, Adam kept the door to his room closed to avoid the temptation of listening to what they were saying or showing too much interest in what they were doing. The cross breeze would have been nice, but the intrusion of official voices could have easily become too distracting. He could still hear them but couldn't hear what they were saying unless they shouted or unless he listened intentionally. And he didn't open his door except to visit the bathroom and get his sandwich from the refrigerator.

It was nearly five when Rosie knocked on his door.

"I have this spray to clean up that messy powder." She came into his room with a spray bottle and a roll of paper towels under her arm.

"I can help, if you'd like," Adam offered.

"Oh, it's alright. Manda has come back, and Henry is helping as well." She began spraying the powder smudges from the dresser.

"Did they find anything?" Adam asked.

"I have no idea but the thought of someone like that in the building is unsettling." She finished wiping down the dresser and scanned the room for more smudges. "They actually fingerprinted me. Can you believe it?"

"Yes, I can." He sat down on the bed. "I think it's for comparison so that they can isolate which prints belong here and which ones don't."

"That's what they said." She wiped a little sweat from her temple with the back of her wrist. "Well, at least the place is getting a good clean." Heading for the door, she sighed. "Well, no rest for the wicked."

"Are you sure there's nothing I can do?"

"No, it's pretty much done. Thanks for the offer."

Adam spent the evening sitting in front of his puzzle, moving pieces and fitting a few, trying others. The challenge of the puzzle was that some pieces seemed to fit, but eventually other pieces around them revealed an error.

He thought of Baxter, with his methodical, linear inquiry methods. Following one question after another, clarifying each step along the way. DePuis had done the same thing back in New Orleans. *Perhaps it works most of the time. They must train them all the same way.* For justice to take place, things for them had to line up, not just complete a picture but be backed by hard evidence. The questions helped them find the evidence.

How often had they gotten the puzzle wrong? How often had a case been closed because most of the pieces fit?

Adam considered his standing in the Ur puzzle. From his perspective, he was a random piece from a completely different puzzle, but to the law in Ur, he had to be considered part of the puzzle they were working on. Where were they trying to fit him into their puzzle? Would he leave Ur without a prison sentence?

As occasionally happened, he noticed three pieces that fit together. He'd need the fourth piece to know if he had it right, and even then, the only way to know for sure would be to flip them over and see if the picture matched the shape. But that would be cheating.

Somebody obviously had it in for Pentecostal clergy. First it was Tommy, then Pastor Lehman. The only person he had met who seemed to dislike that church was Luis, and his wife was an ardent member. Sure, he was pissed about being hornswoggled into a free roof job, but committing two murders? He couldn't have done the first, even if he truly disliked Tommy. Adam had seen the whole thing.

Did the church, namely Tommy and Lehman, have something to do with Baxter's bigger picture investigation? Adam assumed it was drugs of some sort because of the package in his duffel bag but he hadn't seen the package. He didn't exactly know what was in it. But why his bag? Whoever put them in his bag had to do it either at the motel or the bus station. How would they know that they could get them back? Who would have claimed the package, and how would they have done it? More critically, why hadn't they tried to get it back from him yet?

That slightly open drawer meant someone had inexpertly searched his room, probably looking for that package. In Adam's mind, that was a real connection. When could someone have been able to search his room? When he was in the park, certainly. When he was in the shower, possibly.

The sun was setting now. Adam hadn't noticed how late it was, and when, out of frustration, he turned on the desk lamp, he found two more pieces to fit into the puzzle in the upper right-hand corner. They fit the border of the puzzle and were connected to each other. A lucky find, a perfect fit.

Adam had finished his last sub sandwich shortly after he and Rosie left. As the sun was setting, the light in the room turned orange. He wondered if he dared walk to Walmart or eat again at the casino. Baxter had told him to stay in town, but he was feeling hungry, and there was nowhere else in town.

He got up, stretched, and paced. The crime scene people were gone. If he listened for it, he could hear the muffled sound of Henry's television upstairs. It was near eight thirty when someone knocked on his door.

Adam walked over to the door and put his hand on it to brace it. The door wasn't locked, and he wanted to be on the safe side. Leaning into the door, he asked, "Who is it?"

"Baxter."

Adam opened the door. Baxter, looking tired and wearing plain clothes, stood there. He held a pizza box, and two cans of beer dangled by the plastic rings from his fingers. "I thought you might be hungry."

Adam sniffed. 'You thought right. Come in. Is there a pizza place near here?"

Baxter shook his head. "It's one of those cook-your-own premade pizzas from Walmart. My wife heated it up for me." He set the pizza on the dresser and offered Adam a beer. "I hope you like pepperoni."

"Love it." Adam refused the beer. "I don't drink."

"Weren't you a bartender in New Orleans?"

Adam felt a flush of the shadow feeling and blanched.

"Relax. It was in the report DuPuis wrote."

Adam sighed. "Yeah, you might be surprised how many bartenders don't drink. In New Orleans, it was a gay bar—I'm not gay either. Truth is, I'm sober and straight."

"Sorry, I didn't realize. Congratulations. That's great." He seemed flustered, awkward.

"On being sober or straight?"

"Sober, of course."

"You go ahead, though. It won't bother me if you drink. Adam took the pizza and balanced it on top of the dresser. "I think there are paper plates and napkins. There's a kind of little kitchen. I'll be right back."

When Adam returned, Baxter was scrutinizing the face-down puzzle on the table. "Remarkable. You've made progress since I was here earlier. I don't know how you do it."

Adam nodded. "It's the shapes. They look like they're the same, but they aren't."

"Incredible. Do you ever get it wrong?"

"All the time, but when you keep going, problem pieces become obvious. You need at least four together in a kind of square to be sure."

"Yeah." Baxter nodded thoughtfully. "Keep going." He appeared to shake himself out of a trance. "Fuck it. Let's eat. I'm starving."

The pizza hit the spot. Baxter drank both beers. The conversation was informal. Neither said anything about the investigation. It was companionable, nothing serious. Adam knew, however, that Baxter was always on the job. He was careful to be truthful but not overly generous with details about his life. As they stashed the dirty paper plates and napkins into the empty pizza box, Baxter's eyes went back to the puzzle. Adam noticed something in his expression. Was it hesitation? Calculation? Or sizing up the risk of a challenge?

Adam waited but didn't take his eyes off Baxter.

"Mr. Alba..." He hesitated. "I know I shouldn't—it's totally against all the rules, and I hope like hell I don't regret it. I'm going to trust you with some information."

There was a moment while Adam thought carefully. Did he *want* to know what Baxter would say? How much deeper in jeopardy would it place him? Then he decided. "Call me Adam."

"Call me Bax. But only in private, until this is over. We don't want people to think we're too chummy."

They shook hands.

"Hold on," Adam interrupted Baxter. "Shouldn't you be having this discussion with the sheriff?"

"That's the problem. The sheriff's got the whole county to worry about—and he's not from Ur. Right now, this town is a thorn in his reelection campaign. He wants these cases wrapped up yesterday. I think both cases have the same aspects. And I don't even have enough to get an indictment. You see the bind I'm in?"

"Honestly, no."

Baxter dragged his hands down his face. "In Ur, it's just Isi and me. We're the whole damn police force. He needs an indictment—any indictment. But I think both cases are connected."

"But if he understood all the aspects of the case…"

"It's more complicated than that." Baxter swallowed hard. "There were three people in close proximity to one another when Pastor Lehman was shot. All three are influential in Ur. There was Lehman, of course, but the sheriff and the mayor were standing next to him."

"Come on, Bax—first a deacon, then a pastor? Gotta be some anti-religious nutcase, right?"

"That's what the sheriff wants to believe," Baxter admitted.

"What's wrong with it?"

"You sure you're okay hearing all this? I'm trusting you to keep it under wraps… DuPuis said you were good for it."

"I am. Go on. What's wrong with the simple solution?"

"If I chase the easy answer—start grilling every pissed-off Pentecostal who left the church—I might miss the real story. Drugs are passing through Ur. To pull that off, you need a person of considerable influence, someone above suspicion."

"Wait a minute, now. Are you saying you suspect the sheriff?"

"No, I'm not saying that. But of the three big shots who were there, I haven't cleared a single one."

There was a prolonged silence. Baxter continued. "You have an appointment with Sheriff Stacks at 9:00 tomorrow morning."

TWELVE

After an early workout in the park, Adam opted to indulge in a big breakfast before meeting with the sheriff at nine. The music coming from the kitchen seemed louder than usual, but perhaps that was because the only customer in the dining room was Blaine. He was sitting near the back, close to where the group of regulars normally sat at several tables pushed together. Blaine waved an invitation for Adam to join him.

Adam covered his hesitation with a gentle smile. Their first meeting hadn't been pleasant, and it might have ended differently if his wife, Manda, hadn't refereed the situation. Adam wended his way through empty tables, still not certain if he would accept Blaine's offer. He decided to accept mostly because Blaine expressed the rare courtesy of standing up and offering a handshake at his approach. His was a two-handed handshake, his left hand reaching for just above Adam's elbow.

"I hate to eat alone," he said. "Please sit down."

Within seconds of his sitting down, Rosie was pouring him a cup of coffee. "The usual?" she asked.

"The Pioneer with fry bread. It looked good."

"Honey, everything here is good. When it's bad, it's really good," she said in a fair impression of Mae West. She winked coquettishly. She was in her waitress mode, a put-on flirtatiousness for what it was worth, but it felt good all the same. Like he was one of the guys, a normal customer, as if he fit in.

Adam was aware of not having his back to a wall. It bothered him even though the restaurant was empty. Unconsciously, he shifted his chair to an angle so that he could more easily view the rest of the dining room.

"I'm here early today. I usually come in when I take Manda to work, but the kid who works the morning shift called off. Manda is doing double duty today."

"I'm sorry to hear that. I hope he is alright," Adam said.

"What do you mean?" Blaine asked.

"Nothing really. Just if he's not feeling well… "

"Oh, well, Manda thinks he's taking the day off to hang out with Junior Delgado. Best friends. Know what I mean?"

"If best friends means best friends, I do." Adam was thinking about how the kid sized him up when he dropped off his bag. It wasn't something he'd remark on, especially in a small southern town like Ur. He pieced it together with the sincere affection he saw in both of Junior's friends. "I've talked with Junior. He approached me yesterday. I was the one who performed CPR on his father. The kid's pretty broken up. He needs a friend right now."

Rosie brought the hot plates to the table. "Do you need hot sauce?"

"Please." Adam half expected another coquettish remark, but there was none. Then to Blaine, "I met that kid on Friday and saw him yesterday with Junior. He seems nice enough."

"You met Matthew?"

"I didn't know his name, but yeah, when I left my bag at the bus station. Of course, at that time, I didn't know I was going to stay."

"I'm curious. What made you decide to stay?"

"Like I said, I saw the man fall and performed CPR. I just got caught up in the drama. I had to give a statement to the police."

"How long do you think you'll be in town?"

That's what Blaine said but what Adam heard was the unspoken question, "Why are you still here?" There was an edge in his tone. Adam was reminded how aggressive Blaine was when they first met.

"I'll stay for Delgado's memorial service. If it's still on."

Blaine nodded. "It is. The Baptist minister from our church offered to lead the service."

As Adam doused his plate with Tabasco, Blaine looked longingly at Adam's food. On his own plate was an egg-white omelet with spinach and mushrooms and dry wheat toast. "That looks so good."

"Why don't you get it?"

"Heart attack a few years ago." He said it almost too casually. "Haven't been able to work since."

Adam nodded in sympathy. "That's tough." He held up the hot sauce bottle. "Hot sauce won't hurt you. And it will work wonders for… that." He pointed disparagingly at Blaine's breakfast.

Blaine laughed and took the bottle.

Adam's appointment with the sheriff was for 9:00. At 9:20, Deputy Isi led him back through a long corridor to the room the sheriff was using as his office. The desk and the room were too small to contain Sheriff Jim Stacks. His presence was both imposing and intimidating. He glanced up at Adam as Isi ushered him in and asked him to have a seat. He was reading something, leafing back and forth between two pages of typed text. Adam imagined him cross-checking details. Deputy Isi remained and sat on a chair along the wall behind Adam.

Stacks had the aura of the Wild West. His clothes were modern, but his hair, his mustache, even the frame of his reading glasses could have all come from the 1800s. He was the embodiment of a rodeo cowboy and would have intimidated any bull he intended to ride.

Adam had caught glimpses of him the day before and only from a distance. He would stand out in any crowd. Adam felt small and wondered if he was meant to feel that way or if it were all in his imagination. "He needs an indictment, any indictment." Baxter had said. It had been a kind of warning. Adam took it for granted that he should stick to just the facts. He was on his guard but tried to appear as relaxed as he could.

"Mr. Alba, thanks for coming in to see me today. I've read the reports of both Sergeant Baxter and Deputy Isi. I'd like to go over this myself if we could. I may have a few more questions."

At Stacks's prompting, Adam restated the simple facts. Stacks seemed to be listening and watching Adam very carefully. Placing the tip of his pencil on a line of text in the report. "I'm curious. How did you know that there would be a room available for you in the motel?"

"I saw the vacancy sign from the bus when we drove into town. I was relieved to see the sign still lit when I got there."

"You didn't have a reservation?"

"No."

"That was quite a risk on a Friday night before a long weekend. That motel fills up just about every weekend for the casino."

"I didn't know that until later. I guess I was lucky," Adam answered.

Stacks appeared to think. He flipped the page and jabbed another line of text. "How long did you plan on staying in Ur?"

"That's up to you," Adam said. "I'm willing to cooperate any way I can. If I am free to go, I'll stay until the memorial service on Friday."

"Sorry, I meant how long *had* you planned on staying in Ur when you got off the bus?"

"Just the night," Adam said.

He flipped the page again and used his finger this time to indicate his place on the page. "Describe again, please, how you knew that there was a foreign object in your bag."

Was this interview easier than he thought it would be, or is there some sort of trap that he didn't recognize? "I pack my bag in a specific way so that I don't have to unpack the whole bag to get to something I need. I put things in specific places so that I know where they are. When I got my bag back and reached inside, my things weren't in the right place."

"When you got your bag back? Please explain that."

That had to be in the report, but Adam answered honestly. "I dropped it off at the bus station. I intended to continue my journey that evening. After everything happened, I needed to stay, so I picked up my bag."

"Was that the only time the bag was out of your possession?"

"No, I left it in my motel room when I went outside to exercise. That was about half an hour. I went out again after I showered to get a cup of coffee at McDonald's. When I got back, my bag was gone. It was being held in the office."

Stacks glanced up at Isi. "How long were you at McDonald's?" Stacks wasn't writing anything down.

"Twenty minutes, perhaps half an hour."

"It took that long to get a cup of coffee?"

"No, I sat for a few minutes, and then I met and talked to the roofer guys."

"What prompted you to do that?"

That seemed like a stupid question meant to trip him up in some way. Adam felt a little frustrated and tried not to let it get the best of him. "I overheard a comment that one of them made, and they were surprised that I understood. They were speaking Spanish. Tommy Delgado introduced himself and the others and invited me to sit with them."

"What did you talk about?"

"Not much. They looked local, and since I figured I had a few hours before my bus. I thought they might have a suggestion for using that time."

Stacks nodded. "What did they recommend?"

"To be honest, *they* didn't. Tommy Degado mentioned the casino and Walmart, but it wasn't a recommendation. He called it the *corridor of corruption*. He also mentioned the town, and so I decided to explore it, but on my way, Tommy fell. I did CPR, and here I am."

"The previous evening, when you repacked your bag in the laundromat, you did it in your usual way?"

"Certainly. It's automatic. I have a system."

Sheriff Stacks stood up. "I'm wondering if you wouldn't mind demonstrating that for me. It would help me better understand your story." He led the way to the door, opened it, and led him to another room. Baxter and Isi joined them. In the room was a long table. At one end was Adam's bag. His belongings were arranged on the table. They were folded neatly but not the way Adam would have done. They had gone through them carefully.

Adam surveyed the table. "It's not going to be exact because it's not all here. I guess that should be expected."

"What do you mean?"

"I pack tightly. The bag was full. And I know what I put in there and where I put it. Some things are missing, but I guess it was to make room for that package."

Stacks glanced up at Baxter and back to Adam. "What's missing?"

"A pair of jeans, two pairs of socks, and one pair of briefs. Funny that."

"Why is that funny?"

"Funny as in strange. How much room did they gain from a pair of jockey shorts? I understand the jeans and the socks; they're bulky, but underwear?" Adam picked up the duffel bag and set it in the middle of the table. He proceeded to refold and pack the way he normally did. Last to go in was the zip bag with toiletries.

He zipped up the bag and demonstrated the looseness. "It was packed full. I know where everything is. It's all within reach. I don't have to take anything else out of the bag to get it. Test me, if you'd like."

Stacks just shook his head.

Baxter looked approving. "It all fits, sheriff." It sounded like he was endorsing the packing process, but Adam knew it referred to his story— his testimony.

Isi said, "I just learned how to pack." That made Stacks smile. Baxter betrayed no reaction.

"Can I have my stuff back now?" Adam asked.

Sheriff Stacks said, "Deputy, you have the inventory?"

"Yes, sir."

"Give him his stuff back, the backpack as well. Mr. Alba, we may need to talk to you again as our investigation progresses. I hope your stay in Ur is a pleasant one."

He left the substation with his rucksack over one shoulder and carrying his duffel bag in the opposite hand. Whether it was due to his heightened sense of conspicuousness, the amount of activity in the street, or his own sense of shadow, he couldn't say. He was happy to have most of his things back. He was also keenly aware of his surroundings.

A woman who had been smoking a cigarette on the steps of the bank stomped out the filter, picked it up, and went inside when she realized that he noticed her watching him. A car slowed down unnecessarily as it passed him. He watched it park in one of the diagonal spaces in front of the Rest.

Adam felt like basking in the sunshine and simultaneously wanted to get to his room as quickly as possible. He had a lot to think through: the things that Baxter had confided in him, his experience with Stacks, and then getting his stuff back. That little test of packing his bag was just silly, and he guessed it was more about the contents of his bag than his packing.

The talk he had with Baxter the previous evening had done a lot for him. Baxter entrusted him with details that once made things clearer and heightened Adam's awareness of his own situation. The sheriff still considered him a possible conspirator, but the evidence was against his having anything to do with either murder. As for Baxter, he was probably in the clear. Baxter seemed to be on his side. DuPuis must have been persuasive in his endorsement.

The brightness of the day mirrored his pleasure at having his things back. He was lucky to get them back at all. He felt it was a sign that the suspicion that hung over his head was lifting even for Stacks. But then that just might be what Stacks wanted him to feel: safe enough to let his guard down. The possibility that Stacks had put Baxter up to last evening's conversation washed over him like a bucket of cold water. He stopped walking for a second. Then he dismissed the thought. If Baxter was insincere, he was one hell of an actor.

The two young people who were with Junior Delgado the day before got out of the car that had just passed him. At the same time, Junior Delgado walked across the street from the park to meet them. His eyes met Adam's as he passed through the parked cars. They, too, looked in his direction. The group lingered outside the restaurant, waiting for Adam.

Junior seemed more composed than he had been the day before, but stress and perhaps sleepless nights had taken their toll. He looked older than his years. Half-moons of fatigue rested under his eyes. "These are my friends, Matt and Grace." He gestured at them. They both offered their hands.

"We've met." Matt nodded. "At the bus station."

"You probably don't remember me." Grace smiled. "We were on the bus together."

"I thought you looked a little familiar," Adam said politely.

"We're going to have lunch. Will you join us?" Tommy looked at Adam, hopefully.

Adam wasn't hungry and really wanted to get back to his room, but the unexpected invitation felt like an opportunity, so he accepted it.

The music from the kitchen blared as they opened the door. It seemed louder than it had ever been. The clanging of pans rose above the old-school rock and roll. A raspy voice he knew belonged to Henry enthusiastically joined the chorus.

Adam suggested a table over by the wall so that he could set his things down without being in the way. He chose the seat with his back to the wall. To the rear of the dining room, the group of regulars that Rosie nicknamed *the town council* sat at three tables pushed together. Adam recognized the mayor, the woman from the post office, and Blaine, who was having another meal. He didn't know the others.

Rosie brought glasses of water and asked if they wanted coffee. "It's the usual burger and fries, or, today, we've got meatloaf, mashed potatoes with gravy, and fry bread. Of course, you can always get breakfast.

Adam ordered coffee, but the others ordered food. As Rosie retreated, they fell into several moments of awkward silence. Adam half expected them to start fidgeting with their phones. It was Matthew that broke the silence. "Are you leaving today?" he asked, eyeing Adam's duffel bag and rucksack.

"No, I just got them back." It came out of his mouth without thinking, and he wished he hadn't said it.

"Got them back?" Grace said, looking at Matthew. "The bus lost his luggage?"

"Of course not." Matthew was impatient. "What do you mean you just got them back? Who had them?"

Adam was all in it now and decided that any story he could concoct would have been an obvious fabrication. He decided to be honest but cryptic. "The police."

Raised eyebrows all around. "The police? Why did they take your—"

Adam cut Matt off. "It's a long story. I'll make it short; I'm a stranger. I got involved, and they are thorough. You can always ask them, and it looks like you'll get your chance." Adam raised his eyes toward the door. The sheriff and the woman who had been smoking in front of the bank came into the restaurant and joined the town council.

"I'll bet you're sorry you got off that bus." Matt looked directly into Adam's eyes.

"No, I'm not sorry." Then to Tom. "Your father was very nice to me, a total stranger. I'm glad I had the chance to meet him. Men like him are rare. I'll be there on Friday, Tom. I wouldn't miss it." Adam tried to reassure Tom in case that was the question behind their invitation.

Tom looked down, controlling his emotions. "He was always helping somebody."

"I hear you were a state judo champ." Adam tried changing the subject.

Matt sat back, folding his arms like he was tired of hearing the accolade of his friend. Grace rolled her eyes and teasingly backhanded Tom's shoulder. "You're still famous."

"That was four years ago." That picked him up a bit, whether it was an animating topic or he was just grateful for the change of subject. "Who told you that?"

A burst of laughter came from the town council; Rosie was topping off their coffee cups. Adam noticed Blaine looking in his direction, and for a brief second, he wondered if he was the butt of some inside joke.

"Someone mentioned it. Don't ask me who." Adam raised his hands in an I-don't-know gesture.

"Probably Coach Baxter. He was really proud of your team at the time," Grace said.

"Baxter? Sergeant Baxter was your coach?" Adam was more curious than ever.

"Yeah, he wasn't Sergeant Baxter then. He taught civics and phys ed and coached."

"Social studies and AP history too, don't forget," Grace added. "There aren't a lot of kids around here. Most teachers double up."

"It sounds like more than double." Adam was amazed.

Rosie set their plates down on the table. Grace asked Tom to bless the food. And the conversation became even more banal. They expressed interest in him, his travels, where he was headed, that sort of thing. Eyebrows raised again when Adam mentioned he had been a bartender in New Orleans. That sparked questions about Mardi Gras and the French Quarter.

"I've heard it's like Sodom and Gomorrah. That place is just one big sin," Grace commented, dipping a piece of fry bread into her egg yolk.

Matthew interjected. "I'd like to go… just once."

Tom smirked at him. "Not me. Although I have heard of people going to Mardi Gras on mission trips."

Matt rolled his eyes.

"You'd have to be strong in the Lord to do a thing like that," Tom added.

Grace placed her hand on the table and leaned toward Adam. "We probably seem like prudes to you, but Tom and I are in Bible school near Tulsa. Matt here is a heathen, but we still love him."

"I'm not a heathen, but compared to you two, I guess you're being fair. I still love you as well—by the way."

"Bible school, huh? Does that mean you both want to be pastors?"

"I want to work in missions," Tom commented. "People study in Bible school for a lot of reasons: music ministers, youth pastors, evangelists, and missionaries."

"And I'll be happy supporting my husband as a pastor's wife. My boyfriend will be here for the weekend. He has an amazing testimony: sex, drugs, and rock and roll. He'll make a spectacular pastor. We were planning on going back with him on Sunday. Now, we're not so sure." She shot Tom a sideways look.

Tom shook his head. "Classes start again on Monday. Mom insists I go. I think I should stay."

Matt sat up. "Tom, what are you going to do here?"

"I'm the oldest, Matt. My family needs me. They haven't even released my father's body yet."

Grace tried to encourage him. "Your dad wouldn't want you to give up on your studies. You can come back for the funeral. We all will. But your mom needs to know that you—"

Tom cut her off. "My mom needs support."

"Your mom has support. Lots of it. You, me, and Elf will come back for the funeral, and if Elf has to work, we can always borrow his car. We can come back whenever you need or want to."

"I can take the summer off."

"No, you can't. It's the Church Planting Seminar, and it won't be offered again before you graduate. You want to be in missions. You need that seminar," she insisted.

The conversation had left Adam behind. "Alf? Alfred? Alfonso?" Adam was curious.

"No, Elf, with an E, like one of Santa's helpers." Matthew smirked.

"His full name is Elvin. Elvin Lawrence Flemming. Everyone calls him Elf." Grace was proud.

"It suits him. He kind of looks like an elf," Matt added.

"He does not—just because he isn't a big guy…" Grace defended her boyfriend.

"Don't get me wrong," Matt continued. "He's nice and all but he looks like he's ready to play a trick on you. Kind of mischievous."

"He's not like that at all." Grace slapped the table.

"Elf is a great guy." Tom reassured her. "He really is."

"How far away is Tulsa?"

"It's really a suburb, Broken Arrow," Tom said. "About two hours."

Adam sat back while they continued their discussion, sipping his coffee. His mind was tossing ideas back and forth like tennis balls. He wanted to go to his room. He waved at Rosie, signaling that he wanted the check. As he approached, he noticed both Blaine and the sheriff were looking in his direction. He knew he was still under scrutiny.

THIRTEEN

He felt a surprising sense of relief to be back in his space with all his stuff, or most of it, anyway. He set the rucksack and the duffel on the bed. He knew what was in the duffel, as he had packed it himself. He checked the rucksack. Thankfully, they had removed the sandwich, but the chips and water were there. He checked his cell phone. He pulled it out of the front pocket of the rucksack. The charge was down into the single digits. They hadn't bothered to charge it.

He plugged in the charger and powered up the phone, which played a litany of alert notices. There was a frantic text and voice message from his sister. Both were dated the day of Tommy's fall. She was a worrier, especially when he was traveling. Eight years his senior, she had always treated him like she was his second mother. He'd text or call her later after the phone was recharged to tell her he had his real phone back.

There was also a voice message from DuPuis. That surprised Adam. Back in New Orleans, DuPuis started off being a jerk. Now he sounded like a real friend, someone Adam could count on. DuPuis masked his concern with feigned amusement, but Adam could tell the call and the message were serious. "What the hell have you gotten yourself into this time? Call me at this number when you get the chance. If I don't answer, leave a message. And call me if you need me, anytime."

There wasn't enough charge on the phone for much of a conversation, and Adam knew that if he texted DuPuis, he'd call right back. That call would be the first thing he'd do when the phone was charged.

For now, Adam wanted time to clear his head and think. There was a lot of information to process. He connected his phone to the charger and sat down at his puzzle. The simple act of sitting down with the intention of working the puzzle sent his eyes searching for the shapes and his mind considering pieces of information that he had. While they scanned the pieces, his mind processed.

Baxter said he wasn't sure that Pastor Lehman was the intended victim. Apart from Deputy Isi, who had been working at the sheriff's booth? According to Baxter, two other possible targets would have been in sight: the mayor and the sheriff himself.

The only booth clearly visible from that room upstairs was the sheriff's. If the shooter had fired from that room, and the evidence indicates that they had, one of them was the intended victim. Baxter had ruled out himself and Isi as potential victims. Baxter had been too far away, and Isi would have been an easy target. One of those three men was the more likely target.

Baxter also questions whether Delgado was the intended victim. No one knew anything about Chucho. Maybe Delgado got in the way when he stood up. It was possible and offered a valid reason for Chucho to disappear. Was Chucho involved in the drug activity?

He worked on the puzzle until his phone alerted him that it was fully charged. He got up from the table and called and left a message for DuPuis. He also texted his sister that he had his real phone back.

He considered unpacking but decided against it. He liked the idea of having everything in his bag in the right place. He considered the pile of laundry in the corner. *At least I can put those in the laundry bag,* he thought.

He froze. The laundry bag that he kept for dirty clothes wasn't there. It was missing. He checked the side pockets of the duffel bag. They were empty. Had he accidentally left the bag in the laundromat? He sat down on the edge of the bed, his brow furrowed in thought, retracing his steps.

Adam remembered changing in the laundromat, but not his underwear because he had noticed a surveillance camera. He just slipped his shorts over his underwear. He washed the laundry bag with his clothes. He didn't change his underwear until the hotel.

He remembered putting the underwear in the nylon bag at the hotel. He also remembered putting the laundry bag back into the top of his duffel bag, so he hadn't left it behind at the hotel.

That explained the missing gutchies. That word, gutchies, that was his mother's word for boys' underwear. For a moment he was ten years old, watching his mother pack his bag for summer camp. "A clean pair of gutchies for each day and one for good measure." She packed so neatly. There was a special place for everything.

He closed his eyes and luxuriated in the memory. It felt good to think of her like that. There were few such memories for him. Both his parents had worked and worked hard. Most of his childhood memories involved his grandparents, who took care of his sister and him.

A realization intruded upon his memory. His missing underwear was dirty. He had put it in the laundry bag in the motel room. Whoever took that bag had a pair of his dirty gutchies. He laughed out loud. "Hope they enjoy them." He laughed again when he thought of telling Baxter about the pinched laundry bag with dirty underwear.

Adam decided then to unpack. It would only take a few minutes, and somehow the process would put some distance between him and the feeling that strangers, and at least one strange stranger, had been meddling with his things. He'd eventually do laundry and get a new laundry bag and more supplies at Walmart.

An hour later his phone rang. It was his sister. "Finally!" She sounded impatient.

"Cathy, you had the number. I texted you."

"You should have called me."

"Okay, I'm sorry." He knew better than to argue that kind of point with his sister. They chatted about his nephew Jack's plans after high school.

"He's still not sure he even wants to go to college. Dan and I are not thrilled. We tried to get him to go to CCAC for a year to test things out. He and his friend Julian… Who names their kid Julian? He and Julian are going to take a gap year, whatever the hell that means."

"Lots of kids do that. It just means he'll start college a year later. What's he going to do? Just work? Save money?"

She was holding back emotion; Adam thought it might be tears, but he guessed it was anger. "No, at least that would be sensible. They are going to drive around the country and make," she paused, almost forcing out the words, "YouTube videos."

"Cath, think about it. That is the kind of thing you do when you're young. It's not a terrible idea, and if they don't like it, they'll stop."

"And in the meantime, I'll worry."

Of course she would worry. She continued to worry about Adam, her baby brother and a grown man in his thirties. He tried to comfort her. When the call ended, he texted his nephew, starting the text off with "Giacomo, don't show this to your mother… " He figured Jack needed someone on his side. He asked for his YouTube channel so he could subscribe and follow it. He also reminded him that he had an uncle who loved him very much in case he got into a tight spot…"

Adam munched the chips from his rucksack. He went back to his puzzle and was quickly back in flow. While working on the puzzle, he kept thinking about Grace. He could still see her climbing onto the bus in Fort Worth. He remembered thinking she wore the Texas Wesleyan hoodie with pride, like she wanted the people on the bus to see it. If she was in Bible school in Tulsa, why and how did she get to Fort Worth?

Out of curiosity, he picked up his phone and researched buses from Tulsa to Ur. It was cheaper and faster than going to Fort Worth first. It was probably not important, but it was curious. It was like when he found two or three pieces of a jigsaw puzzle that fit together, but you need four pieces in a kind of square to be sure that they came together correctly.

The light in the room shifted and softened. He looked at his watch. It was after five. Apart from the call to his sister, he'd been working on the puzzle for over five hours. Adam had to decide between continuing working on the puzzle and heading to Walmart and the laundromat.

Baxter hadn't exactly lifted his restrictions. He stood up, paced, brushed his teeth, and used his hairbrush. The room began to feel claustrophobic. There'd be no dinner if he didn't go out. Decisively, he gathered his dirty clothes, put them in the duffel, and headed for Walmart and the laundromat.

The feeling of being watched returned with a vengeance as he stepped out of the hotel. It fell on him like a blanket. It clung to the back of his neck and shoulders like the summer heat of the evening sun.

As he approached the First Pentecostal Church, he froze, staring at the roof. He could almost see the men like ghosts up there on the roof. The sounds of their hammers, hand-held and pneumatic, echoed through his memory.

From this angle, he could imagine Luis on his knees by the steeple and Chucho straddling the ridge, using his arms to keep his balance. And he could barely see the top of Tommy's head over the ridge.

As he rounded the bend, the casino became more visible. It became clear with the angle of the properties to one another that the shot had to come from the direction of the casino.

Adam hurried. Excited by the change in perspective, he wanted to double-check. He cut across a dry, overgrown grassy verge into the Walmart parking lot and angled his way toward the far entrance of the building with the food market. He stood as close as he could guess to the spot where he was when he witnessed Tommy's fall.

He closed his eyes. Once again, he could hear Christian music blaring tinnily on the boom box. The echoes of the hammers on the roof. He put the ghosts where he saw them originally. He watched Tommy stand up, wobble a bit, then his body jerked and he fell. The jerk might have been the shot.

The shot had to come from the casino. Chucho was clearly visible. Luis was not. One question remained. When Tommy stood up, did he offer the opportunity of a better shot or did he get in the way of one intended for Chucho? Perhaps it wasn't a murder, but it was homicide, for sure. Baxter wasn't sure if Delgado was the intended victim. Though Adam hadn't heard a shot, the bloodstain on Tommy's chest must have hit his heart and stopped it immediately. Maybe he bled internally.

Alone in the laundromat, Adam leaned the metal folding chair back so he could rest his head on the dryer. The rhythm of the dryer combined with the heat in the laundromat, and he hovered somewhere between being awake and asleep. Half in a dream, he saw Tommy Delgado in McDonald's. He was smiling and proudly showing Adam a picture of his son in a judo gi. Delgado kept touching his chest over his heart where the small bloom of blood had been. As the dream faded, he sank deeper into sleep.

He was aware of the silhouette, the dark shadow that entered the laundromat backed by the brightness of the sun through the picture window. It pulled him out of his slumber stupor. His heart jumped a few beats and began to pound in his chest, making him even more alert. Barely opening one eye, he watched the figure grab a metal folding chair from near the window and approach him. As the figure came closer, he came into focus. It was Baxter.

Adam opened his eyes. "Sergeant Baxter, just the man I want to see." He let the front legs of his folding chair land and stood up in one smooth movement.

Surprised by the statement and the abrupt motion, Baxter stepped back.

Adam spoke and smiled broadly with what he hoped was a telling expression. "It's really hot in here. Why don't we go outside?"

"Sure," Baxter agreed, sounding a little uncertain.

Adam led him to a shady part of the parking lot. His eyes scanned his surroundings. He saw Baxter looking confused. "Listen… Bax. I know I'm acting weird. There's a surveillance camera in there, and I don't know if it records sound. I noticed it the other night when I was washing my clothes. It's why I didn't wash the underwear I was wearing."

"I don't follow."

"I washed *all* my clothes except for my underwear and my shorts. The place was empty. I got undressed, but I noticed the camera and didn't go all the way. Things like that end up on YouTube."

Baxter laughed.

"That's part of what I want to tell you." Baxter focused his attention. "I didn't realize that my laundry bag was missing. It had my *dirty* underwear in it. I noticed the underwear was gone, but I didn't think about the bag."

"There was no laundry bag in your duffel."

"That's the point. It may mean nothing. It may mean a lot. It might just be one more thing missing from my bag. "But…" Adam felt himself blushing. He just had a feeling about the missing bag and underwear. "…A guy once offered me 100 bucks to take off my underwear and give it to him. I know it's creepy, but the underwear and the bag are missing, and I can't get that idea out of my head."

"I don't know anyone involved who has a dirty underwear fetish. Actually, I don't know anyone at all with a dirty underwear fetish," Baxter said.

"You don't know what you don't know." Adam looked him in the eye. "It's just a piece of information, and I'm sorry I didn't realize it earlier. But it might be useful."

"Did you… do it?"

"Do what?"

"Give the guy your underwear." Baxter laughed.

Adam felt the embarrassment lift. "Wouldn't you? A hundred bucks for a pair of jockey shorts? Come on."

"You don't wear fancy Calvin Kleins?" Baxter was not going to let it go.

"Who spends thirty bucks on a pair of gutchies?"

"Gutchies?"

"That's what my mother always used to call them."

Baxter got serious. "Is that how much my wife pays for my underwear?"

It felt good to laugh. It removed any vestige of insecurity he might have felt with Baxter. After all, he barely knew the man, but Bax was genuine, real; he seemed a good balance between intellect and instinct. Adam just hoped that his own instincts weren't wrong.

The sun was nearing the western horizon, and Adam still had a lot to say. The shade felt good, and the day was cooling off. A gentle breeze rustled the leaves, and a stray dog trotted across the parking lot without paying attention to them, as if it had a destination in mind.

"There's a lot more to talk about. How did you know I was here? Am I under surveillance?"

Baxter smiled. "No. My cousin manages the front end of Walmart. She noticed you were buying laundry detergent. So, I came here."

"She called you?"

He chuckled. "No. You weren't in your room, and Walmart was a reasonable guess. Adam, everybody knows you are not from here. Everyone knows that we've had two unexplained deaths. You may not be under surveillance, but you are far from inconspicuous."

As Adam recounted his thoughts about what happened on the roof of the First Pentecostal Church, Baxter listened attentively. He nodded occasionally, letting his mind make connections. Adam was an astute observer and would make a dependable witness if it came to that. Hard evidence was better than a witness statement, and he thought he could get it. It was all coming together. As Adam finished, they sat in silence for a few minutes.

"Listen, Adam. Don't say any of this to anyone. It's possible that the shooter was aiming at Tommy and just waiting for the chance. It's also possible that he was aiming at Chucho."

Adam added. "Did you know that Chucho paid a month's rent up front at the Pioneer's Rest?"

Baxter seemed to freeze. "How do you know that?"

"Rosie said so. Considering the guy was supposed to be surviving on handouts, where did he get that kind of money?"

"Circumstantial but interesting. It's hearsay, but what else did she say about him?"

"Only that she was questioned about him and that she didn't see him much. I can't remember her exact words, but I got the idea that he didn't eat at the Rest, and Rosie feeds her hotel guests one free meal a day. You'd think he would take advantage of that. Hell, I do."

"Interesting."

"Your turn," Adam said.

"Okay, just so you have a clearer picture of where I'm coming from. This is in confidence, now. You're right about the casino. It was the roof. The shot would have been impossible from the parking lot. So, we know it was planned and not a crime of opportunity. Chucho being the target has been raised in discussion, but it's all speculation. No real evidence."

"And how about me? Where do I stand?"

"That's not hard to figure out. Technically you are a person of interest. We know you didn't pull the trigger either time, but we can't eliminate the potentiality of a conspiracy or collaboration. Between you and me. I can't see you as a collaborator. That solution is too easy and too convenient. But in the eyes of the sheriff, that hasn't been ruled out."

Adam sighed.

Baxter continued. "Okay, now I'm going farther than I should. You know someone in this town is involved in trafficking drugs, and I suspect it is a person with some degree of influence. Given the street value of what we took out of your bag, it would have been insane, and I mean deadly insane, for you to turn that in to the police. On the other hand, how and why they choose you to be a blind mule is a big unknown. None of that makes sense… yet."

"Blind mule? What is that?"

"They put it in your bag and hoped you didn't find it. In fact, if you had just gotten on the bus, you wouldn't have found it, right? If you put it in the undercarriage, someone could have taken it out of the bus at any stop where someone was getting off the bus. You had scheduled stopovers in Oklahoma City and Albuquerque. My guess is that somewhere along the line, you would have lost that bag."

Adam sighed. "I've got to get my clothes." He started walking toward the laundromat.

"I'll give you a ride back to the Rest," Baxter called after him.

"I can walk. It's not that far."

"I said I'll give you a ride,"

The tone of Baxter's voice caught Adam off guard. He stopped and turned around. "Am I in danger?"

"I don't know."

FOURTEEN

The puppeteer viewed the daily footage. Usually, it was tedious and boring, but this time the hunk was doing laundry again. It was his lucky day. Would his luck hold out long enough for the guy to strip down again? It was the same duffel bag, though it wasn't as full tonight.

He watched the man empty his bag into a washer, pour in some detergent, and drop the lid. Adam was once again alone in the laundromat. He disappeared. Probably stepped outside for the wash cycle.

He imagined Adam out in the parking lot doing those crazy exercises he always did. He had watched him out in the park once, and once, he had watched him through a peephole. The ease with which he moved his body, the muscles of his torso in a tight T-shirt and the strength of his thighs in those red running shorts made his heart beat hard.

He paused the video. He still had that disturbing feeling that he had seen this guy somewhere before. It gnawed at the back of his mind like a name on the tip of his tongue. Like seeing someone from television but not being able to place them. Perhaps Adam wasn't anybody in particular but just a type. His type. *Hell, that guy would turn heads anywhere.*

He started the footage again and skipped ahead. When Adam reappeared, half-moon-shaped sweat stained the armpits, and there was a vee of sweat down the front of his T-shirt. He could almost feel the heat radiating off his body, the salty, masculine scent. He could feel his own heartbeat.

He looked at his watch. Plenty of time to be alone. He surrendered. He reached down and opened the bottom drawer of his desk. Snaking his hand to the back of the drawer, he felt for the nylon bag and pulled it out. He felt both excitement and shame as he tugged the drawstring loose and tilted the top of the bag toward his face. He inhaled deeply. The scent was intoxicating, masculine, earthy, and primal. He felt that wonderful stirring in his pants.

One hand drifted to his crotch. With the other, he skipped the video ahead. Adam was using the same dryer he had the previous time. He watched as Adam pulled over a metal folding chair, sat back on the back legs of the chair, and rested his head against the humming dryer. His eyes closed. He admired how the denim of his jeans and the dampened T-shirt stretched over his body. He felt himself flush.

He reached into the bag and pulled out a pair of worn jockey shorts—his jockey shorts. He caressed his face with the fabric, inhaling Adam's scent, and sank into his fantasy.

The spell was shattered so quickly he was barely able to take it in. That goon of a police sergeant, Baxter, had arrived and startled Adam out of a deep sleep, making him jump out of his own skin. He'd have to do something about that sergeant someday.

Frustrated, he hit the delete button out of habit. He pulled himself together as he powered down the computer. All that was left on the screen was his own shadowy reflection, a reminder of the man he had become. He felt a wave of disgust.

FIFTEEN

Adam awoke later than usual. The sun was already up. His phone said it was 7:30 and the weather would be pleasant and mild. He went to the park to do his drills. The morning was cooler than he expected. He could hear the coo of morning doves and the scurrying of squirrels as they ran through the canopy of tree branches. The dew soaked his clothes as he did his drills. Having pushed his muscles to the limit, he took a few moments to sit, his back to a tree, and drink in the quiet and solitude of the park at that hour.

As he crossed the road back to the rest, he noticed that the lights of the restaurant were out, and through the window he saw Rosie and Deputy Isi sitting at a table. The sign on the door said closed. It should have been open by now. He tugged at the door. It was locked. Rosie got up and opened the door for him. "Help yourself to coffee," she said, tossing her head toward the counter. "I'll be with you in a few minutes." She locked the door behind him.

There was no music coming from the kitchen, and through the service window, he could see that the kitchen was dark. His coffee in hand, he perched on one of the high stools at the counter and waited. He was in the way. He could feel it. Something was wrong, and he thought he should leave.

He could barely hear their conversation. Isi was jotting down notes. Rosie and Isi eventually stood up. Rosie's expression was resigned, and she didn't have the energy she normally had. Rosie approached him. "What can I get you?"

"I'm not hungry. Coffee is fine. What's wrong? What's happened?"

"Would you mind going over and talking to Aya, I mean Deputy Isi? We can talk after."

Deputy Isi remained standing beside the chair she had occupied. Adam walked over to the table, and they both sat down.

"Do you know Henry Beck?"

"The cook?" Adam wasn't sure, but he was the only Henry he knew of in Ur.

"Yes."

"I know him to see him. I don't know his last name. We've never actually spoken."

"Have you seen him in the past twenty-four hours?"

"No." Adam thought. "I think he cooked me breakfast yesterday, but to be honest, I didn't see him do it. It could have been anybody back there."

She nodded. "When was the last time you saw him?"

"Monday with Sergeant Baxter after the... event in the park. Is he missing?"

Isi nodded. Her face betrayed no emotion. "Will you let us know if you see him or if you hear anything about him?"

Adam agreed. "Deputy, what's going on?"

"Can't really say," she said with a sigh as she stood up.

He watched her leave. Henry was missing, but her answer was enigmatic. Did she not know, or was there some other reason she couldn't say?

He waited for Rosie. The one and only time he got a good look at Henry was when Baxter was checking out the views of the park. He had seen him once from above when he looked out the window one evening and saw him coming back from the bar down the street with a six-pack. Apart from that, he had never seen Henry, and that was the only time he heard him use the front stairs.

All Adam knew about Henry was that he was a vet with PTSD from duty in Iraq. He wasn't allowed to own a gun in an open carry state. He drank a fair amount of beer based on the number of empty cans he had seen in his room. And he was a good short-order cook.

Adam looked up. Rosie was putting chairs up on tables. He got up and started helping her. She stopped; her hands dropped to her side. "I guess the deputy told you that Henry is missing."

"Not in so many words. What happened?"

"I came down to open the dining room, and Henry wasn't in the kitchen. Usually he is in there setting things up for the service. I just figured he slept in a bit." She looked around as if to find an answer to a confusing situation. "By the time I was set up, he still hadn't come down. I went up to see if he was alright, but he wasn't there." Her voice quavered, and a tear fell from her eyes. She pulled a paper napkin from inside her blouse and dabbed it away. "He wasn't in his room, not in the bathroom, nowhere."

"Had he slept in his bed?"

She snorted. "Who could tell?" She shook her head. "He dumped his military discipline after he got discharged." She waved a hand. "Aya asked the same question and got the same answer."

"What are they going to do?"

"Oh, they'll keep an eye out for him. Aya said she'll call the hospitals and police departments and such. Henry's an adult. According to her, without a reasonable suspicion of a crime or foul play, there isn't much they can do. They have to wait twenty-four hours even before filing a missing person's report. Another tear fell. "A lot can happen in twenty-four hours."

Adam winced. "I don't think that wait is a rule but more like general practice. If the deputy is going to do what she said, she's already treating this like a missing person. I mean, at least calling around to make sure he wasn't in an accident or arrested is doing something." He hoped saying so would comfort her. "Can you think of anyone who might know where he is?"

"His cousin Toby, but I'm sure Aya will start there. She's Choctaw, and she knows his family. But I'm afraid something has happened to him. I can't think of anyone who would do him harm. I can't think of any reason for him to go away. He'd have to have a hell of a good reason, and why wouldn't he tell me?" She seemed to fall apart. "I'm worried he's in some ditch somewhere."

They left Toby's old family house in the late afternoon. Toby carried the rifle in one hand and a bag of supplies in the other. Henry carried a shopping bag with supplies and a six-pack in the other. They walked an old familiar route through the prairie behind Toby's house.

Toby had insisted on the gun because Henry was afraid of something or someone. That much he could see. "You sure you don't want to let me in on what's going on?"

"No, I don't want you involved."

"Henry, what did you do?"

"Nothin' you wouldn't do in the same situation. Honestly, I did nothin' but get caught up in something that's none of my business." He sounded rueful and forlorn. Toby believed him.

"I'm leaving the gun."

"I don't want you to do that. A gun alone can send me back in."

"I'll put it under the cot. If you don't touch it, it won't have your prints. Only mine, and I can say I forgot it there. But if you need it, fuckin' use it."

Henry didn't argue. It wasn't a bad plan, and he'd have a defense if he needed it. But why would he? No one knew about the clubhouse. Hell, no one had been there for years.

Acre after acre, they crossed the prairie. There were places where the grass had overgrown the path, but they had walked this way so many times, following it was instinctive. The grass wrapped around their ankles. This stretch of prairie was isolated and expansive. An occasional stand of trees, some large shrubs, but it was all prairie for miles.

The clubhouse was little more than a decent-sized shed. As boys, they played in and around it, building small campfires, toasting marshmallows, and roasting hot dogs on sticks. In their teens, they drank beer, got high, and bragged about their experiences with girls. Henry, Toby, and their friend Jaime spent so much time there that it felt safer than home. It was the first place Henry thought of when he knew he had to disappear.

Toby's parents had known about the shack, but they had no idea what the boys were up to out there. Toby inherited the main house when they passed away. Jaime, the only other person to know about the clubhouse, was gone now as well. Cancer.

The shack seemed smaller than he remembered—smaller and dirtier. It had begun to sag under its own weight or perhaps the weight of the years, much like Henry felt sometimes. There were gaps between some of the clapboards. Blades of light streamed through them, highlighting the dust in the air and creating patterns on the opposite walls. The floor was less even, and some of the boards gave a bit under their feet. It felt dry, parched, lifeless, and fading.

Toby placed the rifle under the cot, back far enough for Henry to claim he hadn't seen it. The cotton padding had mouse holes with visible chewed batting excavated from inside. It was dry-rotted and separated into pieces as they tried to toss it outside. "You'll have to be on the boards tonight. I'll bring you a sleeping bag tomorrow."

"It's okay. I've slept in worse places."

"I still think you should tell me what's going on."

Henry thought for a moment. "The less you know, the safer you'll be. Tell you what. I'll write it down. If anything happens to me, it will be in the stash." He referred to the place where they used to hide the marijuana they grew themselves on the prairie. Henry wondered if, after all these years, he might find some self-seeded plants somewhere.

Toby nodded. He respected his cousin, and whatever Henry was up against, he didn't want him in on it. But he didn't like it. Two heads were always better than one, and they had been through so much together that Henry's refusal to tell his secrets felt like a lack of trust. But he knew better. "If you decide to leave for some reason on your own, put this on the cot." He picked up a stone they used as a doorstop. "If I see it there. I'll know you left because you wanted to."

"Okay." Henry watched him go. He knew Toby could keep a secret. This was the safest place to be. It was at least a twenty-minute walk in any direction before he'd find another human being or even a road. Still, he couldn't stop himself from peering through the gaps in the clapboards just to reassure himself. The breeze shifted, the dust in the shack moved, and the plastic of the grocery bags crackled.

As the sun set, the chirping of prairie dogs comforted him. He didn't remember it being that loud; maybe there were more of them now. When darkness fell, the silence would come. He didn't mind being alone. He preferred it most of the time.

Now, alone on the prairie, in the utter darkness, every sound he couldn't identify sent his imagination soaring. It would be a long night.

By Friday morning, Henry was still missing. There wasn't much more the police could do. Henry was a grown man, and while his disappearance was out of character, there was no indication of a struggle and no evidence that a crime had been committed. The most they could do was file an actual missing person's report.

Deputy Isi had personally reached out to hospitals and police departments in neighboring counties, searching for any sign of Henry—had he been hurt, picked up, or admitted somewhere? She even called his cousin and closest friend, Toby, who told her what she already feared: no one in the family had seen him. He was simply gone. And as Toby pointed out, being gone wasn't illegal.

Adam worked on his puzzle. His mind kept returning to the mystery of Henry's disappearance and how unfair it was on Rosie. She seemed genuinely concerned for his safety and unconcerned that she had a day of business.

As one day stretched to three, Adam debated whether to involve himself. It certainly had nothing to do with him and was none of his business. He had enough experience as a short-order cook that he could easily fill in, and it would give Rosie something to do. As it was, she rarely left her apartment, and when she did, she seemed lost, even dazed.

On Friday, day four of Henry's absence. Adam rose at six in the morning. Decisively, he climbed the steps to the third floor of the Pioneer's Rest and knocked on Rosie's door. The least he could do is make the offer, and if she rejected the suggestion, he'd have gotten the message.

She opened the door quickly, and her disappointment at seeing Adam and not Henry was obvious. Then she blanched. "What's wrong? Did they find Henry?"

"No, I'm sorry. Nothing yet. I thought I'd offer to help. It's no good just sitting around waiting. Over the years, I've been a short-order cook more often than I care to admit. I'm volunteering to fill in for Henry until he gets back."

She squinted, not knowing how to reply.

"I'm not looking for a job. I'm *volunteering*." He stressed the word. "I don't want to be paid. Keeping busy is a good thing to do when there's not much you can do. I think it would be good for you… and for me. The weekend is coming. I've seen how busy it is, and I'm sure I can handle it. It might just help things feel more normal while we wait. I won't be offended if you don't want to do it, but I thought I'd at least offer."

She heard him say *we*—while *we* wait. "Come in." She wasn't sure how to take his offer. It was a rare brand of kindness, especially from a stranger. At the same time, she wasn't sure she wanted to open the restaurant without Henry.

The door opened onto a hallway lined with framed family photos. She led him into a small, fully modern kitchen.

"Have a seat. I was just making a cup of coffee. You take it black, right?"

"Yes, thank you." He was truly grateful for the coffee. He hadn't had a cup in days.

He sat at the table. She pulled a mug from a cabinet shelf, popped a capsule into her coffee maker, and pressed the button. She set her own cup, light with cream, in front of the chair opposite Adam. When his cup was ready, she took it to him and sat down with him.

"I appreciate the offer," she said carefully. "I'm not sure I want to do that. I'm not even sure I *can* do that. If this were just a business, I'd jump, but the Rest is more than that. In some ways, it is one of the few things Ur has left."

"Isn't that even more of a reason to keep it open? The town has been through a lot in the last week. The Pioneer's Rest is the center of town."

She nodded sadly. "Henry has always been part of it ever since he came back from the army."

"He was in Iraq, right?"

She nodded. A smile brushed her face. "He and I go a lot farther back."

"Tell me." He could sense she both wanted and needed to talk.

She looked down, sipped her coffee, and closed her eyes for a second. "I was sixteen. We were at the county fair; me, Eunice, you had breakfast with her and her husband. Her sister's Claudia, that's Tommy Delgado's wife. We were always together."

Adam connected the dots. Luis never said that Tommy was his brother-in-law.

"Henry was there with his cousin Toby and a guy named Jamie. Those three had quite the swagger. They were a few years older than us. Oh, we thought those three were the bees' knees. They strutted around the fair talking to girls and drinking beer. Compared to us, they were mature men. Henry was always so cool. I knew about him. He was one of the bad boys. Had a reputation, you know? I liked that."

Adam smiled encouragingly. The young woman inside her was showing herself.

"At first, he seemed not to notice me at all, but I couldn't get enough of him. We followed them around the fair. Just kept popping up wherever they were. In line for a frosty freeze cone, Henry started talking to me. We spent time together a bit, and yes, we even made out a bit. I fell for him."

"So, you and he are… ?"

She chuckled. "Heaven's, no. Not since we were kids. He was, like I said, one of the bad ones, and he was too old for me according to my folks. They put their foot down. Wouldn't tolerate it. We tried to keep it a secret, but you could never hide much in Ur, even back then. So, when my father found out that I was still seeing Henry, he put his foot down hard… that time on Henry's neck."

"Literally?" Adam raised a brow.

"As good as. So, Henry backed off. He broke my heart. Never told me why until years later, after my father had passed away."

She got up and made herself a second cup. "You want a refill?"

"No, I'm fine." Adam picked up his cup and sipped.

"Anyway. My folks were right. Henry got into trouble with drugs. He tried to grow marijuana out on the prairie. A few plants in the middle of the prairie is one thing, but he went a little overboard. They arrested him. He spent a couple of months in jail because he didn't have money for bail."

"They let him off?" The question he wanted to ask was if she thought Henry was still using drugs. He had heard that Iraq was far from a drug-free experience for many soldiers. Was it possible that Henry was involved in the drug investigation that Baxter said so little about? He couldn't have put the drugs in Adam's bag, but was he involved in some other way? He'd have to mention this to Baxter.

"No. Even if he had gotten the minimum sentence, he would have been in jail for years. The judge gave him a break. He said that Henry 'needed structure' and said he could serve his full sentence in jail, or he could join the army."

"So, he joined the army," Adam concluded.

She nodded. "They made him a cook. He was in one of those mobile kitchens driving around Iraq, following the guys who were fighting." She paused and seemed to be considering a detail that might have been better left unsaid. She shook her head slightly and continued. "When he came back, he wasn't the same guy. His swagger was broken. They said he had PTSD."

Adam leaned back in his chair and laced his fingers behind his head. "Maybe the PTSD is what this is all about. Maybe he just needs to be alone."

She shrugged. "He keeps to himself mostly. He's social when he needs to be, but he's not one for small talk. He takes real pride in the kitchen. It's that army experience that gets us through the weekends."

"When did he start to work at the Rest?"

"He came back from Iraq before my parents died. My father went first, my mother a month later. He came to the funeral despite the way they treated him. I was touched by that."

"It's surprising."

"Not when you think about how he changed. The judge was right. He needed the structure, the discipline. His spit and vinegar were gone, but he came back stronger. That's when he told me what my father did. It really pissed me off even in my grief, but Henry said my father was right to do what he did. He called my father a wise man who saw through his bullshit."

"So that's when you hired Henry?"

"I had to run the business. The hotel was busier back then, but slowing down. The restaurant was still a saloon. My mother ran the hotel, and my father ran the bar. The bar made money, but running a saloon wasn't for me, and Ur didn't have a restaurant. The saloon served food. I decided to make a change."

"I trusted the new Henry. I wasn't a schoolgirl anymore. It just sort of worked out. He could run a kitchen and needed a job and a place to live. The town really rallied around the restaurant. The hotel doesn't do much. You can see that, but it's home."

"So let's do it. Like I said, I'm volunteering to help out—just until Henry gets back. I promise not to mess up his kitchen."

Tears began to fall again. "What if… what if he doesn't come back?"

"He'll come back. I just have a feeling."

"I wish I could trust your feeling. He wouldn't just go off and not tell me. That's not Henry. I'm afraid that something has happened to him."

"Deputy Isi checked everywhere."

They were both thinking about the shooting of the pastor from the third-floor window of the Rest. Neither would voice that thought. Adam wondered if they both shared the same unanswered questions. Did Henry fire the shot? Or did he know who had?

SIXTEEN

Blaine and Manda Lamano were leaving the casino restaurant as Adam and Rosie arrived. Adam had warmed to Manda. She was very kind and thoughtful without expecting anything in return. From the free coffee she had given him at the bus station to her concern for his missing things, she had been a welcome buffer between Adam and her gruff husband, Blaine. Even Blaine, still wearing his intimidating sidearm, seemed to be warming up.

Adam wasn't surprised when Baxter, dining with his wife, acknowledged him with only a simple nod across the dining room when their eyes met. His wife was beautiful in an unpretentious way. She looked completely natural with little to no makeup. Her long chestnut hair hung heavily at her shoulders. Adam would have bet she was enjoying this time out with her husband as a rare treat. They made a handsome couple.

"It looks like other people had the same idea." Rosie tilted her head toward Luis and Eunice. Eunice noticed them and waved. Luis turned around and made a thumbs-up motion. They seemed surprised that he and Rosie would be dining together.

"You won't see her sister Claudia here," Rosie almost whispered. "Tommy hated this casino, and they have too many mouths to feed. I should have taken something over to their house."

"I had the impression that lots of people in Ur hate the casino."

"Not everybody. This casino and Walmart are now the biggest employers in town." They were seated at a small table for two. Adam, not forgetting his manners, held the chair for Rosie. "Wow. You have no idea how long it's been since someone held a chair for me." She smiled but seemed a little embarrassed at the same time.

They were both tired. It hadn't been a hard day, but it was a long one. After agreeing to Adam's encouragement to get back to work, Rosie took him down to the kitchen to show him the ropes.

The only customers in the Rest that day were the regulars that Rosie called the town council. The first to arrive had been Blaine, as usual. It was almost as if he had been camping out hoping the restaurant would open. The sheriff and the woman from the bank arrived. A little later the woman from the post office, the mayor, and a man Adam hadn't seen before joined them. Rosie explained that he was the owner of the bar a couple blocks down the main street. Everyone had asked about Henry except for the bar owner. He already knew Henry hadn't come back because Henry was good for a six-pack a day.

Rosie stayed most of the time in the dining room. With so few orders, Adam was bored. Occasionally Rosie would show him some of the prep for the weekend. "Once these few folks spread the word that we are open again, we'll be packed tomorrow, and Sunday will be business as usual." The only interruption came from a squat elderly woman in an old Volkswagen Beetle delivering partially cooked fry bread. She wore a long, well-worn dress. Her hair was in plaits.

She eyed Adam suspiciously. "Where's Henry?"

Adam shrugged his shoulders. Thinking it best not to say much, he said, "I'm just filling in temporarily."

She was inscrutable. She didn't seem to react. She placed the plastic bags filled with fry bread on the stainless-steel prep table, and nodding slightly, she took it upon herself to train Adam, showing him how to heat the bread in the fryer and how to know when to take it out of the hot oil.

Just as they were both trying the fry bread, the woman sprinkling hers with sugar, Rosie came into the kitchen. "Hatak Ohoyo, you've come early. I'm glad."

"Where's Henry?"

Rosie's face blanched, and tears threatened. "I don't know. I am worried about him. If you see him, tell him to please come home." She took an envelope out of her apron pocket and gave it to the woman. The old woman nodded, took the envelope, and left.

"Why did you tell her to attack Ohio?"

It was the first time she laughed heartily since Henry had disappeared. "It's just a greeting for an old woman in Choctaw. I've known her since I was a kid. She and my mother were good friends."

With his back to the wall, Adam had a broad view of the casino dining room. As their food arrived, Adam pointed out, "The sheriff and his girlfriend just arrived."

"Girlfriend?" Surprised, Rosie turned around to look. She snorted.

"She's not his girlfriend. He's married, and I'm surprised he didn't bring his wife. It's an election year. He's not stupid enough to be seen with a girlfriend."

"How do people know they're not a couple?"

"She shares her house with an old friend from college named Mary. You get my drift?"

Adam smirked. "Do you think he'll win the next election? Adam was thinking about Baxter's comment about the sheriff wanting fast indictments because it was an election year.

"Certainly, he's not a pain in the ass, and as long as he's the sheriff, we keep Baxter and Aya. They make him look good." She looked at her watch. "We should be going soon."

The parking lot of the First Pentecostal Church was packed. Some people were parking in the Walmart parking lot and walking over. Adam and Rosie left her car in the casino lot and crossed the road on foot.

When they entered the church, there was a receiving line that reminded Adam of a wedding. The first person was Junior Delgado. Followed by his two younger brothers and a younger sister. Mrs. Delgado stood next to Mrs. Lehman, the pastor's wife, at the end of the line. Junior greeted everyone warmly. The bags under his eyes made him look tired, but his posture was erect. He looked people in the eye, and his gratitude for the attention to his father and his family was obviously sincere.

There was a gap of at least several years between Junior and his siblings. The second son, a pubescent lad named Benjamin, was struggling. He shifted side to side, putting his weight on one foot and then the other. He was trying to be as composed as his brother but wasn't doing a good job of it.

A man in line in front of Rosie and Adam said something to Benjamin that triggered him. Adam heard the boy say in a cracking voice. "Sure, my dad is with Jesus, but that means he's *not* with us." The man who had made the comment blanched and stepped back. Junior put his arm around his brother's shoulders and pulled him closer while he spoke with Rosie and Adam. The lad seemed to melt into his brother's embrace. The other brother and the sister were even younger. Adam thought to himself, *no wonder Junior felt pressure to stay home and be the man of the family.*

Since the two widows ended the line, it progressed slowly, increasing the awkwardness for the children as the line lingered in front of them. They politely fielded endless banal statements about how big they were getting and questions about how old they were and what grade they were in.

Mrs. Delgado greeted and hugged Rosie. "I love you, Claudia. I'm so sorry." She introduced Adam. "This is the man who tried to help Tommy when he fell."

She hugged and effusively thanked Adam for his kindness and willingness to help her husband. She had tears in her eyes when she broke the embrace.

"I'm sorry I couldn't do more."

She hugged him again. The past week of uncertainty was visible by the sagging lines of her face. Adam wondered if she had been told that her husband had been shot.

Mrs. Lehman acknowledged Rosie cordially and seemed to assume that Adam was Rosie's distant cousin.

They slipped into a pew next to Manda and Blaine. The bus driver, Blake, sat on the far side of his brother. Seeing them together, one could tell the difference between the twins, but apart, they looked enough alike to be confusing. The two women sat together. Adam was at the end of the pew and was glad that he didn't have to engage in small talk with Blaine and Blake.

The music was an unusual mix of traditional hymns and more modern worship songs. Some attendees stood up and seemed to sway or even dance in place. He noticed that Grace, Junior's friend, the girl from the bus, was one of those standing up with her hands raised. Next to her was a shorter, waifish young man doing the same. *He must be Elf, her boyfriend.* She had said that day in the restaurant that she intended to be a pastor's wife. He wondered if they were engaged to be married. Adam noticed that Matt, who sat on the other side of Grace, remained seated.

There was something about Grace that niggled at the back of Adam's mind. It was probably not important, but why had she gone to Fort Worth when going directly to Ur was faster, easier, and cheaper?

The Baptist minister spoke warmly of both Pastor Lehman and Deacon Delgado. "He was a valuable participant at our ministerium meetings," he said of Pastor Lehman, "always bringing a fresh perspective and challenging us to live up to the example of Jesus." He then turned his praise to Tommy, calling him "the very embodiment of Christ's love on earth, showing the kind of devotion that serves both the Lord and the community." Adam glanced at Luis, wondering whether he was rolling his eyes or silently agreeing.

Junior delivered a tearful eulogy for his father, "the greatest dad that ever lived." And Pastor Lehman's brother told the congregation how dedicated and faithful his brother was and how proud their parents had been when he chose the ministry. He tried to joke that they hadn't been so enthusiastic about his own decision to be an engineer, but the joke fell flat.

Adam was relieved that the service didn't end with an altar call where people in the congregation are invited to come forward and accept Jesus. He had been to several funeral services where ministers used the untimely death of a departed loved one to convince some in the congregation that it was time to "get right with God."

The attendees were then invited downstairs to the social hall for light refreshments. No wonder, Adam thought, that the people ate before the service. Trays of packaged cookies, a sheet cake, and a punch bowl filled with sugary orange drink were on offer. Adam grabbed a bottle of water and tried to disappear into the wallpaper. He felt out of place and glad that the feeling did not come with a feeling of being conspicuous.

A few people went out of their way to greet him. Most people knew that he was "the stranger." They asked questions as banal and pointless as those addressed to Junior's siblings. "Where was he from?" "What did he think of Ur?" Some asked that question proudly, as if it were some sort of challenge. Others, almost deprecating, as if they had to apologize for the small, intimate nature of the town.

The sheriff and the mayor shook hands with everyone. The woman from the bank wasn't tagging along with the sheriff. She kept looking at her watch. Maybe it was just a friendship or even an acquaintance. Maybe she was just someone to eat with.

The Baptist minister made sure to speak again with the two widows and Junior before leaving. His departure gave Adam subtle permission to do the same. His promise to Junior complete, Adam wanted to leave as well.

He decided to wait for Rosie upstairs in the quiet of the church. She was talking with a small group of people that included Grace and her boyfriend. He interrupted her briefly to let her know where she would find him when she was ready to leave.

"Oh, here. Let me give you the keys. I can get a ride home."

Realizing that she was comfortable with his leaving, "No need, I can walk."

Grace's boyfriend spoke up. "I can give you a ride. I have my car."

"It's okay, dude. I can walk. It's only a half mile or so."

The young man whispered into Grace's ear. Her eyes darted to Adam, and she nodded. He kissed her on the cheek. "Please," he said. "I'm ready to go anyway." Leaning closer, he whispered. "You're doing me a favor. I gotta get out of here."

He led Adam in the Walmart parking lot to an old Honda Civic that looked to be held together with duct tape and bits of wire. He unlocked the passenger-side door for Adam, and when he got into the driver's seat, he briefly bowed his head and rubbed his eyes.

"That tired?" Adam asked.

Elf shook his head. Looking up, he said, "Just a brief prayer." He started the car.

"Looks like the prayer worked," Adam quipped. The car had started beautifully.

Elf looked at him and laughed. "I know it looks like it's ready for the junkyard, but that's all cosmetic. This car is the best-running car I ever had." He backed out of the parking space and drove to the entrance to the parking lot. "Which way should I turn?"

"I'm at the Pioneer's Rest."

"Okay, which way should I turn? I've never been there before."

"You're not from here then?" Adam asked.

"Not too far away but far enough that I never even heard of the blessed place."

"Turn left. It's less than half a mile."

"Grace told me how you tried to help Tom's dad. That was amazing of you."

Adam shrugged. "I saw him fall."

Elf cringed. "Must have been awful."

"You don't think like that when you're in the middle of it. At least I don't. I just think I have to do something."

"Like there was a reason why you were there," Elf suggested.

Adam would never have described it that way. His life had always seemed to float somewhere in the middle between chaos and destiny. He didn't believe in pure coincidence or happenchance. Neither did he embrace the idea that life was somehow predestined or designed. To Adam, truth lay in the in-between, though he sometimes jealously considered the comparative simplicity of the extremes.

They pulled into one of the diagonal spaces in front of the rest. Adam was surprised when Elf got out of the car.

"I have a room here," he explained. "The lady said she would leave the key in the door for me."

"Wouldn't you normally stay with Grace and her mother?"

"Oh, no." He shook his head. "That would be inappropriate. I stayed overnight at Tom's before, but under the circumstances…" He pulled a backpack out of the trunk of the car.

"So, you came in for the memorial?"

"No. I mean yes—now. I promised Grace and Tom to come and pick them up to take them back to school. I would have come when I heard the news, even without the plan. Tom is a good friend, and his dad was awesome. I would have come earlier but I had to work."

Adam nodded. "So, have you and Grace been dating long?

"A few months. I met her dad a week ago. He teaches at Texas Wesleyan."

Well, that explains part of the mystery of Grace going first to Forth Worth. She was visiting her father. Adam thought. "So, it's getting serious."

Elf hesitated. "Not yet. Never if her mother gets her way. She doesn't like me very much."

"Why do you think that is?"

"I understand why her mother thinks I'm a bad choice. I'm ten years older than Grace. I have a colorful past that Grace likes to share a little too freely. She doesn't understand that when people know things about your past, it can change the way they think about you. It shouldn't be that way, but it is."

"Grace said you had an amazing testimony. Is that your colorful past?" Adam led Elf into the lobby of the Rest.

"See what I mean? Grace is kind of innocent that way. Did she tell you about it?"

Adam shook his head. "Only that it was amazing, and I should ask you."

"That's an improvement on her part."

"Well, she did say something about sex and drugs."

Elf halted and sighed. "You see what I mean? Verbal clickbait, and she doesn't even realize that it's already too much information for casual conversation. It's like she just says whatever she's thinking." He fell silent.

Adam mentally finished Elf's thought in his own way. *Doesn't sound like a good quality for a pastor's wife.*

The lobby of the Pioneer's Rest mesmerized Elf. The Victorian sofa, the player piano, and the electrified wall sconces created a real sense of place. "Wow, it's like stepping back in time. It's right out of an old western movie. It even smells the way you think it would, dusty and dry like a ghost town."

"Except it's apparently real stuff."

They climbed the stairs to the second floor. Elf had the room opposite Adam. Adam showed him around the little kitchen area and the bathroom. "It's just you and me here."

"Grace and her mom will come here for breakfast. Will you join us?"

"Can't. I'll be cooking your breakfast.

"You're kidding. I cook for a diner, too. Just working my way through school. So, you work here?"

Adam was already warming to Elf. Adam reservedly liked most people but at a distance. Elf was making a good impression. "I'm just helping out while the regular guy is out of commission."

"What happened to him?" Elf threw his backpack on the bed.

"No one knows. He just seems to have disappeared."

"He just vanished? That's really weird," Elf muttered; his voice trailed as his thoughts drifted. There was something forlorn in his expression that might have been out of proportion.

"So, are you going to amaze me with your story?"

"Are you a Christian?" Elf asked.

"I was raised Catholic. Lapsed, I guess. I'm not very religious."

"You're safe then. I'll tell you."

"What do you mean I'm safe?"

"Stories like mine change the way people, especially Evangelical and Pentecostal Christians, see and treat me. They like the story, but they change the way they treat me after hearing it. They love the lurid details of someone's testimony." He paused as if deliberating, then repeated himself. "They love the lurid details, but sometimes I wonder if they really believe in the transformation. It's like they don't really trust it—or me."

"Is the transformation the point?"

"Supposed to be. When people tell their story, they spend a long time on the bad stuff and end up with some perfunctory phrase like, 'And then I found Jesus.' Me, I want to hear what happened after that, including the struggles, the questioning, and the doubts. That to me is the real story."

"You know what, I think you're going to be a great pastor." He couldn't explain why, but Adam felt strengthened. Some of the uncertainty of his situation drained away.

"Thanks. Not sure about how great, but just want to be good."

Adam gave Elf one of his bottles of water, and they sat half facing one another on the sofa in the second-floor lobby. "I don't need or really want the lurid details. Just whatever you think communicates your experience, before and after. I've had a few struggles of my own."

"That's easy." He told Adam about his heroin addiction. "I stole, turned tricks, and then dealt to pay for my own drugs. I'll skip those details, though I could write a book. I ended up in jail. Cold turkey detox is an experience I never want to repeat. There are drugs in prison, but something happened in my brain. I saw jail as my chance to straighten up and get my life back, whatever it turned out to be."

"I'll bet that was tough." The thought of drugs being a running theme in his experience of Ur floated in the back of Adan's mind.

Elf continued, "Before you ask, of course, having turned tricks marked me in another way in prison. I'm not a big guy. It was really bad for a while." He fidgeted in his seat, uncomfortable with the memory.

Adam spoke. "For what it's worth, I wouldn't have asked. On the other hand, I've known some very tough wrestlers who were your size."

"Tom gives me judo lessons once in a while. I can't really afford to pay him for them, but I think he thinks it's as much fun as I do. He was a champ, you know. It may come in useful someday, but I hope not. That's how I met Grace. Tom introduced us."

"She takes judo lessons, too?"

"No, she's a friend of Tom's, that's all. Anyway, lots of people find Jesus in prison. There were two guys, two really big guys, who befriended me and protected me. They probably saved my life. They certainly saved my ass—excuse the language."

Adam just shook his head.

"They were really cool and took me to a Bible study. I found Jesus there, and for me, it wasn't about having a better chance at parole like it is for some. I was floundering in my life, and the gospel seemed to explain everything. It was like a map out of darkness. It might sound crazy, but for a while I didn't want to get out. I could spend a lot of time studying the Bible and I had two huge protectors to keep me safe. When I was getting out, the Bible teacher who visited the prison referred me to his school. I was determined to serve the Lord."

Adam took a moment to reflect, then said, "What amazes me most about your story is that you saw prison as a second chance."

"I saw the Lord in that," Elf replied. "The hardest part came after I got out. In prison, I had two beefy guys watching my back. Outside it was just me and the Lord. It was rough. Finding work, affording a place to live. People at church say they want to help, but they don't want you staying in their home. And the temptation of easy money." He rubbed his eyes with the memory of it. "It was real. Sometimes, the voices in your head lie to you. They say you won't make it, that you're no good, that you don't deserve a better life—or even that your conversion wasn't real."

"Do you have any regrets?"

"Yeah, I've got regrets. A whole trail of them. Most came before I got locked up, but I made a few after, too. Still... when I sit with it, I see how all of it—every stumble and fall—brought me here. So, I can't say I'd undo it. I hate that I hurt or used people. That stays with me. But the only regret that really aches now is trusting people with the most honest parts of me—believing they'd see the light in it, not just the dirt."

Elf became pensive. Adam was curious and almost asked how some Christian had used his story against him, but he thought better of it.

Elf appeared to have made a decision. "Look, I kind of used you back there. There were two people in that room I wanted to get away from. I recognized them from before I went to prison. I don't think they recognized me. At least I hope not." He shook his head. "Hypocrisy sucks."

A chill ran down Adam's spine. Everyone at that service seemed honest and respectable. He now wished he'd stayed a bit longer and had paid more attention. Still, Adam started fitting some pieces of the puzzle together. Elf recognized someone from when he was involved in drugs. Hadn't Baxter said something about a person of influence? Was that the connection that Elf had made? Baxter would have had a way of getting him to talk. All Adam had was a forthright question. "Can you tell me who they were?"

Adam could almost see Elf shudder with the same chill that had only moments before traced down his own spine. "No, dude, for two reasons. One, I might be wrong. I was still using drugs back then. Memory is a funny thing. And two, if I really did recognize them for sure, I don't want them as enemies."

SEVENTEEN

Saturday morning shone bright across the prairie. Despite the early warmth, Henry felt cold. He sometimes shivered uncontrollably. The sleeping bag Toby had brought him opened into a blanket he wrapped around himself.

During the day, he might risk building a small fire, but at night when the temperature dropped, he didn't want to risk anyone happening to see the glow on the prairie. He knew people were looking for him, and he wasn't yet ready to be found.

The chills had more to do with the lack of beer than the nightly drop in temperature. Toby, the only person on earth who knew where he was, could be forgetful sometimes. Despite a fridge full of beer, he sometimes forgot. Toby didn't come at all yesterday.

Wrapped in the sleeping bag blanket, Henry peered through a gap in the clapboards on the east side of the clubhouse. There were gaps in the clapboards on all four sides. The view was complete except to the north, where there was a thick grove of trees and shrubs that had once been part of a windbreak.

At first, it was just a dot against the eastern sky. He stared fixedly at it. It could have been anything, but he didn't think it had been there before. He wasn't sure if the constant movement he noticed was real or a figment of his vision. His heart beat a little harder, and he could feel his senses tightening. Henry thought of the gun under the cot and put it out of his mind. No point in overreacting.

His eyes weren't what they used to be. He squinted to see better. The object was a person. They moved slowly and waddled slightly side to side as they walked. They were carrying something. It wasn't Toby. Toby's house was to the south, and Toby didn't waddle.

He waited, unable to stop watching. The figure took shape. Henry was at once relieved to recognize her. Then, like a flood, was it anxiety, fear, or both? *How did she know where to find me? Who else knows?*

She carried two plastic shopping bags, the reusable ones you pay for. They weighed her down and balanced her walk. She held her arms out slightly to avoid the bags brushing against her legs.

Henry was glad to see her but frightened at the same time. What did her coming mean? What news did she bring? She was old, too old to walk the distance that she had to walk, especially carrying those bags. They looked heavy. At least they looked heavy for her.

She paused outside the cabin, and he stepped out of the open door. "Hatak Chito."

"Halito." She greeted him and continued to speak in Choctaw. "Are you well?"

"I am well. Are you well?"

She looked at her eldest grandson. She had been just a girl when his mother was born and barely a woman when he came into the world. Here he stood, already looking like an old man. "I am happy to find you. These bags are heavy."

He walked out to her and took the bags. They were indeed heavy. The aroma of stew filled the air around him. He couldn't see past the fry bread, but he knew he would eat well.

She followed him into the shack. He set the bags on a table. The smell of warm stew quickly filled the cabin. It nearly brought him to tears. He folded the sleeping bag into thirds to increase the cushion for her to sit on the cot. As she sat down, she sighed deeply.

"I brought you some food," she said.

"Thank you. I am hungry." He wanted to tear into the bags. Toby kept him supplied with things to eat, but he wasn't a cook, and what Toby brought him wasn't real food—chips, candy bars, and cold sandwiches bought from the refrigerated section of a convenience store.

"Eat," she said. "It's still warm."

He dug in the bags and found the stew in a large, leaking plastic container that once held sour cream. The fry bread was wrapped in foil and a towel to keep it warm. The other bag held more fry bread and several bottles of water. Opening the stew and breaking a piece of fry bread, he dipped it into the stew. The thick broth coated it and filled the tiny nooks. Eating a little too fast to really savor it, he asked, "How did you know I was here?"

Of course, she couldn't just answer the question. There was more to the story. She told him of her delivery of fry bread to the Pioneer's Rest and the fear she felt when she saw the stranger in his kitchen. "Rosie says, 'please come home.'"

"But how did you know about this place?" He had the feeling that she knew more than she let on. She might have known what he and his friends did in this shack when they were young. Did she worry that he had started using again?

"The prairie dogs told me." It was a silly way to dismiss the question. She had used it ever since he was a child, and he knew to stop asking. If he needed to know something, she'd tell him, but she wouldn't clutter the situation with unimportant details. Of course, her idea of what was and was not important was often unique. That had always been true and added a kind of mystique to her presence in the lives of her grandchildren.

"Did you tell anyone about this place?" Henry was apprehensive.

She shook her head. "I came alone so you could tell me what trouble you have."

He told her the story of what happened the day Pastor Lehman was shot. He told her about the police finding a gun in the old tornado shelter and how they asked him if it was his. "I told them it was not my gun, but I was frightened. I thought they didn't believe me."

"Who asked you these questions, Billy or Aya?"

He shook his head. "Some white deputies from somewhere… not Ur. I didn't know them. I kept thinking about their questions all night. Then I remembered what I saw. I knew I wasn't safe anymore. He saw me. He knows I saw him." He set down his fry bread on a piece of foil.

"Who?"

"No, it is too dangerous. I won't say."

"Why didn't you talk to Billy or Aya? They are Choctaw. They would understand. They would believe you."

"Are you so sure? They are police."

"Things are not the way they used to be. Billy and Aya are Choctaw, and they know you."

"But it is my word about a white man. I am afraid. It's better to let the police solve their crime and not get involved. They can do it without me. I'll go back when they finish."

His words would have rung true forty years earlier. She could hear the voices of many people who thought the old way. She also knew that the old way was so old that it could be forgotten, and forgetting is dangerous.

She was glad of her grandson's caution. "It may be as you say. Your cousin knows you are here?" It was a question.

"He knows I am here. He takes care of me," Henry assured her.

"Did you tell him your story?"

"His anger comes too quickly, so I did not tell him."

"Tell me what you know."

He shook his head. "It is too dangerous. It is a white people's problem."

EIGHTEEN

"They think they're slick," Rosie said, placing dirty plates in a dishwasher rack.

"Who? What do you mean?"

"Aya Isi asking about my missing hotel guest. I told her. He paid a month up front. I don't care whether he stays here or not, but I haven't seen him. Have you?"

Adam shook his head, placing three more plates on the service window. "Not even a sound."

She put her hands on her hips. "He's got two more weeks. This is getting creepy. Two murders and two missing people. How did Ur suddenly turn into New York City?"

She said it so plainly. It was the first time Adam heard anyone openly admit that Tommy Delgado's fall was no accident. He wondered how it had gotten out. Adam thought they were keeping the Delgado shooting under wraps.

She was right, of course. Two murders and two missing people if you count Chucho. *It's odd that no one has seen either of them.* His mind flashed on an old story by Ambrose Bierce. In the story, a man who crossed his field just disappeared. Bierce himself mysteriously disappeared years later.

Chucho was long gone. Presumably, he was scared off by the inevitable involvement of the police. If he were illegal, like Luis thought, police involvement would be the last thing he'd want to be around. But Ur was home for Henry. Henry was like the guy in that story. Just disappeared. It was hard to believe someone like Henry would do that on a whim.

As he dropped two pieces of dough for fry bread into the hot oil, he couldn't stop thinking about Henry. There were only a few possibilities. He ran through them in his mind. He could have gone far enough away so people wouldn't recognize him. But why would he? Was he protecting himself or someone else? Of course, someone could be hiding him closer to home. Why would he need to hide? Was it from the police? Or from someone else? The most unpleasant thought, and the one that plagued Rosie most, was that something had happened to him, either an accident or foul play. But Deputy Isi had checked all the hospitals and police stations.

He wanted to talk to Baxter. He had things to tell him. The conversation with Elf had demanded several hours at the jigsaw puzzle, parsing his thoughts and considering how events might fit together and make sense. Adam was most curious about the two people from Elf's past. Who were they? How did they figure into his past? Elf feared them and would not identify them.

In hindsight, Adam reprimanded himself. If he had only paid more attention at the service and the social gathering after, he might have noticed unusual reactions to or by Elf. The whole thing was normal and weird at the same time. The double memorial, a whole town in mourning, and the feeling that something that no one wanted to talk about hung in the air.

He had tried to think about what he had noticed about Elf. All he could remember was that Grace enthusiastically introduced him to a lot of people, including Adam. Grace did everything with a degree of enthusiasm and innocence. Elf just went along like arm candy. How much information had Grace offered as simple small talk? Could Elf be in some kind of danger? If Adam even remotely guessed he was worth watching more intently, he would have done so.

Adam wondered what it must be like to go through life in a body as small as Elf's. Adam had never been in prison, and he could only imagine the fear Elf must have had. Adam had always been large and strong. Wrestling increased his natural confidence, especially when it came to defending himself and, when necessary, sticking up for others. Elf had awakened the instinct that had first stirred in Adam on the playground when he realized that all schoolyard teasing wasn't good-natured but predatory and cruel. It was an instinct that compelled him to protect and defend victims from predators and innocent kids from bullies. He'd stand up for them and, if necessary, fight even if it meant earning a detention for fighting. He felt a strong urge to protect Elf.

The dining room slowed down about half past one, so Adam began cleaning up. There weren't many more orders. At quarter to two, Rosie popped her head through the door. "No new orders. And I have a message from Sergeant Baxter. He said to tell you that the Pioneers are playing the Pirates at four o'clock. You don't want to miss it."

"What?" Adam was confused. "Who is playing the Pirates? There's no team called the Pioneers." He wondered if Baxter was inviting him to watch the game at his house or if Baxter didn't realize there was no TV in his room.

"Yes, there is. Little League. You like baseball, don't you?"

Adam laughed. "Little League."

"Come on. It'll be fun. We'll change and go. I have to be there early. You can help me carry stuff."

Adam suspected he would be lugging bats and balls, but instead, he was carrying a large electric roasting pan filled with restaurant-sized packages of hot dogs. Rosie carried a trash can-sized bag filled with packages of buns. Over her elbow was another bag with containers of condiments with ketchup, mustard, chopped onions, and relish.

"For two bucks you get a hot dog, a bag of chips, and a drink. The parents' association brings the chips and soft drinks. Best deal in town."

"And they make money?" They crossed the street and started walking through the park.

"Enough to cover uniforms. Kids grow every year, you know. All the supplies are donated. The parents' association has a budget for the chips, and someone drives up to one of those big stores—Sam's or Costco—to get supplies."

"And who pays for this stuff?"

"See if you can guess." She laughed.

"You ought to get Walmart or the casino to sponsor the team."

"They probably would do it but want their name on the uniforms. People around here aren't thrilled with either of those establishments." She snorted. "But if you go to Walmart after the game, it will be packed."

"Tommy said they killed the town."

"We aren't dead yet, but most people think like Tommy." They crossed the street at the far corner of the park. "The field is just behind the school." She threw her chin at a two-story building that couldn't be anything but a school. It was yellow brick with large institutional windows and only one main entrance.

"With all that's going on," Adam shifted his grip on the heavy roaster. "I'm surprised the game wasn't canceled or postponed."

"It's not the kids' fault. Even Claudia Delgado will be there. Her two youngest will be in uniforms. Life is for the living, Adam. Being in mourning gets harder when you stop living. Eunice told me last night that Claudia insisted Junior return to school tomorrow with his friends. He was thinking about taking time off from school. Eunice is Claudia's sister."

"I remember."

They turned the corner around the school building. The concession stand, a semipermanent wood structure, had been erected along the back wall of the building. Rosie told Adam where to place the roaster and suggested he ask Baxter if he needed help. "Usually," she added softly, "Henry helps." Her voice broke, and she quickly busied herself.

The field was multipurpose. Behind the batter's cage, two steel frames for soccer goals were stowed. Permanent football goalposts stood on either end of the field. The whole field was surrounded by a running track. Adam thought it would be a good place to work out.

As he walked toward the field, Adam watched Baxter push a chalk line marker to home plate. A selection of bats was leaning against the cage, and a milk crate with balls was stationed inside the cage behind home plate. They shook hands.

"I'm replacing Henry."

"What?" He seemed disconcerted by the statement.

"Rosie told me Henry usually helps you set up."

"Not me. I'm just doing this because the school custodian is away. I still have a key to the school building. I used to be a teacher."

"And a coach, right? Judo."

"Junior told you."

"He wants to go by Tom now."

"I know. I just haven't gotten used to it. Come inside with me while I put this away."

The sports equipment cage was floor-to-ceiling chain-link and filled with racks of basketballs, soccer balls, and footballs. There were shelves of supplies, folded nets, sacks of rosin, and a rack of nylon over vests for identifying teams in a P.E. class. It was flanked by restrooms on one side and a door marked Tornado Shelter on the other.

They talked. Adam told Baxter about his discussion with Elf.

"You mean that scrawny guy who is Grace's boyfriend?"

Adam nodded. "He told me his story. He's been through a lot."

"Did he try to convert you?"

"What? No. But he told me about his heroin addiction and what he did to bankroll his use. He did time and came out clean."

Baxter's face took on a focused expression as if he were checking off boxes or adding up sums. Adam recognized the look as the way he felt when he was finishing a puzzle and decided to tape up the back to see how he had done.

After a moment of silence that Adam couldn't exactly interpret, Baxter asked, "And he wouldn't tell you who they were?"

"No. He said he could be wrong. It's been a long time, and he was on smack back then."

Baxter nodded thoughtfully.

Then Adam added, "And he said that if he were right, he didn't want them as enemies."

"Did he say if they recognized him?"

"He said he wasn't sure."

The expression on Baxter's face changed again. He became deadpan. "It would be very helpful to know who they were and how they were involved with his old life. I need to talk with him."

"I don't think he'll talk to you, and if you talk to him, he won't trust me anymore. Let me try."

"That's not your job and—"

Adam interrupted him. "Do you want the information or not?"

"I really don't want you to take any chances. Remember, I know what you did in New Orleans. DuPuis told me the whole story."

Adam thought, *DuPuis doesn't know the whole story.* He said, "The situation is different. I think if I tell him I need his help because of the package in my bag—"

"That's not public knowledge."

"I understand that, but the people who put it there know, and as far as my safety goes, they're the ones I need to worry about. I'm telling you we connected. I've already kind of betrayed his trust. Let me take a shot at this."

"You both could be in danger."

"If that's true, we both are *already* in danger."

Baxter looked at his watch. They had been talking for almost half an hour. "People are starting to arrive. You go out first and hang around the concession stand. Help Rosie. She'll shoo you out fast enough. If anybody asks what you were doing, tell them you were using the restroom." He pointed at the doors on the opposite side of the cage.

Adam did as he was told, and within thirty seconds, he was in the way. Claudia Delgado helped her, and there wasn't much more room in the stand. Adam found a place on the bleachers where he could watch the game and as much of a view of the other spectators as he could. He wasn't going to make the same mistake as he had at the memorial social event. If Elf showed up, he'd watch his interactions carefully.

Adam also noticed Baxter watching both the crowd and the game. Every now and then someone would talk to him. The guy was amazing. He didn't miss a beat. He'd be talking to someone, and he'd casually move his head to take in the crowd. He must have also kept one eye on the game because when a little girl hit a double, he cheered her on even though she was playing for the Pirates.

Adam saw Junior, Grace, and Matthew, but Elf was not there. That was probably a wise choice. He wouldn't want to run into those familiar faces again. He considered going back to the hotel on the off chance he found Elf there, but he thought Rosie might need him to carry the roaster back to the Rest. He tried to watch the game and watch the crowd at the same time but lacked the skill he observed in Baxter.

The line at the concession stand had dwindled down to almost nothing. Just chips and soft drinks remained. He emptied the water out of the roaster and carried it back to the Rest. He hoped to see Elf's Honda parked outside. There were cars parked around the park, probably families at the Little League game, but Elf's Civic was nowhere to be seen.

The patron entrance to the restaurant was locked, but anyone who knew about the back stairwell in the hotel knew that it gave easy access to the kitchen and, therefore, the restaurant as well. The security was ridiculous. Access to the alley behind the restaurant was only through the kitchen. A portion of the hallway had been partitioned off and housed a washer and dryer.

The door between the laundry room and the kitchen was propped open. *If Rosie was in the kitchen, it would have been impossible to enter or leave the building through that door without Henry noticing.*

Whoever fired the gun from the second-floor window had to have gone through the kitchen, or they would have been noticed by either Rosie or him. If the shooter went through the kitchen, it had to be someone Henry knew and expected. That meant either Rosie or Manda, the woman who cleaned the rooms. If it was someone other than Rosie or Manda, they would have had to wait or hide somewhere until Henry had left the kitchen.

Adam thought of the hidden master key. He remembered Rosie saying that she would challenge anyone to find it.

"Challenge accepted," he said out loud, though there was no one to hear him. His voice echoed in the tiny laundry room. He first looked up at the ceiling and the corners. No cameras. He looked around the room and asked himself, "If I were a key, where would I hide?"

It had to be in a place that was easy to get to. He opened the door to the dryer and felt around the drum. Nothing. He did the same with the washer. Again, nothing. He ran his hands down the sides of the washer and felt along the back as well. Not there. He did the same with the dryer. Nothing.

The room had no air vents, no windows, nothing but a door to the kitchen. He felt along the top molding of the door. All he got was dirty fingers. He tried the shelf above the washer and dryer. He looked behind the bottles of detergent and bleach. He even looked inside the cap of the laundry detergent. He was enjoying this.

He leaned back against the wall and sank down until he was sitting on the floor. It was then that he realized that the floor wasn't exactly level. The leg on the left side of the washer was taller than the one on the right. He ran his fingers in the gap. There was a small magnetic box under the washer.

He pulled it out. It had a key inside that looked just like his own room key. Bingo.

He put the key back. Now that he knew where it was, he couldn't think of a need for it. As he climbed the back steps, he thought of one. Chucho's room. He retraced his steps, took out the key once again, climbed the stairs to the second floor, and walked down the short dark hallway to the door to the common area.

A dim light shone through a small hole in the door about the height of a peephole. He looked through it. He could see the entire common area. A hint of the shadow feeling flashed over him. He'd never look at that door from the other side again without wondering if someone was watching him through the hole. He opened the door, went to Chucho's room, and turned the knob. It opened. He didn't even need the master key.

If someone had to hide and this door was unlocked, they could have easily hidden in here for a long time without being noticed, especially if they knew Chucho was the guest and Chucho was not coming back. Heck, while he thought about it, they could have hidden themselves in that narrow hallway to the second-floor lobby.

The room was a mirror of his own. The only difference was that the window, which looked out over the back alley, had a small air-conditioning unit. He looked out the window. The alley was empty. The side and back of a Victorian house covered in gingerbread molding seemed dark and abandoned. The paint was peeling, and some of the gingerbread had fallen off the trim. The land around it was mostly dry grass. The lot took up the length of the block. The house faced a side street to the west. He'd been in that alley several times but never paid attention to that house. He'd ask Rosie about it sometime.

Inside the room, there was nothing much to indicate anyone was staying in that room. The bed was made, and the towels on the rack were clean and folded. Of course, Manda had cleaned the room on Monday, and no one had seen Chucho since the Friday before. There were normal toiletries on the small table next to the sink. A tube of toothpaste and a toothbrush were standing upright in a glass. There was an open package of disposable razors, a can of cheap shaving cream, and a stick of deodorant.

Everything looked new. Of course, if Chucho were a homeless drifter, it was likely that the church had supplied these things. The toothbrush looked like it had never been used. He picked up the deodorant. It was a brand he had never seen. He sniffed it. It smelled like soap.

In the drawers, there were a few items of clothing. There were two folded pairs of pants—one still had a thrift shop price tag stapled to the waistband—an open package of tighty-whities, and two long-sleeved shirts. Like the pants, one still had a thrift shop tag stapled to the collar. The musty smell common to secondhand shops was faint but recognizable.

Adam tried to remember the quiet man who sat, arms folded, in the McDonald's. There was nothing more than the sense of coldness and his fascination with his coffee cup. Adam looked under the bed and under the folded clothing. The room was sterile.

For all anyone knew, Chucho was a homeless guy asking for help. But was he? Could he be tied up in some way with the drugs? Was that why he came to town? On the other hand, absconding the way he did, perhaps Luis was right about him possibly being an illegal immigrant. In either case, what did Chucho know?

Adam didn't know what he had expected to find except for some clue to the truth about Chucho. There was nothing at all. If he had ever occupied this room in earnest, he left nothing of himself behind.

Had the police searched this room? Rosie had given them permission to search the whole premises, but since Chucho had rented the room, they needed a search warrant to enter it. If they had searched the room, whether within or outside the law, had they taken anything?

If Chucho fled directly from the church when Tommy fell, he certainly had truly very little to come back here for.

Leaving the room, he locked the door behind him. He didn't know how much time he had before Rosie returned, and he wanted to have the key back where it belonged before she did. He descended the back stairs. Before he could put the key back, another flash of memory. Rosie said there used to be a tornado shelter under the building—*used to be*.

Adam had never seen a tornado shelter before. When Rosie and Baxter mentioned it, he had imagined it having exterior access under a metal door, like the basements of some older houses in Pittsburgh. If the shelter had interior access, it would be a place for the shooter to hide. If it had both interior and exterior access, it could offer a way of entering or leaving the building without notice.

Adam walked through the narrow space beside the stairs that led to the upper floors and, under them, found another flight descending below the building. The stairway was dark, and he didn't see a switch anywhere. He lit his way with the flashlight on his phone. Rosie had said no one had used it for years. He expected to see dust and cobwebs everywhere.

There was a bit of that, but not as much as Adam expected. The stairs themselves had been swept clean. He descended them slowly. His curiosity consumed him. At the bottom of the stairs, there was a heavy steel door to the left and a set of dusty cement steps to the right.

He tried the door. It opened easily. Inside was pitch-black. It reminded Adam of the time his parents took their family to Alcatraz and the tour guide flicked off the lights in the room. The darkness was absolute. People flicked lighters because they were frightened.

Still using his phone as a flashlight, he looked around the bottom of the stairwell. The dusty steps led to precisely the kind of metal door Adam had imagined. He could see tiny chinks of light through the edges of the metal exterior doors.

He turned around and entered the shelter. There was a cool musty scent. The light from his phone revealed a light switch. He tried it. Old-school fluorescent lights flickered to life and revealed a large room, painted white, now dingy with age. Smudges of fingerprint powder dotted the room. The shelves were bare. An old Formica table and chairs were at the far end. Beside them there was a cot with a thin mattress upholstered in gray and white ticking. In the middle of the ceiling, a metal grate blocked the way into some sort of chimney.

Apart from the fingerprint powder smudges, the room was too clean to have been someone's impromptu hiding place. Someone was keeping it clean.

Nineteen

"Well, I'll be damned." Rosie's voice echoed in the empty tornado shelter. Her hands on her hips, she kept looking around as if there was something more to see. "How did you get in here?"

"It wasn't locked." He didn't lie, but he felt a twinge of guilt for not telling her he had found the master key. He'd tell Baxter—eventually. Part of him wondered if entering Chucho's room could be considered unlawful entry. He did have a key, after all, even if he hadn't needed it. He could probably go in there on Monday when Manda cleaned, and then he'd have a more favorable light in which to present his ideas to Baxter.

"Well, I'll be damned." She said it again as she ran her fingertip across the Formica tabletop and looked at it. "No dust." She did the same with the chairs. "Again, no dust. Somebody's been in here and for more than a quick look." She slowly shook her head. "Obviously the fingerprint people were here."

"Did Baxter say anything to you about it?"

"Not about the shelter. He said nothing about the shelter. The only thing he asked me about was a rifle. He asked me if it was mine or Henry's. I don't know where he found it. I asked him, but he didn't answer." She walked over to the cot. "I don't remember this at all."

"Whose gun was it?"

She shrugged her shoulders. "The assassin's, I imagine. It's not mine, and Henry doesn't like guns, never has. I think that's why they made him a cook in the army. Anyway, he's not allowed to own a gun."

Adam waited.

"Even when he was a kid, that Billy Baxter played his cards close to his chest. Don't expect to get a lot out of him. He was always a quiet, respectful boy." She slapped the mattress with the flat of her hand. "It's not very dusty. Why did you come down here?" She seemed to think the idea of doing so was extraordinary.

"I never saw a tornado shelter before. I was curious. I remember Baxter asking about it. It just got me thinking." Again, it wasn't exactly a lie. He couldn't tell if she accepted his explanation or not.

"There used to be provisions and supplies on these shelves. Henry and I threw all that stuff away years ago." She paced aimlessly around the room; the sound of her heels on the cement floor ricocheted around the almost empty room. Her eyes darted in one direction and then another, but there wasn't much to see. She seemed to be in a world of memories.

"We were talking about opening the restaurant for dinner and expanding the dining room. They had just built the casino at the time. We were going to use this room for storage." She paused. "That had to be five or six years ago now." She walked over to the door and indicated access to the alley. "Deliveries would be easy."

"Why didn't you do it?"

She shrugged. "It would have been a hell of an investment. Even back then, there wasn't enough business to hire anyone, not until we knew it would work. Neither one of us wanted to work twelve-hour days." She paused. "Then COVID happened."

"It might be worth thinking about again, if only on the weekends."

She shrugged her shoulders. "I suppose so. But Henry and I aren't getting any younger." Her throat tightened over her last few words.

As they left the shelter, she locked the door behind them. "I wonder if Henry has been keeping the place clean. I can't imagine why he would, though."

"Maybe he's hoping to revisit the idea with you."

She was thoughtful. "Maybe. It still feels a little creepy."

"At least we know it's not a stranger."

Rosie stopped and looked at him. "And how do we know that?"

"Rosie, you said Henry would freak out if he saw a stranger in his kitchen. It's the only way in."

She thought for a moment. "No, there's the alley door."

"Did you see all the dirt on those steps? They haven't been used in a very long time."

"Come with me. Let's check."

They climbed the steps to the first floor and exited through the kitchen door. Rosie walked down to a set of metal doors that leaned against the building. "Look here, the lock is gone. There used to be a padlock there."

Adam reached down and grasped at the handle of the overlapping door and pulled. The hinges resisted and screamed as he pulled. "You'd hear that if you were in your apartment." He pointed up at the windows on the third floor.

"Maybe not if I was using the air-conditioning. Open the other door."

He did. The hinges had been oiled. Light flooded the cement steps. He realized that an intruder only needed to open the overlapping door by a few inches to be able to open the other. A very faint set of footprints hugged the stairwell wall. "Holy shit. Do you see those?"

"Someone has been here. I'll be right back." Rosie bustled into the kitchen. She returned a few minutes later with a round padlock and a bicycle chain. "These are harder to break into than regular locks. I've had it for years. It was Henry's when he had a bike—until he left it in the road and someone ran over it."

The chain wasn't needed. The padlock fitted nicely into the hasp.

"I think you should talk to Baxter or Deputy Isi about this."

"You just try and stop me. I'll see Aya tomorrow."

They went back inside and climbed the stairs. She left him at the second floor and climbed up to her apartment. Until she went to bed, she kept looking out the back windows just to check that there wasn't some weirdo lurking in the alley.

Coming up the back stairs, he was unnerved by the light coming through the hole in the back stairwell door. He grabbed the roll of masking tape from his room, peeled off the cellophane wrapper, and covered the hole with several layers of tape on both sides of the door. It wasn't perfect, but better. He found the sign that had fallen with the bolt. It was behind a narrow table along the wall. The nut was missing. Perhaps after they finished the service tomorrow, he'd walk to Walmart and get a new nut and bolt and reaffix the sign for Rosie.

Adam spent the evening alone with his puzzle. From time to time, he stood up, stretched, and looked out the window, hoping to see Elf's Civic pulling into a parking space. The street and the park were deserted.

He left the door to his room wide open because he wanted to catch Elf when he came back to his room. His goal was to get some idea of who Elf had recognized. He tried to think of different ways he might extract the information that Elf had clearly said he wouldn't disclose.

A text alert from a number in Pennsylvania broke his concentration. It came from an unknown number but had a familiar area code. It was from his nephew.

After decoding a few emojis, it read, "Hey, Uncle Adam, it's Jake. Thanks for the grad gift. I used it to buy this prepaid phone. My mom keeps tabs on the old one 'cause it's on her plan, whatever. She reads everything. If there's anything you wanna tell me that you don't want her to see, hit me up on this number. I'm cool with her knowing most stuff, but just not all of it, ya know?"

Adam replied, "Jake, she only does it because she loves you and is going to worry about you on your adventure. Keep her well-informed about where you are and what you are doing."

He replied almost immediately. "Got it. I promz."

Adam felt a pang of guilt. It had been nearly a week since he sent the selfie in front of the post office to his sister. He texted. "Still in Ur. It's a nice place with a lot of nice people. I'll tell you all about it when I get to Flagstaff. I should be here another week or so."

Adam heard a car door slam out on the street. He looked out the window and saw Elf's Civic parked in front of the hotel. Adam waited for Elf to come up the stairs. It took longer than he expected. He went over to his window and saw Elf pacing the sidewalk talking on his phone. He went out to the common area, sat on the Victorian sofa, and waited.

Elf crested the stairs and was startled to see Adam sitting on the sofa. "Hey there," he said. "You remind me of my mother sitting up waiting for me to come home when I was in high school. The later I stayed out, the more worried and ticked off she'd get."

"My sister does the same thing to my nephew. He just graduated. To be honest, I was waiting for you."

"For me? Why? What's up?"

"I saw Tom, Grace, and Matt at the Little League game. How could you miss that?" There was a hint of sarcasm in his voice.

Elf smiled. "I think you know why I wasn't there. I would have gone, but I didn't know who else would be going. I stayed at Tom's house playing video games with Ben. That's his younger brother. He's having a hard time."

"That was nice of you."

"He's a great kid, and I like video games." He slipped his room key into the lock. "You have any more of that water? I meant to pick some up, but my mind was somewhere else. I just forgot."

"Sure." Adam sprang up and got a bottle from the fridge. Handing him the bottle of water and opening one for himself, "Elf, I hope you can help me with some advice."

"Okay, sure."

Adam continued. "I know you don't like talking about your past, but I'm in an odd situation, and I don't know how to navigate it. Maybe you might have some insights for me." Adam believed this tack to be the best one. He needed to be able to identify the people that Elf was afraid of.

"No problem." Elf said, "Let's talk in my room. I'm tired, and that sofa isn't very comfortable. If I can help, I will."

Adam took it slowly. He outlined the events that led up to his taking his duffel bag to the sheriff's office.

"That's crazy. What was in it, do you know?"

"Fentanyl… fake pills."

He scrunched his face. "Fake fentanyl? You mean they were really fentanyl but were pretending to be something else?"

"Yeah, I think so."

"Wow. They told you that?"

Adam realized that he knew that fact only because Baxter had confided in him. "Not exactly. I think it was a slip."

Warily, Elf said, "A slip… or a trap?"

Adam tensed. "What do you mean by that?"

"Sometimes cops say things to gauge your reaction. They're allowed to lie, you know."

Adam felt destabilized. He hadn't expected that kind of advice. He wondered what Baxter was doing. Had he been trying to gauge Adam's reaction, or was he providing information in confidence? "Yeah, I think I knew that they could lie. And I think I passed the test. Listen, the whole thing doesn't make sense to me. I mean, who did it? Why me? And for the life of me, I can't figure out how they would get it back from me."

"I can't really answer any of those questions. Except they sometimes use blind mules. That's a person who doesn't know what they are carrying or… doesn't even know they are carrying anything." Elf fidgeted. It was clear Elf didn't like talking about the subject.

"I don't even know how to think about those questions. I don't expect you to know what they were thinking or anything, but you know more about that world than I do. I'm in a bizarre situation, and I don't know how to navigate it. After what you said about the people at the service, I just want to know what I should look for. I don't know who to trust. Whatever you can tell me so that I don't get mixed up with them. The police told me they might even try to get the drugs back."

Elf puckered his lips, moving them from side to side, thinking, *I think someone would have tried that by now.*

Adam thought about the bottom drawer of his dresser. "Someone may have searched my room," he said. "A drawer was left partially open."

"If that was the case, be glad they know you no longer have the package."

Adam nodded. "Can you give me a hint about the people you recognized, just so I can be a bit more careful around them?"

"I wish I could tell you more, but even if I was sure of who I saw, that wouldn't help you. In fact, it could only hurt you. If you start acting weird around people, they might get worried or suspicious."

Adam breathed deeply. "Elf, I don't know anyone here. I wish I knew who I could trust and who I should be skeptical of."

Elf's brows lifted with a roll of his eyes. "Who can you trust? That's easy—no one. And I mean *no one*. The only person I trust around here is Tom. I'm seeing Grace, but like I said, she talks too much. I have to watch everything I say around her. Just the other day, I had to shake hands with someone I seriously want nothing to do with."

So, she had introduced him to someone from his past. *At least one of them.*

"Which one was it? Can you describe him? I'd like to know who to steer clear of."

"Don't ask me that again," Elf said sharply. "I'm not telling you, if you start acting strange around them, avoiding them, it'll raise red flags. When you handed that bag over to the cops, you cost them a ton of money—unless, of course, some crooked cop manages to get those pills out of lockup. If they think you've figured out who they are, you're a dead man."

Adam felt the blood drain from his face. "A crooked cop?"

"Don't tell me that surprises you!"

Adam's face fell. "No. It doesn't surprise me. I just hadn't considered it."

The conversation was already surprisingly enlightening, but not in the way Adam had hoped or expected. Adam would have to consider this line of thinking at the table, working his puzzle. He was now genuinely looking for wisdom or understanding from Elf. "Wow, help me out here. Why me? What did I do to make myself vulnerable?"

"That I can answer. You didn't do anything. Understand we're talking a little higher level of the game than I ever played myself. Something must have gone wrong with a regular delivery. The way it happened to you isn't normal. The transport of drugs is usually well-planned. Things go wrong all the time. When you got off the bus and intended to continue the same journey the next day, you probably solved a problem for them. Did you tell people your plans? Like where you were going and what time you were leaving?"

Adam had flippantly delivered that information to everyone. He remembered telling Manda his destination was Flagstaff. The bus driver knew that he was at least going to Oklahoma City, where he had to change buses. And that friendly conversation with that mean woman behind the desk at the motel. Adam gave him the story of his first twenty-four hours in Ur. He added, "If I'm honest, I never stopped talking about it. It was just small talk with strangers."

Elf made a gesture that said, "There you have it," and then said, "It could have happened at the motel or the bus station. Someone moved your bag at the motel, and the bus station had access to your bag for several hours."

"But the lady at the motel didn't seem interested at all."

"Means nothing."

"And the lady at the bus station is really sweet."

"Means even less."

Elf folded his arms over his chest.

Adam rubbed his chin between his forefinger and thumb. "How did they expect to get their stuff back?"

Elf thought for a few moments. "Two messy methods, one perfectly clean."

Adam waited.

"They could mug you, like in the bathroom at a bus station along the way, but that would attract attention. Or they could kill you, again, potentially drawing attention."

"And what's the clean way?"

"They could arrest you."

"Arrest me?" Adam was shocked. "You mean like fake cops?"

"No, not fake cops. Real cops on the take. They'd arrest you and confiscate the evidence."

Adam was stunned.

"Your DNA is all over that package because it was in your bag. If that package had your fingerprints on it, you would be in Oklahoma a lot longer than you planned. They'd get their drugs back and a collar, too. That little demonstration you had to make may well have secured your innocence. Who did you say was there?"

He named them watching Elf for an involuntary response.

"It only takes one corrupt cop. In that room, it could have been any one of them, but definitely not all of them."

"What do you mean?"

"You're not in jail. If the whole department were dirty, you'd be in jail."

"But I turned it in."

"Come on, Adam. Any decent prosecutor could come up with a reason for you to do that. Even if a jury found you not guilty, you'd have been tied up for months. There was at least one ally in that room. Everyone there knew they could all be subpoenaed and could testify to what they saw. It doesn't exactly exonerate you or prove anything, but it weakens the case against you because their testimony is all admissible evidence. My friend, the Lord has blessed you. In my former life, I would have said you were frigging lucky, but I know better now. God has blessed you."

TWENTY

Adam hadn't slept more than brief tumbles into odd dreams. When he looked at his phone, and it said it was ten to five in the morning, he gave up trying to sleep. He put on shorts and a T-shirt and headed over to the sports field behind the school.

It was still dark, so he used the flashlight on his phone to walk the field to make sure some kid hadn't left a bike or other hazardous obstacle. Assured of his safety, he began his wrestling drills, incorporating a long series of tumbles, something the park didn't have enough space open for.

He pushed himself hard. Working in the kitchen was mostly standing, and nothing in the kitchen weighed enough to challenge him. Even at the busiest times, nothing moved fast enough to tire him. He had to push his body to the limit to reach what he called the breakthrough. He once described that breakthrough to DuPuis back in New Orleans as falling through ice into a warm bath. DuPuis, who had never walked on ice in his life, just shook his head.

He went through three sets of drills but still wasn't there. He used the bleachers to do pushups with his feet elevated on the risers. Closer. As light increased, he used the running track at a full sprint. He broke through on his second lap. The tightness and tension were gone. The shadow feeling was almost undetectable. His clothes soaked with sweat and coated in dust and grass from the field, he headed back to shower and get the kitchen ready for the five-hour shift.

Sunday at the Rest was busy but easy, as there was no cooking to order. Patrons chose from three set menu items. Most of it was Friday prep work. Occasionally, someone traded fry bread for toast, but that was nothing. Rosie was busy enough that, apart from placing orders, they said very little to one another.

The only real interruption in the rhythm was a short visit from Elf and Junior, who walked into the kitchen. Adam was startled by the unexpected presence of people in his kitchen and quickly remembered how Rosie had said Henry would react to a stranger in his kitchen. He felt remarkably close to Henry at that moment.

"Hope we're not interrupting too much," Tom said. "I just wanted to thank you again before we head back to Broken Arrow." He extended his hand.

Adam quickly wiped his hands on the towel hanging from his apron. "Back to school, I see. Did Grace talk you into it?"

"She and my mom ganged up on me," Tom admitted.

Elf spoke up. "Good breakfast, and you're all by yourself." He smiled. "If you ever need a job, stop by the Moonstone Grill in Broken Arrow. Tell Frank I sent you. He's always looking for good help."

"Maybe someday." Adam returned his sincere smile.

"We're leaving now. I hope it all works out for you. I'll be praying for you, bro," Elf said.

They bumped fists. "Have a safe drive, and thanks for… everything."

"Stay safe yourself," Elf added as they walked through the swinging door.

Adam enjoyed the feeling that the visit left him. He doubted that he would have noticed if they had gone without saying goodbye, but the fact that they made an effort to do so made him feel warm inside. Tom was a good kid, and Adam felt gratitude toward Elf for all the practical advice he had given him. His frank honesty and his cynicism about the drug world had proved invaluable or would do so when he had time to think it all through—even if he hadn't learned what he had hoped to find out.

Adam's work at the Rest was already routine. He liked the work. It gave him something to do. It added a bit of normalcy to a very abnormal time. It wasn't his town nor his people, but already, his predicament.

Ur was just a stopover, a brief sojourn, but like a fly caught in a spider's web, there was no leaving this place without some kind of resolution. There had to be something he could do to speed up the resolution, but he knew better than to struggle. Struggling is what would get the spider's attention.

If they had enough to arrest him, he'd be in prison. If they let him leave, they could always come and get him if they wanted to. Destroying the web was the only way out, and someone or something bigger than him would need to be involved.

After his shift, he showered again. His pile of dirty clothes was getting bigger. He'd be doing laundry again in a day or two. Now that he was working in Rosie's kitchen, he was going quickly through his meagre wardrobe. Perhaps he would ask Manda to have a look in the thrift store. She had offered to let him take what he could use. Had he felt any permanence in Ur, he would have just bought what he wanted. Instead, he wouldn't mind having a couple of extra pants and shirts he could just toss when he left town.

After their talk the previous evening, he was no closer to knowing who Elf had recognized from his past. Instead, Elf had given Adam a lot to think about. As he sat down to his puzzle, he pondered which of the three people who witnessed his packing was his ally. Deputy Isi had suspected that the package in his bag had been a bomb or something dangerous. She evacuated the building and had a special unit take it away. If that was all an act, she deserved an Oscar.

Adam found three pieces of the puzzle that fit together. Sometimes his perception felt like magic. He saw the three pieces and knew they'd fit. Turning them over to make sure would be cheating, like looking up the answers in an answer key.

What bothered him most at this point in his Ur experience was that Adam didn't know who he could completely trust after talking to Elf and what Rosie had said about Baxter. Rosie said Baxter played his cards close to his chest. It was hard to tell what he was thinking. All he said the day of the packing demonstration was that it all fit. At the time, Adam had thought he was referring to all the stuff fitting in the bag, but in hindsight, he probably meant that Adam's story fit together.

Sheriff Stacks prompted him to do the demonstration, but that didn't mean that he had ordered it. Was it Baxter or Rosie that had said Stacks was more of a politician than he was an active cop?

Who among these was his ally, and who among them might be corrupt?

Another three jigsaw pieces seemed to fit together, but this time it was in a line. It was a combination that couldn't be trusted, at least not until it fit into the main puzzle.

His mind jumped back to the motel. Had he really told the woman who checked him about moving on the next day? What had he said exactly? Had he told her anything useful about his trip, his destination, or when he planned to leave? He couldn't remember.

He remembered thinking that the maid didn't speak English well, but she had said nothing at all. Maybe she spoke great English and understood him perfectly. He remembered telling her how long he would be gone and that she could clean the room if she wanted.

He stood up, stretched his back, and torqued his body to stretch his obliques. He wasn't used to sitting for so long. Even as he stood, he could feel the hardness of the chair on his backside. He dropped to the floor and did push-ups to get his blood flowing again. It was after four in the afternoon. The sun's rays through the window had shifted.

He walked out to the mini kitchen to grab a bottle of water. He realized he had nothing more in the fridge to eat. He didn't feel hungry now, but if he were going to eat at all, he'd have to go to either the Walmart or the casino. He wouldn't feel right feeding himself from the Rest's kitchen unless he was working.

He twisted the cap off a bottle of water and chugged half of it. *I'll give it another hour or so, and if I'm hungry, I'll head out.*

Back in his room, he stretched out on the bed, thinking he'd get a short nap before thinking about food. Within minutes of lying down on the bed just to take a nap, he fell into a deep sleep that lasted until the alarm on his cell phone sounded at five the next morning.

He had slept for nearly twelve hours. While the rest had been long overdue, it left him groggy and nursing a slight headache. Still, he launched into his morning workout with enthusiasm, even adding a few awkward pull-ups after shimmying up one of the football

goalposts. Hanging there, he worked his abs before dropping down to the field. By the time he was done, he felt just as energized as he had the day before—and the headache had vanished.

Manda greeted him warmly when she arrived to clean the rooms. He told her about his pile of laundry and asked if he could take her up on her offer to have a look in the old thrift store. "Working in this kitchen, my clothes get dirty fast."

She seemed delighted by that. "Sure," she beamed. "The key is in the station. If I'm not there, Matthew and Kristy both know where it is. I'll let them know you'll be asking for it."

It was Monday, and restaurant patrons were few. The council was in for late breakfast and lunch. Adam noticed the sheriff was missing when he came out of the kitchen to bus a table. Rosie would usually be the one to do that. She often took plates away while people were still seated. He remembered her saying something about the sheriff not normally being around. However, his friend from the bank was there. So were the mayor, the guy from the bar, and Blaine. Blaine acknowledged him with a nod as he carried the dirty dishes back to the kitchen. Adam heard him asking Rosie for hot sauce.

The shift was so slow that Adam had cleaned the entire kitchen and washed every available dirty dish during the shift. All he had to do when Rosie gave him the all-clear was switch off the fryer and clean the grill.

While Adam scrubbed and scraped the grill, the lady who made the fry bread showed up. She was so quiet; she might have simply materialized. She didn't say anything but just stood there waiting for Adam to notice her. Adam half considered trying to greet her with the phrase Rosie had used, but the best he could do was *attack Ohio* and he knew that was wrong. At least that was how he remembered it. Rosie had chuckled at that and taught him an easier word to use.

"Halito." It was a simple enough word, but he wasn't sure he remembered it correctly.

"Halito." She smiled at him.

If there was something to come after that, he didn't know what it was.

"I want to talk to Rosie." Without another word, she walked through the kitchen and went out into the dining room, where Rosie was sweeping the floor. He thought her a bit odd; she was more reticent than Baxter. There was no need for small talk with her. Adam didn't know whether she acted that way because he was a stranger or if she was like that all the time.

After he finished with the grill, he peered out the service window. He saw the two women sitting at a table with coffee and dessert. Rosie made great desserts and displayed them on glass-domed cake stands. Their conversation seemed serious. He could see the old woman better than Rosie. Rosie was dabbing her eyes with a paper napkin. He was finished and wanted to go, but he decided not to interrupt them. He waited just in case Rosie might need him for something.

He leaned against the stainless-steel prep table, arms folded, half looking for something to do. A flash of memory of Rosie locking the door to the tornado shelter as they left. She hadn't seemed surprised that the door was left open, but when she locked it, was she doing so out of habit or to keep someone out of it? Did she just want to prevent whoever had used and cleaned the room from coming back? Or, not knowing that Adam had found the master key, was she letting Adam know the room was off limits?

Adam glanced through the service window again. They were standing up, and the old woman reached out and hugged Rosie. She was head and shoulders shorter than Rosie, and the gesture would have looked comical if he hadn't known their talk had been emotional for Rosie.

He wondered if the old woman had some news about Henry. Had he or his body been found? If they had discovered Henry's body, it would have been Baxter or Deputy Isa informing her. In his estimation, Rosie would have been hysterical. But if the old woman knew of Henry's whereabouts, would she betray that knowledge even to Rosie?

If Henry were hiding out somewhere, he would be as likely hiding from the police as anyone else. If the old woman knew something about Henry, and he was hiding from the police, she might keep his secret, but would she tell Rosie? If she did, what would Rosie do?

He recalled how Rosie had warned Henry that the three of them were climbing the front stairs. She had shouted, "Don't shoot Henry!" At the time, Adam thought of it as her nervousness, but it could have been a real and intentional warning for Henry.

The two women walked through the swinging door to the kitchen. Rosie had dried her eyes and had composed herself, but it still looked like she had been crying. She didn't look directly at Adam. The old woman didn't even glance at him. The old woman left with a nod and muttered. "I'll bring more bread Wednesday or Thursday."

Rosie looked at Adam, hoping that he would understand. "No news is good news?"

It was a question.

Adam pulled open the door to the bus station. Manda was behind the counter. She smiled seeing him. "You do get around," he said. There was a dim sound of a television in the back.

"I keep busy. Always have." She eyed the laundry bag in his hand. "Back to do laundry again? You know Rosie would let you use the washer and dryer at the Rest. I'm sure she just hasn't thought about telling you that. Ask her." She leaned toward him in mock intimacy and whispered. "You'll save a few bucks.'

"I thought I'd take you up on your offer of the thrift store. I figured if I found something in the store, I'd want to wash it anyway. Two birds with one stone."

"Blaine," she raised her voice toward the door in the back. "I'm going to let this fella into the thrift store. Mind the desk, and I'll be back in a few minutes."

"I'm watching something here."

"Okay." She rolled her eyes theatrically for Adam's benefit. "In the unlikely event that someone walks through the front door, get up off your ass and tell them I'll be back in a few minutes."

There was no response. She reached under the desk and pulled out a lanyard with two keys attached. "Let's go. I'd just give you the key, but the lock is funny sometimes."

She had to jiggle and pull at the door for the deadbolt to slip back. "Let me get the lights. You can take anything you want."

It looked and smelled just like any other thrift store. The shelves and racks were still in place, and that unique scent of a thrift store was stronger than it might have been. Probably a combination of heat and lack of activity. "Why did they go out of business?"

"They didn't, actually. It was run by the Baptist church. They couldn't keep up the rent. Until someone is interested in this space, I just keep it going. You'd be surprised how many people ask to take a look. People still bring donations, but I don't have time to look at the stuff. Every so often, I'll call the church and ask them to send a volunteer or two." She shrugged. "They hang up stuff and throw away the stuff that shouldn't be donated, like broken things or underwear and socks. You're lucky; they came the other day and put it all out."

"Who do I pay if I want something?"

"No, no. It's all free until someone wants to rent this space. They stopped putting tags on things when they stopped paying their rent. I just offered to open the store for people who want to browse or donate. When you're done, just turn out the lights, lock up, and bring me the key."

Adam found several pairs of work pants. They weren't in the best of condition, but they would be fine for the kitchen at the Rest even if they were a little too short. He picked up a paint-splattered pair of work boots in his size and grabbed seven neon yellow t-shirts that looked new. They were branded for a construction company in Oklahoma City.

He eyed the rack of jeans. The Walmart replacement for his missing jeans was a cheap off-brand. He wondered if he might find something of a bit better quality. He could relegate the Walmart brand jeans to work if he could replace the jeans he lost.

As he thumbed through the rack, he came to an abrupt stop. A chill ran down his spine as the pair of jeans looked eerily like the pair he had lost. The wear pattern looked similar. There was the same fading and the same fraying along the right-hand pocket seam. He pulled them off the rack and held them to his waist. They looked like they would fit.

He read the size on the inside of the waistband. They were his size. He sniffed them. They smelled freshly laundered and like the laundry soap he had bought from the vending machine in the laundromat. He stared at them. *These are my jeans,* he thought.

He brought the key back to Manda, holding up his finds. "Wow, that's a good haul." She beamed at him.

"I'll just go down and wash them in the laundromat," Adam said.

"I'm brewing a pot of coffee for Blaine. If you'd like, I'll bring a cup down to you."

"Best coffee in Ur. Don't tell Rosie I said that." He winked, and she winked back.

He emptied his laundry bag into the big washer and added the thrift store clothes except for the jeans. He was so focused on trying on the jeans that he was barely cognizant of the camera. He tried to angle himself so that his lower half would be obscured, dropped his pants, and slipped on the jeans. He was convinced they were the jeans taken from his bag.

He still couldn't wear them without washing. For a moment he wondered if they had some forensic evidential value but decided against it. Off they came and into the washer. He then slipped back into the jeans he had been wearing. Tossed the laundry bag into the washer and filled the slots with quarters.

It wasn't long before he wasn't alone in the laundromat. Manda brought him a cup of coffee, and shortly after that, a woman arrived in a pickup truck. She had six hampers of laundry and three kids who treated the laundromat as a jungle gym. They climbed on the machines, pinched each other, cried, and chased one another in circles around the machines. The woman never said a word. Just dropped soap and coins into eight machines and escaped into the cyber world on her cell phone.

He escaped to the parking lot and waited for his cycles to finish outside. He was on his way back to the hotel when, coming in the opposite direction, Baxter stopped and called to him.

"Get in, Adam." He leaned his head out of the driver's side window.

"I'm okay, I don't need a ride. It's not far."

Baxter revealed a sly grin. "I wasn't offering you a ride back to the hotel. I'm going to meet a friend for real pizza. You'll like him. Get in."

"I'm Italian. I'd be careful with that phrase, 'real pizza,'" he said, walking up to the car.

"Yeah, yeah," Baxter said. "How about not Walmart ready-made pizza?"

"I'm not really hungry."

"It's over an hour's drive. You'll be hungrier when we get there."

Adam studied Baxter's face. He seemed genuine, and something about him inspired trust. He really liked Baxter. He wanted to trust him completely, but victims trust psychopaths. The seeds of suspicion planted by Elf made him want to take it slow and stay alert. If Baxter were on the take or part of the corruption, anything could happen after he got in that car. He could feel his heart speed up and pound in his chest.

He thought of DuPuis. He hadn't liked DuPuis at first. In fact, he didn't trust DuPuis until almost at the end. He hadn't suspected DuPuis of anything more than disinterest, but that had been enough. He eliminated only one cop in Ur from corruption. Deputy Isi's reaction to his claim that something was in his bag was too genuine. If she had been a corrupt cop and in on the deal, she'd have just taken the bag. Calling in the bomb squad made that scenario impossible.

Baxter seemed genuine, but would he really trust Adam based on a conversation with DuPuis? But he liked Baxter, really liked him. The way he liked Elf. He wanted to trust Baxter completely but wouldn't until he was sure. It was a risk, but he thought it was one worth taking. If something bad happened, at least he'd know.

He walked around to the passenger side. He heard the unlock function click on the door. He slipped in. They traveled to the highway exchange and headed north. Adam told Baxter about finding his jeans in the thrift store.

"Are you sure?"

"I'm convinced."

"That's weird. So, whoever planted the drugs in your bag also donated the jeans? Are you suggesting we have an ethical, community-minded drug trafficker? Baxter said with exaggerated sarcasm.

"They can't be all bad." He was trying to make a joke, but it fell flat. "I don't know how my jeans got there, but apparently people just leave bags of stuff by the door as donations."

Adam told him about finding the shelter and showing it to Rosie. He didn't say anything about having found the master key.

When Adam had finished, Baxter only asked one question. "If you had to rate Rosie's surprise at how clean that room was on a scale of zero to ten, zero being not surprised at all and ten being bowled over, what score would you give it?"

"Seven or eight. I think she was genuinely surprised. She said it was creepy, but she didn't freak out. She seemed more curious than frightened. She was more bothered by discovering that the cellar doors in the alley had been used."

"What are you talking about?"

"The metal doors in the back that lead down to the shelter. Somebody used them. There were footprints in the dust."

Baxter appeared thoughtful. "Huh, we didn't see them. We looked."

"Maybe they were made after your crew left. The padlock was gone."

Baxter sighed. "That's very useful, Adam. Well done. Did Rosie say anything about what we found down there?"

"She didn't say anything about that."

"This is between you and me and no one else. Don't let it slip. We found a recently fired AR-15 with a suppressor in that shelter. We had to make sure it wasn't Miss Rosie's, and that's why she knows about it. We removed it as evidence, and it's with ballistics. The suppressor explains the sound of firecrackers."

"Holy shit."

"I suspect that the person who used that back entrance was simply trying to recover their weapon. Did you and Rosie disturb those footprints?"

"Not at all. I mean, we didn't sweep the steps. We opened the door, and air might have blown things around a little."

Baxter adjusted the frequency on his radio and grabbed the mic. He spoke into it, and Deputy Isi responded. He gave her instructions to gather what might be important evidence. They were to document the footprints, and take shoes from Henry's room."

"Henry?"

"We have to make sure those footprints aren't Henry's."

They were driving through suburban roads now. Baxter put on his turn signal and edged into a left turn lane.

Adam was stunned and disappointed. "Did we seriously drive over an hour to come to Pizza Hut? I just have to go on record. This is not real pizza."

"It is to me." Baxter was suppressing a smile. "Would you have come if I said we were going to Pizza Hut?"

"I doubt it, but making a one-hour drive just for Pizza Hut has me seriously questioning your sanity."

Baxter looked Adam straight in the eyes. "It's not about the pizza. I want you to meet someone. This is a good place because no one ever comes here."

"There's a reason no one comes here, Bax."

Baxter laughed. "Don't kid yourself. They're still in business. It's just mostly takeout now."

Adam hadn't been in Pizza Hut since high school. The décor hadn't changed much, and by the aroma, neither had the pizza. The place was set up differently now. There was a small counter where you could place or pick up your order and a self-serve soda machine. The dining room was completely empty except for one guy sitting at a table in the farthest corner of the dining room.

"That's my friend. Let's order first." Baxter said, ringing the bell on the service desk to call someone from the back.

The clerk, a kid no older than sixteen, wearing a tomato-sauce-stained apron and dusted with flour, handed them paper cups and promised to bring their order to their table. They filled their cups at the self-serve soft drink dispenser and walked into the dining room and up to a table where the man was sitting, sipping his own soft drink. As he came into focus, Adam froze and squinted as if it would make the image of the man clearer. In a hesitant voice he said, "Chucho?"

TWENTY-ONE

I t was the brightness of the halogen light that woke him up. His eyes
snapped open and closed at once. He was back in Iraq. He could hear
the ordnance in the distance. He lay on his back, eyes clamped shut. His
pulse thundering in his ears, and a cold sweat breaking out all over his
body. Someone was close; he could feel it. He thought he could even hear
breathing.

He lay on his back, frozen. The hard cot felt like stone beneath him.
The voice was an eerie falsetto. It sent nightmarish shivers down his spine.

"Henry," the intruder said softly. "I've been worried about you." The
tone was mocking, like a schoolyard taunt. The American accent made his
mind swim. It didn't make sense. Enemies didn't have American accents.
There was something familiar about that voice. His mind tried to swim to
shore. Then he knew. *Shit.*

He was back home, in the shack, and he recognized the voice. He
would have given anything in life for it to be Toby playing a sick joke.
This was sick, but it was no joke.

"Henry," the voice said again. "I've been looking for you. Why are
you hiding? Who are you hiding from?"

"What do you want?" His eyes squeezed shut against the blinding
light. His voice was deep from sleep. He spoke with intention and what

he hoped sounded like confidence. He knew exactly who it was. He almost called him by name but held it back.

"I want to know why you're hiding. I told you. I've been worried about you."

"I ain't hiding." It was, of course, a lie, but worth trying.

"Yes, you are."

"Get that fucking light out of my eyes." Henry used his bravest tone.

"The better to see you, my dear."

The tone of his voice made Henry sick to his stomach. "Listen. I ain't said nothing to nobody."

"And you won't say anything to anyone, right? Do you promise? Cross your heart and hope to die?" He strung out the word die.

"Why do you think I'm here?" Henry said, thinking, *You asshole.* "It's so nobody asks me questions. He tried to fill his voice with calm confidence, but inside he was shivering. He knew the intruder had always been unstable, and there was no telling what this guy would do. "I thought you could figure that out. I never told anyone your other secret."

There was a long pause. The tone of the falsetto became more serious, less taunting but still a falsetto. "Which secret is that, Henry?"

This fucker is more fucked up than I thought. Henry thought and said, "You know which secret I'm talking about."

"You mean *our* secret, Henry?" He stressed the word our. "We were both there."

"It's not my secret. I'm way past shame for anything I did when I was a kid or when I was high."

"Well, perhaps I should kill you now. Never know when you'll let something slip—maybe after a couple of beers. After all, dead men tell no tales."

Henry could tell he was enjoying this. *The sick son of a bitch.* "Oh, you won't kill me now. I haven't suffered enough. Now get that light out of my eyes!"

"When I'm ready, Henry."

Henry couldn't tell if he was standing upright or bending down. The voice was not close in his ear but came from a slight distance. The shack, as small as it was, distorted space. It looked tiny, like a shed from outside but didn't feel small inside, had never felt small. It had always felt safe. That safe feeling now was gone, probably forever. All he could tell was that the came from above him.

He thinks I'm helpless. He thinks I'm trapped and scared. He thinks I'm too old to do anything at all. As much to get the light out of his face as to make this fucker pay–just a little, Henry stilled and steeled himself. He wasn't as strong as he used to be, but over the years he had lost nothing in quick reflexes. Surprise was his best weapon.

His right had never been as powerful as his left. While laying down, he couldn't put his weight behind it. He squirmed a bit, trying to get even a slightly better position.

"What are you doing?"

"The light. I told you…" Without knowing where he was aiming, the punch hit deep into the intruder's flabby belly and in the effort, Henry fell off the cot onto the floor.

The intruder fell back. The punch had taken him by surprise and had knocked the wind out of him. The flashlight swayed, and he heard it fall to the ground. Henry opened his eyes and sprang to his feet. But before he could do anything else, he heard the click of a revolver being cocked. The indirect light now illuminated the inside of the shack. The gun was pointed directly at him. It was an old-school six-shooter.

"Don't try that again," the intruder gasped. "I have no reason to keep you alive." He found the flashlight with his open hand and picked it up.

"I can think of at least one." The flashlight focused again on Henry's face.

"Yes, what?"

Henry smiled insincerely. "Forget I said anything." He tried to mimic the taunting tone of the intruder's voice. Henry felt the balance of power shift slightly but not entirely in his favor. "Go ahead and kill me." The gun was still pointed at him, but he knew the intruder well enough that he would use it only if he felt physically threatened.

"Let's go," the intruder said.

"Where?"

"Somewhere I can keep tabs on you."

Henry tripped on the doorstop, kicking it through the door out onto the ground. It hurt his foot but was worth it. He limped out into the darkness of the prairie, the intruder following him with the flashlight and the gun. He said a silent prayer that Toby would visit the shack sooner than he promised and the doorstop wouldn't be on the cot. Toby would know to look where they hid the stash when they were young.

The intruder stood behind Henry, shining the flashlight on Henry's back. "Put your hands behind your back."

"You're going to cuff me?"

"I could shackle you, if you prefer."

Henry swallowed hard. He knew this bastard was nuts, but being cuffed was worse than he might have guessed. He put his hands behind his back. He wanted to try and reason with him but knew it was useless. His captor was enjoying the power too much. He felt the cuffs tighten. He wasn't taking chances. There was no playing chicken with this guy. Not anymore.

As they walked through the prairie, Henry could almost feel the gun pointed at his back. The light from the flashlight was so powerful, Henry cast a shadow on the grass in front of him. It made it even more difficult for him to see what lay in front of him. He tried to use his legs to cut through the grass—already tall for the season. It cut across his pant legs. They were not walking fast, and he could feel the longer blades of grass wrapping around his ankles like tendrils.

He tried feeling his way along the ground and was sure his captor was merely following the path Henry cut through the grass. The familiar smell of the grass and the feeling of a gentle breeze made him think of taking daytime walks with his cousin Toby when they were kids, watching the wind like waves travel across the top blades of grass.

They were heading west. Toby's house was to the east. Henry had no idea where he was being led. To the west of the shack, there was nothing but prairie, grassland, and long stretches of road, some unmaintained.

He could kill Henry at any time, and in this landscape, his body could easily become bones before anyone found him. In his memory he saw a large hole in the ground. His crew was mobile, keeping up with the movement of troops. They drove around the crater from either a landmine or an IED. Struggling, Henry brought himself back to the present. At least he wouldn't have to dig it himself.

Henry tripped twice and fell both times. Both times, his kidnapper refused to help him get up. "My hands are full, you know." *You're enjoying this, you fucking pervert, you bastard.* It took all his ingenuity and agility to figure out a way of getting back on his feet.

The first time he lost his balance, tall grass had wrapped around his lower leg and took hold. That time, he was able to fall to his side. The grass broke his fall. He was okay. The second time, a prairie dog hole caught him off guard. He felt a strong twinge of pain in his right ankle as it twisted into the hole, and he fell headlong and face down, leaving now a trail of blood from what he imagined was a broken nose. It dripped liberally for what seemed like ages.

He limped now, depending on his left foot, the foot that had tripped over the doorstop. He kept telling himself, *It ain't over till it's over.* He kept thinking about Toby. Unreliable at the best of times, it might be days before Toby went back to the shack. Mentally, he tried to send Toby a message through the air.

Henry realized that putting on the cuffs might have been his last chance. A flashlight, a revolver, and cuffs? It would have been risky, but he could have elbowed his captor in the face. *It might have worked. Or,* he thought, *Toby might have found my body.*

Now he realized *why* he was cuffed. It was dark enough and the grass was tall enough that a well-timed fall could have helped him disappear if he could have stayed low to the ground. Cuffed as he was, he didn't stand a chance. He couldn't move fast enough.

In the distance, he could see a faint blue glow. Henry squinted to improve his sight. There was someone, he couldn't tell who, sitting in a vehicle looking at a cell phone. All he could see was the faint image of an inclined face, white, looking down at a phone. He couldn't even tell if it were a man or a woman, a boy or a girl.

Henry nearly jumped out of his skin when he heard a loud whistle behind him. The phone went dark. *So, there are two of them. Not just one. And one of them doesn't want to be recognized.*

When they got to the road, Henry could see the vehicle was a pickup truck. His captor lowered the tailgate and told Henry to climb in. The accomplice, now wearing some sort of mask, got out of the truck and took the gun from the captor.

"Lay down over here," the captor barked.

Henry scooted over to the side of the bed, hoping he was leaving bloodstains in the back of this truck. A chain was threaded through his flexi cuffs and padlocked to a tiedown loop on the side of the truck bed. The shackles his captor had threatened him with were used to attach one ankle to another tie-down ring. It was his injured ankle, and the shackle felt like a hot knife cutting into his swelling flesh.

They had every reason to kill him and, from what he could see, no reason to keep him alive—but they were, even though he had recognized his intruder and captor's voice and had made it clear. They were taking him somewhere. How was keeping him alive to their advantage?

As they drove down the road, Henry lay on his back, the chain from the cuffs to the tie-down cutting into his back. He could feel the rippled liner of the bed under him and each bump in the road caused a spasm of pain in his ankle. *After you kill me, I'll fucking haunt you for the rest of your life.*

He tried to zone out. A six-pack of beer would be easier, but he knew how to go into a world of his own. They taught him how to do it in a class at the VA. He looked up at the night sky. It was a clear night. The darkness of the prairie made stargazing easy and mesmerizing. Henry let his mind drift to the days of his youth, sitting out on the prairie with Toby and Jaime, getting high or drunk or both and looking at the sky that grew more dramatic as their fire died to embers and their high became more intense.

This would actually be quite pleasant if they weren't going to kill me, he amused to himself.

He became aware that they were in town when he could see buildings in his peripheral vision. He tried to sit up as the truck slowed down, but it was too awkward, and he couldn't see much anyway. Ur had very few lampposts. The upper windows in buildings were dark, though there was a glow from lights attached to the fronts of businesses. He guessed he was close to home. It didn't make any sense. Why would they bring him back here?

The truck drove onto a gravel surface. When they stopped near the back basement door of the school, he was uncuffed and forced to walk at gunpoint into the tornado shelter. The brightness in the shelter caused Henry to close his eyes once again. How or why they had keys to the school was a mystery. Looking on the bright side, the shelter was more comfortable than the shack. There was electricity, plumbing, and even survival food.

When he was sure they were gone, he limped to the door and tried the breaker bar. As he expected, the mechanism had been disengaged. He searched for tools. He needed an Allen wrench to re-engage the mechanism, that is, if it hadn't been disabled completely. It had been worth a try, and it gave him something to do while he waited.

TWENTY-TWO

Adam's eyes darted to Baxter with aggressive suspicion. He didn't know what kind of freaky game this was, but he didn't think he wanted to play. "What do you mean friend?"

Baxter and Chucho both relaxed. It was as if they had expected his reaction and were relieved to see it. Baxter said calmly. "Chucho is a nickname for Jesus. Adam, I'd like to introduce you to Special Agent Jesus Ramirez of the DEA. Sorry to have kept you in the dark about him. We weren't completely sure his cover had been blown."

Chucho was a DEA agent. In Adam's mind those were two circles of a Venn diagram that didn't overlap. It should have made him feel more secure, but the memory of his discussion with Elf kept replaying in the back of his mind. He could still hear Elf say, "Trust no one."

Baxter's strange, deceptive invitation and driving an hour to a Pizza Hut increased his suspicion. Did the corruption go higher, or was this going to prove to be a better reason to trust Baxter? Could he trust either, both, or neither of them?

Adam's mind continued to reel as he hesitantly sat down at the table.

"He's not comfortable," Ramirez said. His smile became more patient than pleasant.

"He'll get there. He's just upset we're at Pizza Hut and not someplace better," Baxter quipped. "Adam, I know it's a shock. Maybe I should have warned you in the car, but that would have opened up a conversation that Ramirez should be in on."

Adam grappled for bearings. "Are there any more big surprises?"

"I don't think so. Not as shocking as this. You might have guessed most of what we want to talk about. Bax says you're pretty quick off the mark," said Ramirez.

Adam looked him in the eye. "DEA?"

Ramirez nodded. "I can show you my ID if you want."

Adam waved the offer away with his hands. "How would I be able to tell if it was fake?"

Chucho's eyebrows rose in response.

"I told you he was a fast thinker." There was a touch of pride in Baxter's voice.

"We are all but certain that my cover was blown," Ramirez said flatly.

"What do you think went wrong?"

Baxter spoke. "We're not sure."

Ramirez added, "That part is circumstantial. The shot would have hit me if Delgado hadn't stood up."

"Hard evidence is pretty thin, but it's clear that the scope of this case is bigger than it looks." Chucho's eyes darted to the service counter. Someone walked into the restaurant and was standing at the counter. Adam turned to look when they rang the bell. "This place is usually empty. I've never seen anyone come in and eat here."

He's just picking up," Chucho said quietly.

What the hell have I gotten myself into? Adam couldn't be sure which side these guys were on. "If your cover was blown, why are you still around? Hell, why *am I* here now?"

"I'll answer the first question; Bax will answer the second." He sat back in his chair. The man at the counter left with a pizza box. "I'm still here because the case got complicated. I assume I was the intended victim up on the roof of the church. My cover was blown too quickly."

Baxter spoke up. "We're still not sure about that."

"Especially after Pastor Lehman was shot," Chucho inserted.

Adam felt himself sliding into the flow. "I thought there was a question about the pastor being the intended victim?" He addressed the question to Baxter.

Chucho started talking about baseball. The kid who took their order placed two large pizzas and some paper plates on the table. "We never considered a church connection. We knew there was someone of influence in Ur involved, but we weren't sure who or how. The church became a new avenue of investigation."

Baxter leaned in and almost whispered. "Gambling is illegal in Oklahoma except under tribal contract. Lehman, Delgado, and a bunch of people with him fought the casino, but they really didn't have a chance. They couldn't do much to stop it because of the tribal agreement."

"So, the casino is Choctaw?"

"No." Baxter shook his head. "The Choctaw reservation is on the east side of Oklahoma. I'll explain how we Choctaw got here on the way back to Ur if you're interested, but this isn't the time. As of now, the casino is beside the point."

"I thought the shot that killed Tommy came from there?" Adam asked.

"That's the most likely place, but we don't think the casino organization is behind it. Getting on the roof wouldn't be difficult, especially if the shooter knew someone who works in the casino. Everybody knows at least one person who works in the casino, not to mention the people who drive into town for work."

Ramirez swallowed a bite of pizza and spoke up. "We first considered the casino because it is an obvious choice. Large sums of money exchanging hands, people coming in and out, and out of town seemed like the ideal setup."

"So, the casino *isn't* involved?"

"We don't know either way. We have an agent working in the casino. Nothing useful yet. Let's just say we're taking a more panoramic view now," Ramirez replied. "If we consider the two killings, we come up with only three alternatives."

Baxter said, "Argument One: Both victims were the intended targets. That begs the question, why? Does it have anything at all to do with drug trafficking, or is there some nutball out there that has it in for Pentecostal clergy?"

Ramirez picked up the narrative. "Argument Two: Neither Delgado nor Lehman were the intended targets. Either the shooter is the unluckiest person in the world or is a piss-poor marksman. In other words, an amateur. Possible but unlikely considering the stakes involved."

Baxter finished it off. "Final argument: One or the other of them was the intended victim: the other a victim of circumstance. In that case, which is which? Since no one else has been shot, we might conclude that Lehman was the intended target all along. If that is the case, did the shooter mistake Delgado for Lehman to begin with, or was Delgado the intended victim and Lehman a shot gone bad? Which would mean… "

"Someone else is going to die." The words flowed out of Adam's mouth like unconscious drool.

"Told you he was fast," Baxter said sounding even more proud.

Adam was now mentally fully participating in this game. "If Lehman was not the intended victim, who is your best guess for the next victim?"

With a gesture of his hand, Ramirez handed the podium over to Baxter.

"There were three drivers in the casino deal. One against, two in favor. It may be just a coincidence, but the same three were in very close proximity when the shots were fired from the Pioneer's Rest. Lehman stood opposed to the casino. The mayor openly endorsed the casino project, saying it would bring jobs to the area and would be of economic benefit."

"Let me guess who the last guy was—Sheriff Stacks."

Baxter nodded. Stacks is not dumb by any stretch of imagination. His reputation for the years he was on the force as a peon like me is pretty good. Stacks didn't open his mouth about the casino, probably because he knew legally it was a done deal.

"What did he get out of it?" Adam asked. "How did he benefit?"

"I don't think he personally benefitted much. He got a raise. But there were big funding increases. We have got several new deputies in the county. There was an upgrade to the 9-1-1 system. We now have a small crime scene tech team who, until recently, had extraordinarily little to do, so Stacks lends them out to surrounding counties when they're not busy."

"And Baxter got promoted." Ramirez raised his brow and nodded his head.

Baxter's face flushed. "I was a part-time deputy. I had to go full-time to be a sergeant," he admitted. "Teachers don't make a lot of money. I got kids."

"Okay, why are you telling me all this?" Adam looked from one to the other.

"We're not giving up completely on the casino. We have someone on the inside, and if there is anything there, we'll get it, but for now it doesn't look all that promising. So far, the casino looks clean… as far as casinos go."

"I see. What do you need from me?"

Ramirez explained. "We don't know as much as we thought we knew, and we, that is Bax, thought… "

"It would be helpful if you found Jesus." Baxter completed the sentence.

Ramirez added, "Or at least if it looked like you were looking for him."

Adam waited.

Baxter made their request clear. "We're not asking you to *investigate*," he said, adding air quotes around the word. "Just attend services, stick around for cookies and punch, and mingle. The more they get used to you, the more likely they are to let something slip."

"Am I looking for anything specific?" Adam asked.

"Not really. You'll know it when you hear it."

"I can't do Sunday morning—I'm cooking for Rosie. But Wednesday night, Friday night, and Sunday evening work," Adam offered.

"That's when it's mostly insiders anyway," Baxter said.

"You'll do it then?" Ramirez was hopeful.

"I'll do it," Adam agreed. He wondered if they were trying to use reverse psychology. They kept telling him *not* to investigate, but they wanted him to gather information. Baxter knew what he had done in New Orleans. Ramirez likely knew it now as well. *Don't investigate, my ass*, Adam thought. What did they really expect him to do?

A deacon and a pastor were dead. What did the church have to do with the drugs? If Delgado and Lehman were the intended targets, how were they involved? Did they know too much or were they more involved than anyone might expect?

He otherwise didn't have much contact with people other than Rosie. He occasionally spoke to Manda, but since he started working in the kitchen at the rest, there was little or no opportunity to meet other people. The old Choctaw woman said next to nothing to him.

Adam had described the encounters that he had with her. It was hard for Baxter not to betray his interest in the second encounter, the private conversation that brought tears to Rosie.

"I know who you're talking about," Baxter had said. "You won't get anything out of her that she doesn't want you to know. You say they talked for half an hour."

"About that," Adam guessed.

Baxter and Chucho glanced at one another but said nothing.

Ramirez had been more interested in Adam's conversation with Elf.

"He wouldn't even describe the people he recognized?"

"Nope. Refused flat out. He just told me to trust no one."

"And here you are talking to us." Ramirez remarked. "And you say it was specifically related to his drug activity?" he pressed.

Adam halted. He took a moment to retrace his conversation with Elf. "Actually, I'm not sure about that. Now that I think about it, it could have been related to his turning tricks for drug money. All Elf said was they were from his past and he didn't want them as enemies. I naturally assumed it was the drugs because we were talking about the drugs being found in my bag."

Adam said nothing about Elf's speculation of corrupt cops. That was a card he might need to play later, and it was better that they not know for sure that he had it in his hand. He would have been curious to see their reaction to that idea, but it was worth keeping to himself for now.

"Sounds like you and I need to take a ride to Broken Arrow," Ramirez said to Baxter.

"He won't talk to you," Adam asserted.

"He'll talk to us." Ramirez' face looked hard. "He's still on parole. I'll bet he didn't tell you that."

Adam fixed his eyes on a discarded pizza crust, not wanting to reveal his reaction. If Elf were still on parole, he could lose everything for the slightest slip. No wonder he didn't mention his parole. Adam felt like he had betrayed Elf's confidence and that Elf would soon learn of his betrayal.

Baxter hadn't lied when he said no one would see him drop Adam off in town. By 9 p.m., the only activity that might be expected in downtown Ur would be around the bar at the end of the main street. He had passed the main highway exit for Ur, drove to the next exit, and backtracked on lonely, unlit roads. He dropped Adam off at the sports field behind the school.

"Don't assume that people don't know you are working out here in the mornings. You might not see anyone, but you never know. I've heard there are some who like to watch you."

"That's a bit weird." Adam could feel the shadow of being watched getting stronger. "Why are you telling me this? I've never seen anyone watching me."

"I don't think it's anything menacing. There is this thing you do that looks kind of odd—you crawl around your own head? I'd love to see that."

Adam sighed. The thought of people watching him didn't bother him as much as not knowing they were watching him. "Yeah, a neck bridge and walk-around would look funny to a lot of people. Having a strong neck is really important. It's a mistake for a wrestler to neglect that." He refused to allow his mind to reflect on an injury he once experienced. "Be spying on me around 5:30 tomorrow morning, and you'll see it."

"Unlikely," Baxter said.

"Who told you about that?"

"It's hearsay. Someone told Stacks, and Stacks made a joke about it. I don't know who told Stacks. Also, make sure you're wearing underwear under those shorts." He couldn't hold back his laugh. "Apparently you're… *special*."

Embarrassed, Adam felt his face turn red and was glad that it was dark in the car. "Ask me, and I'll show you sometime."

"I don't need to know how special you are."

It was Adam's turn to laugh. "I meant the neck bridge and walk around." He shook his head as if to clear it. "Okay, I'm done. I'll see you." As he climbed out of the car, Baxter stopped him.

"If you need me, call or text me on your prepaid phone. I'll do the same. Don't come to the substation unless you must. We don't want people to think we're too friendly."

TWENTY-THREE

Now that he knew that his workout was sometimes observed, Adam was hyperalert to possible watchers while he moved in the playing field. He kept scanning his perimeter, checking for movement behind windows, and even looking for cameras. There was no one and nothing in sight.

During his shift, he took a few minutes to wash his hands and step out into the dining room. The town council was there. The sheriff was back in town, and young Matthew, who had come in alone, had been invited to join them. Both Blaine and Blake Lamano were there. The two women regulars, the one from the post office and the other from the bank, were there as well. It was an easy shift.

Adam showered, shaved, and walked to the First Pentecostal Church to look at the sign out front. He remembered that it listed the services and the time but couldn't remember the exact time they started. He wasn't Pentecostal, but his connection to Tommy Delgado, he thought, might give him an in, or at least an excuse for his interest in the church.

He knew he could have probably asked anyone about the service times, including Rosie, but would that seem like too much investigation? What if they asked why he was interested? He would enjoy the walk anyway, and he could pick up a few snacks in Walmart as well.

Back in his room, he spent two hours working on his puzzle. At half past six, he headed to the church for the Wednesday evening Bible study that was to begin at 7 p.m.

There were more cars in the church parking lot than Adam had expected. When he walked in, he was greeted by a few people who loosely lingered in the church lobby. They welcomed him, and one of them, a forward girl named Laura, introduced herself and invited him to sit with her family. Of course, Adam accepted.

There must have been twenty people already sitting close to the front of the church when a young man began playing soft music on an electric keyboard, a signal that the service was starting.

Eunice, Luis' wife, led the songs that began the service, accompanied by the keyboard player. She had a strong voice, more enthusiastic than melodic. Her singing style was a mixture of singing and shouting. The sound of her tambourine echoed in the gabled ceiling.

Her sister Claudia sat in the first row, but the children were either somewhere else in the building, perhaps in the social hall downstairs, or they had been left at home with a babysitter or Ben supervising. The rest were unfamiliar to him.

He thought of Tommy, Luis, and Chucho up on the roof. Unless he were somewhere else in the church. Luis wasn't in attendance.

When the woman in front of him stood up during a song, Adam did too, thinking it was time to do that. But he soon realized that sitting or standing was a personal choice. He had grown up in the Roman Catholic faith and had been an altar boy. There were specific times to sit or stand or kneel. This church had no kneelers.

After several songs, a man got up and stood behind a podium. He announced that over the next five or six weeks, they would have guest speakers, potential pastors, delivering sermons on Sunday mornings. He encouraged everyone to spread the word so that all members would be in attendance so they could take part in the choice of the new pastor.

He also welcomed their guests, and Adam had to stand up and introduce himself. He remembered Baxter's words, that everyone in town knew who he was, and he wondered at the need for introductions.

"My name is Adam Alba. I've been in Ur two weeks. He didn't know what else to say, so he sat back down. They welcomed him like an Alcoholics Anonymous meeting. He felt conspicuous. He was aware that eyes were on him, and until he was no longer interesting, it would stay that way.

The man asked people to open their Bibles to 1 John 1:9. Adam had no Bible and couldn't have found the verse without a table of contents. Everyone in the church found the verse so quickly, they might have had it bookmarked.

The girl named Laura shared her Bible with him. It was filled with margin notes in green and purple ink. He wondered if she was as good at school homework as she was with Bible study. The man read the verse out loud. "If we confess our sins, He is faithful and just to forgive our sins and cleanse us from all unrighteousness."

Adam thought of Elf and how he had said that Christians preferred the juicy details of his past and wouldn't let him put the past behind him. Adam also recalled going to confession when he was a kid and making up sins to confess because he couldn't think of anything that he had done that qualified as a sin. Priests are sworn to secrecy, and he wondered if Pentecostal deacons and pastors shared the same privilege. Perhaps it was a confession that doomed Delgado and Lehman.

The man droned on about the process of being cleansed from unrighteousness that Adam found simplistic, something about genuine repentance and asking God for forgiveness. Adam thought of his own past. While embracing sobriety, he had tried to make amends with those he had hurt. Wasn't making amends a better sign of repentance than just making confessions to some clergyman and praying about it? Not everyone had accepted his apology, and he could see firsthand the damage he had caused others. He genuinely felt remorse.

There were lots of things he could look back on and say they had been mistakes, even sins, but he had learned something from his mistakes and from making amends, even the acknowledgement that making amends was important. Not penance, a few prayers and a promise to do better, like the way he was raised but trying to make things right. Wasn't that the point? Wasn't that part of the cleansing process? This guy didn't seem to understand that forgiveness wasn't merely for the purpose of coming clean and asking God for forgiveness.

Adam thought about how Elf had said about not being allowed to put his past behind him. It unsettled Adam. He knew Baxter and Ramirez would eventually speak with Elf. He could still hear the confident relish in Ramirez's voice: "He'll talk to us. He's still on parole."

Ramirez's statement came from a position of assumed power, and it made Adam uneasy. It sounded like he could *make* Elf talk. If Elf were truly still on parole, they'd know exactly where to find him and would have power to coerce him. Adam rarely prayed, and what came to his mind that evening could hardly be called a prayer. More, it was a promise to himself to ask Elf to forgive him for his breach of confidence.

After the Bible teacher shared his message, everyone was invited to share their reactions to the mini sermon and were encouraged to add to the message. Adam remained silent. He could have said a lot. He wanted to say something, but he reminded himself why he was there in the first place. He didn't want to say anything that might increase the distance between him and the people at this service, but he had the impression that their belief system was both simplistic and sincere.

Eventually, everyone went downstairs for more packaged cookies and iced sweet tea.

The room had been rearranged. Sofas and chairs had been pulled away from the wall. It looked more like a large living room than a basement of a church. Racks of folding tables and chairs were stored along the back wall. Women were sitting and men were standing in tiny groups, the way they might have done in high school.

His social cachet had increased since the memorial service. As he wandered through the room hoping to catch snippets of conversation that Baxter might think useful, he was waylaid and invited into several conversations. Most of it was small talk, but he learned three things he considered important. First everyone knew about Henry. Most were hoping for the best and praying for him. Several, however, suggested that he was reaping the natural harvest of a life of drinking and drugs.

Among the older men he heard reminiscences of Henry's youthful antics. Those too young to have known Henry back then listened with rapt attention. Elf was right about people liking the lurid details.

The most disturbing part of the things that people said about Henry was that it was all said in the past tense. No one talked about his PTSD or the way he had pulled his life together after his deployment in Iraq. Adam's gut churned when one of the men said, "The wages of sin is death." Adam thought the statement was cruel and uncalled-for. It all went into Adam's mind. Baxter would hear about him.

As he passed by the seated women, one grabbed his arm and introduced herself as Grace's mother. She was in her early forties and quite beautiful. She rattled off in rapid, nervous, speech. She reminded him of women who were coming on to him a little too strong. They would be too animated and a little out of breath. Without thinking, she offered up two bits of information. She betrayed her lack of enthusiasm about Elf. "I just hope she knows what she's getting into. I've warned her."

She also bragged about how often Grace came home. "Every other weekend. Sometimes every weekend." She was so proud. The word *clockwork* passed through Adam's mind. That degree of regularity could easily be exploited. He'd want to mention that to Baxter. Given the insular environment of Ur, Baxter probably already knew it. But he'd mention it, nonetheless.

Adam noticed a slight crevice in her rambling. "Does she always visit her father in Fort Worth first?"

The woman seemed to freeze. The question stopped her speaking entirely.

Adam tried to salvage the conversation. "Let me explain. I was on the same bus as she was. We ate together with her friends, Matt and Tom. I believe she mentioned visiting her father there."

"Was it Matt and Tom that mentioned her father, or was it Grace?" she had asked.

"It was Grace. I think she really enjoys those visits."

The woman gradually thawed while she processed what he had said. "Yes, she spends Fridays with him. Neither of them has class on Fridays. He teaches at Texas Wesleyan."

"I'm sorry if I brought up a sensitive topic."

"No, no. Don't be sorry. It's not sensitive. I shouldn't be surprised that she mentioned her father. It's only that she took it very hard when her father and I separated. She never speaks about him to me, and I imagine she does the same about me to him. You know what the Bible says about being unequally yoked."

Adam didn't know what the Bible said about being yoked, unequally or otherwise, to anyone and didn't want to ask. He could google it later if he found himself thinking about it.

She changed the subject. 'We're all praying for Eunice. Luis is so stiff-necked. Not sure how long she'll be able to stand it."

Adam looked around to see if Eunice was in earshot. *Stiff-necked?* If Adam thought anything about Luis, it would have been that he was henpecked. He wanted to come to the man's defense, but he reminded himself as to why he was there.

Seeing and accurately reading Adam's reaction, another woman who had been listening to the conversation joined in. "Oh, it's no secret. Eunice asks for prayer all the time. It's so difficult when your husband isn't," she hesitated to find a polite euphemism. She settled on "...an *active* member of the congregation."

This was a theme among the women of the church. One of the women went as far as saying, "It's so difficult being married to an unsaved husband. Until my Steve was baptized, we were all praying for him. And look at him now. He's one of the church elders and teaches Bible study," she said, full of pride.

"Was he the teacher tonight?" Adam feigned interest.

"Oh, yes. Wasn't it a wonderful lesson?"

Adam hadn't thought the lesson wonderful but just smiled and nodded in response.

Adam left the church with a very uneasy feeling. As he walked home, he wished he had somehow defended Luis, but among his thoughts, that was the least consequential. Grace's clockwork returns to Ur could be significant. What did her mother really mean by unequally yoked? Even more troublesome was that no one expressed an interest in finding Henry. Either he'd turn up or he wouldn't. All Baxter had said about Henry was that Deputy Isi had made all the necessary calls to find him if he had been hurt or arrested.

Henry's absence didn't seem to bother anyone other than Rosie. Why did no one think Henry was worth looking for?

The Thursday shift was as slow as the Wednesday shift had been. On most weekdays, the restaurant existed mostly for that tiny group of people Rosie called the town council. On weekends, it had become a hub of the community of Ur. More and more, Adam was realizing how much a labor of love the Pioneer's Rest had become for Rosie and Henry.

The door to the alley was propped open. Adam was draining the oil from the fryer when the old, stout Choctaw woman arrived with more fry bread. A young man carried in the sacks of bread for her and went back to sit in the driver's seat of the Volkswagen Beetle.

"Halito." He smiled at her and shrugged his shoulders. "Still waiting for Henry. I hope he comes back soon."

"Halito." She looked at him skeptically.

"Your grandson?" He glanced out the door toward the young man sitting in the car.

"He is my great-grandson."

"I'll get Rosie."

She didn't wait. "I'll go through."

Adam figured that they'd be having another visit. After a few minutes, he looked through the service window. They were sitting with coffee again. He thought of the young man waiting outside. He imagined an antsy kid impatiently waiting. Instead, as he walked around the car, he saw the boy, face glued to his cell phone, his thumbs dancing on the screen. He looked up as Adam approached.

He was much younger than Adam had earlier guessed. Adam doubted he was even old enough to drive. "Waiting can be tough. You want a pop or something?"

"I'm okay. I don't mind waiting."

"Looks like they're going to be there a while. Are you sure?"

He considered. "Okay, a Coke, whatever you have." He got out of the car.

"What's your name?" Adam asked as they walked back into the kitchen.

"Jeremy."

"I'm Adam. Wait here. Jeremy. I'll get it for you." The Rest didn't serve fountain drinks. Cans of various soft drinks were kept in a fridge behind the bar. When Adam stepped into the dining room, the conversation stopped. They both looked at him. "Just getting Jeremy a Coke." They both smiled and nodded to him. Their conversation didn't continue until he was back in the kitchen.

"Thanks." Jeremy leaned against the prep table and accepted the can of Coke. Wanting to make conversation, he said, "I'm used to waiting for my grandmother."

"Does she bring bread to other places?"

"No. But she knows I like driving, so she makes me take her places. I only have a permit and need the practice."

"You're a good grandson," Adam said, sounding too paternal for his own comfort. He sometimes surprised himself by how much he sounded like his father.

Jeremy shrugged and popped the top of the can. The can hissed and threatened to spill over. but the boy caught it with a sip. "Cold." He raised the can as if in toast to Adam.

"Where else do you take her? There's not much around."

"There's Walmart, of course. We're going there after here. Sometimes we visit relatives. Sometimes we just drive and talk. I think I'm her favorite." He almost blushed. "Actually, I'm just the youngest… and the most handsome." He winked, and his eyes twinkled.

Adam liked the boy. Somehow he felt proud of him. Something about the way he talked about his great-grandmother convinced Adam of his genuine affection for her. *Sometimes we just drive and talk. What a remarkable statement from a kid!*

The old woman and Rosie came out into the kitchen. This time, Rosie hadn't been crying. She seemed stronger, even happier. Adam would have liked to know what they had been talking about. The change was remarkable.

The boy's grandmother said something to the boy in Choctaw. In response, he thanked Adam again for the Coke, calling him sir.

They followed them out to the alley. Rosie opened the passenger-side door for the old woman and said, "Yakoke Fehna Hoke. Chukmàt mika."

Together, Rosie and Adam watched them drive off. "I didn't know you were fluent in that language."

"I'm not fluent," Rosie confided. "I learned a few formal phrases out of respect. Henry is fluent. She's his grandmother."

He hadn't known that, and he wondered if Baxter knew it. He probably did. "What did you say to her?"

"Thanks very much and goodbye."

"Can you teach me to say that?"

"Adam, you had enough trouble with *Hatak Ohoyo*. She speaks English. By the way, she thinks you're sweet for keeping Henry's place for him. Honestly, *Halito* is enough.

It wasn't long before his work was interrupted again. The call had come just as he refilled the fryer with fresh oil.

"Ready for another road trip?" Baxter's voice on the line.

"Not Pizza Hut."

"No, just good old American diner food. No Ramirez either."

"Where are we going?"

"I'll explain while we drive."

Adam arrived a little early at the place where Baxter told him to wait. Wait, he did. Baxter was late.

There was very little traffic on this side of town. In the ten minutes it took him to reach the spot, only one car passed him. Manda and her husband slowed down to ask him if he needed a lift somewhere.

"I'm just out for a walk, thanks."

"Ain't nothing but road and miles of it out this side of town," Blaine warned.

Adam thanked them again and said he'd turn back sooner or later.

Adam felt exposed. He paced around a picnic table in an isolated section about a quarter mile outside of town. He couldn't imagine anyone choosing to come to this spot for a picnic. An old, rusty cast-iron grill was mounted to a small cement pad about ten feet from the table. *Somebody must use this place.* There was cold ash in the grill. In boredom, he prodded it with a stick. It was dry and soft. Something had been burned in the grill, though it didn't look like residue from charcoal briquettes.

He had things to tell Baxter, but in his mind they didn't mean much. After his talk with Baxter and Ramirez, he was unclear about what he was really supposed to do. Telling him not to investigate but to listen for information that might be useful sounded good at the time, but after his visit to the church Bible study, he wasn't sure he could help the way they expected.

He paced around the picnic area and mindlessly picked up some litter, an empty soda can, and a decaying potato chip bag, and tossed them in the rusty fifty-gallon drum meant to serve as a trash bin. The cooling day had been hot, not sticky but hot. Now a breeze rustled the leaves of the trees and stirred the fine dust that had built up by the pavement. Tiny dust devils rose up and died by the side of the road.

There was a perfume smell, some flower that Adam couldn't identify, that carried on the breeze. It seemed to come and go. The scent was light, not heavy, not cloying like the night-blooming jasmine that had grown outside his dorm room window in college.

Lost in his thoughts, he barely noticed the arrival of a Toyota Prius pulling off the road.

Baxter leaned out the window. "Sorry, I had a flat. This is my wife's car. Get in."

"It's not hard to change a tire." Adam slipped into the passenger seat.

"I hate riding on donuts." Baxter said as he pulled back out onto the road. "My wife is getting the tire repaired. She'll take the kids to Mr. Softie while she waits. Kids love it.

"What's Mr. Softie?"

"Soft ice cream," Baxter said. "It's a treat for the kids."

"Where is it? I could go for that."

"It's off the next exit on the highway. About eight miles."

"I'm curious. Where are we going now?" Adam fiddled with the strap of his seat belt.

"Listen, Adam. I saw your reaction when Ramirez talked about getting Elf to talk. He wanted to pick him up right away. I talked him out of it. Convinced him that the soft touch was a better way to go. I figured you and I could talk to him, just talk to him. No threats, no muscle. Just common sense and decency."

Adam was silent for a moment. He tried to imagine how Elf might react, and there were too many possibilities. "I guess it's better this way."

Baxter assured him. "Whatever he knows, it's unlikely to have much evidential value. It's not likely to pull him into the case even as a witness. I don't know what kind of muscle Ramirez wanted to use on the guy, but pulling him in could cost Elf a lot. He could lose his job, his friends, and his confidence. I read his sheet. The guy's got a history, and the progress he's made deserves respect and consideration," Baxter paused in thought. "His parole officer has a reputation for being a hard-ass ballbuster." Baxter shook his head as if to clear it. "The kid knows the system and what it's capable of. This way, it's a bit more respectful and less disruptive."

"That matters to you." Adam had a habit of making statements that weren't questions but got answers.

Baxter waited to speak. When he spoke, he was cool and definite. "Yeah. It does. And if I correctly understood your reaction when Ramirez talked about getting Elf to talk, it matters to you as well." Baxter drove up the on-ramp, gaining speed.

"I didn't like what he said or how he said it. In fact, I didn't like *him* at that moment."

"Honestly, neither did I—*at that moment*. I think he's a good cop, and if ruthlessness were needed, I'd feel better knowing that he was on my side."

Adam was impressed by the honesty and the humanity of the statement. "Who blew his cover? Do you know?"

Baxter glanced at him, apparently impressed. "Good question! I got only half an answer. It might have been someone at the DEA who either had it in for him or wanted to keep the drugs operation going, at least for a while. Like I said then, only two people in town knew who he was, me and Stacks—unless Stacks told someone and if he did, he'd never admit to it. Probably wouldn't even remember it." He sighed deeply. "The rest is speculation—a hypothesis that needs to be tested."

"His cover was blown for sure then?"

"'For sure' is too strong. I put it at a 90 percent chance." He exited the highway and headed down a two-lane road. "It's just hard to believe that anyone had it in for Tommy Delgado." He slowed down and turned left at a crossroads. The setting sun was now to their left. The angle of the sun made the land around them glow in yellow-tinged green for miles.

"You think it was Sheriff Stacks who blew Chucho's cover?"

"I think it *could* have been. That's why we met out of town yesterday. That's why I want you to use your prepaid phone. That's why I took

DuPuis' word and trusted you. That's why I think he might have been the target of the shooting at the festival."

Adam noticed an open fence gate wide enough for a truck to drive through, then looked over at Baxter to gauge his reaction. "Elf told me to watch out for crooked cops! He said if I had gotten on that bus as planned, I might have been arrested to get the drugs back," Adam confided.

"And here you are, driving with me in the middle of nowhere. Does that mean you trust me now?"

"Ramirez picked up on that yesterday." Adam was evasive.

"I know. So did I, but I don't think I let it show." He slowed down and veered into the oncoming lane and then back again."

"What was that all about?" Adam asked.

"There was a snake stretching across the lane. I didn't want to kill it. They do that sometimes for warmth."

"That was a snake?"

"It wasn't a broom handle. Anyway, there wasn't anyone coming, and I had room to save its life. Hopefully, it will move on before someone else comes along."

"That was a big snake!"

"Yep, it was. Listen, I don't think Stacks has enough greed to be directly mixed up in what's going on. He likes to be liked. He likes his job. Voters are important. He gets chummy with people sometimes. I think he could have run at the mouth without realizing what he was saying."

"He's the sheriff!" Adam didn't exactly know what he was implying apart from a sheriff should know police work.

"He's a cop, but he only had less than ten years on the force, and then he won an election. He wouldn't intentionally risk his popularity for money. But he wouldn't be inclined to risk his job by not being the kind of guy people would vote for either."

Adam thought for a moment, remembering how Baxter had once said that Stacks wanted their open cases closed before the election.

After a few moments, Baxter injected. "In case you're wondering, I am the one who suggested he question you. I suggested he make you do that bag-packing demonstration. And I made sure Deputy Isi was present for it. Pinning those drugs on you is impossible now."

"So you saved my ass."

"Your ass performed admirably."

"So, Isi didn't know who Chucho was?"

"Not unless Stacks let it slip. We agreed with the DEA to keep his identity under wraps."

"Do you think he might have?" Adam asked.

"What, let it slip to Isi?

"Yeah,"

"Probably not. They don't socialize in the same circles. He might be a little less careful in social circles with people he thinks he can trust."

Adam let that settle in. Did that include Rosie's town council? Did Stacks eat with them to maintain voter support, to listen to gossip, or simply because the Rest was the only place to eat in town? What might he have divulged without thinking while chummily dining with them? Adam found it a little hard to believe that an experienced cop would be so loose-tongued, but then, this was Ur, where everyone thought they knew everyone.

The possibility of a crooked cop seemed slight unless it was what Baxter called top-down, meaning someone in the DEA. If that were the case, that bag packing scene he had performed might well have saved him from an easy conviction, at least on possession charges.

There were long stretches of quiet during which Adam stared out the window at the endless rural terrain, dotted occasionally by a ranch gate, a dirt driveway, a house in the distance, or an occasional business like a convenience store or gas station.

Throughout the trip, his mind was far from idle, despite the stretches of silence. Adam suspected Baxter was strategizing while he found himself rehearsing the conversation with Elf. He had the distinct feeling that the freedom Elf had in sharing his story and his opinion was made in confidence. And that confidence was now broken. Would he clam up? Would he lie to avoid getting involved, perhaps in fear of losing his own freedom?

"There's a cooler in the back seat with some bottled water. Would you grab me one and get one for yourself?"

Adam undid his seat belt and leaned over behind Baxter. He popped the cooler with one hand and pulled out two bottles of water. He replaced his seatbelt, opened one bottle, and handed it to Baxter. The other he held close to his temple, feeling the cold. Then he opened it and gulped, the cold water tracing its way through his chest.

As they approached the outskirts of Broken Arrow, the rural landscape gently but quickly grew more suburban. At first there were a few housing developments with undeveloped space in between. They seemed out of place.

Then suddenly, Broken Arrow became like every suburb in America that had room to sprawl. Strip malls and chain restaurants flanked long stretches of main roads with side streets leading into housing developments. The streets were cleaner than New Orleans and were busy enough to be called traffic.

At the first red light, Baxter pressed a button on his phone screen. The mechanical voice instructed him to turn left in 1,000 feet. "We'll be there soon," he said. "It's only another mile or so."

They pulled into the parking lot. The Moonstone Grill was a permanent structure stylized like an old-school diner from the nineteen fifties. Ribbons of gleaming chrome-like trim wrapped around the trailer or railroad car-shaped building clad in dull silver vertical siding. It was, Adam thought, a work of nostalgic art.

The glass front door made a sucking sound when Baxter pulled it open. There was another set of glass doors just beyond, forming a tiny airlock foyer. A bulletin board filled with business cards attached with pushpins covered one wall of the foyer above a bench lined with flyers and pamphlets. Adam opened the second door, and they stepped into the diner. A metal stand bore a sign asking patrons to "Please Wait to be Seated."

There were only a few occupied tables and only one server. "Anywhere you'd like, fellas," called a middle-aged woman who was pouring coffee for a lone man sitting at the counter. "Be with you in a jiff." She wore a uniform that was a cross between a carhop and a French maid. Her ample bosom donned a folded napkin like a corsage. The blonde hair piled on top of her head seemed to be fraying around the edges. Behind her, an anonymous hand turned a stainless-steel wheel with a couple of orders attached.

They sat down at a booth by the window. Adam watched a hand reach up to the wheel, grab a check, place it on the sill of the service window, and set a plate on top of it. The fingers tapped a little bell. "Must be Elf," Adam commented. "He's not a big guy."

She approached their table with glasses of water and menus tucked under her elbow. "I'm Brook. I'll be taking care of you today." She set down a couple of menus. "What would you like to drink?" Baxter ordered coffee. Adam said. "Just the water is fine. Is that Elf back there?"

She nodded. "Elf, we got a couple of your friends out here," she shouted.

Everyone in the diner turned to look at them. Baxter laughed.

A pair of eyes appeared through the service window, eyebrows raised in surprise. "I didn't expect her to do that," Adam said under his breath as she went off.

"Let's hope it didn't freak him out," Baxter said.

"I'm kind of feeling guilty about this."

"You're doing him a favor. Otherwise, he'd be talking to his parole officer and Ramirez. This has got to be a big step up from that."

Brook came back to their table with Baxter's coffee and some creamer. "Don't mean to rush you but the kitchen closes in about twenty minutes. Have you had enough time to decide?" She took their order. "Elf takes a dinner break when the kitchen closes. Do you want to wait for him?"

They both nodded.

Brook left them. *The home stretch*, Adam thought, his heartbeat racing with the beat of his fingers drumming on the table. In half an hour, they'd be talking to Elf. How would he react when he found out Baxter was a cop? Then ice ran down Adam's spine. What if Baxter was one of the people Elf recognized at the memorial service? Was he about to drag Elf into his worst nightmare?

TWENTY-FOUR

Rosie stood in the alleyway behind the Pioneers Rest, her hands on her hips. The day was beginning to cool down. The alley was now fully shaded by her building. She waited for the trash collectors to arrive. Willy Brown had come and gone, taking the kitchen waste for his pigs. Every Monday and Thursday, he picked up the food waste in the wheeled bin he provided and left a clean wheeled bin for the next pickup.

The trash collection was once a week, and if she weren't standing watch, they'd leave a mess. Half the trash would be blowing around the alley. She wondered if other businesses had the same problem with them. There wasn't ever much trash from the Rest. Mostly paper napkins from the restaurant and the few things she, Henry, and the rare guests of the hotel might generate. Still, they charged her for a dumpster, a small one but a dumpster all the same, and emptied it once a week because she was a business.

She could have cut her trash bill by 75 percent if she cheated and simply used a small, wheeled bin as residential waste for her house across the alley. One bin would have easily been enough. But everyone knew she didn't live there anymore and that the house was vacant.

There had been a few ridiculous offers for the property, but she had never seriously considered them. She knew those offers were most likely for the original antique fixtures that were inside the old Victorian house, built in 1861.

She was tired. Usually, Henry waited for the trash pickup. He had a way with those guys that made them want to be neater. Or was it that he would just clean up after them? She knew he was friendly with them. He'd sometimes make a couple of burgers and fries to-go for them as a kind of a tip.

Hugging herself against a chill, she stopped herself from tearing up. *Henry, come home,* she thought, sending her message like a prayer through the air. She followed the thought with a real prayer. *Dear God, keep him safe and bring him home.* They had been through so much for so long. There were moments when she looked at him that she could still see the young man he had once been, even if he were a little more crusty and a lot less cocky.

She closed her eyes, and once again she was young, with her friends at the county fair. She could see him strutting down the midway, the chain that anchored his wallet to his belt swinging on his hip and the wear ring from a can of snuff on his other back pocket.

Back then she could imagine him in all sorts of futures: a rancher, a country music star, and even a famous rodeo bull rider. She imagined him as a doting husband, a wonderful father, and a responsible businessman taking over her family business. None of that happened, of course, thanks to her father.

But they had settled down, in a way. Life had its twists and turns but, in the end, they faced the second half of life together. It felt good, safe, just knowing that someone she could trust, someone she believed in lived in the same building, slept close by. Shared her life, if not her bed. It was what life had given her, and now it seemed to have taken it away. She repeated her prayer. "Dear God, please keep him safe and bring him home," she said this out loud for anyone to hear, but no one heard.

She paced the alley waiting. She didn't trust herself to go inside. She'd get distracted, or she'd sit down and not want to get up. Time after time she passed the metal doors that led down to the tornado shelter. Each time her eyes lingered on the lock she and Adam had used to secure them.

She smiled at the thought of the teenager still living inside her, practicing signing her name with Henry's last name in her notebook. Mrs. Rosalinda Beck, Rose Beck, Rosie Beck. Her chest tightened. She could feel the old pain and anger she felt when her father had scared Henry away.

The old lock was nowhere to be seen. She had walked the whole alleyway looking for where it might have been discarded. There was no sign of it. Whoever broke in must have been neat enough to toss it in the trash.

Each time she looked at the new lock, she got that vulnerable feeling of a stranger breaking into the Rest. The thought frightened her. Without Henry, dependable Henry, rough around the edges, Henry. She just didn't feel safe.

The window air conditioner in her third-floor apartment kicked on. It seemed loud enough that it could have hidden the creak of the rusty metal hinges.

The real source of unease in her mind, and the creepiest aspect of the missing lock, was that it was not likely a total stranger. Whoever broke that lock and entered the building had to know where it would lead, had to know about the shelter. *They had been there long enough to clean the damned place, for heaven's sake. Who would do that?*

In a bigger town or city, she thought, *it might be a homeless person. But we don't have any homeless people in Ur.* The casino attracted strangers, but few ventured past the casino. The casino is *why* they came to Ur. Only on the rarest of occasions did anyone explore Ur, and most of them were looking for antique stores.

With the slight movement of a cooling breeze, she crossed and pulled in her arms, hugging herself. But it wasn't a stranger, was it? It couldn't have been. Whoever broke that lock and used those stairs couldn't have been a stranger. She remembered distinctly, the footprints that clung to the wall of the stairwell faced in, not out. Someone had come in and had left by another means and the only way was either through the lobby of the hotel or the kitchen.

It baffled her. The footprints in the dust had been clear. It wasn't like the person habitually used the alley entrance. Yet, someone had cleaned that room as if they were using it over a longer period of time. How could anyone do that without her or Henry being aware of it?

When she had shown the well to Deputy Isi, she took a few notes but seemed to believe that whoever entered the basement through the alley had to do so after the building had been processed. She had insisted that they wouldn't overlook something like that. But she still took notes and used her phone to take pictures. Rosie had learned about the AR-15 they had found in the shelter when Baxter asked her if she owned one. Isi thought they might have tried to come back for it only to discover that it had been taken into evidence.

If that were true, they had to come when the restaurant was closed or they had to get past Henry, not something easy to do. Was it the same person who had cleaned the shelter?

She shook her head, and a strand of hair fell out of her bun and into her face. Without thinking, she tucked it behind her ear. The sound of the trash collection truck coming down the alleyway interrupted her rumination.

She turned toward them and waited. They pulled up alongside the dumpster. A kind of forklift scooped up the dumpster, lifted it, and tipped it over the truck. As they returned it to its place, a couple napkins fell out of it. At least it wasn't a big mess.

She sighed, picked up the two napkins that had blown out of the dumpster and tossed them back in the bin. As she headed toward the kitchen door, she froze. If the lock was broken and someone came in after the police were done with the building, what if it was Henry?

She turned around and considered her old family house across the alley. It was as good a place to hide as any. What if Henry was camped in there and just needed some food? She decided to go and check when a goosebump stopped her. Henry had keys to the building. What if it wasn't Henry in the house? She'd wait and bring Adam with her.

While waiting for Elf, the diner slowly emptied. Adam shifted his position toward the aisle of the booth. He hoped to encourage Elf to sit across from him next to Baxter to observe Elf's reactions. The sense that he had betrayed someone by bringing Baxter to Broken Arrow frayed the edges of his emotions. If he could only have the chance to warn Elf in some way. He didn't want Elf to feel as if he had been broadsided.

As luck would have it, Elf came through the kitchen door and turned toward the small alcove where the restrooms were located. Thinking quickly and pretending he hadn't noticed Elf, Adam shifted on the booth bench. "Excuse me, I need to use the restroom."

Baxter nodded.

Adam walked to the alcove that housed the restroom doors. He tried the doorknob, hoping the restroom would accommodate more than one guy at a time. It would be easy to get in a brief word before Elf joined them at the table. He stood outside the locked bathroom door until Elf came out.

Startled, Elf nearly walked into Adam as he exited the restroom. He backed up and froze. An involuntary "Excuse me" escaped his lips.

Adam dove into what he wanted to say but tripped over the words, not knowing if he was even making sense. "Listen, I'm really sorry about coming here, but believe me, it's better this way."

Elf tried to interrupt.

"No, listen. If the guy I'm sitting with is one of the people you were afraid of at the memorial service, just say you hate pickles."

Elf looked confused. "I do hate pickles."

Adam thought for a minute. "Are you saying you recognize the guy already?"

"No. I really do hate pickles."

"Good, then it won't be a lie." Adam shook off the confusion. "When you get to our table, if he was one of the people…"

"He isn't. Who is he?"

"He's a cop. Sergeant Baxter. "

Elf stiffened.

"Believe me. It's better this way. The other cop wanted to get your parole officer involved."

Elf's eyes widened, and the color drained from his face. He stiffened. "What's going on?" His voice was cautious, serious but with a hint of panic.

"He's probably trying to find out if I'm a crooked cop." Elf jumped, and Adam blanched. Baxter stood grinning at the door to the restroom alcove. "Adam, you ought to consider joining the force. I'm not offended. If Ramirez had been at that service, I would have been thinking the same thing about him." He extended a hand toward Elf, introducing himself. "When we're all done peeing, let's go eat. Brook has our food on the table. It's my turn to pee." He walked past them and into the men's room.

"He's not someone I recognize except from the service. That doesn't mean I'd trust him, but he's not one of the people that I wanted to get away from." A blanket of resignation covered Elf. "That's what this is all about?"

Adam admitted it.

It purposely took longer for Baxter to empty his bladder than one would estimate. They sat in the booth opposite one another. Before Baxter returned, Adam tried to apologize, and it felt distinctly like a confession of sin telling Elf of his conversations with Baxter and Chucho. Elf listened intently, pulling himself together.

"We're cool, Adam. I half expected it after our talk. I'm grateful that my parole officer isn't involved. I'd like to spend as little time with that guy as I can. If this meeting has to happen, this way really is better."

Elf saw Baxter coming back to the booth, and he slid out and sat back down again next to Adam. "I think the officer would like to see me clearly as we talk." He said it under his breath but was fairly sure that Baxter heard him. "Shall I call you Officer or Sergeant?" he said as Baxter slid into the booth.

"My name is Baxter. Most people I know treat it like my first name. If you're more comfortable with sergeant, feel free. But this is an unofficial visit, Mr... ?"

"Elvin Lawrence Fleming. Everyone calls me Elf. It fits better. When I hear someone call me Mr. Fleming or Elvin, I think of my father."

"These burgers look wonderful, er... Elf. I'm starving," Baxter continued, passing the ketchup bottle to Adam, who in turn passed it to Elf.

Brook came to the table offering to refill drinks. Baxter asked for a cup of coffee as he'd have a long drive back to Ur.

"I really do only have half an hour. I need to clean the kitchen before I leave, so what is it you want from me?" His frankness bordered on hostility, but he covered it well. "You wouldn't have driven this far for a hamburger and a friendly visit." He smiled thinly and bit into his burger.

Baxter swallowed his own bite of burger, sipped his coffee, and said, "Adam has told you about the drugs that were put into his bag."

Elf nodded. "I'm clean. Glad to take a test. I have nothing to do with that world anymore."

"I believe you. I'm not here for that." Baxter made sure that his eyes met Elf's when he said it. "But Adam said you recognized someone from your past at the memorial service for Deacon Delgado. I believe his son, Tom, is a friend of yours."

"A good friend," Elf added.

"I understand why you might not want to identify that person."

"Two people," Elf added, and a sinking feeling came over him.

"I've got two murders and drug activity dating back over a year. The other cop that Adam mentioned is DEA."

The last patrons were leaving the diner. Brook was wiping down tables and the counter and shutting down counter equipment. "Anybody want coffee before I toss this?" she called to the table where they sat. Baxter raised his cup. She filled it.

Adam had the distinct feeling she was working slowly to overhear snippets of their conversation.

Elf dipped a fry in ketchup and popped it into his mouth. "Unfortunately, Sergeant, it's not what you might hope. The only connection to drugs is that I was using at the time and needed money."

Brook walked through the swinging door to the kitchen.

Elf leaned into the table. "Look, I did a lot of things to get the money for drugs back then. If I had seen someone who was mixed up in dealing drugs, I wouldn't have said anything at all; not to Adam, not to anyone. I want to live."

"You just admitted that you wouldn't tell me if they were."

"Right. But I will tell you honestly. If they have anything to do with drugs, I don't know about it. I can't help you with that. However, in good faith, I'll tell you about them," he seemed to flush with embarrassment. "But neither of them has broken any laws that I know of."

"Any laws?"

"None that would stick. None that would be worth pursuing. Let's just say they had been repeat clients of mine, and I'm not talking about selling drugs. You get my meaning?"

Baxter thought. "Tricks," he whispered.

Adam busied himself with his own dinner.

"They compensated me for my… time. I'm not proud of it. But I don't have to be ashamed of it either. I've been cleansed by the blood of the lamb."

Adam thought about the Bible study. Elf was certainly standing up in his understanding of forgiveness.

Elf continued. "I think they might have recognized me. I didn't want to interact with them. I'm sure, in the circumstances, they didn't want to interact with me either. But my girlfriend, Grace, is a pretty chatty girl. I live in fear of either of them finding me here. When Brook shouted that I had friends here, well. I feared the worst."

"You fear violence?"

"Sort of. I fear they might try to renew our acquaintance. I would refuse, of course, but one of them has leverage, and I don't think the other would take kindly to being rejected."

"Adam, what was it you said that gave you the idea that Elf was afraid of these guys?" Baxter asked.

Adam wished he had been left out of the conversation but answered the question. "Elf, I thought you said you didn't want them as enemies."

"Right, absolutely right. I don't. And as long as I can stay away from them, it won't be much of a problem. At least I don't think so. They're both married, or at least they were back then. They might be nervous about what I might say. If I say anything to you, they might find out. You won't be able to do anything to them, but they would be able to do something to me. Which is why I don't want to disclose that information."

Baxter nodded knowingly. Adam knew him now well enough to imagine the gears working in his head.

Adam spoke up. "Elf, I'm really sorry to put you in this position."

Elf shook his head and halfheartedly chuckled. "Adam, you didn't put me in this position; I did. Old sins cast long shadows. I've been forgiven. I've been redeemed, but I carry the consequences of what I've done." He turned and looked at Adam.

"Dude." Adam returned his gaze. "You and me, we're cool. okay?" He put his fist to his chest, and he extended it slightly toward Adam. They bumped fists. Adam felt relief.

"Thank you," Adam said.

Careful of his words, Elf continued. "Let me tell you. One guy with considerable influence likes to…" he thought of how to phrase it politely. He knew what he might have said back in the day, but he preferred to avoid that kind of language. "… insinuate himself into tight places, and he prefers young men of a certain stature for that activity."

The mayor and the sheriff were the only people of authority Adam could think of. He tried to read Baxter's face, but Bax was good at his job.

Baxter wished he hadn't heard that, but he pressed on. "And the other?"

"The other is a sick, sexual sadist that frankly scared the crap out of me. It's amazing what a person is willing to do, even more than once, to get a fix. I want nothing to do with that guy. I think he could really be dangerous." He visibly shook. "I think the only reason I survived was because he knew he wanted to come back for more. I had given him the performance he wanted. But each time it got weirder and more difficult." He turned to Adam. "Believe it or not, I believe that getting arrested was

God's way of saving me from the life I had created. I thank God for prison."

Baxter leaned back. Adam could see the gears still working. "Mr. Fleming, Elf," he corrected himself. "You've been very helpful. I really appreciate your honesty. I can't thank you enough." He pulled a card out of his wallet and handed it to Elf. "If either of these men shows up or bothers you, I want you to call me." He handed Elf a card. "This is my personal cell phone number. Use it without fear. I'm not that far away, and I have good friends in Tulsa. If something happens to your parole, tell your lawyer to call me. Don't hesitate."

TWENTY-FIVE

The camera he had hidden in the tornado shelter worked perfectly. The electric panel had a wide-angle view of the entire shelter. Apart from the occasional kid who parked outside the school to use the free Wi-Fi, his camera had use of the entire bandwidth. The resolution of the video was exceptional. It was a good thing his young friend knew how to change settings on the school's system so that his camera and the connection with his video storage would go unnoticed. The most remarkable thing is that he did it remotely. He didn't even have to go into the building.

This was almost as much fun as watching that guy strip off in the laundromat. That extra camera had really paid off when the hunk had gone all the way to try on those jeans. Henry was a resourceful guy. Watching him try to figure his way out of the room was entertaining. He was like a mouse trapped in a maze with no exit and only one treat, a bottle of whiskey.

He tried to imagine the elation Henry would feel when he found it and the convulsions he would experience after drinking it. This was going to be good. It was just a matter of time, and it would all be recorded so that he could watch it again and again and again.

Henry could not get the breaker bar to function. He had tried everything he could think of, trying to fashion tools out of what he could find. He had tried hard—for hours. And occasionally he tried again. The mechanism was completely disabled. It would have to be replaced, and that heavy door had to be opened from the outside.

He shifted in his chair, which squeaked as it swiveled under his weight.

He enjoyed watching Henry suffer. He didn't have to bother with him again. There was nothing to do until Henry found the whiskey. Surely, he would find it long before the next home Little League game. And even then, no one would bother with the tornado shelter. Once he found it, he'd drink it, for sure. He knew Henry wouldn't... couldn't resist.

There wasn't much in the bottle. Enough for one big swig, and that was all it would take.

Once Henry was silenced, he could sneak back into the shelter, remove the bottle and the camera, and walk away. Whoever found the body would assume that Henry just got trapped and died. He was no spring chicken and had lived a hard life. Even if an autopsy eventually found the poison, they couldn't pin it on him, and if all went as planned, someone else might get the blame. That too would be fun to watch.

Not having to dispose of a body was key to his plan. Whoever got the blame would be the icing rose on the top of the cake. He raised his own glass of whiskey and toasted the monitor of the laptop.

How long would it take for the smell to cause someone to open the shelter door and find Henry's body? What if they accidentally got locked in there with the body? That would be funny. Too bad by then the camera would be gone.

The custodian wouldn't return until Labor Day weekend. *It would be awful,* a taunting, sardonic expression falling across his face, *for the kids to start their academic year off with the discovery of a rotted corpse in the basement of the school.*

Until Henry found the whiskey, he'd have the pleasure of watching him suffer. He could hear the frustration in Henry's voice as he talked to himself, planning, figuring out the maze, not knowing there was no escape. He sped up the video to the end. Henry was still sober and still alive. With a final click, he archived the day's footage. Henry would die soon enough, and all the important bits would be recorded, and with a little editing, he could keep the best parts forever.

TWENTY-SIX

The Friday shift went both smoothly and slowly. Adam had plenty of time to prepare for the weekend rush. He spent most of his time slicing tomatoes and dicing potatoes and storing them in containers of cold salty water. He sliced onions into rings and diced onions and peppers for the home-fried potatoes.

As had become his custom on weekdays, he ventured out into the dining room to greet the patrons, always hoping to hear a phrase or snippet of conversation that Baxter would find informative or useful. Both Baxter and Deputy Isi had joined the town council for lunch. The sheriff and the mayor were both absent. He smiled in satisfaction when he saw Blaine, Manda's husband, dousing his eggs and potatoes with hot sauce. At least he did something nice for that guy.

The fry-bread lady returned with her grandson, Jeremy, who insisted on coming in with her to the kitchen. Business was so slow, Adam offered to make them breakfast, his treat. He thought Jeremy would have accepted but instead acquiesced to his grandmother's decision to forego the offer. The old woman told Jeremy to wait for her in the car, she'd only be a minute. Adam assumed she went out to the dining room to be paid because she was out there less than five minutes. As she walked through the kitchen and out the door, she smiled at Adam, saying, "Chukfa haiyo."

Adam tried to remember the phrase so he could ask Rosie, but it escaped him. He repeated it again and again in his mind, but the phrase disappeared the moment Rosie stomped into the kitchen.

"That pain in the ass!"

"What's wrong?" Adam had already finished cleaning the kitchen.

"Blaine Lamano. He has nothing to do all day. You know he doesn't work." She said it as if it were sinful gossip. "He thinks he can just spend all day here drinking my coffee. He's the only one out there now and won't take the hint. The man irks me to no end."

"Tell you what, Rosie. I think he's a lonely guy. You go rest up. I'll eat my lunch down here and sit with him for a while. When I start cleaning up the dining room, he'll get the idea."

"Ha! Only if you ask him to get off his fat ass and help you. That will get rid of him."

Adam thought that was funny.

"Thanks, honey, I'll take you up on that. I've got a lot on my mind." She hesitated for a moment. "And I wanted to ask a favor of you."

"Anything," Adam said, looking her in the eye. She had never asked him for anything other than to carry hot dogs to the Little League field. "Another Little League game?"

She shook her head. "You know the house across the alley. It was my parents' house."

"I don't know if I knew that." Adam tried to remember.

"Well, it's been a long time since I've been over there, and I'm uncomfortable going over there by myself. Would you mind?"

"Not at all." He opened a container and spooned something out onto his plate. It looked like a pile of cut-up seasoned tomatoes.

"What's that?" She bent over his plate. "Smells wonderful."

"My mom called it tomato salad. It's really bruschetta without the toasted bread."

"Sounds wonderful. May I taste it?"

Of course. He gave her the spoon with salad on it.

"It's amazing," she said. "But what did you do to that poor sandwich? It looks like you sat on it."

"It's an Italian habit. I just kind of press them down. It gets everything to mix well, stick together."

"Curious. I've never seen anyone do that. Of course you do lots of things I've never seen anyone do before; the way you do puzzles, those exercises you did in the park."

"You saw them?"

"Back when you did them in the park. How could I miss them?" She smiled. "You sure you don't mind finishing up in the dining room?"

"Not at all," Adam assured her.

She walked over to the door that led out to the alleyway. It had been propped open for air. She gazed out into the alleyway and at the house that had once been her home. "Just let me know when you have a few minutes, and we'll go over."

"Right after I shower." He nodded.

She pulled the door closed and made sure it was locked. "Ever since that business about the tornado shelter, I can't shake that creepy feeling." She turned toward the back stairs. She seemed more tired than usual.

He took a sympathetic deep breath. "Oh, Rosie?"

She turned around.

"That lady said something to me in her language when she left." He tried to recall it. His mouth moved, but the sound wouldn't come back to him.

She watched him struggle. "Did it sound like, "chukfá haiyo?"

Adam brightened. "Yes, that's it!"

"It means see you later. She likes you."

With his plate in hand, he backed through the swinging door to the dining room.

Blaine was staring out the large windows toward the park when Adam set his plate down on the table. "You don't mind if I join you, do you?"

Slightly startled, Blaine looked up at him. "No, not at all. Where's Rosie?"

"I offered to close for her to give her an early day. She works hard every day, you know."

"She's like my Manda. Needs to keep busy."

Adam nodded, understanding but factoring in the detail that Manda likely had to make up for Blaine's loss of income since his heart attack. "It's part of feeling you have a purpose."

"Is that why you're working here? To feel like you have a purpose?" His tone was almost brutal. He turned toward Adam, his fingers tapping on the side of his coffee cup.

Adam wondered at his sensitivity. Maybe he didn't feel like he had a purpose since his heart attack. Adam felt sorry for him. "Not really. I'm kind of stuck here. The folks in town are nice enough, but leaving here right now would leave things unsettled. As a stranger in town, I'm naturally under a certain amount of suspicion."

Blaine sat back, crossed his arms, and considered. "I don't think anyone really suspects you. Though leaving abruptly might make them wonder."

"Helping Rosie a few hours a day gives me something to do, but I would be very happy to see Henry walk through that door." Adam sopped up some of the juice from his tomato salad with a piece of bread.

Blaine snorted at the thought. "I doubt that's going to happen. Henry was always a bit of a troublemaker. Just naturally stirred things up. He'd as likely pick a fight as watch television. If he comes back at all, it will be at the most incendiary moment."

"I take it you didn't like him very much." Adam bit into his sandwich, marking every word that Blaine said.

Blaine actually laughed. "Mind if I get myself a refill?" He held up his coffee cup.

"I'll get it for you." Adam stood up and walked behind the counter to the coffee machine. He pulled the carafe from the heater. It smelled stale, even burned. "I'll have to make another pot. This has gone off."

Blane shook his head. "Don't bother. I'm fine."

Adam rinsed out the pot in the sink and returned to the table.

As he sat back down, Blaine continued. "There was a time I idolized him."

"Henry?"

"Henry and my brother Jaime. They were best friends. You know when you are a kid, four years makes a lot of difference. Jaime and Henry always seemed to be in the center of things. They were tough and cool. Henry's cousin Toby hung out with them too, but he wasn't really cool like them. He was cool by association."

"Maybe Jaime knows what happened to Henry."

"Jamie is dead."

"I'm sorry."

Blaine shook his head, then shrugged his shoulders. "It's been almost ten years since he died. Cancer. Jaime never liked us very much anyway. We were never close."

"Us?"

Blake and me. Blake's my twin…"

"He drives the bus, right?" Adam injected.

"Yeah. I really looked up to Jaime. I think Jaime resented it when we were born. There were two of us and one of him. Twins can be a handful, and our mother babied us a lot. Jaime didn't seem to want to bother with either of us very much. Blake never cared. He was always good on his own."

Adam waited, taking another bite of his sandwich as an excuse to avoid saying anything.

Blaine mused. "I think I was a little jealous of Henry, his being so close to my big brother. Anyway, that's what Blake says. I don't know why I'm telling you this." His eyes were fixed on nothing in the park.

Adam swallowed. "Sometimes we just need to say stuff. I imagine Henry being gone brings up a lot more thoughts about your brother Jaime. What do you think happened to Henry? Nobody seems to worry about him except for Rosie."

Blaine looked at Adam with an expression that was difficult to read. It was somewhere between fear and anger, the way Adam had felt when his Alcoholics Anonymous sponsor asked questions that hit close to home. "Henry always did whatever he wanted and got away with almost all of it. Maybe he just went away. Maybe he's had an accident somewhere. Maybe his past has caught up with him."

"His past?"

"Henry was into a lot of shit. Drugs, women, sex. Sometimes he just used people. Hate to admit it, but Jaime did too. He and Jaime just did what they wanted like they were invincible or immune to consequences. Some role models, huh?"

"We all make mistakes, especially when we're young," Adam said.

"Old sins cast long shadows. Consequences are consequences." Blain said.

For the second time in two days, Adam heard that phrase. His stomach tightened. Looking at the wall clock, it was closing in on two. He stood up and muttered something about letting Blaine out through the now-locked front door. It was hard for him to fight off the thought that his own shadow, that feeling that haunted him, was long, very long indeed, and he wondered if he'd ever escape it.

As he unlocked the door for Blaine to leave, he spoke almost unconsciously. "Old sins can cast very long shadows, but sometimes it's just best to let sleeping dogs lie."

Blaine paused mid-step, brow furrowing at Adam's words. He just shrugged and walked out into the heat of the day. Afternoon sunlight slanted through the window. Adam squinted as he watched Blaine cross the street and into the shade of the park.

He genuinely felt sorry for that lonely old man whose usefulness was a thing of the past.

When she took hold of his arm, he thought of his mother who, on the day of his sister's wedding, as he ushered her to her seat in the church, whispered that women took the arms of men because they were wearing high heels and wanted to steady themselves.

"I thought they just wanted to feel my muscles, Ma."

She laughed. "That too, son, That too. But I'm your mother."

Rosie wasn't wearing high heels, and Adam guessed she needed steadying for reasons that were more emotional than physical. The alley was quiet, and the shade cast by the Pioneer's Rest reached in angles across the road surface.

They walked the alley to the corner. The only key Rosie had was to the front door. The grass in the front yard of the old Victorian house was turning yellow with neglect. Empty flower boxes hung off the porch railing. The porch steps creaked under their shared weight. She hadn't directly answered when he had asked her about this visit to the house. All she said was, "Just checking on things."

She stopped at the gate and looked up at the house. "It wouldn't kill me to have the place painted, and it wouldn't take much to put flowers in those flower boxes."

"Who cuts the grass?"

She paused. "Henry."

The key she used to open the front door was larger than most modern keys, and turning the deadbolt seemed hard work. A spray of WD-40 would have been helpful. As she pushed the door open. A dry, dusty smell slipped past them through the open door.

Rosie reached for a light switch to the right of the front door, and old sconce lights that previously had worked on gas, similar to those in the lobby of the Rest, dimly lit the interior hallway. A flight of dusty stairs rose to the second floor on their left. "That's the sitting room." She pointed to a room to their right with furniture draped in dusty bedsheets of various colors and patterns. A large fireplace flanked the far wall. Sunlight filtered through the dust-covered picture window.

"This place belonged to my grandparents. I was raised here."

They walked directly down the hall, passing an under-the-stairs door to their left, and through another door to a large kitchen. The woodwork under the stairs had been quality work. The shellac finishing was yellowed and, in places, blistered. The molding carried a layer of dust. As they walked, dust and dust bunnies swirled and danced around their feet.

The refrigerator, an antique model with the compressor on the top, was propped open, and the old white enameled stove was covered in dust. The 1930s sink and drainboard were a single unit of enameled furniture. Paint peeled in spots on the walls and from the ceiling.

A 1960s Formica-topped table formed a kind of island in the middle of the room. Adam could imagine the table covered with flour, instead of dust, while women made homemade pasta. The memory stirred inside him and grounded him.

He knew the memory was his, not hers, and he wondered what she would remember if she closed her eyes and just thought about that table.

Rosie walked straight through the kitchen, through a mud porch to the back door. A dusty old wool coat still hung on a hook to one side of the door, and an old pair of work boots, covered in dust, laces akimbo, rested under a picnic table-style bench.

She tried the knob and tugged on the door to see if it was still secure. It was.

A door in the middle of the wall to the right led to an empty room. "That was a formal dining room," she said. "We normally ate in the kitchen." Between the kitchen and the empty dining room was a kind of narrow hallway with wall-to-wall cabinetry. "That's the butler's pantry. My grandparents were rather well off."

"They had a butler?"

"Not in my memory. And I don't think all the time. When my mother was a little girl, they sometimes entertained distinguished guests at the hotel and would invite them to dinner." She rested her fingertips on the kitchen table. "Halona's mother worked in the house. She brought Halona with her and Halona took care of my mother, watched her, played with her. They were five or six years apart."

"Halona?"

"Sorry, the lady who brings the fry bread. Her name is Halona, though I never call her that."

"What do you call her?"

"Pokni. I think it means grandmother. She's older than she looks, bless her."

Adam waited.

"Well, nothing's been disturbed. Let's go upstairs."

Like the hotel, each bedroom had a wash-up sink, which Adam imagined replaced an old washstand. There was nothing under the beds, and she had Adam open each closet door.

There was only one bathroom for four bedrooms. It was furnished much in the same way the bathrooms in the hotel were. Clawfoot tubs with a steel ring surrounding a showerhead to hang a shower curtain. "My mother told me this used to be a bedroom before they got plumbing. Can you imagine that? It was probably a nursery. It's too small for a normal-sized bed."

They descended the stairs, and she once again put her hand on his arm. 'Would you mind checking the basement for me? I've always hated going down there."

She led him to a doorway under the stairs, opened it, picked up a flashlight. Checking that it worked, she gave it to him. "Stupidly, the light switch is at the bottom of the steps to the right."

"What am I looking for?"

"There should be nothing down there but spiders." She paused. "Or maybe a snake. Be careful." She stood at the top of the steps waiting for him.

Using the flashlight, Adam carefully descended the wooden steps. He could feel them give a little under his weight. He wasn't sure of his footing and tested each wooden step. He could feel cobwebs, or spider webs, brushing by his face as he descended. At the bottom of the steps, he found a pushbutton switch and pressed it. An old-school fluorescent fixture illuminated the room. The smell of dusty dry rot was mixed with a musty smell that belied occasional dampness.

He looked around, walked into the room and looked under the stairs. All he saw was cobwebs. The shelves were empty except for a few empty old blue canning jars, the kind his grandmother used to preserve tomatoes from her garden.

Back at the bottom of the steps he looked up at her. "Nothing but a few old canning jars."

She looked relieved. "No snakes?"

He shook his head.

"Not even dead ones?"

"No."

"Thanks."

After locking up the house, she took his arm once again. "I can't thank you enough." Her mood hadn't improved. "I've made a chocolate cake. Can I tempt you?" There were always desserts available on the weekend.

"Sure." He thought she'd lead him up to her apartment, but instead, she led him into the restaurant dining room. Indeed, there were now several desserts in cake stands on the counter. A chocolate cake and two pies. She must have brought them down while he was in the shower.

The piece of cake she placed in front of him looked like a quarter of the whole cake. "Rosie, I can't eat that much cake."

"Oh, go on. If you can't finish it now, take it upstairs and have it later." She poured coffee. Before sitting down, she went behind the counter and pulled out a bottle of whiskey. "I could use a drink. How about you?"

Adam gently shook his head. "No, thank you. I don't drink."

"Not even just a little?" she asked encouragingly.

He waited a beat to decide whether to tell her that he was sober. He decided against it and simply said, "Really, no, thank you. But you go ahead."

They sat companionably in the corner of the dining room. They weren't really visible through the forest of chair legs balanced on the tabletops. The conversation was casual and grew into a companionable silence that Adam decided to break. "What did you expect to find over there?" referring to their inspection of her old family home.

She appeared to consider his question and whether or not to answer it honestly. "I was at once hoping to find Henry hiding there and, at the same time, fearing that I'd find him hurt or worse." She took a bite of chocolate cake and washed it down with coffee. "Of course, there could have been someone else there, but that was less likely."

Adam could feel his chest tighten in empathy. She was worried about Henry, and her fear that something had happened to him was palpable. More than once in the past week, he had thought that it was more likely that something terrible had happened to Henry. If he had just run away, he could have called her, texted her, or even sent a postcard in that time. He must know that his absence would torment her.

The silence lasted a while, and Rosie broke it by changing the subject. "How did you finally get rid of Blaine Lamano?"

"We talked while I ate my lunch, and then I told him I had to clean up. I just led him out the front door."

"I wish I could do that. Hell, I wish I had seen it. He can be a real pain in the ass. Always has been. I don't know what Manda sees in that man."

"You know what they say." Adam raised a brow.

She waited.

"Love is blind… but the neighbors ain't."

At that, she laughed heartily. "That's a good one. Where did you hear that?"

"From a gossipy woman who ran a laundromat in New Orleans." He paused for a moment, then added, "Our conversation was interesting, though; we talked about his brother Jaimie and Henry."

Her eyebrows raised. "Did you now? That's something. I'm curious."

"He said he didn't think his brother liked him and that Henry was his brother's best friend."

"That was true enough, though I wouldn't say that Jaimie disliked him or Blake. He was a good three or four years older than they were. No teenager wants a kid hanging around him, especially some of the things teenagers get up to." She leaned into the table and lowered her voice in a gossipy, confidential way. "Even when he was a kid, he was such a pain in the ass. Henry, Jamie, and Henry's cousin Toby were a kind of posse. They were always together. When you saw one, you always saw another, if not all three. Blaine dogged them like a lost puppy. He never left them alone. Always trailing after them. They had to hide to get away from him. Everyone knew it. It became almost a running joke."

"When he talked, it sounded like he really looked up to his brother."

"I'm sure he did, at least at first." She thought for a moment and then continued. "They were in high school when Blaine and Blake turned thirteen. Blaine's voice changed, and they kind of let him hang out with them sometimes. Then it just stopped. This was before Henry and I got together, so I don't really know what happened. I never asked Henry. And Henry never said a word about it."

TWENTY-SEVEN

The Friday evening service at the First Pentecostal Church of Ur was uneventful, mostly because Adam's company was monopolized by Elf's girlfriend Grace and Tom (Junior) Delgado. Why they chose to sit with him rather than with their respective families puzzled Adam. Perhaps they felt some affinity toward him, or perhaps they just wanted to make him feel welcome; he wasn't sure.

Unsurprisingly, Elf was not with them. Adam doubted that he would ever return to Ur, especially if Grace's mother didn't warm up to him.

Elf's other misgivings about Grace had to do with their age difference and Grace's indiscreet chattiness. She was needlessly expository. Because he wasn't sure what Grace had said about him after he left the service to take Adam back to the Pioneer's Rest, he now worried that one or both of the people he was hoping to avoid might try to contact him again if Grace gave them enough information. He had pointedly said that one was a man *of* influence and the other was a sexual sadist. Both had been his clients when, under the influence of addiction, he would do anything to get the money for a fix.

Tambourine in hand, Eunice led the singing again. Adam wondered if it were her regular gig. She didn't have a bad voice, but it wasn't great either. The same young man accompanied her on the keyboard. They were joined by a middle-aged man on an electric guitar. Again, Luis wasn't there.

Claudia, the widow of Tommy Delgado, sat in the front row with her three youngest children. Pastor Lehman's widow did not attend.

A guest speaker, perhaps one of the new pastoral hopefuls, delivered a fire and brimstone service that ended in an altar call with two people going forward to be saved. At that point, Adam once again felt glances as if the congregation were waiting for him to get up and get saved.

Adam heard a woman sitting behind him say, "Those two again. You wonder what they get up to between services that they feel the need to be re-saved every time there's an altar call." Tom had heard them too and seemed to find it funny, while Grace was scandalized. "They shouldn't say things like that," she whispered to Adam. "You never know."

These people talk in code, Adam thought. "You never know what?" he asked, thinking she'd quote some Bible verse he was unfamiliar with.

"They may have fallen from grace," she said.

Tom sighed meaningfully.

Adam had no idea what his reaction meant. Adam wondered if Pentecostals believe in mortal and venial sins the way Roman Catholics do. "Well, God always does, even in advance, right?"

She furrowed her brow. "Does what?"

"He always knows."

"Amen," she said.

Adam blinked. He wasn't sure if he understood anything of the conversation. He would never make a good Pentecostal, not that he had been considering it. Growing up, he could never fully understand how God could know what would happen and then blame the sinner for doing it. In religious environments, this one in particular, he was conscious of his own ignorance of contextual cues. At least as an altar boy he knew when to sit, when to stand, and when to kneel but never had any real idea as to why. A CCD teacher once tried to explain it all to him, but when he asked too many questions, she got frustrated, patted him on the shoulder, and told him he would understand one day. Even then, he wondered if she had understood or even listened to his questions. Grace reminded him of her.

Tom and Grace both continued to cling to Adam during the social time after the service. He couldn't find a reason to drift away from them. He had hoped to hear more of the gossip he had heard the previous Wednesday. Surely someone would let something slip, something other people might not notice, but to him, as a stranger, it might stick out or catch his attention.

Standing near the back wall of the social hall, with his hands in his pockets and trying to make conversation with quiet Tom and chatty Grace, Tom's younger brother Ben, the one who had seemed the least tolerant of the customs of the memorial service, joined them. He asked Grace, "Where's your boyfriend?"

Elf had spent an evening playing video games with the boy the previous week. Adam guessed he was hoping to do it again. Adam felt his heart sink, thinking how lost the kid must feel in the confusion of having lost his father. He must have connected with Elf. Adam smiled to himself. *Elf was easy to connect to.*

Briefly, Adam thought of reaching out to Ben, saying something like, *I hear you like video games. What is your favorite?* However, he wasn't in that room to make young Ben feel better after losing his dad. He was there to *not investigate*, as per the instructions of Baxter and Chucho. Of course, an evening of video games with a kid that needed to talk might be useful.

Tom answered his brother's question. "Elf has to work."

"How's Elf doing?" Adam interjected. He wondered if Elf had said anything about the visit they had in the diner.

"Okay, I guess," Tom answered again. "Not a lot of free time."

"He's working double shifts these days. The diner just lost another cook," Grace added.

"Doesn't that interfere with his classes?" Adam asked.

Both Grace and Tom nodded. "He's pretty close with his teachers," Tom said. "A lot of the assignments are online. He's keeping up."

Adam pretended to be merely curious. "Did he ever say why he wanted to leave the service that night? He seemed to insist on giving me a ride back to my room." Adam was relatively certain that Elf would have really debated whether to confide in her about why he wanted to get away.

"No, he just said he was tired and knew you were both staying at the Rest."

"Did Matt pick you up at the bus station?" Tom directed his question to Grace.

"Of course. He always does. We had dinner at the casino, and then I walked here."

"Still won't come in, huh?"

She shook her head. "He was here last Friday, of course. I hoped it would make a difference. Keep him in prayer, please."

So, Tom and Grace hadn't traveled from Broken Arrow together. Adam wondered if Grace had spent a day or more with her father, but given her mother's reaction to his asking about him, he decided against asking her. It was, after all, a pretty safe assumption.

Grace excused herself to visit the restroom, and Ben went for more cookies.

"Matthew is a good friend of yours?"

Tom nodded. "He is closer to Grace, though."

"He seems to really like you both," Adam said.

Tom shifted his gaze. The pained expression on his face revealed his struggle between discretion and honesty. He glanced from side to side to make sure he could be discreet. "It's kind of a secret. Matt is Grace's half-brother—from another mother. It's why her parents divorced. Nobody that knows about it talks about it. Their dad just went away. He tried to support his children, but two women and two kids is a lot, so both families had a rough time. I probably shouldn't have said anything." He seemed to take his last statement to heart.

"Don't worry, I won't say anything about that."

He shrugged his shoulders. "Grace says that her dad is doing better and trying harder now, but Matt isn't much interested. She visits her dad all the time. Matt doesn't. He thinks it's too little, too late. His dad bought his truck for him, and he keeps sending Matt presents. They talk once in a while, but not too often."

"I had the impression that Matt was a really good friend of yours, not just Grace. That you were the glue between the two of them."

Tom shook his head. "When we were kids, me and Matt were pretty good friends. School, scouts, judo lessons, but… " he hesitated, looking for the right words, "… it's different now."

Adam stared at him. Instinctively he knew, or thought he knew, what Tom was saying. The way Matt had scanned Adam's body with his eyes had reminded him of the way patrons in the gay bar back in New Orleans had done. That day when the three of them sat together on the bench in the park consoling Tom, Adam had the distinct feeling that Matt was too solicitous. He lowered his voice to barely above a whisper. "Is it because Matt is in love with you?"

Tom almost jumped out of his skin. "I'm a Christian, and I'm not gay. And keep your voice down."

Adam felt his guts tighten. "I didn't say you were. But that would make things kind of awkward between you."

"Look, Matt has a hard time here. I love him, but not that way. People aren't exactly accepting him. And Grace and I, we're his only real friends. If he could get out of Ur, he would. I wish he would. Grace wants him to stay and come to church. After hearing Elf's story, Grace thinks the Lord can fix Matt, make him straight, but… " He shrugged. His eyes grew distant.

"I don't think it really works that way," Adam said. "I've known a lot of gay people."

Tom sighed. "With God, all things are possible, but I'm not so sure that God is interested in that. The school I go to won't accept people who still struggle with same-sex attraction, no matter what."

Adam could almost see questions like flotsam swirling in Tom's mind. "Tom, I'm sorry I brought it up."

"Don't be. It's alright. But it's not something we talk openly about."

Adam silently nodded. He couldn't help wondering how many secrets the small town of Ur harbored. In many ways, from the outside, Ur might almost seem an idyllic place, but from the moment he arrived, he could sense something too nice, too idyllic, a superficial tranquility that disguised a seething underbelly.

The room was dark. The only light came from his laptop screen. The Puppeteer had invested in a gaming chair. It swiveled, and he could lean back comfortably without feeling like he was going to topple over. A window fan to vent the smoke from the occasional cigarette hummed. This was his private place.

It had been years since he and his wife stopped sleeping in the same room. They got along. They both cared immensely for one another. After intimacy had lost its luster, there was no point. She was a morning person; he was a night owl. They had grown comfortably apart.

There were now three cameras, two in the laundromat and a wide-angled one in the school tornado shelter. His young friend had helped him set up the ability to live stream and record video so he could watch in real time and archive the footage he wanted to keep. He had even learned how to edit just to save the best bits. He wanted to watch Henry suffer, and he wanted to keep that memory forever.

He liked that phrase, *young friend*. He thought it was funny. It was so easy to manipulate that kid. He could get him to do anything he wanted him to do. Controlling him was enough—for now. He smirked at how a simple offer of friendship, a little of, I-know-what-it's-like, and the offer more money than he'd ever earn in Ur. He seemed amenable, so approaching him had been easy. He was eager to do anything for the adventure, for the profit, and a bit of revenge. More than anything, he wanted to show them all there was more to him than they thought.

In those hours he had spent waiting quietly in the shelter at the Pioneer's Rest, a fantasy germinated and grew. No windows, only artificial light, the monotony of an environment designed to accommodate people only long enough to outlast a storm. It was to be for only a month or two but turned into six. It was the only way at the time.

The isolation inspired him. He was supposed to be resting, but while the body rests, the mind travels. The sounds of Henry banging away in the kitchen upstairs, playing his rock music, working just a few hours a day and living his life without worry, without struggle, always getting that stupid woman Rosie to take care of him. Life wasn't fair, and sometimes, you want to, need to, settle the score.

When Henry finally put two and two together, the idiot that he was, and when he ran away with his secret, it finally gave him a reason to convert a dream into reality.

The problem was Henry wasn't suffering. Every time he looked at the footage or opened the live stream, he saw Henry not suffering. He watched Henry pace. He watched Henry do push-ups, crunches, and jumping jacks. When Henry broke into the emergency food stores, he hoped, really hoped, to see him find the whiskey. He saw Henry looking for tools, trying to fix the breaker bar on the door. There wasn't much he could do with a can opener, but there was the Allen wrench. He hadn't found it yet, but oh, it would be so good to see Henry's disappointment when it didn't work.

He sat up and reached for the wireless mouse. He could never get used to the square patch on the laptop meant to be used as a touch mouse. Opening the channel to live stream of the shelter, he saw Henry lying on a cot, his face to the wall, his back to the camera. He strained his eyes to see if Henry was still breathing. He turned up the volume on his speaker, and to his disappointment, he could hear a gentle snore. *The man was good for a six-pack of beer a day, for Christ's sake. You'd think the DTs would have him shaking by now.*

He looked at his watch. It was nearly 7:15 p.m. He switched channels to the two cameras in the laundromat. His screen split into a gallery view so he could watch both cameras at the same time. He knew the package arrived between four and five p.m., but the drop was scheduled for 7:30.

This was the first time they were trying this dead drop system. It meant a little less profit; after all, someone had to pick up the drop in Ur, not Oklahoma City, and they had to get their cut. With the casino so close, no one even looked at strangers on that side of town anymore, at least not on a Friday night.

The laundromat was the perfect place, especially on a Friday evening. The loss of the last shipment, not to mention the penalty he had to pay to make up for that lost shipment. The choice was no choice. Make up for it or your lights go out.

With Lehman out of the way, somebody had to take over the operation. It might as well be him. It might have been easier for Lehman to run the money through the church, but he had businesses too and could do it just as well. He looked at his watch again and compared it to the time on his computer screen. It was close. He waited, watching intently.

Finally, when the timestamp reached 7:30, the kid walked into the laundromat carrying a basket of laundry. He walked down the line of washers and set his basket on the top loader next to the machine with the jammed coin slot, the one that had been vandalized and couldn't be repaired. He reached to the bottom of his basket. Casually checking his surroundings, he pulled out the vacuum-sealed, gift-wrapped package, placed it in the bottom of the out-of-service washer, and dumped the clothes on top of the package. Closing the lid, he placed the empty basket on top of the washer and walked out.

The drop was half complete. Now for the pickup.

The timestamp had reached 7:50 when the person for the pickup came in. As planned, he walked directly to the washer with the basket on top. The laundromat was empty, but he still surreptitiously checked his surroundings. That guy was good but not good enough to notice the cameras. He picked out the package, covered it with the clothes, and carried the basket out of the laundromat. He had just watched two kilos of fentanyl pills walk out of his laundromat with a street value of nearly half a million dollars. Of course he wouldn't get all that. He'd get part of Lehman's cut, but his laundromat business was not tax-exempt like the church was. He couldn't get away with cooking the books that much.

Perfect. It worked just the way they planned. This way was smoother, faster, and, at least for him, safer. Even if the cops or the DEA caught on, what would they do except subpoena the recordings? What did that have to do with him?

"Oh no, officer, I had no idea." He said it out loud, and it sounded good to him. He was out of the loop entirely. This was perfection itself. Clicking the archive button, he muttered to himself. "Who says spy movies are useless?"

He pulled a bottle of beer out of the tiny fridge under his desk. He didn't drink often these days, but this was worth celebrating. He popped the top, leaned back in his new chair, and drank, savoring the flavor, wanting to make it last.

Things were coming together. Delgado got what was coming to him. The idiot was too stupid for words, and all his self-righteous bullshit was sickening. His constant droning about serving the lord maddened him. When Delgado started asking questions, Lehman said he had to go. Silencing that sanctimonious asshole was a pleasure, and watching him fall from that church roof was like Lucifer falling from heaven, beautiful.

The timing was off, though. It made that guy, Adam, stay in town and messed up the delivery of the package. It took a lot to clean up that mess, especially when he took it to the police. If they had only gotten to him sooner! At least he wasn't too nosey. But it's time for him to go before he messes things up again.

He closed down the program and switched off the laptop. It won't be long now. Henry will find that whiskey, and he'll drink. And that loose end will be all tied up.

Halona Beck had walked the distance from the road carrying more food for her eldest grandson, Henry. The place where Jeremy parked had a phone signal, so he was happy to sit and play on his phone while he waited for her.

She hadn't been to the shack for a couple of days. Henry had plenty of food. After all, Toby was taking care of him, or, at least, he was supposed to be taking care of him—if he remembered. Toby wasn't so good at remembering, especially after his wife died. His wife had been particularly good at remembering and everyone knew that she did his remembering for him.

The walk had tired her out. The grass was already tall and made it hard to walk. She had to keep her eyes to the ground to be careful about holes, and with the higher grass, snakes were probably under a rock or in one of those holes. It was too hot in the day. She kept her eyes open and her ears too for the sound of a rattle. She wasn't scared.

She muttered to herself. "Don't bother them, and they won't bother you." That rattle was a warning. It was fair play in her mind.

She saw the shack in the distance. Chuckling to herself, she remembered how surprised Henry had been when she found him, as if he and Toby, or any of her grandchildren, ever did anything she didn't know about. She shook her head thinking of it. *At least not when they were kids.*

She found the shack empty, the door wide open, bits of paper on the floor, and animals had been inside eating Henry's food. How long had he been gone? She turned and headed toward Toby's house. The walk was almost as long as it would have been back to where Jeremy waited, but if she found Henry and Toby together, they could both have a good meal. And Toby could ride her back to Jeremy.

The back door to Toby's house was open. She went in and put her bags on the kitchen counter. She called out for Toby and Henry. There was only silence. The only sound came from Toby's cat expecting a treat. She walked through the house to the living room and looked out the window. Toby was parking his car. She opened the front door and stood outside.

Toby was surprised but glad to see her. "Hatak Chita," he greeted her.

They exchanged a few words in Choctaw, and she asked him where Henry had gone.

He wasn't sure how to answer her. He knew she had found Henry at the shack and wondered why she was here looking for Henry.

"You know where he is," he answered vaguely.

"He's not there."

"Maybe he's walking," he suggested.

"Maybe he hasn't been there long enough for the animals to claim his food."

Toby stopped short. She could see him pondering. Suddenly, with alarm, he ran around the house. Going back through the house, she could see him running in the direction of the shack. *For a fat man, he could still run,* she thought.

She busied herself in the kitchen, wiping down counters and washing the few dishes in the sink, always looking out the back window toward the shack. Her heart was beating in her chest, and though her hands were in warm water, they felt cold.

Eventually he came into view. It looked like he was carrying a rifle. As he approached the house, she went out onto the back porch.

"How did you get here, Grandmother?"

"Jeremy is parked on the road. Where is Henry?"

Toby was loath to answer and wasn't sure what to say. "Come on. I'll take you to Jeremy. You give this to Baxter." He handed her a piece of folded paper.

She opened it. Her eyes passed over the words and then over them again, more slowly. She found herself shaking inside, partly in anger and the rest in fear. Finally looking up, Toby was already in the car.

"Come grandmother," he called to her.

She moved more quickly than she thought she could. "Is this true?" She held up the paper.

"Henry thinks so."

She remembered how Henry's voice had trembled last time they spoke—alone, drained. He hadn't told her everything. He hadn't told her about this. Then she thought of how Toby would be feeling. How long had it been since he saw Henry? If he forgot Henry for even a day, he'd be blaming himself as much as the man named in this note.

As he drove, he explained about Henry's reluctance to talk about his predicament, the signal of the doorstop, and their agreement to hide the story in the place they used to keep their marijuana."

"The tin box in the hollow tree," she said.

In shock, he turned and looked at her. "How did you know about that?"

She shook her head and used the explanation she gave to them as children. "The prairie dogs told me. Besides, it's my job to know."

He pulled up across from the beetle. They were facing in opposite directions.

"Where did you get that rifle?"

"I left it for Henry in case he needed it."

"Why are you bringing it now?" she asked, fearing she already knew the answer.

"If he's done anything to Henry," he tried to control himself, "I might need it."

She could see the anger inside his eyes even as they flickered toward Jeremy while waving at him from across the street. She knew that nothing she could say would change what would happen. She bit her lip, knowing Toby's threat was no empty boast. And if he found the man responsible before the cops did, another of her grandsons would be in jail or worse.

TWENTY-EIGHT

Adam reached the sports field early. More than an hour would pass before sunrise. The field was absolutely black. He paced off an area big enough to do his wrestling drills. Having checked for obstacles, he laid his flashlight on its side as a reference point and began his routine.

Suddenly, he was not alone. There was only time for half a thought, a ninja covered in black. The throw took him completely by surprise. Someone grabbed at him and was flying through the air. He had no sense of how close or far away the ground was. He landed on his neck. He felt his neck muscles spasm and swell while flashes of bright lights from inside his brain blinded him. Then it was dark, absolutely black. He couldn't even find the light of his flashlight.

He time-traveled like in a dream to his last wrestling match, the accident, the loss of time and the long recovery. It might have been seconds, minutes, or hours, or years. Nothing made sense. He was immediately nauseous and dizzy with pain.

Then he could feel the grass spiking through his hair, and he was back in Ur. *Not again*, he thought. *I can't go through this again.* He heard voices and tried to focus, but the effort was too much.

"Is he dead?" someone asked. The voice was spine-chilling, a put-on falsetto psychotic voice. Adam heard the response in spurts. "I don't...

knocked out… still breathing." This voice sounded younger, less weathered, and less confident.

He could feel his heartbeat in his ears and a metallic taste in his mouth. Was it blood? Too dry to be blood. The voice came into focus. "He hit his head pretty hard," the younger man said. "I really don't like this. It's going too far. I don't know why we had to do this."

"Because he's too close. He started asking questions. He's got to go. If he dies, he had an accident doing his crazy exercises. If he lives, he'll get the message. He's been sniffing around. He knows about your father, and eventually, he'll figure it out. Especially since he knows about your boyfriend, Tom. You want to get paid, don't you?"

"He's not my boyfriend."

"You'd suck him off if he let you."

His face burned. He ripped off the mask. "He's not gay."

"What does he care as long as he gets serviced?"

Adam's mind continued to swim in a sea of confusion. He could hear their voices, but what they were saying didn't make sense. Was it a dream? Instinctively, he knew he shouldn't move or try to get up. He had landed on his neck. Moving might not only be painful but might also cause more damage. Even the thought of movement sent excruciating pain shooting through his head and down his back. The muscles in his neck kept getting tighter and tighter. He remained still, his head swimming in and out of consciousness.

"He hit his head pretty hard. He'll need a doctor," the younger one said, having second thoughts.

"You mean he hit his pretty head hard." He snickered. Fingertips traced Adam's jawbone and chin and then ran across his lips. "Such a pretty man. So handsome. So strong. And such beautiful pain. Too bad we won't be here to see you wake up. If you wake up, that is. With a nitrile-gloved hand, he pulled a folded piece of paper out of his shirt pocket and slipped it into Adam's shorts, taking the opportunity to grope him.

Adam didn't process the unpleasant sensation. At that moment, he had time-traveled back to the Moonstone Diner. He could hear Elf's fear and disgust as he spoke about the sexual sadist who had been one of his johns back then. He could hear him lower his voice so as to not be overheard, though, by that time, the booths around them were empty.

The eyes of the younger man flashed in anger and disgust. The more he got to know this guy, the creepier he became. He was enjoying this. He turned away in disgust. "Fuck," he whispered under his breath. "This isn't what it was supposed to be. I never signed up for this."

The throw had been harder than he planned. He was used to practicing with people who knew how to fall and who knew what to expect. He had never actually used judo outside of practice. It surprised him how easy it was, and at the same time, it sickened him. *That was just practice, you idiot. Who gives a rat's ass that he found out about who my father is, except for the job.* He reprimanded himself, and it made him sick.

He wanted to get away, to anonymously report this so Adam could get help, but he knew he couldn't do that. He needed the money too badly. He couldn't endanger the operation. They just needed to keep Henry on ice for a while until the money came in and then he'd be out of Ur forever. As long as he got the money soon.

The last thing Adam heard made no sense at all. "Should we put him in the shelter with Henry?"

Then it was total darkness inside and out.

She was nearly finished prepping the dining room. Saturdays were consistently busy from open to close. On Sundays there were two rushes, one before and another after church services. The ones who wanted breakfast before church kept looking at their watches and wondering what was taking so long. The lunch-after-church crowd was less intense, but they lingered longer, many well after closing time. Saturday was nice and steady.

She started talking to Adam as she pushed the swinging door to the kitchen. She stopped short. He wasn't there. She placed her hand above the surface of the grill. It was still cold. She looked at her watch just to be sure she wasn't early.

He's probably running late, she told herself. She turned on the grill, switched on the fryer, and began taking trays out of the cooler. She set them on the prep table. Adam had done a great job preparing for the weekend. She tried to remember the order in which he laid out his trays. When she finished doing that, he still hadn't come down.

She crossed her arms over her chest, trying to suppress the flutter of alarm she felt in her chest. She told herself she was just too sensitive because of Henry. Adam was probably just in the shower. He'd be down straight away. He'd be glad of her help.

The tension rose with each passing minute, and she could feel it tightening in her chest. It was too much for her. She walked through the laundry room and up the back steps to the second floor. She stood in the middle of the common area. The doors to both bathrooms and the door to Adam's room were wide open. She was confused. The space was unnaturally empty. Over the last couple of weeks, she had been close to either tears or panic. Now both came to the surface.

Had he left without telling her?

She calmed slightly walking into his room. A small pile of laundry lay in the corner. Both his bags, the rucksack and the duffel bag were on the floor beside the wash-up stand. She looked out his window at the park, hoping to see him walking back to the rest.

He just lost track of time. She reasoned. She knew he did his exercises in the sports field behind the school. She didn't see him. His puzzle was nearly finished. She shook her head to clear it. "Really. He just lost track of time."

She imagined walking around the school, seeing him bounce and roll around the way he did. There might not be time now for him to shower, or would she just tell people to wait a few minutes? She was glad it wasn't Sunday when the early crowd was always pressed for time. *Good thing I started up the grill and the fryer.*

Half determined and half desperate, she went down the front steps, out of the lobby, and across the street. The morning air still carried a freshness that the sun would burn off quickly. She strode through the park and around the school. There didn't seem to be anyone there. The place was empty, still, and strangely silent.

Then she saw him in the middle of the field, lying flat on his back. She darted across the field.

Falling to her knees, she called, "Adam, Adam. Are you alright? Adam?" His skin was pale. His breathing shallow. She shook him by the shoulder. He winced, and a cry of pain rumbled in his chest, but he did not open his eyes. "Adam? Adam?" Her cries became more urgent.

With the sharp stab of pain in his neck, his eyes sprang open, and in the light of the sun, closed again immediately.

"What happened? Are you alright? Can you sit up?"

In his confusion, he didn't know which question to answer or even if he knew the answers. Through a dry throat, all he could say was "No" and whisper, "my neck." He seemed to be in such pain she could almost feel it herself.

"Your neck. Oh, Jesus. Don't move." She spoke through restrained sobs.

She pulled her cell phone out of her pocket. Her hands were shaking. She dialed 911.

"Just stay still, honey. I'm calling for help."

Jeremy parked the Beetle in one of the diagonal spaces in front of the sheriff's substation. "Do you want me to come in with you, Gram?"

"No. We have to talk business." She had said nothing to him about what happened. When he asked her how she met up with Toby, she didn't answer. She had told no one about Henry in the shack, especially not Jeremy. "If it takes too long, go to the Rest and have breakfast. Tell Rosie I'll pay her later. Maybe I'll meet you there."

She got out of the car. The day was starting to heat up, but it would never be as hot as Toby seemed. She worried about him. She worried about Henry. What had happened to him? He didn't run away. He didn't take the gun. He didn't put the doorstop where he and Toby agreed for a signal. She hoped that Toby would not find that man. She didn't want to have another grandson in prison.

The front desk at the substation was empty so she walked past it and down the corridor. There was a faint smell of cigarette smoke and air freshener. *That other one, the sheriff, he smokes.* She could see Baxter sitting at the big desk at the end of the hall. He was typing on his computer.

He was startled when she walked into his office. "Hatak Ohoyo," he said.

She spoke to him in Choctaw, but he didn't seem to understand.

"Henry is missing," she said in English.

"I know. We've been looking for him."

She breathed deeply. Shaking her head, she said, "Before now he just wasn't here. He wasn't missing. Now he is missing. I'm afraid for him."

He paused and thought. "Please sit down," he said. He indicated the chair on the other side of the desk. "What do you mean?"

"He wasn't lost. He just wasn't here."

"You knew where he was?"

She dipped her chin in a single nod. "He's my grandson. I found him. I knew where he would hide. I brought him food."

"Did you tell anyone?"

"I didn't tell anyone anything, not even Rosie when she was crying so much. That was what he wanted me to do."

"Why not?"

She kept her face calm, but surely, he could figure out the answer to that question. "Henry was *hiding*." She stressed the last word. "He was *safe* where he was. He didn't do anything wrong. I told him he should talk to you, but he was afraid to come back."

The chair squeaked as Baxter sat back. He considered. "And now he isn't where he was?"

She shook her head. "No, I went there, and he's gone. I'm very worried."

"Tell me so I can help."

She proceeded to tell him the story. She tried to skip through the story to be quicker, but he kept asking questions, so she slowed down and told him like it happened. As she finished, she said "Now, I can give this to you." She pulled out the piece of folded paper. "You will understand why Henry was afraid to come back."

Baxter opened the paper and began reading. His eyes followed the text. It was

hand written in a careful cursive hand." He cleared the desk in front of him and flattened the paper down on the desk. Forensically, the paper itself was already compromised, but the content was revealing. He read intently, in the back of his mind, he also recalled Henry's reaction when he had been asked about the gun in the old tornado shelter.

Baxter finished the note and read it a second time. She was watching him. He read with even more intensity, his mind putting details in chronological order. When Baxter had asked him about the rifle in the shelter, his answer had been that he had never seen it before. That could have been a perfectly honest answer. He wasn't lying. He had doubted the answer at the time. He had thought it possible that Henry simply didn't want to be associated with the gun.

Baxter felt his heart sink. He could hear his own question to Henry, "Had anyone you didn't know come through the kitchen or go out through the back door?" Again, Henry had answered the questions honestly, without embellishment.

Fuck, he thought. *Of course he knew him. Henry knew who put the rifle in the shelter. He knew it. He knew him! Why didn't he open his mouth?*

Baxter had sensed that he was holding something back but decided to follow up with him another time. By the time he was ready to question Henry again, Henry was gone.

"Why didn't you give this to me right away?" He looked up at the old woman.

Her hands were gripping the hard wooden arms of the chair as if she were getting ready to stand up. "I just got it today. I came straight here," she answered plainly.

"I mean, why didn't you give this to me when you first arrived?"

"I was telling you about this and answering your questions. What can you do with that piece of paper without knowing the story behind it?"

He held it up. "This is evidence."

"And I gave it to you and told you where I got it."

"Did Toby read this?"

"Toby read it before I read it." She hoped he would understand what that might mean.

An alert came over Baxter's cell phone. It was a text message from the 911 dispatcher.

The sun had already dried the dew from the grass, but the scent of wet grass remained in the air. Deputy Isi was the first to arrive. She tried to clear the area around Adam to make room for the paramedics. Rosie refused to move.

"I'm staying with him." She was caressing the back of his hand with the tip of her finger. She thought her gentle touch should be alright and would remind him that he wasn't alone. Someone who cared was with him.

"Okay, but we need the room for the paramedics to work."

"Ayasha." Rosie used her full name to mean business. "Until then, I'm staying with him."

Isi walked around the area trying to determine if it was a crime scene or merely the scene of an accident. There was a flashlight lying on the ground some distance away, but there was nothing to indicate the scene of a crime. There were no external wounds that she could see. No other objects to be found.

Adam's mind swam to the surface. He was aware of Rosie's touch. Somehow he knew it was her, and she made him feel safe. He wanted to tell her that Henry was in the shelter in the school. He didn't know how he knew that, but he was sure of it.

He tried hard to speak. He stirred. His face twitched, and tears dripped from his closed eyes. He could feel the sun on his face and didn't want to open his eyes.

"Just relax, Adam. The paramedics are on the way. Don't worry. Just stay calm and don't move, honey." Rosie tried to comfort him.

He tried to speak. In his mind he was carrying on full conversations, trying to communicate with her. Why couldn't she understand? Rosie, check the shelter. Henry is in the shelter. His cracked lips moved only slightly, and sound barely came out. Rosie was reminded of old women saying the rosary in church. All she could make out was the word *shelter*.

Baxter was next to arrive. He had sprinted from the substation. When he saw the location on the dispatcher alert, he knew it had to be Adam, and he didn't believe even for a moment that this was an accident. Breathing hard, sweat beading on his temples. He scanned the scene out of habit.

"Deputy, secure the scene."

"I've looked. There's no evidence of a crime scene. There's just nothing here but a flashlight."

"Bag it. It might be evidence."

He crouched down next to Adam. "Hey buddy. What happened?"

"He can't move or talk," Rosie said. "All I know is that he said something about his neck. And he keeps muttering something about the shelter."

"The shelter?"

Rosie explained. "He must be delirious. There's nothing down there. We were just down there the other day. We think someone might have broken in through the alley entrance. I told Aya about it. We just put on a new lock."

Just then they heard the ambulance circling the school through the gravel parking lot. The ambulance drove out onto the playing field. As the EMTs emerged, Rosie, Baxter and Deputy Isi gave them space.

The EMTs worked on him for a short while. They took his vitals, stabilized his neck. And prepared a stretcher. As they moved him to a stretcher, in a burst of pain he screamed, "HENRY SHELTER."

The stretcher disappeared into the back of the ambulance.

"I'm going to the hospital with him," Rosie insisted, beginning to move toward the ambulance.

Baxter stopped her. "The hospital won't talk to you anyway. You're not next of kin. But I'll bring you with me when I go."

"I want to go now," she insisted.

"Yes, right away."

He turned to Deputy Isi. "Deputy, go with them and stick with him as long as they let you. If he says anything, write it down. I'll be there as soon as I can. Miss Rosie will come with me."

Deputy Isi climbed into the back of the ambulance with the paramedics. Together they watch the ambulance drive away, sirens blaring. They began to walk back toward the Pioneer's Rest. Before they reached the curb, however, they both stopped, looked at one another, and said at the same time. "The other shelter."

Rosie padded her pockets. "I don't have my keys."

"I have mine," Baxter said, turning around. "Let's go."

Baxter was already finding the right key as they approached the back door of the school. "Rosie, perhaps you should wait here."

"The hell I will."

They entered the basement of the school and switched on the lights. Their footsteps on the concrete floor echoed against the hard cement block walls. A faint electric hum from overhead fluorescents became the background for the sound of their hearts beating in their ears.

Baxter turned the handle and pulled. The door opened, and there stood Henry in the middle of the room holding a bottle of whiskey. He was thinner, had dark circles under his eyes, and his hair was unkempt. He clutched a bottle of whiskey in one trembling hand.

Henry's shoulders sagged when he spotted Baxter and Rosie. "Hey, Rosie… Bax… Don't let that door close behind you or we'll all be stuck in here," he said, his voice quivering with an odd mix of relief and anxiety."

Silent tears streamed down Rosie's face. Only when she hugged him, and he put his arms around her, did they turn into sobs.

Toby sat in his car, looking out the driver-side window, staring at one man in the crowd. Anger burned in his chest. His hand involuntarily reaching for the rifle. *One shot would end him*, Toby thought, his pulse thrumming. *But if I pull that trigger now, Henry might never come home— and I'd be locked up forever.* Out of the corner of his eye, he could see his grandmother and young Jeremy walking down the street toward the Rest. The very sight of her instilled control in him.

He got out of the car and walked across the street to join the crowd. Jeremy waved, and his grandmother looked up and saw him. It wouldn't be today. *It might not be today, but the day would come,* Toby vowed to himself. What was most important was getting Henry back.

There he was next to his wife, genially talking to other people waiting, smiling, shaking hands. His shirt tails hanging down like curtains from his belly. Combed hair, shining watch flashing in the sun. He seemed so natural, so comfortable. *He's a fucking psychopath.* No remorse, no fear, not even a hint of his true nature.

His grandmother had her eyes on Toby, not the man that had kidnapped Henry. He could feel her telling him to hold his temper. As he approached his grandmother and Jeremy, Toby slowed. He could sense his uncle's anger. It made him feel afraid even though he knew it wasn't directed at him.

She spoke to Toby in Choctaw. Her words made him breathe deep and slow. Anyone who knew him well might recognize him wrapping himself in an added blanket of control. He wanted to confront the bastard and demand that he tell him where Henry was. He wanted to grab him by the neck and beat the living shit out of him. His grandmother put her arm through his and held him tight. Her touch steadied him.

Jeremy saw a couple of his friends talking to Grace and Tom and took the opportunity to join them. Grace's mother was talking to the Lamanos. Eunice and her sister Claudia stood on either side of Luis, who kept looking at his watch. Others milled among the group. The general murmur was occasionally punctuated with laughter. Some of them were restless. One cupped his hands around his eyes to peer through the window. The lights in the Rest were on. What was taking so long?

His grandmother squeezed Toby's arm and jerked her head, pointing with her chin across the street. Sergeant Baxter was coming out of the park and crossing the street. He was greeted with waves and friendly calls of "Hey, Bax."

He joined the crowd, and in a gentle voice meant to draw understanding and patience, he explained that Adam, the cook, had had an accident while working out in the sports field. There were general indistinguishable murmurs. Manda Lamano looked horrified, covering her mouth with her hand. Luis looked concerned, and his eyes seemed to dart around the group. Blaine muttered under his breath in a soft voice, "Oh, dear God."

Baxter explained that the Pioneer's Rest wouldn't be opening today as Miss Rosie would be at the hospital with Adam. "... since he has no family here."

The group began to disperse to their cars, some agreeing to meet at the casino for their buffet. The eyes of Toby and his grandmother bored into Baxter's face. He could feel the pull of their stare. He approached them but was cut off by Jeremy.

"Gram, my friends want to go to McDonald's. Is it okay?"

She nodded.

"Take the car. Uncle Toby will take me home."

"I'm not allowed to drive without someone else." His eyes flickered toward Baxter.

"Take one of them with you," Toby said, indicating one of the older kids.

"Just be careful." Baxter winked at him.

He ran back to his friends.

As the crowd cleared, Baxter leaned close to them and whispered, "We have Henry. He's okay."

The immediate reaction, the reduction in tension, anger, and fear was palpable. Toby was visibly relieved, but the anger still burned in him.

"He's been through a lot. I'm going to take him to the hospital just to have a doctor look at him to make sure. I'll need to interview him, but you can come to the hospital to see him. He'll be glad of that."

"Help him to heal." His grandmother nodded.

"What about *him*? You're just going to let him go?" Toby's gaze was a tracer beam toward the man opening the car door for his wife.

Baxter put his hand on Toby's shoulder. "Soon. I promise. I've already requested the warrants."

Henry shifted in the seat, being careful of his ankle. When Baxter had gone to get his car, Rosie was full of questions, but he evaded answering her directly. He wouldn't admit that he had been frightened, frustrated, or, at times, felt hopeless. It had been his anger that kept him going, but even that was running out. All he would say was, "I'm sorry I couldn't tell you."

They stopped at the back door to the Rest, so Rosie could get her purse and turn off the kitchen equipment. Once she was out of earshot he said, "I didn't want to scare Rosie, but I got lots to tell you, Bax."

Baxter held up his hand. "Not yet," he said. "We need your statement to be clean. We need to do this by the book."

Rosie came out the back door of the Rest and slid into the back seat. "Any news about Adam?"

"Not yet." Baxter pulled out of the alley and headed toward the highway.

"Who's Adam?" Henry asked.

"The guest who's been filling in for you in the kitchen."

"Ah, right. My grandmother told me about him."

Rosie leaned forward in her seat, her seatbelt stretching across her bosom. "So, she knew where you were? She didn't tell me!"

Baxter interrupted. "Please, with all respect for what you've both been through, we'll need formal statements from both of you. If we all talk in the car, it might muddy the official record. So, for the time being, let's not catch-up just yet, please."

They fell silent. He could feel the tension rise in the car. "There will be plenty of time after you've seen the doctor."

"But I don't need a doctor, Bax. I'm fine. I'd rather just give my statement and go home." Henry protested, unconsciously flexing his ankle.

Baxter knew there would be no going home for Henry, not until his captor was in custody. "No, you have to see a doctor."

"There's nothing wrong with me."

"You're limping."

"Just a little. I twisted my ankle. It's okay. I'm fine."

Baxter was trying to be careful about what he said and what he allowed Henry to say in the car. He had already appealed on behalf of procedure. He'd try the personal touch. "Listen, Henry. Two things, and then the subject is closed. First, even if I was sure that you were fine, you have to give a statement. I couldn't let you go home before that. But if I don't take you to a doctor and you really need to see one, it'll be my ass. So, just do it for me."

"And how much of that whiskey did you drink before we found you, Henry Beck?" Rosie spoke up from the back seat.

"Not even a sip, Rose. I just found it. Probably some kids hid it there."

"Uh-huh." She didn't believe him. "I thought you gave up the hard stuff."

Out of the corner of his eye, Baxter could see the sly smile on Henry's face. "I did give it up. Not a drop. Nothing but beer for a long time." He glanced back at her. "If I'm honest, I think I might have if you didn't find me. I was considering it, but I didn't drink it." He paused. "A little while ago you were glad I'm alive, and now you're on me about a little whiskey. I'm telling you, I didn't even have a taste. But could you blame me if I had? I was trapped in there for Christ's sake."

She rummaged in her purse looking for chewing gum. "Here, get that whiskey off your breath before the doctor sees you."

"I'm telling you. I didn't drink any," he said.

"And how long has it been since you brushed your teeth?"

He took the gum. Baxter refused the offer, turned on his lights, and hit the gas.

TWENTY-NINE

Adam had uttered only three words since being placed into the ambulance. Deputy Aya Isi wrote them down in her notebook. The first two, a repeat from the field, "Henry" and "shelter," he said with the most force. They seemed to bother him most. He muttered the third as he sank back into unconsciousness. It sounded like ninja.

Despite the speeding with sirens blaring, it felt like the drive to the hospital took forever. She admired the EMTs and the ER staff for their efficiency. Everyone knew their job, knew what to do, and did it. Adam Alba was taken immediately for x-rays and an MRI.

Adam now lay in an examination room in Emergency, waiting to be admitted. They had asked Deputy Isi for information she didn't have. He hadn't had a wallet, ID, or any insurance information with him when the accident happened, and that unnecessarily slowed things up. They had cut off his clothes and covered him loosely with a hospital gown. The folded piece of paper they found in his shorts now lay in a plastic bag on the tray table beside his bed. Adam was now taped up with an IV. An oxygen hose pinched his nostrils. Sensor pads connected to a machine beeped his vitals—blood pressure and heart rate.

While the doctors and nurses came and went, Aya stood guard outside the examination room. Occasionally they asked her a question about how the accident happened or his medical history. She couldn't answer, but she tried her best.

When he was alone, she went back into the exam room, stood by his bed and grasped his hand just to let him know that someone was there. On one occasion, it felt like he tried to grasp back, but she couldn't be sure. Still, the gesture made her heart sink. He was a stranger in town. He was alone. He appeared peacefully asleep most of the time, but occasionally he'd surface, his eyes would flicker, and in a dry, raspy voice he would repeat, "Henry… shelter."

In a calm voice. Deputy Isi would reassure him. "Thank you. We found him. He's going to be alright." Her voice and her touch seemed to calm him, and back down he'd go.

When Sergeant Baxter arrived with Henry and Rosie, his badge got Henry, though apparently in good health and spirits, to an isolated room in the ER right away, ahead of everyone in the waiting room hoping to be seen. Rosie had to remain in the waiting room, but Isi suspected that it was more to keep their official statements clean than for any privacy or HIPAA regulation. Though he was in the isolated room, he still had to wait while the doctor tended to more urgent patients.

The doctor, a tall, robust woman who might have been in her forties, reviewed information about Adam on a computer in the nurses' station. Before the doctor went in to check Henry, she spoke to both Baxter and Isi about Adam. "There appears to be no obvious damage to the vertebrae or the spinal cord."

A nurse skirted by them and entered Adam's room. She carried a neck brace.

Both Baxter and Isi relaxed visibly. They listened carefully. "There is a concussion. Severe trauma to the neck muscles. We'll want to keep him for a while for observation. He has the strongest neck muscles I've ever seen."

Baxter offered information. "He was a wrestler and still keeps in shape. He once mentioned a severe injury in the past, but I don't know the details."

The doctor appeared to consider. "There were signs of a previous injury that looked severe. In any case, it looks like the trauma is muscular. For now, we've sedated him. He's going to be in pain when he wakes up."

"Any idea how long he'll be out?" Baxter asked, trying not to look at his watch.

"Tomorrow, most likely. He may drift in and out. There wasn't much of a description of the event in the record. All it says is he was exercising at the time of the accident."

"Exercising was his habit. He was found on the playing field behind Ur School Building." Baxter peeked between a one-inch gap in the curtains. Adam lay in his bed, brace around his neck. He somehow looked smaller, weaker, more vulnerable.

Baxter could feel his own neck muscles tightening in sympathy. Unconsciously he rubbed the back of his neck. "I'm afraid that's all we know for sure."

"I really shouldn't speculate, but the trauma seems excessive for exercising alone on a grassy field. Considering the development of his neck muscles, he would have to have fallen from a significant distance or with force greater than his own weight." She looked at Baxter in a way that made him feel like he had missed something.

Isi fixed her gaze on Baxter. She heard what the doctor said, and she could easily imagine the cogs moving in Sergeant Baxter's brain. She knew him well enough to let him think things through before she added another piece to the puzzle.

The doctor's last words echoed in Baxter's mind. He pressed his lips together in thought and rubbed his chin. What if Adam had learned something and didn't recognize the danger of knowing it? It wasn't beyond Adam to take risks. Baxter knew that from DuPuis.

Baxter had the sickening feeling that his asking Adam for help may have endangered him. Had Elf said anything to Adam about who he recognized, and had Adam done anything risky about it? He spoke more to himself than anyone around him. "How did he know that Henry was in the shelter?"

Deputy Isi saw her way in. "Maybe the ninja told him." It sounded silly. That word, or something close, had come out of Adam's mouth. At the time, she had attributed it to his delirium.

"What?"

"He said it a few times." She took her notebook out of her pocket. "Once in the ambulance right after we left and a couple times when I was sitting with him. He said, 'Henry, Shelter' and something that sounded like ninja. If he was right about Henry in the shelter, there's something to the ninja…"

"A ninja in Ur." Baxter nodded thoughtfully. The old judo coach naturally thought of judo. His mind sorted through the names of people he might know who he had coached in Judo. Too many to think about. What would any of them have against Adam? The only one good enough to consider facing Adam would have been Junior Delgado. Was he in town? "We'd better keep a guard on his room."

Isi remembered the piece of folded paper. "Wait, let me get something." She picked up the plastic bag that held the folded paper and plucked a couple of gloves from a dispenser. Returning to the sergeant, "Here. They said they found this while cutting off his clothes. They were gloved. They put it in this bag."

Baxter stretched on the gloves, reached into the bag, and extracted the folded paper. He read: "Leave Ur. You don't belong here. We don't want you here." His first thought was that the note was juvenile—

something a kid would write. Baxter folded it back up and put it back into the bag. "We'll need the name of the person who found this."

"It's in my notebook," Isi said flatly.

Baxter nodded. "It's evidence. Have it checked for prints. Get a photocopy for me."

The doctor nearly collided with a nurse as she emerged from Henry's room. The nurse stopped and looked up at her and tilted her head toward the examination room that held Henry. "I'll be there in a minute to write up the order. No rush. We'll do an X-ray on the sprained ankle, a saline IV, and a CBC. He says he doesn't need anything for pain, but I'll put in something PRN."

To Baxter and Isi, "He's a little dehydrated and has a sprained ankle." He's a tough cookie and he might be covering up some of the pain, but he doesn't want anything for it."

Baxter suppressed a laugh. He knew Henry well enough. He was relieved when she said, "We'll keep him for observation overnight. If we need to keep him longer, we'll have to transfer him to the VA. I'm told there are a couple of family members out there. Shall I send them back?"

Baxter would have preferred to make them wait until after he and Cayce had taken Henry's statement, but he knew Henry would want to see his family and Rosie. They would all be itching to see him. A short visit would do them all good. "Aya, It's his grandmother, his cousin Toby Beck and Rosie Valez. If his family starts speaking Choctaw, I won't be able to keep up."

"My first language," she offered.

"We'll let them visit for a few minutes. Deputy Isi will brief them and then bring them in," he said to the doctor. She went to the nurses' station, which was situated just behind the ER reception window. Then to Deputy Isi, "You'll stay in the room. I'd like Henry to see them, but I don't want them to compare notes. You understand what I mean." It wasn't a question. "Listen carefully and stop them from going too far. You might as well be the one to get statements from both of them, and Rosie, too."

His instructions were routine. He shouldn't have felt the need to say them. She could see he wanted to say more. Slightly exasperated, she interrupted him. "The statements, one at a time, of course, and I'll record them as well."

Baxter mentally took a step back. "Right. You already know all that. Ask at the information desk in the lobby. I've asked the hospital for a private space for you to take statements.

The woman who staffed the window to the ER waiting room approached. "There is an Agent Cayce from the FBI who is asking for you, Sergeant. He says you're expecting him."

"Thank you. Send him back. We're also expecting Jesus Ramirez of the DEA. When he gets here, just send him back. Sorry to be such a bother."

"No problem, officer." She walked back to her desk.

Then speaking to Deputy Isi, Baxter instructed, "Introduce yourself to Cayce and, if you get the chance, Ramirez as well. They'll be working with us."

Us. He said us, not me. Calling in the feds elevated the stakes, and she was going to be in on the case. It was real validation. It felt like a promotion. "Shall I update the sheriff?"

He paused and exhaled a deep breath slowly. He ran his fingers through his hair as if it might help him think or decide. His mind raced trying to connect the dots. They *should* be keeping the sheriff informed. It was protocol. The sheriff might involve himself, or he might not. If he did, it would be merely to take credit for the investigation during his next political speeches. Stacks wasn't a stupid man. He wouldn't get involved until a positive outcome would be more certain.

"Not yet. I woke him up to request the arrest and search warrants. He's the one that brought in the FBI. Let's not bother him yet. Let's see where we get to."

Something about this whole case felt off. Too many pieces just didn't fit together. The thought reminded him of Adam's puzzle. "How do you fit the pieces together without looking at the picture?" he had asked him.

"Looks can be distracting," he had answered. "The shape is all that really counts." Adam's injury didn't make sense, not even to the doctor. Henry runs away to a place of safety, only to somehow end up trapped in the tornado shelter. Adam somehow knows that Henry is in the shelter. And he runs into or imagines a ninja in Ur.

According to Ramirez, another fentanyl shipment had reached its destination. How Ramirez knew that Baxter would soon learn, but he also recalled Elf's caution to Adam about *trusting no one.* Elf had recognized someone from his past who could *easily mess up* his parole. Was it the sheriff or the mayor? If not one of them, who else could it have been?"

The buzzer unlocked the door to the ER examination area. A tall, muscular man with a determined look on his face walked through and made a beeline for the two uniformed officers.

"Sergeant William Baxter," Baxter extended his hand. "I take it you're Cayce."

He replied with a single nod. His voice was surprisingly low. "FBI. Just call me Cayce."

"And you? How shall I call you?"

"Just call me Bax. This is Deputy Isi."

He offered his and nodded once. She returned his handshake.

"Ramirez should be here shortly," Baxter added, glancing at his watch.

"I've met him," Cayce added without nuance of any kind. "It would help me if we conferred before proceeding. Just all get on the same page.

I, for one, know next to nothing about this case. All I know is it was a kidnapping, and you recovered the hostage. Well done."

Baxter had trouble interpreting it. Was he hiding a dislike? Suspicion? Or just didn't have an opinion."

"Ramiriz knows the whole story, but I'll let him tell it from his angle. I'll try and fill you in while we wait." He led Cayce to the end of the corridor.

As the group of Henry's visitors passed Adam's room, Baxter saw Rosie peek through the gap in the curtains. She raised her fingertips to her lips and visibly tried to pull herself together.

Baxter excused himself and approached her.

Miss Rosie, I want to ask you a favor. He followed her into Henry's room, where his family was already flying streaks in Choctaw. They quieted when he entered. "I want to ask you all a favor."

They looked at him expectantly.

"Please don't let anyone know that we have found Henry."

Henry tried to speak up, and the look on Toby's face could split logs. "We know who did this and you're just going to let him stay free? The fucker should already be in jail."

"Please. Just give me a little time."

Adam opened his eyes and found himself in a hospital bed with the top of the bed slightly elevated and his neck in a brace. He was immediately aware of his neck muscles. Bits and pieces of his memory began to fit together, as if he were differentiating real events from those of a dream.

He closed his eyes again. It felt better to close his eyes, and it was easier to think about the dream.

He remembered pacing off the space for his drills in the stark darkness of the poorly lit sports field behind the school. He could remember the smell of dew-covered grass and the feeling of the dew soaking through his sneakers.

Then, as incongruent as a dream, a man in black wearing a ski mask. Then he was tumbling through the air. He had no time to plan how he would land. There was a bright flash of pain, then a darkness even darker than the sports field before sunrise.

Had it been the conversation that pulled him from the depths? Were there two of them talking, or was there one talking to, perhaps with, him?

There was sudden knowledge that Henry was hiding in the tornado shelter. Adam's mind flashed to the shelter in the basement of the Rest. Then his mind shifted to walking down the steps to the dark basement in the house across the alley. There was a jump in continuity, and he knew it was the shelter in the school, not the one in the Rest. All he could remember about that shelter was the sign on the door.

Rosie came into his dream. She had been selling hot dogs. She kept asking him if he wanted one, and then Deputy Isi was trying to shoo her away.

No, there were two of them at least. Rosie and Deputy Isi must have scared them off. Had he died? He tried to remember if he had died. Then Baxter showed up and took charge. What a crazy dream! Swimming through air and not knowing how to swim.

He opened his eyes again and squinted against the barrage of light filling the room through the window. The slightest move sharpened the pulsing soreness in his neck into a dagger that traveled up through the back of his head and down through his shoulders. With it, the explosion of a headache, a sense of swimming, nausea. He closed his eyes again.

In the recesses of his mind, he was drinking again, lying on a filthy secondhand sofa that smelled of cigarette smoke, the room spinning, and on the floor next to him, a bucket to catch the vomit. With that memory came the same sense of defeat he felt when he would fall off the wagon, and he would beat himself up for having given in. One is too much; a thousand is never enough.

Coming back to himself, he talked his way through his thoughts. He hadn't started drinking again. That he would have remembered. He tried to open his eyes and sit up. The pain brought him back to himself and back to the moment. He was in a hospital somewhere. He had no memory of how he came to be there and no sense of how long he had been there. He slowly opened his eyes, trying to adjust to the light.

Through squinted eyes, Adam tried to scan the room without moving his head. Rosie! Holy shit! Rosie was slouched in an uncomfortable-looking chair, asleep. Her chin resting at an angle to her bosom. He wanted to sit up, but the throbbing in his neck muscles reminded him that moving wasn't something he wanted to do.

"Rosie," he whispered. His throat felt dry.

She didn't stir.

"Rosie," he said a bit more forcefully—his voice deeper in the morning. "Rosie Valez, wake up!"

She started, looked up, and her face contorted into an expression that Adam couldn't read. "Oh, mother of God, you're awake." She stood up at the side of his bed. "I vowed a thousand rosaries for your recovery."

He was still squinting. "Are there curtains or blinds? It's so bright!"

Drawing the vertical blinds on the window, she said, "Is that better?" She knew it must be because he had fully opened his eyes.

"Where am I?"

She started to tell him, but seeing him wince in pain, she said, "I'll get the nurse." She pressed the call button resting next to his head. She tugged at the cord and placed it beside his hand. "There," she said. "It's right there if you need it." She moved it so that it touched his hand.

At the sound of their voices, a man who had been standing outside the open door to Adam's room, stepped inside. He looked familiar, but Adam couldn't place him.

"Who's that?" he asked, pointing with his eyes.

"Sheriff's deputy." She looked over at him. "Whiteoak, isn't it?"

He nodded.

"He's been here all night. Keeping you safe." Rosie patted down a wrinkle in the

bedsheet.

"Thank you, sir. Why do I need protection?"

The question seemed to baffle the deputy and left him speechless.

Rosie answered. "Well. There is reason to believe that your injury wasn't the result of an accident."

"You mean the ninja."

Now it was Rosie's turn to be speechless. "I'll let you discuss that with Sergeant Baxter."

A nurse entered the room. She smiled and asked him how he was feeling.

Rosie rolled her eyes. It made Adam chuckle, but the chuckle made him wince in pain.

"The doctor has prescribed something for that pain. It's marked as needed. Do you need it now?"

The deputy spoke up. Can we wait until the sergeant gets here? Mr. Alba, are you able to manage for now? He's only a couple of miles away."

Adam said he could manage the pain if he didn't move and confided to the nurse his urgency to pee. "But I don't think I can move."

"Never fear, we have that covered. I'll be right back." She left the room.

The deputy remained. "I have to stay with you until Sarge gets here," he explained.

"It's okay, Dude. I'm not shy." Adam assumed he was referring to being in the room while Adam emptied his bladder.

"Sergeant's orders, you see."

Rosie's face turned a little pink. "Well, I'll just leave the room for the next event. I'll visit Henry." She stopped, paused, and took a breath. She looked into Adam's eyes with a motherly expression that he hadn't seen directed his way since his own mother had passed away. "Adam, honey, you are a sight for sore eyes."

"Wait, Rosie. Henry. Did you say Henry?"

She interrupted him. "Henry is fine, thanks to you. He's just down the hall. He even has a deputy of his own. And he's well enough to visit you. I'm sure he will want to."

Adam felt confused. "Thanks to me? What do you mean?"

"Thanks to you. You're the one that told us where he was. We'll talk later. For now, just rest."

"And when did I do that?" he said as she left the room.

The deputy just shrugged his shoulders.

The nurse walked into the room carrying a plastic urinal device. She moved the sheets aside and handed him the bottle. "Can you do it, or do you need help?"

He tried to position the bottle but fumbled. He felt his face redden. "Sorry, it's really painful to move my head and I can't see what I'm doing."

"It's okay. I'll help you."

Deputy Whiteoak looked everywhere but at Adam. He, too, was red in the face. After the nurse left, they shared some awkward small talk until the sergeant arrived.

Baxter forced what he hoped was a cheerful smile on his face before he walked into the room. "Hey buddy. Glad to see you're up." To Whiteoak he said, "You can leave me alone with him. Oh, and Whiteoak, you pass downtown Ur on your way home, don't you?"

"Yes, I can, sir. I live south of the town."

"Do me a favor and give Miss Rosie a ride back to the Pioneer's Rest in Ur. She's been here all night."

"Yes, sir." Whiteoak left the room and closed the door behind him.

"How are you feeling?" Baxter sat down on the chair that Rosie had vacated.

"If I move, it hurts. I can't wait to hear what the doctor says."

"I can tell you one thing she did say," Baxter said.

"Yeah?"

"She said you have the strongest neck muscles she'd ever seen. Given the circumstances, I guess it will be a while before I can watch you crawl around your own head."

Adam smiled through a wince. "Anything broken?"

"She didn't see anything on the X-ray or the MRI, but I'd better let her talk to you about that. Actually, the doctor I talked to was the ER doctor. They'll probably give you someone else now."

"Can you tell me how I got here?"

"Miss Rosie didn't tell you?"

"No. She went to see Henry when I had to pee. Speaking of which, how the hell did you find Henry?"

Baxter glowed. "The ramblings of a suffering man… you!"

Adam furrowed his brow. "I don't think I understand."

"After Ms. Rosie found you on the field, you kept saying Henry… shelter." After the ambulance took you, Miss Rosie and I checked out the shelter in the school. There he was."

"Is he alright?"

"Forgive me, but better than you. They're keeping him for observation for a day or so, but he seems fine. What I want to know is how you knew?"

"I'm not sure. I don't remember saying that, but I sort of remember knowing it. So how did you find me?"

"I didn't. Miss Rosie went to look for you when you didn't show up for work. She found you and called in the emergency. Deputy Isi responded first. When I heard it was you, I went right away. What happened?" He pulled out his notebook to take notes.

"Honestly, things are pretty jumbled."

"Try and take me through it," Baxter encouraged.

"It was still dark when I got to the field. I paced off the space I needed for my drills. I put a flashlight on the ground as a point of reference. I started doing my drills. Then there was something there in the dark. At first, I thought it was a big dog or something. It was a person. He just materialized out of the darkness. His eyes were all I could see. He grabbed me. Then ran into me. Suddenly I was sailing through the air. It was so smooth. I was confused, disoriented and couldn't tell where the ground was until I landed—badly. After that, it's all bits and pieces. I don't even know if the bits and pieces are real or—dreams."

"Can you describe him at all>? Like how tall was he? How was he built?" Baxter's voice was smooth and calming.

Adam instinctively tried to shake his head, which made him stiffen with pain. "No. It was dark. He was dressed all in black and wearing a kind of ski mask."

"The ninja." Baxter nodded.

"Yeah, he looked like a ninja. I remember thinking that."

"When you were in and out, you also said the word *ninja* a couple of times to Deputy Isi. She didn't know what to make of it, but she wrote it down. You're doing exceptionally well, Adam, under the circumstances. Anything else you can tell me about him?"

"I caught a flash of his eyes, but I couldn't tell you the color. He was pretty tall, maybe six feet. He wasn't big. I mean, he wasn't beefy, but he sure was strong and quick. I must be getting old. Before I knew it, I was hitting the ground, and everything went black."

Baxter mentally flipped through a series of judo throws, some of them no longer legal for competition and rarely taught or learned. It sounded like *gan seki otoshi,* but he couldn't know for sure, and there were a number of similar throws that he had taught when he was coaching. It could have been any one of them. Of course it could have been a different martial art.

Some of those throws could be done with more force than was necessary. It would have to be malicious to add the force. If the *uke,* that is the guy being thrown, didn't expect to be thrown or didn't know how to fall safely, accidents like Adam's could happen.

"You're sure it was a man?"

Adam was surprised. "He was pretty strong." He thought about it. "Honestly, I couldn't say." Something stirred inside Adam. It was a memory, but was he remembering a dream or something that really happened? "I think it was a guy because he didn't sound like a girl."

"He talked?"

"I think so."

"What did he say?"

"I'm not sure." He closed his eyes, trying to remember and only felt his head pound. "Maybe it will come to me, but it isn't there now."

Baxter pulled a folded piece of paper out of his notebook. He unfolded it and held it up for Adam to read it. "Where did you get this?" Baxter watched him carefully.

"Me? I've never seen it in my life."

"This is just a photocopy. You had the original on you when they cut off your shorts."

"What? My shorts?" Adam was confused.

"It was in your shorts when they cut them off you," Baxter insisted. "It was shoved down the front of your shorts."

"Wait a minute." Adam searched his mind. "He said I was pretty."

"Who said you were pretty, the ninja?"

"No, the other guy?"

"So, there were two?"

"I think so. He had an eerie way of talking. High and sick."

"What did he say?"

Adam spoke very slowly, as if his words rose to the surface of his mind in tiny clusters. He was halfway between right now and back then. "He said I was pretty and touched my face and my… I guess that's when he put the paper in my shorts. Creepy."

They sat in silence for a moment. Baxter was giving him time to process, to remember.

"They talked to each other. They wondered if I was dead or going to die. The ninja had a younger, more normal voice. He wanted to put me in the shelter with Henry." Adam's words bubbled slowly, rising up from the depths of his psyche, surfacing one by one into his mind. "Then the creepy one told me I was pretty. Holy shit. I think I know who the ninja might be."

THIRTY

After the successful delivery of the latest package on Friday, the promise of a wonderful weekend loomed. The plan to lose the stranger in town was simple enough, but it hadn't gone to plan. The impact had been more than his young friend had anticipated. Now the kid was getting nervous. That was a problem.

Saturday felt like a campfire that got out of control. The kid texted him almost constantly for news. *That's what you get when you ask a kid to do a man's job. He worries like a woman. The little faggot.* His wife, a real woman, spent her day on the Ur grapevine. Every call, every overheard conversation glued his ears to her voice, and his brain creaked, trying to discern the other half of the conversations. Everyone was talking about it.

What was meant to be a simple but powerful message to leave town turned into a siren-blaring ambulance that got the attention of the whole town. Somehow, the stranger had moved from slightly uncomfortable curiosity to an object of affection and compassion. It was sickening. It all came down to Rosie. By Saturday afternoon everyone in town knew how she had found him, why she had looked for him, and that he had been seriously injured.

As far as he could tell, no one suspected that it was anything but an accident, but the whole town was rallying to take care of the poor guy. The poor guy!

Rosie had stayed in the hospital with him, and she had a lot of time to answer the phone.

Sunday morning was the first time he indulged in looking in on Henry. He hoped to see him finally collapsed in a heap on the floor in the middle of the shelter. He would have missed the actual death throes but they'd be recorded. At least he could enjoy the reruns.

The livestream was down. There was something wrong with it. The sound was gone, and the image was warped, and if he hadn't known what it was supposed to be, he wouldn't have known what he was looking at. The warping sometimes jumped, but he couldn't make out any details. He could feel his heart beating in his chest. What if he had missed everything?

He pulled up the recording from the day before. Something was indeed wrong with the camera. The sound was gone, and the focus was no longer wide-angled. He couldn't see the whole room, and he couldn't see Henry. Where the hell was he?

He wondered if Henry had found the camera. But no, there would at least be an image of him finding the camera and putting it back.

Then something moved to one side. He stared at it. He realized it was the edge of Henry's bony backside bending over something. The figure stood up. He stepped out of frame and in a few seconds was walking across the frame holding… He hit pause. He wanted to savor the moment. Henry was holding the whiskey bottle.

He slowed the playback to half speed and hoped Henry would drink it in a shot. He was sure Henry wouldn't wait because he was sure Henry couldn't resist. There wasn't much more than a big swig, and that was all that was necessary. His heart raced, and he felt that stirring in his pants that over the years had become increasingly rare.

Henry slowly unscrewed the cap of the bottle.

He paused the film again. He was enjoying his own suffering, the pain of anticipation. It was delicious.

He set the playback speed so slow, it was little more than a series of stills. Something seemed to surprise Henry. He looked in the direction of the door. He said something. That was nothing. Henry talked to himself sometimes.

He moved the cursor to a little earlier and reset the playback to normal speed. He watched Henry walk across the frame with the whiskey bottle. He stopped beautifully in the center of the frame. Something surprised him. He said something, and everything seemed to stop as if the camera had frozen. It hadn't, but that split second felt like an eternity.

The puppeteer's world collapsed. "How the fuck did she know?" It came out as a shout.

"Language, dear. It's the Lord's day," his wife called from the kitchen. She was cooking breakfast. Usually, they ate breakfast out at the Rest on Sunday mornings, but since the Rest was closed indefinitely… "How did who know what?"

He had to think fast. "I was just thinking about the stranger. How did she know where to look for him?"

"You mean Rosie?" He could hear her walking down the hall. He flipped the screen of his laptop down, which put the computer into sleep mode. Just in time.

"I imagine she was waiting for him and got worried. You said yourself that you once saw him bouncing around the field doing those exercises he does. I'm sure she just got worried and went to look for him." She stood in the doorway, her normally friendly face contorted into a scowl.

He was still in his robe.

"You'd better start getting ready for church. Why don't you take your shower? Breakfast will be ready in about fifteen minutes."

Just her looking into the room felt like an invasion of privacy. It was the smallest room in the house. It was his space. He hated seeing her there. Fire burned in his chest, but he knew better than to argue with her.

She glanced up at the humming window fan. Shaking her head and tsk-tsking, she moved her hands to her waist in an assertive posture. "You know, if you think I don't know you're smoking in here," she seemed to struggle for words. "If you're going to kill yourself with cigarettes, then get on with it, but do it outside from now on." She stormed back down the hallway, calling behind her, "I can still smell it on your clothes!"

He got up, slammed the door shut, and pressed the little button on the doorknob to lock the door. Invaded and berated on this, the worst day of his life. He was pissed off. He opened the computer. He viewed the footage once again. He watched Henry find the bottle of whiskey and walk into the center of the room. Then all hope was lost.

He set the whiskey bottle on a table, and they walked together toward the door. Why hadn't the door closed and locked them both in there? It had a heavy swing. Was there someone outside holding the door open? Or had she propped it open? His heart dropped down into his stomach, and it was replaced with panic. "Fuck, Henry is on the loose." He could feel his throat going dry and his hands and feet going cold.

He wanted to go, to just go. But it was time for damage control. According to his wife's end of the conversations he had heard, no one mentioned finding Henry. If there was any luck left in the world, Henry would go back into hiding, perhaps with Rosie in tow.

He decided to play it cool. He would shower, shave, eat his breakfast, and take his wife to church. He'd make up some excuse to drop her off. He'd have more than an hour to get to the shelter, wipe the place down, and extract the camera and the whiskey bottle. At least there was that.

The parking lot of the Baptist Church was full. By the license plates, even some of the folks who had left the church for the Pentecostal one had returned. He pulled into the lot, alongside the side entrance.

"I hate being late," his wife complained.

"You won't be as late as me. I'll go find a place to park."

She carefully stepped down out of his truck and headed inside, not bothering to look where he went. He pulled out of the lot and did not notice the car idling across the street, facing in the direction of town. He didn't notice it pulling out behind him, lagging behind at a distance.

Toby's hand caressed the rifle in the passenger seat as he watched them drive up to the church. He knew his wife wouldn't miss church. She was one of the few Christians who seemed to live up to their own standards. She wasn't an overtly pious woman, but she went to church and always seemed to be doing her best. She didn't deserve to have a husband like him, and doubly, he didn't deserve to have a wife like her.

He followed. He thought he knew where he was going but was surprised when he passed town and drove into the parking lot of the laundromat and the bus station. He parked his truck where a bus would park to load and unload passengers. What the hell was he doing?

Toby pulled into the parking lot and parked in front of the laundromat. It didn't matter. If the bastard got on a bus, he'd follow the bus. All he needed was a clean shot. That guy had always been a pain in the ass and a secret freak.

He'd always been a weird kid. As Toby waited, eyes fixed on the bus station door, his mind went back to the time he watched the bastard tear one wing off a butterfly just to watch it struggle to fly. Later, when he decided to perform favors to get into the good graces of the older boys, he threatened them with exposing them. Toby was the only one who never let him do that because he could imagine that freak biting it off. Too bad they didn't just kill him back then and make it look like it was an accident.

One clean shot with no witnesses and I'd be home clean." He pulled his hand away from the gun. "But not before we find my cousin."

Finally, he came out and got back into his truck. Right behind him, the kid who worked at the bus station came out and got into his own truck. They pulled out of the lot in opposite directions. Toby wasn't interested in the kid. He wanted the man.

Toby followed him, not too close but close enough to see where he went. When he parked behind the school, Toby thought he had him. Maybe that was the reason Baxter wanted them to keep quiet about Henry. He was coming to check on Henry.

Toby watched Blaine Lamano get out of his truck and take something out of his pocket. He was wearing that sidearm he always wore, and Toby knew it was time for stealth and tactics. *Lamano thinks he is going to do something to Henry. He doesn't know that Henry is safe. I'm going to get to him first. This is the perfect place.*

Toby parked on the street in front of the school. He took his rifle, quietly opened his door, and gingerly stepped onto the gravel lot. He moved close to the building to hug the wall. There, grass was growing through the gravel, quieting the sound of his footsteps. He crept along the wall as quickly as he could.

As he passed Lamano's truck, he looked inside. Lamano's cell phone was on the passenger seat. Peering around the corner of the building, he watched Lamano open the back door to the school. Once he stepped inside, Toby moved to the door.

The basement lights came on, and Toby peered around the frame of the door. He watched Lamano open the shelter door, prop it open with a broom, and step inside.

Gotcha, he thought. *I might not even need the gun. Henry had said the door was broken.* As quickly and silently as he could, Toby stepped inside and walked lightly to the door. With one swift kick, he knocked the broom away from the door and watched the door close with a satisfying thud.

Toby stood up straight and gently tugged on the door to make sure it was closed. Pleased, he thought to himself, *There you go, you motherfucker, see how it feels.*

He walked away as he heard Lamano trying in vain to push the breaker bar inside the door. If Henry couldn't jerry-rig that breaker bar, no one could. He slipped out of the school, closed the outside door, and got back into his truck, no one the wiser. Oh, they'll find him, Toby thought, and they'll have him. *I can't wait to tell Henry.*

Manda Lamano stood outside the Baptist church, watching everyone leave, all the while her eyes scanning the area for their truck. He said he was going to park the truck but never returned. He had been on edge for days. When he dropped her off, she recognized that he was too tightly wound to sit through a service and thought it was an excuse. But she fully expected him to be in the parking lot when she came out of the church, complaining about how long she had spent socializing.

After his heart attack, she made a lot of excuses to ward off her own resentment of all the extra work. He was frail. He needed help. Even now, he was still a bit weak. She believed he was depressed. He felt useless since he couldn't work. His newfound fascination with electronics, she had hoped, would help pull him out of his slump.

It bothered her that he still smoked, though he had cut down a lot. And in fairness, a beer now and then never hurt anyone. As long as it was just now and then.

Of course, he no longer needed her constant ministrations. He seemed afraid to overexert himself. It had been a couple of years of subsisting on his disability payments and her meager earnings. If she could only rent out the empty units at the strip mall, it would make all the difference. If it weren't for the bus station rent, they'd be behind in their taxes on the property.

It had come as a relief when Blaine started to spend time at the Rest. It meant an added expense for the food, but at least for those few hours a day, he was out of her hair. And what else did he have?

Blaine spent a lot of time at the Rest. If she hadn't known better, she might have wondered about him and Rosie. It wasn't so much her trust in Blaine, but she knew that Rosie barely tolerated him. She'd never thought much of him even when they were kids.

As adults, Blaine liked to needle her. He'd complain about this or that being too hot or too cold and could he have a fresh cup of coffee instead of the one Rosie would top off. She unabashedly called him a pain in the ass in front of anyone who happened to be around, and she had to admit that Rosie had a point. Blaine could really be a pain in the ass, unless, of course, you knew him well enough to know he was harmless.

She had more than once reminded herself that her marriage vows were *for better or worse.* They were just stuck in *worse.*

She tried calling and texting him, but there was no response. *He probably let the battery die. Honestly, if I don't do everything for that man!* Frustrated, she paced the cement walkway, dodging and apologizing to the folks leaving the church. "Oh, Blaine must be hung up somewhere. He'll be here soon enough" became a kind of refrain as folks offered her a ride.

At least it was a beautiful day. The sun now high in the sky, the air warm but not hot, and there was an occasional gentle scent of some early blooming flowers in the air. She tried calling Blaine again, then texting. Nothing.

The pastor and his wife were the last to leave the church. It was a full hour after the end of the service. Of course, they offered her a ride. "I just don't know what happened to him. He's not answering his phone." The pastor's wife tried to reassure her, suggesting a flat tire and a low phone battery. "It must be something like that."

The pastor tried to lighten her concern. "Maybe he's just lost track of time. He's wandering around a Tractor Supply and left his phone in the car. Let's be honest, it's not the first time he's ducked out on one of my sermons."

"It was a fine sermon," his wife insisted.

The entire length of the drive, while trying to keep up small talk with the pastor, Manda scanned the road for signs of Blaine's truck. She was worried. The delay could have been anything, but the idea that he had experienced another heart attack and was now slumped somewhere over his steering wheel lingered behind her thoughts. *Oh lord, please let him be alright*, was her silent prayer.

She beat back the thought of what it would mean for her if he weren't alright—how much more she'd have to do… or, though she barely let herself consider it, how much less. Internally, she scolded herself for being so selfish—especially right after leaving church!

The parking lot of the bus station was empty when the pastor and his wife dropped her off at the bus station. She wondered what happened to Matthew's truck. Usually his huge Dodge Ram was parked in clear view of the window. Matthew was very finicky about that truck.

She called out to him as she walked into the station. There was no reply. Manda looked at her watch, fearing she was somehow late. But even if she were, he was supposed to wait for her to arrive. It was twenty minutes to twelve and Matthew wasn't there. She tried calling his cell phone. He didn't answer. She left a voice-mail message. *Kids don't do much with voicemail these days,* she reminded herself, and texted him to check his voicemail.

She called his mother, who told her he left for work as usual this morning. She searched the desk and the till. There was no note explaining his absence, but the front door had been unlocked when she arrived. There was a mug of coffee on the counter. It was still a little warm. He or someone had at least been there.

She opened up the till. The money was still there, the same fifty dollars in change they started out with each day. Most people paid with a credit card anyway.

She checked in the back. No Matthew. She walked down to the laundromat, stopping to cup her eyes on the windows between the two businesses. No Matthew. No Blaine. If she hadn't just been to church and just got out of the pastor's car, she mused to herself, she would have suspected she'd missed the rapture.

She called Blaine's brother Blake. He answered the phone. Some sports channel blared in his background. He hadn't seen Blaine or heard from him. If the Rest was open, she would have called Rosie. But who else was there to call?

At 5 p.m., unable to stand the wait any longer, she called Matthew's mother again. She hadn't heard anything from Matthew. "No, it's surprising. He would have had lunch with Tom and Grace before they left to go back to school."

"Neither of them has boarded a bus since I got here at noon. Do you think they went back in the morning?"

"No, according to Matt, Claudia gave Tom his father's truck. They drove back."

"Well, I'm really worried about them both. This is so unusual. I'm going to report Blaine as missing. Maybe you should do the same about Matthew."

"I'll wait a while. I saw on TV that you have to wait twenty-four hours."

Manda rolled her eyes. *A lot can happen in twenty-four hours,* she thought. She hung up the phone.

Baxter leaned closer to the bed to better hear Adam. Adam's words had grown more faint, more distant, and more ethereal as he traveled through his thoughts. He was recalling more and more, and like one of his puzzles, two difficult pieces just fit together.

"Bax, do you remember your dreams?"

Baxter was bewildered at the left-field question. "Rarely," he said.

"I remember mine a lot. Sometimes during the day, something happens, and it comes out in a dream in a crazy sort of way. The dream makes perfect sense when you're dreaming. It doesn't' have to be logical but when you wake up, and try to piece it together, the dream doesn't actually make sense anymore. That doesn't matter because when you're awake you can put the pieces together."

"Adam, you're losing me."

"Okay, okay. Bear with me. I went to the Friday night service at the Pentecostal church. Grace and Junior, I mean Tom Delgado, he prefers to be called Tom, not Tommy like his dad but Tom, sat with me, and we talked in the social hall after the service.

"It was just normal conversation, and I thought I was really wasting my time. I wanted to get away from them because they were monopolizing my time, and I had to *not* investigate. He emphasized the word NOT. They were talking about their friend Matt not going to church. He, Matt, had picked Grace up from the bus station. They had dinner, but Matt wouldn't come to church. I'm thinking, what's the big deal? A friend is a friend. If I were gay, I wouldn't go to that church either."

"Wait. We're talking about Matthew Cummings, right?"

"I don't know his last name, but he hangs out with Tom and Grace."

Baxter nodded. "Okay. What makes you say he's gay? Did he come on to you or something?"

Adam dismissed the thought. "No. I noticed him check me out a couple of times, but he never tried anything. What convinced me was that day in the park. The three of them were sitting together. Tom was in the middle, and they were comforting him. Matt's attention was too… " he floundered for the right term, "too attentive, caring, solicitous—not the kind of comfort that comes from a guy who's a friend. It was obvious to me that he was in love with Tom, but…"

"Tom isn't gay." Baxter finished the sentence. "That explains a lot."

"It really shook Tom up when I asked him about that."

"Of course it did. What did he say?"

"He said they weren't as close friends as they had been. That Grace was closer to Matt because he's her brother."

Baxter sat back down.

Adam continued. "Knowing Elf's story, she believes that if Matt comes to church, God will fix him."

Baxter closed and rubbed his eyes with his thumb and forefinger.

Adam went on. "They have the same father. The one she visits in Texas. It sounds like there is a lot going on there. The father has been trying to make things up with Matt. He bought his truck for him. Now, here's the clincher. He sends him gifts all the time–through Grace. Remember she was on the same bus as I was.

Baxter sat up as if he had had a shock. "Adam, all the time? He sends gifts all the time?"

"That's what it sounded like to me. But I'm not done. There's another piece that fits. On the field, in my dream, but now I don't think it was a dream, the creepy guy said that they had to get rid of me because the ninja's boyfriend betrayed their secret. I had that feeling when Tom told me Matt was Grace's brother."

"Are you telling me that Tom and Matt are lovers?" Baxter was incredulous.

"No, but I do think that Matt is still hung up on Tom and the creepy guy uses it. And, I think Tom might have told Matt about our talk in the social hall."

Baxter spoke into the mic on his shoulder.

"Do you know who the creepy guy is?" Adam focused on Baxter's eyes. "I have a guess, but it's just a guess."

"Tell me your guess."

"It's just a guess."

"Tell me anyway."

"I think it was Blaine Lamano."

"Adam, you just put the last few pieces in that puzzle of yours. The package of fentanyl in your bag was gift-wrapped."

From the moment the door slammed shut and he knew that there was no way out, he began planning, rehearsing, what his next move would be.

Eventually, he set the stage, moved a single hardback chair to the middle of the room and placed it directly in front of the door. When it opened, he would be the first thing they would see. On the table next to the chair he placed the camera, the bottle of whiskey and his revolver—

loaded and cocked. He removed the side holster and tossed it on the cot where he had once watched Henry sleeping.

He has several plans of action and would decide which to use when the time came.

He wasn't sure how he'd use the revolver. He might place it in his mouth and shoot his own brains out when the door opened. That would be exceptionally dramatic and would certainly leave a scar on whoever walked through the door. It also might leave unanswered questions. That would be delicious. Too bad he wouldn't be around to watch it.

He might shoot the person who walked through the door and then himself? The thought of just one more kill and his victim being unpredictable was titillating. It would be a good ending to the story, also leaving questions unanswered.

What if he decided to do nothing at all and remain in complete control of what they knew? He didn't have to tell them anything. He couldn't talk his way out of the murders. Once they got the AR-15, he figured that it might be just a matter of time. He had handled the gun, left casings on the roof of the casino, and ballistics could match the bullets. He might have even drooled a bit while aiming, such a delicious moment, and they'd have DNA as well. If they ever had a reason to fingerprint him, they have him signed, sealed and delivered.

He could always do nothing and remain silent. How long would they interrogate him? What cop games would they play? What questions might they use to trip him up? Oh, that would be good fun. He'd see how stupid the cops were. It would be like playing chess with a novice.

How much could he talk his way out of? He was good at talking his way out of things. Most people were so insipidly stupid. Or, would he more enjoy spilling his guts with all the lurid details, weaving a tale of suspense with a backstory of neglect and abuse? They'd eat it up.

What if the person who discovered him was armed? A cop, perhaps? He could just pick up the gun, even fire it without aiming and they would fire. Suicide by cop, they call it. They probably wouldn't shoot to kill, though. If they did somehow kill him with the shot, that would leave a scar of a different kind.

He enjoyed these ruminations. Too bad there'd be only one performance.

He had dismissed the thought of drinking the whiskey. Death would be quick but not easy and it lacked theatrical gravitas. It risked them thinking he had merely died of a heart attack. Some might even feel sorry for him in the end. He couldn't bear the thought of being an object of the pity of idiots.

He waited, ears attentive to the sound of someone unlocking the basement door. They'd see his truck. They'd guess he was inside, trapped just like Henry had been. For a long time, he played a solo game of musical chairs without music. He circled the chair and table until he felt like sitting. He'd sit a while staring at the door. Then up again, circling in the opposite direction, just to balance out his experience.

The puppeteer still held the strings for his final performance.

Baxter flicked the screen of his cell phone with his thumb. Held it to his ear and said, "Baxter."

"Ramirez here. We have Steven Bishop and Matthew Cummings in custody."

"Well, that's one missing person accounted for." Baxter sighed. "Did they talk?"

"Bishop lawyered up. Cummings never stopped yammering." The background of the call sounded like Ramirez was walking across a busy street.

"Okay, Chucho, cut the suspense. How right or how wrong were we?"

"Half and half, Bax. We analyzed the sample from Alba's bag and matched it to a distribution point in Nuevo Laredo. Bishop has an old Toyota held together with chewing gum and Jesus bumper stickers. We've been watching him for quite a while. A couple of times a month, he'd load it up with a couple of trash bags full of used clothes he took from one of those donation bins. He'd drive into Nuevo Laredo on mission work."

Baxter could imagine the air quotes Ramirez put around "mission work."

"Couple of hours later, he drives back with some Mexican food and two or three kilos of fenty pills. Lehman handled the money through the church and the mission. How about that? Tax-exempt drug money."

"So, it *was* Lehman. That's a relief. We didn't have to go after anyone else."

"Now for something you don't know." Chucho paused for effect.

"Come on, Chucho."

"According to Cummings, Delgado had to go because he was asking too many questions about church funds. Turns out my cover wasn't blown after all. Delgado was definitely the target."

"Lehman order the hit?"

"Lehman ordered the hit."

Baxter cast his eyes on the floor. He was suddenly sad. He wondered how much pain it caused Matthew to know why his friend's father had been killed. Did the rejection from Tom make that easier for him? He felt sick about the human costs.

"And Bishop sent the drugs to Cummings with his daughter?

"The guy's a sociopath. He involved both his children."

"So she knew?"

"No proof of that. We think she was a blind mule. Every couple of weeks, she'd visit her father on Thursday night and spend Friday with him doing father-daughter shit. Then he'd put her on a bus with pocket money and a present for Cummings. Alba was right. Bishop is Cummings's father. Here's something else you might not know."

"Chucho, spill it. No more dramatic pauses for suspense."

"It's fucking sick. Cummings wanted to go to college and wanted Bishop's faculty tuition waiver. It turns out he wasn't a professor at all. He didn't even work there. He just gave his daughter gifts from the campus store. So, he offered Cummings something else: a way to earn enough money to go to any school he wanted."

Baxter sighed loud enough for Ramirez to comment. "Sucks, doesn't it?"

"Okay. Did Cummings say anything about Lamano?"

"Spilled it all. If he had lawyered up, he could have worked a sweet deal, but he just kept talking like he was applying for a job. Between the evidence you have and what Cummings has said, Lamano is done. He'll find himself on death row. The two killings and the kidnapping. Cummings even talked about the sexual assault on Alba."

"Did you tell this to Cayce?"

"Absolutely. They are probably executing search warrants as we speak. I take it Lamano is still missing."

"Cayce thinks he's a fugitive. My gut says he's still local."

After spotting Blaine Lamano's truck parked behind the school, Deputy Isa leaned against her fender waiting for Sergeant Baxter to arrive.

He warned her not to do anything alone. As she well knew, Lamano was always armed.

She couldn't have done anything anyway since she didn't have a key to the school. Baxter still had one from when he was a teacher. In fact, he had taught her civics. Until she met Mr. Baxter, as she called him back then, she hadn't been much interested in government.

Raised in a traditional Choctaw family with Choctaw values, she always felt a little out of sync with the world around her. Growing up, she imagined, even intended to move to the reservation one day.

Baxter was Choctaw. He looked Choctaw. He held Choctaw values and understood many things in the Choctaw way. He lived in both worlds and was successful in both. It was true that he didn't speak much Choctaw, and his wife was white, but he was still Choctaw. That impressed her enough to expand her view and experience of the world she lived in.

When Sergeant Baxter arrived, he seemed to move more slowly or *deliberately* than usual. He had a serious look on his face. "I don't know what we're going to find in there. Let's just take it easy and go slow. It could be dangerous. You know what to do. But if I go down, no heroics. Get out of the way and let him go. Then call Cayce and leave it to him and the U.S. Marshals."

"You didn't call them in?"

"I did. Cayce wants me to wait, but he knows I won't. He's after a kidnapper, and we're after a cold-blooded murderer. I want him alive. I don't know how he would react if he were confronted with a squad of Marshalls."

"You're confident." It was almost a question. Isi felt guilty about the hint of doubt and fear in her voice.

"I'm confident with you backing me up, yes."

Trying to be as quiet as possible, he slipped the key into the lock on the door and gingerly opened it. The basement of the school was garishly lit with overhead fluorescent lighting.

Baxter glanced around the area, focusing on the shelter door. It was closed. If Lamano were in there, and it was a decent guess that he was, according to Henry Beck, the door could not be opened from the inside. He just hoped they hadn't made enough noise for Lamano to set up some sort of defense.

He pulled out his gun and silently indicated that the deputy should do the same. He made a slight detour into the sports cage and grabbed a cement block as gingerly and quietly as he could. He gently set the block down by the doorjamb. He whispered to his deputy. "Once I open the door, I'll go in. Use the block to keep the door open. Be prepared to defend yourself."

She nodded. Her heart had never beaten so hard in her chest, not even when she called the bomb squad for Adam Alba's duffel bag.

Baxter could feel sweat under his grip of the firearm. He held the gun in his other hand, wiped his palm on his pants, returned the gun, and prepared to open the door. He gently gripped the lever and, as quietly as possible, pushed it down. Then, in one swift motion, he swung the door open and straight-armed his pistol at the man standing in front of a wooden chair. "Freeze!"

Lamano turned, startled, didn't move but seemed to remain calm.

Baxter's eyes scanned the display on the table and noted Lamano was not wearing his sidearm holster.

Lamano's eyes were fixed on Baxter's eyes, not his weapon. "Well, if it isn't little Billy Baxter." His voice was higher, unnatural, in a creepy tempo and tone like a cinematic psychopath.

Baxter stepped forward. "Lay face down on the floor and put your hands behind your back." Baxter's voice filled the shelter. Behind, he could hear Deputy Isi putting the cement block in place.

"Oh, now, now. Is that necessary?" His right arm began to move. Baxter was aware of the gun on the table next to him.

He stepped forward again. He held his gun with both hands. "Go for the gun, and you'll never use your right hand again."

Lamano stopped. "Oh, you won't hurt me. You want to know. You need to know what I know, don't you?" His voice took on a falsetto pitch, and he spoke in a Hollywood psychopath rhythm. "Oh, the things I can tell you. I know things about your sheriff, about your friend, and even about how well one of your students has turned out, thanks to you."

Baxter stepped forward again, but this time, he appeared to relax. He watched Lamano notice this. He also knew that Deputy Isi had entered the room and that there were now two guns aimed at Lamano. "If you must shoot, Aya, go for the balls. On this guy, they are completely expendable."

He watched the offensive statement change something about Lamano's demeanor. Baxter calmly latched the safety on his weapon and holstered it. "This is your last chance. On the floor, face down, hands behind your back."

Lamano didn't move. He was defiant.

Baxter rushed him, and instinctively Lamano raised his arms in defense. Grabbing Lamano's sleeve and collar, Baxter stepped into him, turned, and Lamano was now rolling over Baxter's back to land with a thud on the concrete floor of the shelter.

With the wind knocked out of him, a wave of fear crossed Lamano's face.

With force, Baxter rolled Lamano over, pulled the cuffs from his belt, and cuffed him. "When I said get down on the floor, I meant it."

Lamano groaned.

"Deputy, arrest him."

"So, I have to do the paperwork?" She holstered her weapon.

"You got it! It's your collar."

Deputy Isi holstered her weapon and approached the perp. "Blaine Lamano, you are under arrest for the murders of Tomas Delgado and Patrick Lehman. You have the right to remain silent."

Lamano groaned again.

"Anything you say can and will be used against you in a court of law."

Lamano squirmed, trying to right himself. He was like an upside-down tortoise but on his belly.

As she finished the proper warning, Baxter heard vehicles approaching and looked out the door. "That'll be the U.S. Marshals coming to the rescue. They can have him—for now."

The tension was broken. They both laughed. "Sergeant," she said. "That was amazing."

EPILOGUE

"It smells good in here. Like my mother's house." Baxter stood in the doorway to Adam's room at the Rest. He visited almost every day.

"Henry heated up some of his grandmother's stew for me."

"Any left?" Baxter asked hopefully.

"Sorry."

The evening sun turned the interior of the room orange, and a slight breeze gently moved the sheer curtains.

"You're not wearing your brace.' Bax walked across the room and sat backward on the hardback chair next to the bed, his arms stretched across the back of the chair.

"I'll put it back on later. I'll never get back to normal if I wear it all the time. Any news?"

Baxter shook his head. "No bail for Lamano. It's up to the prosecutors now. My reports are complete. They'll call me to testify, of course."

"And Manda Lamano? What's going to happen to her?"

Baxter looked out the window. "The searches really upset her. She's not implicated in any way that I can see. Tongues wag, of course, but mostly in sympathy with her. She'll be alright."

Baxter stood up and looked at Adam's puzzle. There were only two pieces yet to be placed. "Interesting that the whiskey bottle in the shelter contained potassium cyanide. Putting Henry in that shelter was attempted murder."

"Will they prosecute that?" Adam sat up on his bed, pillows at his back. He bit into the Walmart bake-it-at-home pizza Baxter's wife sent with him. On a previous visit, Baxter had shown up with a half-melted soft serve ice cream cone upside down in a cup.

"I doubt it. They can include it in the trial disclosures, but there is no concrete evidence one way or another that Lamano put it there. The bottle only had Henry's fingerprints. On the other hand, the evidence for the sexual assault is a little stronger… but I don't think they'll actually try and prosecute it."

"What assault?"

"The groping of your crotch. Matt Cummings included it in his statement, and we have that note that the hospital staff found in your shorts. Your crotch is now part of the federal record backed up by the physical evidence of that note." The laughter he had been trying to restrain escaped.

Adam pursed his lips, suppressing his own laughter, but he didn't know why it was funny. It could be just that Bax found it funny and was laughing. "I don't really remember him doing that."

"I don't think they'll ask you to testify about it."

"I guess at some point, heaping up charges won't increase the punishment," Adam ventured. "It just serves to show how truly messed up he was. Henry told me some stories about Lamano when they were young. He was odd, even as a kid."

"There are three gaps and only two pieces left. You're missing a piece."

"It's on top of the dresser. It fell to the floor early on, and I set it aside. Call it superstition. The first piece to fall on the floor has to be the last piece put into the puzzle. It's silly, but I've done that ever since I was a kid."

Baxter recovered the piece from the dresser. He slipped it into its space.

"Satisfying, isn't it?" Adam was aware that Baxter had broken the superstition and wondered if he had done it consciously.

"Baxter asked, "How about these other two?"

"Go ahead."

"How do I decide? They're the same." He stacked one on the other. "They're exactly the same."

"Believe it or not, it probably happens in every puzzle. This is the first time it has come down to the last two pieces." Adam put the brace back on his neck.

"Are you in pain?"

"No, but the muscles get tired after a while. It will take me months to get back to normal."

Baxter continued pushing the two pieces around the back of the puzzle. "It really is a guess. What if I look at the picture? Is that cheating?"

"If you think it would help, but the puzzle could be upside down. How do unsolved puzzles make you feel?"

"I hate them," Baxter admitted. "I once had a book of puzzles from Mensa, that group you have to be a genius to join. I could do a lot of them, but some were so hard I just gave up and looked up the answer in the back of the book."

"I've learned to live without an answer key. That doesn't stop me from trying though," Adam admitted. "But I've learned to be comfortable with ambiguity. Only in hindsight are we likely to judge our choices as good or bad."

"Like your decision to get off that bus in Ur? I'll bet you think that was a pretty bad decision."

Adam snorted a short laugh. "With the information I had at the time, it was the best decision I could make." He slouched a little more into his pillow. "If I had stayed on that bus, I would have never met you, Rosie, or Henry. It was no more a mistake than destiny. You can look at it any way you like."

"I'm glad you got off that bus. As we get older, it gets harder to find real friends." It was an uncomfortable statement to make and to hear. "I guess you'll soon be heading to Flagstaff."

"Flagstaff has lost its luster for me."

"Thinking of staying?" Baxter turned to look at Adam. Adam thought he looked hopeful, and it both flattered and saddened him.

Adam shook his head. "I need to work. And after bustling New Orleans and quiet Ur, I think I'm ready for some suburban sprawl. I'll give Broken Arrow a try."

Baxter looked back at the puzzle. "Gonna hang out with Elf?"

"I don't know if we'll ever hang out, but I'll look him up. Tom Delgado too. Once I'm settled, that is."

"Will you ever settle anywhere, Adam?" He was pushing the pieces back and forth on the puzzle back.

"Bax, the odds are fifty-fifty. Just like those two pieces. It's not about being right or wrong anymore. It's about moving forward."

Baxter looked at Adam, then back to the puzzle. He placed both puzzle pieces. The puzzle was complete.

"Perfect." Adam slid off the bed. "Now let's tape up the back so that we can see what it is supposed to look like. Pass me that masking tape."

Together they covered the entire back of the puzzle, laying down strips in multiple directions. They used the whole roll. Carefully, they flipped the puzzle.

Baxter's expression fell. "Shit, I was wrong."

The entire puzzle was perfect, except the tan teddy bear had a black eye and the black teddy bear had a tan belly button.

"No. You made the best choice you could with the information you had. Think about it in those terms."

Baxter looked Adam in the eye. It was sinking in. He felt like he understood what Adam meant. "What are you going to do with this puzzle now?"

"Throw it away."

Baxter hesitated. He felt silly, but he knew if he didn't ask, he'd regret it. "Can I have it?"

ABOUT THE AUTHOR

Joseph Onesta is an author and board-certified clinical hypnotist known for his compelling storytelling and transformative work in the field of hypnosis. A Pittsburgh native, he shares his home with his husband and their beloved, aging cat, Abbey. When he's not writing or helping clients unlock  their potential, Joseph enjoys cultivating his vegetable garden—a peaceful retreat that keeps him grounded between crafting mysteries and exploring the complexities of the human mind.

Learn more about Joseph and his work at **josephonesta.com**.

NOTE FROM THE AUTHOR

I hope you have enjoyed reading this book, the first in the Adam Alba series. If you'd like to get in early on Adam's future adventures, please visit and subscribe at https://www.AdamAlbaMysteries.com. You'll be alerted when the next episode drops and benefit from an early publication price for both paperback and e-book versions.